NEW SIGHT

New Sight Book 1

Jo Schneider

Copyright Information
All rights Reserved
© 2017 by Jo Schneider
ISBN-13: 978-1544038612

For Mom, who took me to the creaky , stuffy bookmobile once a week to feed my story addiction. Viva-la-bookmobile!

Chapter 1

Lysandra Blake chose to dwell on the peeling corner of the flowered wallpaper instead of why she sat imprisoned in the psych ward. Yet another tear balled in the corner of her good eye. She rubbed her cheek on her shoulder, expanding the already dark, damp spot on her pink hospital gown.

Closing her eye, Lys took a breath, allowing the drugs the doctors gave her to do their job and keep her numb. She preferred the feeling of floating on the ocean, gently bobbing over the waves, to facing the fear, pain, and horror of the last week.

It didn't help.

Another tear came, and she tried to wipe it away, but the Velcro straps that bound her wrists to the bed stopped her. Red, raw rings circled her arms where the straps bit into her skin despite the padding around the edges, and each time she moved, she felt the unforgiving plastic dig in deeper, as if they meant to latch onto her bones. Out of spite, she jerked her arms around. The pulling didn't help, but she did it anyway. She knew she should be grateful—restrained, she couldn't hurt anyone else. But somehow that knowledge didn't make being tied down like a caged animal any easier to bear.

The door to her mental ward room opened with a squeak. "Lys?"

Lys turned her head to see her dad walk in. Wrinkles covered his usually immaculate suit, his tie hung loosely around his neck. His dark hair poked out as if he'd been running his hands through it. "How's my little girl?" he asked, scratching the stubble on his chin.

She raised an eyebrow. "Little girl?"

"Well, I can't call you old," he said. "That would make me ancient."

1

"You *are* ancient," Lys teased, more out of habit than actual humor. She didn't feel much like laughing at the moment.

"The ingratitude," he said, waggling a finger. Lys noticed that he left plenty of space between them.

She tried to ignore it. "Teenagers," Lys said, shaking her head in sympathy. The grin on her dad's face grew more natural—less forced. His eyes held sympathy and love. Two emotions Lys knew she didn't deserve.

Her insides churned, and Lys averted her gaze—she didn't mean to look at her father's eyes, but she felt drawn to them like moths to a flame. Even though she knew it was a bad idea, even though she knew it would lead to the Need which would lead to her trying to rip someone else's eyes out.

She didn't want to think about that. "So, what's a nice guy like you doing in a place like this?" she asked, focusing on the gold chain of his tie tack.

The top half of him leaned forward, as if to move, but his legs remained riveted in place. She saw his chest rise and fall with the intake of a breath before he walked over and pulled a tissue from the box on the bedside table. "I heard they have killer food here." He sat down in a chair, and after another breath, he slowly reached out toward her face and dabbed her tears away. "Do you have any recommendations?"

Lys held perfectly still, afraid that she might frighten him away. He hadn't been this close since she'd arrived. "Well, I'd have to say the green Jell-O. I just can't help myself—you know what it does to me." The words came out clunky.

This elicited a small snort. "And here I thought it might be the peanut butter bars."

"They only give you those if you're good." The tight ball in her chest unraveled a tiny bit. Lys didn't think that having to be physically restrained qualified her as being good, but having her dad sit next to her allowed a tiny ray of hope through her despair.

Hope that couldn't last. Would she ever get to leave this room again?

"This sucks," she whispered.

He nodded. "Yeah, it does."

Why was this happening to her? She'd been living her life—shopping, hanging out with her friends, going to high school—and then she'd...what? Gone crazy? Psychotic? Berserk? Reason told her she was crazy, but if she was crazy could she trust reason?

"Honey," he put his hand on her forehead, his fingers trembling slightly. "Honey, look at me." His voice was serious. "Please Lys, we need to talk."

Lys shifted her gaze to the wall, where she caught a glimpse of her long, dark hair and pale face in the mirror. She glared at herself. "I'm tired of talking."

"I know." Her dad hesitated. "But things have changed. There's a man in the other room. He says he might be able to help you."

"Another doctor?" Lys asked. She'd had about as much as she could take from them.

"No," he said, "they still don't know what's going on." Pain laced his voice. "But this man says he knows what happened to you."

"How can he?" Lys whispered. Fear gripped her heart, and Lys didn't know if she'd ever be herself again. If she could ever look at her mom without remembering the euphoria that filled Lys when she attacked her.

"I don't know." Her dad sat forward in the chair, rubbing his hands together. He paused before letting out a deep sigh. "But you know what I say about gentlemen callers."

The words jerked her out of the stifling despair and back into herself. "Dad," Lys managed an eye roll. "Seriously? Have you seen the doctors in this place?"

He held up a finger. "Never turn one down just because you

don't like his shoes."

She couldn't help herself—a smile creased her lips. She almost felt normal. "Does he really have bad shoes? Because you know how I feel about that and missing teeth."

Her dad shrugged. "His teeth looked intact. Not sure about the shoes, your mother buys mine."

The mere mention of her mother caused her heart to drop into her stomach. The image of her mom, clutching her bloody face and screaming would never fade. Ever. At least her mother would keep her eye.

Her dad pressed on. "His name is Jeremiah Mason. He says you emailed him a few weeks ago, and came by to see if he could talk to you."

Lys frowned. "I emailed him?" She shook her head, trying to clear away the cobwebs. When had she emailed a man she didn't know?

"Something about a research project based on addiction?"

Furrowing her brow, Lys tried to think. She couldn't remember emailing anyone. But huge chunks of this past week were mired in dark fog. She shook her head. "I don't remember."

"He says he can help."

Could he help her, or was he just another person to tell her sad tale to? Lys didn't want to hope. Hope bred nice thoughts, which led to her wondering if she might have a normal life again. Would she ever be able to meet her father's eyes, or anyone's for that matter, without having the Need to rip them out rise up in her like a storm?

He went on. "I've called everyone I know, trying to see if they can tell me what happened to you." Their eyes met—Lys' gaze drawn to his. "Mr. Mason called the house yesterday, and he says he can help. He is the *only* person who has said he can help."

Lys had to look away. She found herself struggling against her bonds. Her fingers flexed, itching to reach up and encircle his eye and take it for her own. They came out easy, once you got behind the...No! Not her dad. She would *not* hurt him. She managed to swivel her head toward the camera in the corner. Was this Mr. Mason observing her from the other room? Watching her? The thought made Lys struggle harder. How dare he look at her! She should be the one to see everything. She should be looking, not him.

The thought was absurd, and Lys knew it. That didn't stop her from thinking it—*feeling* it. She grit her teeth and took a breath, once again imagining the ocean.

Lys' dad waited until she stopped struggling. "You don't have to talk to him."

"Dad," Lys said, swallowing hard. "Everyone thinks I'm crazy. And I'm starting to believe them. I don't want to hear it from anyone else."

"Oh honey." Her dad reached out to put his arms around her.

"No!" Lys cried. She recoiled from the advance like a magnet pushing off another magnet. He couldn't be that close, even if she longed for him to be. Sitting in this room for days had given her too much time to think. If he got closer, Lys knew she would try for his eyes. Her dad stopped. "Don't, please," she said.

He sat back, reaching out to hold her twitching hand, his fingers rubbing hers. "Mr. Mason specifically said that he thinks there is another explanation—something the doctors don't know about."

"Like what?" Lys asked, her mind going through the possibilities they'd already presented: schizophrenia, a psychotic disorder, acute anxiety, post-traumatic stress something or other...

"I don't know. He said he wanted to speak with you before he would tell me."

Lys pulled on her restraints again. How could she go on like this? Strapped down to a hospital bed, never knowing when she

5

would be consumed by the Need. This was no life, she was dead already. If this Mr. Mason could help her, if he could do anything at all that would make life go back to normal, she would speak to him. She had to. "I'll talk to him," she whispered.

"Good," he said. "But if he makes you uncomfortable at all, give me a nod. I'll be in the observation room."

"Okay."

"We're going to get through this." He gave her hand one last, steady squeeze.

Lys watched her dad retreat through door, leaving her alone in her prison. For the hundredth time she glanced around the small room. It looked more like an apartment than a mental ward, no doubt in an attempt to make the chained-down patients feel "at home".

Unfortunately her room at home didn't contain paintings of puppies, cheap linoleum floors, badly hung wallpaper or harsh, fluorescent lighting. Nor did it smell like thinly disguised ammonia. She really missed her own bed.

While she mused, Mr. Mason came through the door. Tall and thin, he wore an expensive suit, much like the kind her dad usually bought. He strode toward her with confidence in his steps. This man looked a little older than her dad, maybe fifty or so. Lys tried to keep her gaze down, but it wouldn't obey. Her eye met his— they were an aquamarine color that reminded Lys of turquoise. The white skin in the crows feet around his eyes provided a stark contrast against his tan face. The smell of pine came with him. Maybe they'd just cleaned the hallway.

"Lysandra?" He asked, smiling. "I'm Jeremiah Mason." He sat down in the chair next to the bed.

She struggled to pull her eye away from his face as he studied her. He didn't have a notebook, like most of the doctors had, and he didn't look at her like a complicated puzzle to be solved. No, he wore a different expression on his face. Curiosity. And he didn't hesitate to meet her eye. Surely they'd warned him not to.

Ripping her gaze away, she spoke. "Everybody calls me Lys, like bliss," she said.

He nodded. "Lys, I run a facility that may be able to help you. I'm going to need to ask you a few, unusual, questions."

"About what?"

"No one else is listening, I've asked them to turn off the sound in the observation room, and I won't tell anyone what you tell me." He leaned forward, talking slowly. "But if you're not honest with me, I won't be able to help you. Can you do that for me?" His low voice grated on Lys' nerves.

"Sure," Lys muttered. She kept her gaze on her knees. She didn't like being talked to like she was ten. Her parents never talked to her like that, even when she was ten. Maybe this guy would be worse than the doctors.

"Good." He put his elbows on his knees and clasped his hands together. "Have you ever had an out of body experience?"

Lys blinked. "No." What kind of facility did this guy run?

"What about hallucinations or demonstrating more than average feats of strength?"

"Uh, no."

Mason nodded, and an "I don't believe you" tone came out in his words. "Do you use drugs or alcohol excessively?"

"No." She wanted to mention that she didn't dress up in costume and run around her neighborhood either, but he didn't give her the chance.

"You need to be honest with me, Lys. Your parents told me that addiction runs in your family." She felt Mr. Mason's eyes boring into her skull.

"No," Lys snapped. She'd endured too many stories about her Aunt Della, the woman's fall into addiction and subsequent death to get heavily involved with either drugs or alcohol.

"Is there anything that you haven't told your parents about

what happened? Anything at all?"

"NO!" Lys yelled this time. Angry, she turned to look at him. Mr. Mason smiled. His eyes were that strange aquamarine color, and simply having them look at her made Lys feel the Need.

Reason shut down, and her whole body started to tremble—full of explosive energy that would only be released if she did one thing. Her hands struggled against their bonds, and in her mind she begged him to come closer. It would only take a moment. She could do it with her teeth.

He watched her, not flinching away as she lunged for him; her face just inches shy of her target.

Rage boiled up inside, and she took in a great gulp of air so she could scream, but the scream didn't come. Instead she choked down the pine scent from the hall. It caught in her throat and broke the spell. She coughed and gagged, the feeling that she might vomit interrupting the Need.

She took another breath and sat back, trying not to throw up.

"Tell me about this unnatural appetite that drove you to attack your mother."

Appetite? Lys clutched at the sheets on her bed, balling them up in her fists. She didn't answer. How did he know?

"When did it begin?" Mr. Mason asked.

The words spilled out before she could stop them—like he pulled them out of her. "Not until I ripped the eyes out of a frog in science class."

The scene would forever be burned into her conscious like a brand on a cow. She could still taste the formaldehyde fumes that came off the frog. The flickering light in the corner above the teacher's desk, the squeak of Billy's sneakers on the linoleum floors—it was all still in her mind's eye.

One second the frog was lying there, cut open, and the next Lys could have sworn it was staring up at her, watching her. For some reason this infuriated her. Lys had never felt anger like that before. She'd never wanted to hurt something so badly.

"How did it feel when you took the frog's eyes?" Mr. Mason asked.

"Good," Lys answered, licking her lips. He wouldn't get it even if she told him.

"How good?"

Better than she ever thought anything could feel. Better than getting to pee after holding it all night in a freezing cold tent. Better than waking up after a bad dream and finding yourself safe in your bed. Better than her first kiss. Better than she ever imagined sex would be.

"Really good," she said.

"So good you'd kill to feel it again?"

"Yes." The answer came out of Lys' mouth before she could stop it. Then the realization hit her. Lys *would* kill to feel it again.

"Did the same thing happen when you attacked your mother?"

Guilt punched Lys in the stomach. All her mother had done was bring her some soup for dinner. The scene flashed through her memory. The soup, her mom being worried and insisting that Lys look at her. The spoon. Her mother's beautiful, blue eyes.

"Lys," Mr. Mason prompted. "Why did you attack her?"

"She made me look at her!" she said, surprising herself with the intensity. "She made me look at her and when I saw her eyes all I wanted to do was take them. I had to have them!" Lys stopped. Saying it reminded her that this was all real. She'd tried to take her mother's eye out with a spoon. Would her mother ever forgive her? Did she deserve forgiveness?

"Lys," Mr. Mason's voice cut into her thoughts. "What were you trying to do to yourself?"

I was trying to end my pain! Lys wanted to scream.

After coming to her senses, and seeing her mom bleeding on the floor, Lys had tried to take her own eye. If she couldn't see

9

anyone else then she wouldn't ever feel the Need again.

A giant weight settled on her chest. She could hardly breathe, and she began to shake. "Please, just go." She looked straight at the camera. "I want you to go."

Mr. Mason leaned forward, his face moving into her view. "What do you want right now?"

He was too close. She couldn't help herself, Lys lunged forward. All reason gone, she only felt the Need. If she had his eyes, she could see what he could see. If she had everyone's eyes, she'd see everything. And that's what she wanted.

The bonds held, but that didn't stop Lys from leaning as far as she could toward Mr. Mason. "I want your eyes too." She didn't recognize the cold voice.

Mr. Mason held her gaze for a moment longer before he leaned back.

"You need to go," Lys said through gritted teeth. Her dad burst through the door.

Smiling, Mr. Mason stood. His gaze remained on Lys.

"I can help you," he said, "but you're going to have to trust me."

Chapter 2

When Mr. Mason had said she would be going through detox in a hospital, Lys had pictured a large, white building with lots of windows, four or five floors, rooms smelling of air fresheners that didn't quite disguise the tang of antiseptic, an emergency room and dozens of smiling doctors and nurses. Not an unfamiliar deserted road that wound through foothills lined with large, leaning trees that reached for them as they went by.

"Are you sure we're going the right way?" Lys asked, trying to keep the tremor out of her voice. She sat in the back seat of an SUV with her hands cuffed together and attached to the floor with a silver aircraft cable. The metal cuffs cut into her already chafed and swollen wrists using every bump in the road to remind her that she was still a prisoner.

Taking her fist steps out of the psych ward had given Lys' heart the room to beat again, and for a moment she could believe that everything was going to be okay. But the hope had plunged to the pit of her stomach when Mr. Mason's associates came with a wheelchair, the handcuffs and a sedative to help her sleep.

"This is it, mate" one of the men in the front seat said. Mark, if Lys remembered right. Short and stocky with dark hair, he talked with an Australian accent, which in any other circumstance Lys would have found hot. But after losing the last two and a half hours to a drug induced black out, Lys didn't much care about accents.

The SUV slowed and turned onto a driveway—more like a glorified dirt path that grudgingly allowed them passage than anything else. The already leaning trees seemed to cinch their branches together, closing off Lys' view of the road behind and the sky above. As the sedative wore off, Lys found her heart pounding harder and faster with every foot that separated her from the main road. She swallowed, trying to clear the lump of fear from her throat.

"Don't worry," the other man said over his shoulder, seeing her in the rear view mirror. "Mason likes his privacy. Your parents can call anytime."

Sweat coated her palms, and Lys wiped them on her jeans, adding to the already damp spots on the knees. She looked out the side window again. A long, sharp branch screeched along the glass, causing a shiver to run up her spine.

What had she been thinking? Lys opened her mouth to ask them to take her back, but her vision blurred, and she clamped her lips together, fighting off the wave of nausea that swelled up in her throat.

The trees continued to twist and blur, and Lys closed her eyes.

For a second she saw what could have been a view of the vehicle she rode in from the outside. It towered above her vantage point, like she stood the same height as a mouse. The vehicle disturbed a wave of dust that rolled away from the wheels, engulfing everything. She continued to watch as the SUV moved away, whipping through the branches and kicking up a wake of dirt. The gritty cloud began to turn and roil, looking like a pallet full of paints being sucked down a drain, before the whole vision dissolved back into black.

"You okay?" the driver asked in a voice that sounded far away.

Lys took a shallow breath, willing her mind to stay focused, and opened her eyes.

"Of course she's not okay," Mark said, grinning over his shoulder at Lys. "You're driving like an old man. We're not going to get there until tomorrow."

The driver, he'd introduced himself as Ayden, shook his head. "I'm trying not to take out the suspension, like someone else I know." He shot Mark a side-long glance.

Mark rolled his eyes and shook his head. He saw Lys' face,

which had to be white as a sheet, and made a patting gesture with his hand. "I'm joking, we're almost there."

Lys swallowed. This had all sounded like such a good idea when she had been strapped down in the psych ward. Now the entire scenario, along with Mr. Mason's explanation, seemed more than a little farfetched.

* * *

Addicted. That's what Mr. Mason told her and her parents at the hospital.

"My little girl? Addicted?" Lys' mom had asked in a trembling voice.

"Mrs. Blake," Mr. Mason said patiently, "your daughter has been exposed to a rare and highly addictive drug referred to as Pop. If she doesn't receive the correct treatment right away she may never recover."

"But if it's a drug, won't she just go through withdrawal?"

At that point Lys had risked a look up. Her mom's bandaged face mirrored Lys' own, and her good eye glistened with worry and tears.

It had taken her dad almost an hour to convince Lys to see her mom. Guilt sat like an Olympic-sized weight on her chest, making breathing almost impossible.

Her mom had burst into the room and rushed to Lys' side. But she didn't do more than give Lys' hand a small squeeze before she stepped away, and Lys could feel the tremor in her mom's fingers. Her own mother knew she was a monster. Lys decided right then that she would do whatever it took to make things right—to get her life back to normal.

"Not with Pop." Mr. Mason said. "Pop is manufactured to addict people, but it's unstable. It shuts down the senses before it shuts down other more important systems of the body."

Lys' mom turned to her dad. He hugged her close and spoke to Mr. Mason. "How did this happen?"

"Pop comes from central South America. The drug makers are still looking for the perfect formula—one that doesn't kill the users. They are hoping to come up with the next big drug, new products so to speak. When they think they've got a formula that works they send it out to test it, which must be how Lys came in contact with it. Probably at a party. You said you went to a party after the Homecoming game."

Lys nodded. She kept her gaze away from the others faces. She watched her parent's shuffling feet and Mr. Mason's statue-like stance, and knew that she would have to ask the hard question. "What will happen to me?" Her voice came out as a tiny squeak.

Mr. Mason turned to face her. "I'm sorry, Lys, but without treatment your body will continue to shut down, and you will die."

Lys felt the fragile hope that had been cautiously growing shatter. Die? Part of her wanted to die, but the rest of her—the sane part—hoped this would pass. Doctors had treatments for everything, right?

Her mom lost it. Sobbing and pleading she asked what they could do to save her little girl so she didn't end up like her Aunt Della. Mr. Mason pulled her parents into another room.

The next day she and her dad had had a chat.

"But dad," Lys said, wishing she could use her hands to talk. "He says I'm going to die!"

"We don't have any other confirmation of that, Lys," her dad said. "Who is this man, and why should we simply believe him?"

Lys banged the back of her head against the stiff pillow. They'd been through this twice already.

"Look, honey," her dad said, sitting on the same chair that Mr. Mason had sat in the day before. "I know you feel like this man is your only hope, but I can't let him take you away like he wants to."

Lys shook her head. "But dad, he's the only one who doesn't think I'm completely insane."

"I don't think you're insane."

"You should," Lys said. "Because only a psychopath would want to rip their mother's eyes out."

The words caused her dad to flinch, but he recovered a moment later. "Lys." He reached out and took her hand. "Don't ever say that. I know you're not crazy. You're my baby girl, and nothing could ever change that."

She could tell by the tone in his voice that he was not going to budge on this. So Lys did the last thing she wanted to and the only thing she knew would convince him. She raised her eye and met her father's gaze.

The next dose of her medication sat in a cup by her bed, ready to be taken. The dislocated feeling that it gave her—that floating on an air mattress on a slowly rolling ocean—had started to evaporate about an hour before. Lys knew that the Need could get through. And for the first time, she encouraged it.

The feeling of want started at the base of her neck and spread like frost through her veins. Her fingers twitched, and she latched onto her dad's hand. The buzz of the Need filled her ears, and rose like the climax of a symphony, drowning out her dad's shout of surprise when she lunged as far as she could toward him, teeth bared. He jumped off the chair, jerking his hand away from hers, and stumbled back. The fear Lys knew had been lurking in her dad surfaced, twisting his face into a conflicted expression of disgust and terror.

The clear, blue orbs of his eyes called to her—sung like sirens luring her to her death. She had to have them—would kill or die for them, and he knew it. He raised a shaking hand to cover his lips that hung agape in horror.

* * *

The memory filled Lys with shame, but it also reminded her why she'd agreed to go with Mr. Mason. She tried to ignore the rising feeling of panic and told herself that she had to do this.

Mark continued to watch her. "You look nervous."

"Uh." Lys didn't know how to answer that. Nervous would mean that she would laugh a little too loudly at Mark's jokes and say something stupid in reply. Considering right now she wanted to scream, cry and rip her wrists out of the handcuffs so she could jump out of a moving vehicle and escape into unknown woods Lys figured she was way past nervous.

"Relax," Mark said, "we've had meaner characters than you in here. We can handle it." He exchanged a look with Ayden, and the other man nodded. "You'll be feeling better in no time."

Whatever sedative they'd given her muted the Need, but her mind felt more alive than it had since she'd gone into the psych ward. Lys decided to try questions to distract herself.

"Do you guys, uh, know what's going to happen to me?"

"We'll let Mason explain that to you. He's here at the hospital," Ayden said in a soft voice.

Hospital? Part of Lys still didn't believe in the supposed hospital lurking here in the backwoods of who knew where. She balled her hands into fists. Maybe her dad was right, maybe she should have held out for a different option.

No. Mr. Mason believed her; he said he could help her. Lys would hold on to that until she knew otherwise. Her mind cradled the fragile hope, not wanting to let it fall and shatter into shards of nothing.

"Here we go," Mark said. He pointed out the front of the SUV.

They came around a sharp corner, and Lys leaned forward, following Mark's gesture.

Sure enough a hospital sat nestled in a clearing at the end of the road. Nothing big, just a two story, white building with a drop off spot. Three cars sat in the parking lot, not even filling it a quarter of the way. Mr. Mason stood outside the main doors.

"What is this place?" Lys asked. A hospital in the middle of the woods? Secluded, small, off the beaten path. Creepy.

"It used to be a privately run facility that treated people suffering from PTSD," Ayden said, maneuvering the SUV toward the door. "Mostly for war veterans that couldn't get help anywhere else."

Old veterans? Lys' mind jumped to the guys she saw begging for money on street corners. Some of them had signs saying they were veterans. Their haunted expressions—their eyes that Lys knew had seen things that no person should have to see—made Lys shiver. Partly because she now wanted to see what they saw, and partly because she now felt like she'd just entered a horror movie. This sank below creepy. "So why do I have to detox here?"

"Mr. Mason will explain," Mark said as the SUV came to a stop at the drop off point.

Did either of these guys ever answer a question? She wanted to call them out on it, but Mr. Mason stepped up to Mark's window. He leaned in, and Lys could see that his lips were drawn into a thin line.

"Is something wrong?" Mark asked.

"We've got one inside who could use your help." Mr. Mason's voice was soft, like Ayden's, but insistent.

"Got it," Mark said, turning around and giving Lys a smile. "Ayden will take it from here. Let me know if he's not a gracious host."

Ayden glared as the other man got out of the vehicle, passing Mr. Mason and jogging in the front doors.

Lys watched him go. She shifted in her seat, trying to remain calm.

"Come on," Ayden said. He got out and opened Lys' door. "Let's get you inside."

While having handcuffs on made her feel like a prisoner, they also made her feel safe. Not safe from others, but from herself and what she might do to whoever got too close. As Ayden unfastened her from the aircraft cable, Lys' breathing sped up. She silently begged him not to undo the cuffs, but with steady hands, he drew a key from his pocket, inserted it into a metal lock and twisted. The cuffs sprung open, leaving Lys free.

She didn't want to be free anymore.

"You won't be needing those from now on," Mr. Mason said from the other side of the vehicle, gesturing with a hand. "Come inside."

The cobblestone driveway looked about a thousand miles below her. Lys slid over and dipped one toe out of the SUV. The tennis shoes she wore hit the ground, and she let the bottom of her foot succumb to gravity. The other foot followed, and as she stood, Lys felt her knees wobble. One hand reached out to use the roof of the vehicle for support, and she took a step. She tried another, but her foot stopped in mid-air, her body distracted by something much more insistent than gravity. The Need.

Emotions, a week repressed by medication, came bubbling up from the bottom of a cauldron. Anger, fear, hunger—the Need. It swelled in her stomach and ached to make her fingers move. She doubled over, trying to contain it.

"Lys, what's wrong?" Someone pulled on her arm.

"Get away!" she pleaded, "please." She felt herself start to shake. She fell to her hands and knees and put her head down on the cobblestones, squeezing her eye shut. A voice said her name, but she didn't care.

She wanted the feeling back. The feeling like after she ripped the frog's eyes out—euphoria. She was a hungry monster, demanding to be fed. The Need gnawed through her mind, screaming at her to do something. To hurt someone.

On their own accord, Lys' fingers began to twitch. Why did he take the handcuffs off?

The image of her mom's bandaged face sprung into her mind. All of the times her dad flinched away from her, and all of the looks the doctors gave her paraded through her memory. No, she wouldn't hurt anyone else. Not while she had an ounce of control left in her. She laced her fingers together and squeezed until her arms shook.

The dark behind her eyelids flared to life, and she found herself in another place. She stood in her room, looking at her bed. Everything was exactly as she'd left it, except the blood on the carpet. Someone had cleaned that up. Her MP3 player sat on the dresser, and her school bag lay on the chair.

Lys tried to look over at the mirror. Her head wouldn't move. She attempted to look up. Nothing happened. What was this? She floated out of her body. Had it taken too long to get here? Was she dead?

Panic filled her mind, and she wanted to scream. The picture of her room faded, replaced by the dark.

For a moment she thought that death had come, but a voice broke through. "Lysandra, can you hear me?"

The familiar voice penetrated her mind, and Lys smelled the pine scent from the surrounding trees. Memories of camping and hiking and outings with her friends and her parents filled her thoughts to overflowing. A small measure of peace came with them, allowing Lys to focus.

"Do you understand me?"

Lys nodded, latching onto the memories like a rescue rope thrown from a raft.

Footsteps sounded behind her and another voice spoke. "Here"

"I'm sorry, Lys, I didn't think the dose they gave you at the hospital would wear off so fast." Mr. Mason tugged Lys into a sitting position. Tremors wracked her body, and Lys kept her hands clasped together. She didn't dare open her eye.

Ayden placed a cup to her lips. "Drink this. It'll help."

The Need still demanded to be fed, but the image of her mother's face coupled with the good memories kept her from acting. Lys tried to drink. Most of the liquid sloshed down the front of her shirt, the cold biting into her hot skin, but she gulped enough in for a few swallows. The liquid had the same flat, sugary taste as old Sprite—nasty—but within seconds the Need retreated. It didn't leave, so much as something hit the mute button. Lys could still feel it, but she didn't have to listen anymore. She took a deep, shuttering breath and let it out, her limbs still trembling. After another, she opened her eye and stared at her hands.

"Better?" Mr. Mason asked. He knelt on the ground next to her.

"Better," Lys whispered.

"I apologize," Mr. Mason said, "usually the inhibitor lasts a bit longer."

"I could have hurt someone." She didn't look up. "I *wanted* to hurt you."

"You may not believe me, but it happens all the time." Ayden said it, and his words held a smile. "We can handle it. Like Mark said, we've had much meaner characters than you come through here."

Mr. Mason cleared his throat before silence filled the air. It reminded Lys of times when her parents gave her the "we'll talk about this later" look.

"Do you think you can stand?" Mr. Mason asked.

Lys didn't want to stand. She wanted to stay curled up here, in the driveway, safe from the demands of the Need. But she didn't think that they would let her, so she nodded. "I think so." Lys allowed Ayden to pull her to her feet—the world tilted and her legs shook. Mr. Mason stepped back and gestured toward the open door again. Lys kept her eye on the stones.

"Come inside and meet the others, then we'll get you settled in."

Chapter 3

It's a good thing Ayden went slow, because Lys' legs wouldn't stop shaking, and she could have sworn that the ground kept pitching back and forth beneath her feet. He led her—half dragging her really—around the vehicle and to the entrance.

With the Need almost breaking free, everything felt more sinister than it had a few minutes before. Lys glanced up at the doors, and instead of standing open and inviting, they now seemed to be a gaping hole, ready to swallow her whole. The sun hit the exterior of the building, shooting rays of hot, white light into her eye. She looked back down at her feet and regarded the cobble stone walkway that led to the doors. The cracks between stones lay like reaching traps that wanted to snatch her as she passed. Part of her conscious knew that she was being irrational, but the other part, the one that had pretty much taken over since all of this started, knew that the ground wanted to suck her down into hell.

Ayden led Lys though the doors. He kept talking, but she couldn't understand what he was saying. The Need still churned inside, angry at having been denied. Cool, treated air flew in her face, replacing the warm air from outside. She felt like she'd just walked into death. She shivered, chills running through her body.

"Easy," Ayden said, getting a better grip around her arm. "You're okay."

Why did everyone keep saying that? She was *not* okay.

"Brady is in the waiting room," Mr. Mason said. "We'll take Lys there."

As long as there was a chair. All Lys wanted to do was sit down; she didn't care much about anything else.

Lucky for her, they didn't have to go far. Inside the entrance sat a long, deserted desk. They turned left and walked down the hall and through the second open door.

A young man sat in a poufy tan couch, lounging with one foot up on the cushions. Comfortable looking chairs and another couch surrounded a table that sat in the middle of the room.

"Howdo," the young man said, jerking his head back in greeting. He had a British accent.

"Hi," she said, wondering if this kid suffered from the Need too.

"Lys," Mr. Mason said, following her and Ayden into the room. "This is Brady Moore. Brady, this is Lysandra Blake."

"Nice to meet you, Lysandra Blake," he said, smiling.

"Just Lys. Like bliss," she said automatically. He seemed normal enough.

In an attempt to keep from staring at his face, Lys settled on his hands. What looked like a wooden ball lay at the end of each of his arms. She eyed her own wrists and wondered why Mr. Mason had made her give up her restraints—it didn't seem fair.

"Please, sit down," Mr. Mason said.

Lys did so, taking it slow. From the outside it may have looked graceful, from the inside she felt like her knees had given out and that she'd narrowly avoided sprawling all over the floor.

Brady watched her with interest. He shook his head back and forth, trying to rid his eyes of his scraggly, dark hair.

Eyes! Lys jerked her gaze down to his chest. Was she stupid? What was she doing looking anywhere near his eyes? And why was he staring at her face?

Then she remembered that she had a bandage over one eye. Duh.

"Since the two of you have arrived so close together, I thought I would only do the orientation once." Mr. Mason sat down in a chair across from Lys, completing the triangle around the table.

"I'm just glad I get to hang out with a cute girl," Brady said with a contagious smile. His arms and legs looked longer than the rest of him, and Lys thought he had to be a couple of years younger than her.

"The two of you will join another young man that just arrived," Mr. Mason said. "It is unusual for us to have so many new guests here at once."

Three of them? Three people with the Need? Lys wondered if Brady's hands were bound because he had succeeded where Lys had failed.

"Both of you know about Pop. You've both been exposed to it, and without treatment it will eventually start shutting down vital systems of your body." Lys could feel Mr. Mason looking at her, but she kept her eye on his shirt. "After we get you settled in, we'll have dinner. You will begin your treatments tonight."

"How long will this take?" Brady asked.

"It depends." Mr. Mason shrugged. "For some it takes a few days. For others it may be closer to two weeks."

"But then we go to your rehab facility?" Lys asked, remembering what he told her before.

"That is correct."

"Why have us here?" Brady asked. "Why not just send us straight to this facility?"

"Pop is extremely slippery. Trace amounts of it will come out in your sweat, breath and waste for at least a week after treatment starts. For anyone who wasn't affected by it in the first place this is not a concern. However, even those small amounts can—and will—set those trying to recover back days, if not months."

"Months?" Lys asked.

"For some." Mr. Mason nodded. "Everyone is different."

Lys could feel him looking at her again. She studied the candle that sat in the middle of the table. Orange scent, she thought.

"So, what now?" Lys asked.

"The drug to which you are all addicted is one hundred

24

percent deadly. Without help you will die in withdrawal." Mr. Mason glanced around. "Each of you has had different side effects from the drug. The staff is here to help. Only you know what the drug has done to you. There is no way to know what it has done to anyone else—how it affects them. The staff is aware of these things, and they are prepared to intervene in any situation that comes up."

So the effects *were* different for everyone. Her eye moved to Brady and she wondered again what he'd done. How different did it get?

Mr. Mason kept talking. "Please, if you see any of the counselors restraining another guest, keep your distance. One guest may feel the urge to sing at the top of his lungs, while another feels the need to braid your intestines together and another will attack anyone who wears a blue shirt."

Why couldn't she have been infected with the urge to sing at the top of her lungs? Not that Lys was a good singer—really, not good at all—but it sounded so much better than the urge to take eyes, or ...what had he said about intestines?

"We have a few rules to go over before we take you up to your rooms. The first is our you-tell policy." He turned to meet Lys' eye. She looked away. "Everyone here, including the staff, has been affected by this drug. The staff knows enough to keep the rest of you safe, but none of the other guests have any idea what the drug did to you. It is considered impolite to ask someone about this. However, there is no way to patrol this, so you are at your own discretion on the matter. If you feel you want to tell someone, that choice is entirely up to you, but you must know that no one is compelled to answer. Keep your own matters as private as you like."

Lys felt some of her anxiety unwind. She didn't like to think about what happened with her mom, but if she had to tell some support group about it Lys thought she might die. Not to mention what people would think of her. Then again, looking at Brady's hands, maybe everyone here had problems at least as twisted as hers.

"While you are here, you will not leave your room unescorted." Mr. Mason went on. "If a counselor asks you to do something, you will do it immediately and you will do it without question. You are required to come down to meal times in the private dining room. If you need anything, simply press the call button next to your door and a counselor will assist you."

He glanced down at his watch. "I've got a meeting in a few minutes, so I'll have you escorted to your rooms." He pulled a pager off his belt and pressed a button. "Dinner will be at five o'clock. One of the counselors will bring you down."

A moment later Ayden reappeared accompanied by a woman with short, blond hair. One of them smelled of damp earth.

Mr. Mason stood. Lys and Brady followed suit. "Lys, this is Genni. She will be your counselor during your stay."

Lys smiled, not looking at the other woman's face.

"Brady, this is Ayden. Ayden and Mark, who you've met, will be taking care of you and Kamau."

"Kamau?" Brady asked.

"He is the young man who joined us a few days ago." Mr. Mason gestured for Lys to follow Genni. "Why don't the two of you go up to your rooms and get some rest?"

A moment before she'd felt fine, but suddenly Lys could hardly keep her eye open. Gravity seemed to have doubled, and her feet felt like lead weights.

"Come on," Genni said, stepping forward and gently taking her by the arm. "Let's get you upstairs."

Lys allowed herself to be steered toward the door. Each step got harder than the last, and she felt like she could curl up on the floor and go to sleep for a week. Genni tightened her grip on Lys' arm, and a little bit of the grogginess went away. "You can rest

26

once we're upstairs," she promised.

Upstairs? Lys hoped they had an elevator. Her brain started to go fuzzy.

Genni pulled her through the door and into the hall. "So you're from the L.A. area?" Genni asked.

Lys nodded. Her brain rallied, grasping for a reasonable response. The best she could come up with was, "Yeah."

"Have you ever seen the—"

An ear piercing scream shot down the hall like an arrow, grinding in Lys' ears. Genni's head swiveled around and stopped as she said, "Uh-oh."

Chapter 4

Lys tensed, turning to see what held Genni's attention. A young man stood in the middle of the hallway, his red hair and freckles a bright contrast to the taupe and white.

"Kenny!" Mr. Mason said, darting around Lys and Genni, heading straight for the young man.

A power Lys couldn't control seized hold of her gaze and forced it to look up at Kenny's face. A gasp caught in her throat when she saw his eyes. Swirling, smoky black covered his irises, like those contacts you could get for Halloween, only somehow alive.

The Need battered at the barrier that held it back, frenzied like a wild animal. Lys' fingers twitched and without meaning to, she took a step forward.

Mr. Mason stopped a dozen feet shy of the young man. "Kenny, what are you doing?"

Kenny reached a trembling hand toward Mr. Mason. "Don't you see?"

"You know I can't see what you see," Mr. Mason said in a calm voice. "Why don't you stop this and tell me what you see? You know I'll listen to you."

So Kenny *could* see too? Lys wondered what he saw, and the Need began its assault anew. Lys wiggled her arm, trying to get it out of Genni's grip.

Brady's voice came from behind her. "Bloody hell, how did that get in here?"

Lys blinked, distracted by the thought that Brady could see something she couldn't. She glanced past her shoulder and saw Brady crawling over the back of the couch. The wide-eyed, silent scream on his face made Lys wonder what he could see. Across the room, Ayden snatched something out of a drawer.

28

Next to her, Genni kept shaking her head and blinking her eyes. "It's not real," she muttered to herself.

Everyone could see something that she couldn't. The Need wavered—not sure where to concentrate its focus—until Kenny spoke.

"You don't understand what you're doing! You don't realize what will happen!" Kenny's voice went up an octave. He looked so desperate, so pleading.

Lys felt Genni's hand on her arm tighten again. "It's not real, Lys," she said. "Don't be afraid."

Afraid of what?

"Kenny!" Mr. Mason said. "Remember what you know. You can fight this." He took a tentative step forward. "Stop using it."

Kenny started to twitch before he doubled over on himself. Mr. Mason rushed forward, trying to catch Kenny, but the young man screamed again—a sound brought straight up from Hell— and pushed Mr. Mason away.

"You don't understand!" Kenny said, spittle flying from his mouth. "Everything will be destroyed!" He turned away from Mr. Mason, who was picking himself up off the floor, and looked straight at Lys.

"You can see it," he said, pointing at her. "You'll see it all."

See it all? Just what the Need wanted. Kenny's words felt like an invitation, and Lys pulled hard against Genni's hold.

Before she could get away, Mark appeared next to Kenny. A brief flash came from his hands, and Kenny jerked back, his whole body wracking with a spasm. Ayden ran in from behind Lys and plunged a needle into Kenny's neck.

Lys stared, her mouth hanging open. Needles? Shocks? Those eyes? What was this place?

"Is he out?" Genni asked, keeping her grasp on Lys' arm.

Ayden lowered Kenny to the floor and pulled one of his eyelids open. "He's out."

29

"Sorry about that," Mark said, addressing his words to Mr. Mason. "That was the strongest attack I've seen in a while."

Mr. Mason looked more concerned than annoyed. "I'm surprised he reverted so far."

Ayden looked up at Genni and Lys. "You okay?"

Genni nodded and squeezed Lys' arm. "It's okay; there is nothing here that is going to hurt you." Hurt her? Lys felt like she'd missed something. She was the one who wanted to hurt people.

Brady stumbled out of the waiting room, sweating and pale. "Where did the dragon go?" he asked.

"Dragon?" Lys asked, checking behind her.

"You didn't see the dragon?" Brady asked.

"Uh, no." Lys said.

Mr. Mason left Mark with Kenny and stood. "You saw nothing out of the ordinary?" he asked Lys.

"Just his eyes," Lys said, trying not to think about how much the Need wanted them. "They were black. Sort of."

Mr. Mason studied her for a moment. "You're lucky. The inhibitor we just gave you saved you from the effects."

"What just happened?" Brady asked. "I saw a dragon, and it was about to have me for lunch."

Mr. Mason held up his hands. "Pop is very potent. Remember what I said about trace amounts of the drug coming from you? Kenny came in and got a whiff of what the two of you have left in your systems. He escalated off that, and you escalated off him."

"But it was so real," Brady said, glancing around.

"A hallucination. Nothing more," Mr. Mason said.

"Hallucinations don't smell like fire."

Mr. Mason's lips spread into a grin. "That depends on how powerful the hallucination is."

* * *

30

Up in her room, and after a brief nap, Lys still didn't know if she believed Mr. Mason's explanation. Brady swore that he saw a dragon, and Genni had seen something as well, but all Lys saw were Kenny's black, swirling eyes.

She pushed herself off the bed and walked over to the window. Pulling the thick, green curtains to one side, Lys saw the sun on its way to meet the hills beyond the trees. Lys could still make out a group of three people walking on a path below. The scene reminded her of a post card, but with the beauty came the seclusion. And with the seclusion came feelings of despair and fear. Lys tried to suppress them, but with nothing else to think about, and the drugs from the psych ward wearing off, her emotions ran wild. Thoughts of her parents pained her, wondering about school and her friends depressed her, and trying to figure out if her life would ever be normal again was agonizingly futile.

The curtains fell back as Lys turned around. The simple room consisted of a bed, a dresser with a mirror, a rocking chair and a window. Lys glanced at the door. Genni, the counselor, had bolted it shut on her way out.

"If you have any problems, just press the button. One of the counselors will be close by."

Lys shook her head. The creepy feeling from when she'd first arrived had not abated. It was probably all those ghost hunting shows she'd watched on television; gloom wafted through the halls like fog. Most of it was probably hers.

A knock came at the door, causing Lys to jump. A moment later it opened. Genni stood outside wearing her uniform of a green shirt and khaki shorts. "Ready?" she asked.

Lys nodded, taking a breath. She could feel the Need getting frisky—awakening from its own afternoon nap. Mr. Mason had assured her that the handcuffs would no longer be necessary, but so far, she didn't agree.

Genni gestured for Lys to go ahead of her. They walked down

the sterile, off-white hall to the stairs—the elevators in the middle of the building didn't get used much according to Genni—and made their way back to the first floor.

As they descended, Lys risked a question. "How many people are here?"

"There are seven guests and ten or twelve people on staff," Genni said. "But a few of the guests are moving tomorrow, so the number will go down."

"How did you meet Mr. Mason?" Lys asked. She wondered how all of these people had gotten involved with Mr. Mason and his treatment facility. Lys really wanted to know if Genni had been addicted to Pop, but she didn't think it would be polite to ask.

"It's a long story," Genni said. "Once you're through your first few days maybe I'll tell you about it."

Lys didn't get much more than that. She tried a few more questions, but Genni dodged them. It didn't feel like the woman was trying to be overly secretive, but she didn't seem terribly open either.

They moved past the front desk and into the other side of the building. Lys caught a glimpse of a large dining area to their right, but Genni kept going down the hall and through a different door.

A round table sat in the center of the square room. Seven or eight chairs surrounded the table, and Lys saw a little kitchen off to the side.

"There she is!" Brady's bright voice said. "Why is it you're always the last one to arrive?"

Lys focused on an appropriate response. "It's a girl thing."

Brady turned to the young man sitting next to him and grinned. "Told you she would be here. Nice patch, by the way." The last he aimed at Lys.

"Thanks," Lys said, brushing at her eye with her fingers. She'd traded the bandages for a tie dye patch that her dad had given her. The doctors said she could start wearing it tomorrow, but she didn't want to wait. At least no one laughed at her, although a grin stretched across Brady's face.

Lys figured Brady was maybe fourteen. The new guy next to him had to be a year or two older than Lys—seventeen or eighteen. He had skin the color of ebony—darker than she had ever seen. His tall, lean figure sat with perfect posture, and he held his head with confidence. He nodded, and Lys remembered to avoid his gaze. He didn't look nearly as paranoid as she felt, and she wondered if he was the guy who wanted to sing at the top of his lungs. The mental picture of this proper young man belting out opera almost made her laugh out loud.

Mr. Mason walked in from the kitchen with Mark in tow.

"Ah, Lys, good. Sit down and we'll get started."

She took the seat opposite the boys. Mark and Mr. Mason sat as well, but Genni left. Lys felt a bit outnumbered.

"Did you get some rest?" Mr. Mason asked.

Lys nodded. "A little."

"I'm glad. Dinner should be out in a moment." Mr. Mason paused. "I thought it might be nice for the three of you to get to know one another."

Lys glanced up at the others. She couldn't think of a more diverse group. Where the new guy seemed very proper, Brady looked to be totally at ease. Mark sat with one arm up on the chair next to him, and Mr. Mason watched them all expectantly. She wasn't sure she wanted to share much about herself. She didn't know who these people were. Mr. Mason she trusted, and maybe Mark because she knew him a little, but not the others.

"You're an Auzie." Brady said to Mark.

"That's right," he answered. "What part of England are you from?"

"Just north of London," Brady said. "I lived out in the country until my mum and dad divorced a few years ago. Last summer I moved in with my mum so I could go to a better school."

"You a rugby player?" Mark asked.

Brady shook his head. "Naw, my mum would never let me. You?"

Mark shrugged. "It's been a long time."

Brady sat forward. "So what's the craziest thing you've ever cooked? Kangaroo?"

Laughing, Mark shook his head. "I shouldn't mention it at the table."

Everyone chuckled, and the conversation stopped as dinner arrived. Two more counselors served them, setting platters of delicious smelling food down on the table. Steam rose from the chicken and rice, and Lys' stomach gave a rather vocal growl. Apple salad, beans and bread were passed around, and Lys took a large portion. She ate with an appetite she hadn't noticed in weeks, trying not to look like a pig.

If the committee for good manners needed a new poster boy, the newcomer could be their guy. He ate with ease, grace and precision, not unlike the people in old Jane Austen movies Lys and her friends watched. He listened politely to the conversation that was going on around him and spoke easily when Mr. Mason asked him to introduce himself.

"My name is Kamau. My family is from Mozambique," he said in a smooth, deep voice. "My father is the chief of our tribe. I have been going to university for a few months in Maputo Cidade."

"Whoa, you're in a tribe?" Brady interrupted.

Nodding once, Kamau said, "Yes, where I am from, the old traditions of our people still run very strong. My father has made it his goal to integrate technology and the outside world into our culture without disrespecting or destroying our traditions."

"Do you have to squeeze water from plants to have stuff to drink?" Brady asked leaning forward.

Kamau smiled, his face breaking from the polite mask. "Not

normally, but I have done so."

He must have felt her gaze on him, because Kamau looked right at her, and Lys had to turn her attention to his neck. She cleared her throat. "If your father is the chief of your tribe, does that make you his successor?"

"Yes."

"So you're like a prince?" Brady asked, drawing Kamau's attention. "Wow, that's cool."

"More like the next in line to do the hardest job I could ever imagine."

"Do you have any brothers and sisters?" Mark asked, speaking for the first time.

Kamau's friendly manner cracked as his lips drew into a thin line. "I had a younger sister, but she is gone."

Lys didn't think gone meant gone away to school or on vacation.

"I'm sorry, mate." Mark said.

"It was a long time ago."

Mr. Mason turned the conversation. "Lys, you haven't told us anything about yourself."

Lys hardly heard him. Against her own better judgment, she was watching Kamau's face, and the moment Mr. Mason turned his attention from him, Kamau's whole countenance transformed from a polite young man into that of a predator.

Lys had been little, maybe six or seven years old, the first time she'd seen that expression. She was at the store with her mom, shopping for a present for her dad's birthday. They'd walked up and down all the aisles, trying to find just the right thing. Lys' mom hadn't even noticed the man, but Lys had.

Tall, with scraggly hair, he followed them like a shadow. Lys was shy, so she looked away every time she saw the man watching her. But after he followed them for three or four aisles, Lys proved too slow and she met his eyes.

35

They were horrible. Angry, dark eyes that looked at Lys as if she were dinner, not a little girl. Lys started to cry. When her mother asked her what was wrong, Lys told her about the scary man.

Naturally the scary man disappeared, and Lys never saw him again, but she'd seen the look since then. She saw it whenever they showed a cold-blooded killer on the news. Kamau's eyes were the same, and they watched Mr. Mason with deadly interest. Lys' idea that he might be the guy who felt the need to sing at the top of his lungs evaporated. What if he was the one who wanted to braid intestines together? What lay under that polite facade? Suddenly Lys' budding interest in him faltered.

"Lys?" Mr. Mason prompted.

"Oh!" Lys looked around, distracted from Kamau. What had Mr. Mason asked? "I, uh, I'm from California, but because of my dad's job we've moved around a lot. It's just me and my parents." She paused. "I, I love art and movies and hanging out with my friends." It sounded really stupid coming out like that—nothing like being the prince of a tribe.

Brady saved her. "What kind of art do you like? Do you draw or paint?"

"I like painting, but I'm better at drawing."

"I have the greatest idea for a manga, but I can't draw. You could teach me!"

A comic book? "Uh, sure."

Brady's attention span was about two seconds. "Can I have more chicken?"

"Have all you want," Mark said, laughing as he passed the plate.

Brady looked at Lys' plate. "Is that all you're going to eat?"

She glanced down. "Yes?" It was more than she'd eaten at once in a long time.

"I don't understand you light eaters. Personally, breakfast is my favorite meal of the day. Although I prefer tomatoes," Brady pronounced it ta-mah-toes, "and beans to your American cold cereal."

"That's sick." Lys made a face, imagining eating any sort of bean for breakfast. It must be a boy thing.

"What do you eat?" Brady asked Kamau. It was obvious the younger boy was dying to know more about this African tribe.

Kamau grinned, glancing at Lys. "I'd rather not say at the table."

"Are you sure you don't want any beans?" Brady asked Lys, raising the bowl.

"I'm good," she held up a hand.

"What's your story?" Brady asked Mark.

Mark finished chewing before he wiped his mouth with a napkin. "Mr. Mason here found me and helped me go through what you're going through. That was a few years ago. I decided I wanted to stay on and help everyone else. We're kind of a tight family here."

"We're lucky to have a lot of dedicated, resourceful people to help us," Mr. Mason said.

Mark nodded. "You're in good hands."

The conversation paused. Lys felt like they were dancing around the proverbial elephant in the room—the question they were all thinking but no one wanted to ask. Knowing everyone's names was nice, but she had bigger reasons for being here.

"So," she said, turning to Mr. Mason "You mentioned that we would start treatments tonight?"

Chapter 5

Genni smiled. "Are you ready?" How could Genni be so casual? The question reminded Lys of something her mother would ask her like, "Do you have your keys?" or, "Do we need milk?" Not, "I'm about to give you some 'tonic' that's going to counteract the deadly drug that's in your system, trying to kill you. It might be uncomfortable. You're going to feel horrible for the next week or so, but trust me, you'll live." That's not exactly the way Mr. Mason described it, but that was the gist.

"Sure," Lys said aloud. "Why wait?"

The woman handed Lys a large glass of cloudy, white liquid. "You might want to sit down on the bed first," she said.

"Will it affect me that fast?" Lys asked, eying the liquid with new suspicion.

"It does some people."

Lys sat. She stared at the glass in her hand, wondering how something that looked like the dregs of a science experiment could cure her.

How bad could it be? She'd seen TV. Movies. Sure, people went through withdrawal all the time. Flu like symptoms, puking everywhere, looking like a bus just ran over you, and probably feeling that way too. Lys swallowed. I can handle this, she told herself. She'd had the flu last year. She'd been hit in the face by more than one volleyball in her gym classes. Feeling like crap— she could take it.

Bringing the glass to her lips, Lys sniffed. No smell. Of course she couldn't smell much anyway. As Mr. Mason had predicted, her other senses had started to dull over the past few days, with her sense of smell going the quickest. Lys could feel Genni watching her, waiting. So in one, daring chug, Lys tipped the glass back and drank.

It was the same liquid Ayden had given to her when she'd collapsed on the front stairs. At least it tasted the same—flat Sprite.

"Good job." Genni took the glass. "You might want to lie down."

Lys went to swing her legs up.

"Take your shoes off first."

Wow, bossy. Lys kicked off her shoes and lay down. She didn't feel any different. When Ayden gave her the drink it only took a few seconds to…

Lys gasped. Her intestines suddenly felt like they were being grabbed and wrung out, like someone squeezing the water from a towel. Her senses exploded. Whereas a moment before she hadn't been able to smell anything, now she could smell everything. Mountain air, musty carpet, old people stench, antiseptic and the woman's body odor beside her, thinly disguised by deodorant. It all hit her like a hammer on an anvil. Lys felt herself gagging.

A roaring that put a rock concert to shame started in her ears. It got louder and louder, pulsing with new chords that were so dissonant that it hurt. Lys could hear herself screaming. Her insides burst into flames; her skin went cold like clammy ice. Dark lights blinked behind her closed eyes. Was this the end? Mr. Mason said if she didn't get treatment fast enough that the drug would kill her. She wondered if she should have taken that option.

Black—a word she'd never really thought about. Black was dark, it usually represented evil, loneliness or pain. Now Lys would forever associate black with fear. She'd never been afraid of the dark, but after spending so much time in a deep well she couldn't penetrate with any of her senses, Lys changed her mind.

She didn't know how long she stayed in the dark. It could have been an hour, but it felt more like eternity. Her life before this madness was gone, hidden away—hardly even aware of its own existence. When the light came, Lys wept with gratitude.

It shone through the black like a ray of hope after the worst day of her life. The blue light came toward her, and Lys thought it might be the most beautiful thing she'd ever seen. It shot past her awareness, looped around her and then flew off back to where it had come from. The light left behind a trail of spreading joy, eating the black away, leaving hope.

As the world appeared around her, Lys found herself on the front porch of her house. The Halloween decorations sat by the stairs—a few hay bales and a scarecrow. She reached out a hand and opened the door, walking inside. She took a breath, trying to inhale the sweet scent of home, but it didn't work. She smelled nothing.

Lys glanced around. The pictures hung on the walls, and her mom's purse sat on the edge of the table. However, the feeling of home that rushed over her each time she walked in the door didn't come. Nothing came. The house felt more like an empty shell than the place she lived.

Lys didn't want to be alone. So she went back outside, looking for her parents.

That's when she noticed the yard. Her attention had been directed at the house before, but now that she looked around at everything else, she knew something was very wrong.

A gigantic hole filled the spot where the driveway should be. Her father's car sat smoldering, blown in half like in a movie. Lys panicked. She ran toward the car, hoping—praying—that her father was not inside. When she got to the driver's side she stopped. Someone was in the front seat. Only two people drove this car. She swallowed and looked away.

This must be a dream. She closed her eyes, and then opened them again. Eyes? Two? Lys reached up a trembling hand to touch the right side of her face. There was no patch or bandage there. She let her eyelashes brush her fingers as she blinked. She had two eyes. Two good eyes—she could clearly see out of both. She had her eye back, but she'd lost her parents?

No, this couldn't be. Her eye was ruined. The doctors said she could keep it, but she'd never see out of it again. This had to be a dream. She could control a dream. Lys closed her eyes and concentrated on waking up.

Nothing happened. She took a breath, not sure it would help, and tried again, filling her mind with thoughts of the real world. The light faded, and she felt herself being pulled back into the dark.

Lys sat up, gasping for breath, her sheets drenched in sweat. She immediately doubled over, dry-heaving into a bucket that resided next to her bed.

Was this the second or the third time she'd woken up? Lys didn't know. She remembered Genni giving her more tonic, but she had no idea when that had been. Yesterday? Five minutes ago? Time meant nothing in the darkness, and since each time she closed her eyes that's where she ended up, she didn't have any idea how many minutes, hours or days had passed.

Lying back in the bed, Lys kept one hand on the lip of the bucket. She held it like a rescue rope. Sleep came for her again. The darkness crept in, and no matter how hard she tried, Lys was helpless to keep it at bay.

This time she didn't start out trapped in the abyss. This time she recognized her surroundings immediately. She floated above Los Angeles; it was burning. The center of the city—all of the sky scrapers—smoldered. Like a giant torch, they lit the smoke-filled sky with an eerie glow.

Somehow Lys was flying. For reasons she didn't understand, she flew closer, drawn to the scene by the desire to know what had happened. Below her, the streets lay mostly deserted. The first person she saw was a little girl. Not more than five or six years old, the little girl stood in the middle of the street, surrounded by holes that looked like they had been punched into the roadway by a giant hammer.

When Lys moved closer she could see that the little girl was giggling, but she couldn't hear anything. To Lys' surprise, the little girl bent over and tapped the ground with her hand, like packing sand. When she did so, the ground gave way as if a wrecking ball had hit it. The asphalt spider-webbed out for a dozen feet in each direction.

What in the world? Lys stopped, shocked. She fluttered over the little girl, who must have noticed her presence because the little girl looked up. Lys met her eyes. They were filled with a blue-green swirling vortex. Lys recoiled from the alien orbs, flying away, arms pin-wheeling. But she didn't get far before the Need swelled up inside of her. It stopped her retreat and propelled her forward again until Lys hovered within reach of the girl. The little girl waved, and Lys pounced.

Lys woke with a gasp. Her whole body shook. She always woke up shaking. These withdrawals made the flu feel like a sniffle. Sometimes she wished that the option of dying was still on the table. She had to use the bucket again. The lack of contents in her stomach almost made Lys wish she'd eaten more at her last meal. Whenever that had been.

They were expected to come down to meals. Nobody ate much—appetites were no real concern for anyone. Lys didn't care if she never ate anything again. Ever.

But, three times a day a knock came at her door. One of the women on the staff would be outside, dressed in their green and khaki uniforms, ready to escort her down to breakfast, lunch or dinner. Sometimes it was all Lys could do to not yell at them to go away.

Lys thought that sleep would drag her in again, but this time the dream left her wide awake. She lay there, one arm dangling off the bed touching the bucket, wondering if a knock would sound. Maybe that's why she woke up.

Had it been three days since they arrived, or four? She could clearly remember her arrival, Kenny and dinner, with Mr. Mason's explanation that the drug's effects were long lasting if not handled properly, and she remembered breakfast from this morning. Or was it yesterday?

Sleep did not come. Lys was grateful. She rolled onto her back and glanced at the window. No light filtered in through the green curtains. Could it be morning? She didn't want to get up.

Lying on the bed was the only thing that felt remotely comfortable. Standing, walking, talking and pretty much everything else was, well, it was hard. It hurt, and she didn't want to do it. Any of it.

Unfortunately she had to pee.

Sitting sent waves of excruciating pain through her entire body. Working up to the effort of swinging her legs off the bed took a good ten seconds. Her head felt like it might split in half. The pain had begun after she'd drunk her first round of tonic, and it hadn't stopped since—an angry little man with a big hammer was whacking the inside of her skull.

She placed her hands on the bed, one on each side of her hips. This was the really horrible part. Lys took a breath, which caused her head to throb even harder, and stood. She only got halfway before she doubled over, and she had to wait for a wave of dizziness to pass. Or at least abate. Reaching out for the dresser, Lys straightened up.

The first step was always iffy; having only one good eye didn't help. Lys shuffled her right foot along the thin carpet, moving the heel of her right foot just past the toe of her left foot. Good, no falling.

The second step she actually lifted her left foot off the ground. Her hand stayed on the dresser. The foot made a tiny arch and came back down onto the rug, right on an orange patch of the pattern. If she could hit the orange patches all along the floor she would be at the bathroom in five steps. She'd tried to follow the greenish patches once, and the counselor had had to come in and pick her up off the floor.

She made her way slowly to the door that led into her private bathroom. It seemed to take forever to do anything, and using the toilet was no exception. However, by the time she finished, she felt even more awake than before.

An impulse from another life hit Lys, and she turned to look at herself in the mirror. Needles of pain ripped through the base of her skull. The dim light gave her just enough illumination to see by. Her eye met itself in the mirror and she glared.

Was that her? So haggard and sallow? Her sunken cheeks looked yellow. At least she thought it was yellow. Lys still saw things that weren't there. As a matter of fact, suddenly, staring back at her in the mirror was her face from before. Her young, beautiful, perfect face. Not this horror that she had become—no eye patch, no deathly pallor.

Lys' teeth ground together. She used to cry, in the beginning, but now she got angry. When she got angry the Need came, and when the Need came she wanted to hurt people. More and more she wanted to give in, to just let her body and her emotions do what they wanted to, but a small part of her was still sane, still Lys. She wondered how long it would last. The tonic helped, but not enough.

She turned away from the mirror, not bothering to brush her long, dark hair back or straighten her shirt. She went to flush the toilet, and nothing happened.

Another try didn't improve the situation. "Figures," she said to herself.

With a sigh, Lys moved out, following the orange spots until she reached the call button and pressed it. Nothing happened. Lys frowned and pressed it again. Still nothing.

A few seconds went by. There was supposed to be a counselor at the desk at all times. Usually one of them knocked on the door or buzzed the room right away. Strange that no one answered.

Lys took a firm grasp on the door handle. Once she balanced, she lifted her other hand and knocked.

"Hello?" Lys said as loudly as she could in a gravelly voice. It felt like talking through a mouthful of marbles. No one answered.

Okay, now she was concerned. Lys jiggled the knob and knocked again. To her surprise, the knob turned. It wasn't locked?

Lys opened the door and slowly stepped into the hall.

Moonlight streamed in through the windows at the end of the hall, leaving illuminated squares on the linoleum. The rest of the lights were off. Lys took a few more steps. She felt her balance begin to return as she moved.

Well, since the door was open, and Lys didn't want her toilet overflowing, she decided to make her way to the main desk. That's where the call button should be directed to, right?

The world tilted back and forth as she followed the linoleum squares. Her fingertips stayed on the handrail attached to the wall, lightly caressing the wood surface.

Silence surrounded her. Lys could hear the sound of her own heart beating, and the slap of her bare feet landing on the floor. When she got around the corner she stopped. A single reading lamp lit the desk, but she didn't see a counselor.

Lys turned, looking back toward her room. Where was everyone?

The light from the main desk darkened for a moment. Lys turned back, hoping to find that the counselor had returned. No luck.

"Hello?" she whispered. "Is anyone there?" Her pale wisp of a voice hardly penetrated the air around her. No answer.

Someone, or something, had just moved between her and the lamp. Lys was certain of it. Or she could be hallucinating again. She didn't like either option, so she turned to go back to her room. She didn't want to meet anyone else. It could be Kenny, or one of the other guests. What if this person was about to give into their Need—whatever it might be? What if they hurt someone? Went on a rampage of killing, or whatever. Yeah, she would go back to her room.

But as she started to walk back, she heard a slapping noise, and she stopped in her tracks. It sounded like running feet. The footsteps, if that's what they were, were headed away from Lys.

She went to take another step, but darkness engulfed her.

Lys tried to blink away the gloom, but nothing happened. Had she passed out? Was this another dream?

A fuzzy light came from her right, and Lys turned her head to look. A figure, roughly shaped like a woman in a flowing dress, floated forward, driving back the darkness as it came. Lys wondered if she was seeing a ghost.

Lys didn't move, but her perspective did. Her vision turned and she found herself running away from the anamorphic shape. The hallway looked similar to the one outside her room, but dust covered everything. The linoleum peeled back in places—several chunks were missing, making a "U" shape on the floor—and the handrail hung loosely from the brackets on the wall.

The light began to fade the longer she ran. Or whatever body she was trapped in ran. It could be another dream. She felt like she was watching the scene through someone's helmet camera.

An open door appeared on her right, and Lys bolted inside. Darkness filled the room, but she could see the light getting brighter in a mirror that hung on the wall. Her perspective looked around, maybe searching for a place to hide. The light continued to get brighter, and just before she turned back, Lys spotted a reflection in the mirror. She didn't see herself, instead she saw Brady.

The light rose to a blinding level, and Lys saw Brady's hands go up in front of his eyes. The floating apparition came through the door, fingers like fabric ribbons reaching for Brady. He stumbled back, falling...

Lys' own eyes shot open. She stood in the hallway outside her room, hand gripping the rail along the wall so hard that her whole arm shook. One thought flashed through her mind. Brady was in trouble. Someone had to help him!

Logic told her that withdrawal caused the hallucination, but something else, a feeling she couldn't explain, said otherwise. It was real and it was happening right now.

She turned back to the desk where the reading light glowed, illuminating some of the surrounding space. There should be a counselor. Where were they? The bathroom? That could be it. She started to move in the direction of the desk again, but her legs turned to spaghetti and she almost fell flat on her face. Lys managed to stumble over to the desk before she ended up on the floor.

The hallucination had left her weak. Well, not weak, she thought as she got her feet under her again, just feeling strange. Excited and shaking. Maybe a little terrified too. Lys couldn't decide. She glanced down, hoping to find a note there about where the counselor had gone, but found nothing.

How much time had passed since she'd buzzed the desk? Two minutes? Five? Surely if the counselor had been in the bathroom they'd be back by now.

She glanced around. Where else would there be a counselor? Downstairs? She hadn't seen anyone at the desk down there at all. Upstairs? Where were their rooms?

In order to get downstairs Lys had to get to the far end of the hall. That didn't sound fun. Lys turned her head to look at the elevator. She hadn't noticed before, but the elevator light glowed B.

The basement? That might explain the dust and run-down hall that Lys saw Brady in. He must be down there. She'd go down to the main floor and start yelling. That should wake someone up.

Walking to the elevator almost took more concentration than Lys had in her. Her legs started working again, but they didn't respond with their normal speed. The trip felt like it took an hour, but it couldn't have been more than a few seconds. She willed herself to move faster, knowing that whatever was after Brady would surely have him before she got help.

The down arrow lit up as soon as Lys pushed it, and she waited as the lights above the elevator went from "B" to "L" to "2". The world paused before the doors slid open with a ding, releasing a soft wall of light.

Part of Lys hoped to find a counselor behind the doors, or Brady even, but that didn't work out. Instead she found only empty air.

Before the doors could shut again, Lys stepped inside. She caught her reflection in the mirrors along the back wall. Her reflection, not Brady's. She looked as bad as she felt, but Lys couldn't stop thinking about Brady and the terror in his eyes.

Lys turned around and pressed the button to go down to the lobby. She watched the reading lamp until the doors slid shut. She willed the elevator to hurry. Why was it that when you needed to get somewhere fast everything seemed to go twice as slow as normal? The ride down one floor shouldn't take so long. Lys glanced up at the lighted numbers above the door and found that she'd passed the lobby level and was going into the basement.

"What?" she asked herself, pressing the lobby button again. The "B" above the door lit up, and the elevator settled to a stop.

Lys didn't want to go to the basement. The doors opened, but Lys kept pressing the lobby button. Then the double arrows to close the doors. Neither button worked. The light coming from the elevator only penetrated a few feet past the door.

Lys glared into the dark. She backed up against the far wall of the elevator, her fingers gripping the rail. After a moment, details started to stand out.

Dust covered the floor, Lys could see that. She could also see several sets of new footprints. One of them walked by the door and the other stepped right out of the elevator. One set had to be Brady's. The apparition following Brady didn't have feet, at least not that Lys had seen, so the other set must belong to someone else. A counselor? Maybe they followed him down here in the elevator. Would she be in trouble for being out of bed?

The thought seemed absurd. All she wanted to do was help Brady. He had looked terrified. Who in their right mind wouldn't go after him? All of this flew through her mind, but Lys didn't move to get off the elevator. She waited for the doors to slide shut, but it never happened. Go out? Lys didn't want to do that.

A moan floated through the darkness, and Lys jumped. Was that Brady? Her own fear was overcome by worry—worry that something was down here chasing him. Lys stepped forward once, twice and then out of the elevator into the dark hallway.

"Brady?" she said. It felt like yelling would lose the ghosts of fifty years, so she kept her voice down.

A scraping came from her left, and Lys turned that way and started to walk. Her hands shook, and a chill crawled up her spine. The sound of her heart beating had to be audible to everyone in the building. She took a dozen steps before the light from the elevator started to retreat, the dark replacing it.

"No!" She turned in time to see the doors sliding shut. Lys tried to run back, but her legs still refused to be rushed. She thrust her hand out, trying to get it into the gap, but the sliver of light disappeared just before she got there.

Darkness descended. Her shaking hands rubbed along the wall, trying to find the up arrow button. The hard surface gave way to the round indent. She pressed it again and again, but it wouldn't light up. Another moan floated through the dusty air. Lys twirled around, keeping her back against the wall. Brady was down here. Something else was down here. Now she was down here, and she was trapped.

Chapter 6

The stairs. Where were the stairs from here? They had to come all the way to the basement. Weren't there fire codes or something? There had to be a way out. Heart pounding, and hands still shaking, Lys pushed off and started down the hall. One trembling finger kept contact with the wall, and in order to distract herself from the dark closing in around her, Lys imagined the trail it would leave in the dust.

After a dozen or so steps, the surface stopped, leaving nothing but air. She groped ahead until she found the next corner. The opening was too small to be a hallway, so she kept going. The stairs had to be this way.

The dark pressed in on Lys, making it hard to breathe. Even though there were no eyes down here, at least none that she could see, the Need stirred inside of her. She imagined veterans walking these halls, their eyes wild, their memories haunted with things that Lys didn't even want to think about. Stale air filled her nostrils—she could taste the old around her.

A whimper poked through the air, reminding Lys of the reason she came down here in the first place. Brady. Her eyes must be getting used to the dark, because she could make out the gaping black hole that was the next doorway ahead of her.

Another step caused something to crunch beneath her feet. It felt like gravel or dirt. She stopped, flicking her foot like a cat. More crunching. But she hadn't moved. Someone else was close. The sound stopped.

If she could barely see down here, no one else could either. Who would be sneaking around in the basement? Why would anyone be here in the middle of the night?

"Brady?" she whispered. She hadn't meant to; it just came out. Fear pulsed through her body faster than her blood.

A dark figure emerged from the gaping hole to her right, heading straight for her. Lys took a step back.

She drew in a breath to scream, hoping that someone would hear her. Before she got it out, a flashlight flipped on, illuminating the shadowy world around her.

Her scream came out as a strangled cry. The light split the dark, much like it had in her dreams. But instead of a shimmering ghost, a dark figure with shinning eyes stood before her.

"Kamau?" she asked, placing a hand over her fluttering heart.

"Lys?" he said, taking a small step back. "What are you doing down here?"

"I—" she stopped, dropping her gaze. What was she supposed to say? I thought I had a vision of Brady down here running from a ghost? Yeah, that would go over well. So she countered. "What are you doing down here?"

Kamau glanced around. "I was looking for Brady. He is not in his room."

The two of them started at one another. Kamau's gaze shot through her, and Lys felt the Need stir. She shifted her eyes to the ground.

"You should go back upstairs." Kamau said.

Lys swallowed. "I'm fine." Her voice held an edge that scared her. Her memory turned to Kenny and his swirling eyes. What was Kamau's need? His guarded expression told Lys that Kamau was wondering the same thing about her.

The two of them stood there, the gloom pressing in around them, trying to penetrate the small pocket of light they resided in.

"We should go upstairs," Kamau said after a few breaths of oppressive tension. He lifted a hand as if to gesture her back down the hall.

She couldn't help it; Lys took a step away from him.

Kamau froze. "I am not going to hurt you."

He meant it. At least it felt like he meant it. Lys didn't get the impression that he was about to break into crazy. However, Kamau kept shifting his weight back and forth on his feet and glancing around, as if he expected someone else to be close by.

"Sorry," she said, willing herself to stop moving. "I, uh—"

A cry filled the hallway. This one started out as a sob, and then escalated into a full blown, blood curdling scream. Lys' heart turned to ice in her chest.

"Is that Brady?" she asked, her voice trembling.

"I hope not," Kamau whispered. He stepped closer, and this time Lys didn't step away. She would risk him wanting to braid her intestines together just so she could have someone real standing next to her. Unless he turned out to be a hallucination.

"Maybe we should go back upstairs," he said.

"No," Lys shook her head. "We have to help him." The words came unbidden. She would much rather run to the end of the hall and up the stairs than go after the apparition in the basement. But she couldn't get the image of Brady's terrified face out of her mind.

Another scream came, this one louder than the first. If any of Lys' blood still flowed, it froze in that instant. However, a warmth came from inside of her. From depths she hadn't accessed in years.

She'd always had a protective streak in her. She never got busted for ditching class or writing on the bathroom walls. No, she got in trouble for being overprotective. Back in junior high, a kid in her gym class had pushed down one of the overweight girls. He and his buddies kept shoving her and laughing as the girl struggled to get back up. Lys had become so mad that she began to shake all over. Her vision blurred and she screamed at the boys to leave the girl alone. She still didn't remember what happened after that. She must have attacked the boys, because the gym teacher had to come over and pull Lys off the leader of the pack.

She hadn't considered it before, but the knee jerk reaction to help her friends rivaled the insistence of the Need. Not as frightening, but just as persistent.

"You saw Brady come down here?" she asked Kamau.

He hesitated. "I did not see him, but I heard him leave and followed him down the stairs."

"Come on," she said, grabbing Kamau by the arm. "Let's go get him." It was stupid. Bordering on insane really, but she didn't see any other course of action. She had to find Brady. Kamau had the flashlight, so she was determined to drag him along too. Besides, she didn't want to go alone. And a tiny part of her didn't want him lurking in the dark behind her.

"Go get him?" Kamau asked.

Now that she had back-up, Lys felt better about being loud. "Brady!" she cried. "Where are you?"

Her voice drove through the air, bouncing off the walls and shooting down the hallway.

A moan answered her. It came from their left.

"Lys, maybe we should..." Kamau started.

Lys ignored him. She kept a hold of his arm and took them down the next hall toward the sound of what she hoped was Brady.

The beam from Kamau's flashlight bobbed up and down as they moved, almost at a run now.

The same gray haze as she'd experienced upstairs blurred her vision, and Lys gripped Kamau's arm tighter for support. She could see herself out of the corner of her eye, like she was looking from Kamau's vantage point.

She shook her head, tossing the strange vision away, and kept running. They got to the corner and turned. She saw the "U" shape of missing linoleum on the floor.

"Come on," she said, leading them to the doorway. "He's in here."

And she was right. Brady crouched on his hands and knees,

shaking.

"Brady!" she said, rushing forward.

"Wait." Kamau's hand shot out, holding her back.

"But—"

"Look at him," he said.

The flashlight beam cut through the settling dust. Lys got the reflection of it right in her eye as Kamau shined it across the mirror behind Brady. A crack ran the length of the glass, and a spread of shards lay on the floor. Blood trailed from the mirror to Brady's hands. Lys followed the spot of light as it moved up to Brady's head. Sweat dripped from his hair, and his whole body shook.

"Brady?" Kamau said, gently pushing past Lys and into the room.

Brady flinched at the sound of his name, moving away like a frightened dog.

"Brady," Kamau repeated, "can you hear me? Do you understand what I'm saying?" He stepped forward, holding his hand out behind him to keep Lys from coming any closer.

Lys couldn't see around Kamau, but she heard Brady whimper, as well as the scraping of glass shards on the linoleum floor.

The light around her faded, once again replaced by the gray haze. She could see the hallway, and her perspective followed the footprints in the dust with its eyes. Up ahead a glow came from one of the rooms.

She shook her head. Hallucinating again? Is this what happened to the others when Kenny freaked out? Seeing things that weren't there, remembering things that hadn't happened?

"Brady," Kamau said again, moving closer to Brady and squatting down next to him. "Can you hear me?"

"Get away," Brady said, pleading in his tone. Lys knew that tone, she knew those words.

"Get back," she said, going after Kamau and pulling him up.

He turned on her, a questioning look in his eyes.

For a moment she was mesmerized by his dark, deep eyes. They'd seen things she never had. Why couldn't she see them too?

Another scream from Brady brought her out of it. The sound cut through the silent room, severing Lys from herself for a moment.

"We need to find a counselor," Kamau said.

"Help me," Brady whimpered, gasping for air after screaming. He writhed on the floor, curling up into a ball. "Please."

"What's that?" Kamau asked, looking behind Lys.

She whipped her head around. Behind her, at the end of another hallway, floated the sneering, glowing head of a wolf as big as a table. It snapped its jaws and slowly came toward them.

"We have to get out of here!" she said, going to Brady and trying to pull him to his feet.

Kamau stood transfixed, watching the light come toward him.

"Help me!" Lys said. All of the ghost hunting shows she'd ever watched late at night were coming back to her. They'd never seen anything like this!

Kamau finally turned and came to help her. Brady twitched and moaned, but it didn't sound like pain. Lys' thoughts turned back to the Need, and how she felt after she took the eyes from the frog. Pure ecstasy.

She almost dropped Brady and ran for it, but Kamau grabbed his other arm—the one with a deep gash in it from the mirror—and hauled the smaller boy to his feet.

"This way," Kamau said, pulling them both out the door and away from the advancing wolf head.

"Is there an exit down here?" Lys asked, glancing back over her shoulder. The glowing apparition glided at them.

"There's an exit sign," Kamau said, pointing his flashlight ahead.

Sure enough, a steel door stood at the end of the hall, and above it, an exit sign.

"Uh, that door is locked," Lys said, noticing the security bar and stout lock.

"I can open it," Brady said in a hoarse voice. Lys barely recognized it as human.

The light behind them grew brighter as they moved. Lys and Kamau dragged Brady between them. He couldn't get his feet under him. How did he plan to open the door?

Unfortunately, they had no other direction to choose from. Everything else along the corridor led into rooms. She couldn't see any other hallways or turns to take. It was either the exit door or go back and face the apparition behind them.

Kamau brought them to a halt. He studied the lock, like maybe he could pick it, but before he could do anything, Brady let go of Lys and flung himself at the door, hands first.

The door crumpled like newspaper, caving in around his hands and folding almost in half. Brady shook his arms, like he was trying to get his sleeves down, and the door flew outside into the night. He fell to his knees, looking at his hands in wonder.

Lys glanced back. The light around the approaching head grew steadily brighter.

"Let's get out of here," she said, stepping forward, not taking her eye off the thing behind them.

Brady nodded and stumbled to his feet. They followed him out the door. Three concrete steps led up. Lys misjudged the first one and tripped, hitting her elbow and scraping both hands.

"Come on," Kamau said, practically picking her up and setting her back on her feet. Once they reached the top Brady went to the left. Kamau flipped off the flashlight.

"No!" she said quickly. "Go this way." She pointed. Not far from their position she could see the path that went around the hospital."Why?" Brady asked, shaking his head as if trying to clear it.

"The path is right over here," Lys said, pushing past him.

"Lys," Kamau said, reaching out and taking her hand to stop her. "How can you tell?"

She looked back. He looked concerned.

"I can see it," she said, tugging him along. "We can get back to the front doors if we follow it."

"You can see it?" Brady slurred, sounding drunk.

"Yes," Lys said. They had to get back inside and tell Mr. Mason what had happened.

The two boys followed Lys. Kamau kept a hold of her hand—Lys didn't mind.

Twigs dotted the path, and Lys wished again that she had put her shoes on. Come to think of it, why did the boys think to put shoes on?

Her thoughts hurtled ahead, and Lys couldn't clear her mind of insane questions. How had Brady just ripped through a metal door?

"Guys," Brady said, "I don't feel so good."

"Here," she said, reaching out with her other hand for Brady's. "Just follow me."

Where Kamau's hand felt warm in hers, Brady's was ice cold. The moment their fingers touched Lys felt a shock, and she jumped back.

Kamau must have felt it too, because he pulled her away from Brady, placing her behind him.

Her hand remained cold where Brady's fingers had brushed it. The chill began to spread up her hand and wrist toward her shoulder. She shook her arm, trying to get the tingling sensation to go away.

"What was that?" she asked Brady.

He didn't answer; instead he looked intently at his hands. Turning them face down, his fingers began to twitch like they were moving across an imaginary keyboard. "This is so weird."

"I think we should get around to the front of the hospital," Kamau said.

Lys whole heatedly agreed. "Yeah, come on." She looked back toward the crumpled door. There was no light coming after them—no ghostly form. Had she been hallucinating? What about Kamau? He obviously saw something that scared him enough to run.

"Someone's coming," Brady said.

Lys turned her head. She couldn't see through the thick trees. Anything could be hiding in the shadows.

"Let's get back inside," Kamau said. This time he pulled Lys by the hand.

She started to follow him, but stopped when Brady didn't move. Her heart beat insistently in her chest—something felt wrong.

"Brady," she said, "let's go back."

Brady sank to his knees, placing the palms of his hands on the ground. "I can feel everything."

Lys glanced at Kamau, who watched Brady with a frown.

"What do you mean?" Lys asked.

"I can feel it all," he said, rubbing his hands along the dirt path. He turned to look at Lys. "It's wicked!" The excitement in his voice caught Lys off guard. Instead of sounding haggard, his voice grew strong and deeper than Lys remembered. And he sounded like he'd just learned that he didn't have to go back to school for a month.

"You've got to try this!" Brady said.

Kamau still had a hold of her hand. He tugged her back as he flipped on the flashlight and shined it at Brady.

Brady knelt on the ground, with both hands still pressed against the dirt. His whole body shook, but Lys hardly noticed. She only cared about his eyes. They were black. Not just the pupils or even the irises. His entire eyeball looked as if it was covered in black oil. The surface swirled, calling to Lys.

Those eyes! That's what she really wanted. The Need broke free of its prison, engulfing reason like an ocean wave. Whatever barrier the tonic had erected washed away in an instant. Lys felt herself lunge forward. If she had those eyes, she would be satisfied.

"No!" Kamau wrapped his arms around her, pinning her hands to her sides.

Lys struggled. She didn't care about Kamau, even though his face lay only inches away. She wanted Brady's eyes, and she wanted them now.

"Lys!" Kamau said. "Stop it! Control it."

The command went unheeded. Lys kicked and wriggled, trying to get free. "Let me go!" she yelled.

"No." He held her fast. "Get a hold of yourself." The beam from the flashlight waved around, hitting trees, the ground and finally Brady again.

The Need pulsed inside of her, forcing her to fight Kamau's vice grip, but she couldn't break free. All Lys wanted was Brady's eyes. If she could get them the Need would go away. It would be satisfied. At least she thought it would be satisfied.

Kamau grunted. "Brady, you need to listen to me. You need to control it. You need to harness the energy and control it. Move it where you want it. Don't let it consume you." There was a highly compelling quality to his instructions.

Brady stood, tilted his head to the side and then walked to the nearest tree. He placed his hand on it. The trunk, thicker than Lys' whole body, exploded into splinters. Kamau moved back as the tree wobbled and fell away from them.

A shock wave ran through Lys. It felt like a line of people had dragged their feet across the carpet and then touched a screw. The electricity went through Kamau and into her. The wall went back up around the Need. She stopped struggling.

Before the tree hit the ground, Brady picked up a rock the size of a softball. He crushed it in his hand like it was a potato chip, crumbs pouring out from between his fingers.

"What's wrong with him?" Lys asked. Was it the drug or something worse?

"Do not let him touch you," Kamau said, releasing her.

Kamau tried talking to Brady again. "You can control it," he urged. "It does not have to control you."

Seeing Brady, Lys knew he couldn't be in control. Of course, in a second she might not be either.

Lys saw a dark shadow moving toward them. "Someone's coming," she said.

"Don't get too close to him!" Mark's voice shouted through the trees. Lys could see his outline running at them, darting between trees and bushes.

Brady turned at the sound of the voice. "You don't understand," he said, "this is incredible. I had no idea how much..." Then he doubled over, going back to his knees. The ground crumpled in on itself where he landed. He tried to stand, but stumbled and fell again. This time the dirt exploded around him. Lys felt rock shards hit her face as she turned away.

"Brady!" Mark commanded. "You have to control it! Do *not* go into it." He ran past Lys and Kamau, heading straight for Brady.

Lys didn't understand. Control it? Go into it? Kamau had just said the same thing. Were they talking about the drug? What did Kamau know about it? What wasn't he telling her?

The ground around them started to shake, and small cracks appeared at their feet. Brady, still on his hands and knees, let out a primal scream—Lys had never heard anything like it. The sound lanced through her body like glass, shattering her link to reality.

Just before Mark got to Brady, someone in black stepped in

61

front of him. Lys heard a twang, and Mark fell to the ground. More figures dressed in black came at them through the trees.

People started to yell, and Lys felt Kamau take her arm and attempt to pull her away. Lys tried to move, but couldn't. The world fractured in front of her eyes.

Suddenly she could see everything. She could see from her own eyes, she could see herself from Kamau's eyes. She could see all of them from above, she could see more figures in black and she could see the crumpled doorway behind them. She was flying, she was running, she was standing and she was dying.

Chapter 7

Fuzzy gray surrounded Lys. She quickly decided she liked the black better. At least with the black she knew what to expect. The gray gave her hope that the light might come. It hurt to hope. What would she hope for? Half-remembered scenes replayed in her mind.

"Get a net on him. This kid is going to kill us all. Cut that girl off before she goes crazy too. Where is Mason? We'll have to take them back to the city…"

She thought she remembered being chased through the forest by people in black, but the memory wouldn't solidify. Other voices asked her if she was using, but Lys couldn't see the faces that went with them. Instead she saw outlines and shadows hidden in the fuzzy gray.

She tried to get the images in her mind in some sort of order; the hospital, dreaming, the ghost, running, falling—Brady!

That thought jolted her awake. Her eye opened. She expected to see stars, with trees overhead and dirt beneath her. Instead a sterile, white ceiling lit by a fluorescent light greeted her.

Lys turned her head. White surrounded her: white walls, white ceiling and white floor. She propped herself up on her elbows, even the sheets, blankets and box frame under the bed were white.

Her head swam with the effort of lifting it, so Lys lay back down. Was she in some new part of the hospital? The sequence of events from the night before still lacked clarity. Another dream? Lys hoped so, but she didn't think so.

The door to the room had bars on it. A cell? How did she get in an all-white prison cell? She glanced around slowly, taking in the bed, a toilet, a sink and about three feet square of free space right in front of the door. The bed touched three of the four walls. Why was she in prison? Surely Mr. Mason wouldn't toss her in here for going after Brady. Especially since he hadn't even given her a chance to explain.

Her new clothes consisted of a shirt and a pair of pants—both white and resembling scrubs more than anything else. Thin, white slippers covered her feet.

The slap of a foot on the floor drew Lys' attention. She wasn't alone. Before she could talk herself out of it, Lys sat up and swung her legs off the bed. Her head continued to pound, and her stomach objected, but she didn't throw up or pass out. So far so good.

"Hello?" a deep voice asked.

"Kamau?" Lys said, rising to her feet. Having such a small cell proved to be handy. She had to reach out to steady herself as she walked to the door.

Outside her cell lay a white hallway. The walls curved, more like a tube than a hall, with a flat spot running down the floor and the ceiling. She could see three other cell doors.

Kamau stood in at the door across from Lys. His polite mask gone, replaced by a scowl.

"Where are we?" Lys asked, looking around. It was like they'd been abducted and placed in some alien space ship. Or a bad reality television show.

"I'm not sure," Kamau said, a stony look on his face. "But I do not think we are in the hospital."

Neither did Lys. Mr. Mason didn't seem the type to let them wake up wondering. He'd have someone there to tell them what was going on. Wouldn't he?

"Is anyone else here?" Lys asked, craning her head to try to look into the other cells.

"No," Kamau said. "But someone has been screaming from far away."

Brady. He had plenty to scream about: being addicted to a drug, running from ghosts, or suffering from the Need.

Lys' mind halted on that subject. The Need. It was gone. She explored it, not wanting to wake the Need, but wanting to see if it was still around. Lys poked at it like she would a canker sore. It stirred, but only a little. Like it had been buried under a mound of heavy blankets. Buried? The tonic sort of repressed the Need; it never felt like this.

Lys risked meeting Kamau's eyes and found them glaring at her.

"What?" she asked. What was his problem?

"Why were you out of your bed?"

"Uh." Seriously? Weren't there more important things to discuss? Like where they were.

"What were you doing in the basement?"

Lys shook her head. "I, uh, the toilet in my room clogged, so I buzzed the counselor. No one answered, and the door was open, so I went looking for someone to help." She didn't think he'd believe the truth! Visions and dreams? Now that she really thought about it, the whole fiasco was probably a hallucination brought on by Pop. Or the tonic.

"How did you get into the basement?"

"I took the elevator down, trying to find someone, and it took me to the basement. The elevator wouldn't go back up, so I stepped out. Then it closed and wouldn't open again."

"Why were you wandering the halls?" His eyes bore in to hers.

"Why were *you* wandering the halls?" she asked, returning the glare. "Down there in the dark? And why did you have a flashlight with you? You just usually carry one around in your pocket?"

She hadn't meant it to come out so forcefully. Too late now.

"I told you, I was searching for Brady," Kamau said.

"Why didn't you just tell the counselor that he was missing?"

Kamau rubbed the bridge of his nose with a hand. "There was no counselor when I called."

Lys opened her mouth to reply, then stopped.

"What is it?" he asked.

"There was no counselor when I called either," she said.

Kamau's scowl turned into a thoughtful frown. "Are you sure?"

Hadn't she just gone over this? "I went to the desk and didn't find anyone. Why do you think I got on the elevator?"

The two of them regarded one another. Lys broke the silence. "Why was Brady out of his room?" Finally the most important question hit her, floating up from the dredges of her mind. "What happened with him, anyway?"

"I do not know," Kamau said. It looked like he wanted to say more.

"What was with the door? How did he do that?" Lys asked, leaning forward and pressing her face between the bars.

"The door?" Kamau asked, shifting his eyes to a spot above her head.

"You saw it," she said. "He hit it and the whole thing crumpled like a piece of paper. How did he do that?"

"It was an old door."

That was his explanation? "Oh come on," Lys said, "You saw it too."

"I only saw him open the door."

"You're totally lying." Again, not what she meant to say out loud.

His scowl deepened. "I do not know what you saw, but I saw Brady push the door."

Lys opened her mouth to rebuttal, but stopped. Her mind jumped again. Maybe she could get him with this one. "What did you see coming down the hall after us?"

"I do not know what you mean." Kamau looked away.

"The glowing ball of, whatever? What did it look like to you?" He didn't answer. Lys went on. "I know you saw it."

Kamau hesitated before answering. "The figure of my

66

grandfather in his ceremonial robes."

So they all saw different things. Lys saw a wolf head, Kamau saw his grandfather and Brady saw a woman in a flowing dress. Or at least she thought that's what he saw. "Maybe it was all a hallucination," she said aloud. Only she hadn't seen anything when Kenny freaked out and the others had.

"Perhaps." He frowned.

"Do you think Brady is okay?" Lys asked. "He seemed pretty messed up."

"You should have listened to me and stayed away from him." The words sounded more like advice than a censure.

"But he was in trouble!" Lys said, waving a hand through the bars. "We couldn't leave him there."

"Why are you so concerned about him?" Kamau asked, his voice finally breaking back into the realm of friendly.

"I dunno." She shrugged, looking down. "I just felt like he needed our help. Well, my help. I couldn't leave him there, not when he looked so scared." She risked a glance back up. "Thanks for coming with me."

"You did not give me much of a choice." His lips tugged into a tiny grin.

She had been a bit forceful. "Yeah, sorry about that. I hope I don't get you in trouble."

Kamau looked around. "I think we might be in more trouble than we know about."

"Why do you say—"

A squeak followed by a slam interrupted them. Two men in black suits came from the end of the hall. Both men stood taller than Kamau and filled out their suits like body builders. One of them had brown hair and the other had blond. The blond haired man spoke first.

"Oh good, I see you're finally awake." The heavy tone belayed the light-hearted words. "It's about time." His eyes, which Lys quickly berated herself for looking at, even if the Need was buried right now, held nothing but contempt for her. And when he turned to Kamau, a deep scowl surfaced.

"Mr. Doyle will be happy to see that you're both okay," the man with the brown hair said.

The man with blond hair stepped forward, stopping in front of Lys. "Time for you to see the boss."

The man was huge. He towered over Lys, gazing down at her with both curiosity and repulsion. Mostly repulsion. Lys didn't understand.

"Who are you?" she asked. "Where is Mr. Mason?"

The two men exchanged a knowing glance before the dark haired one spoke. "We'll let Mr. Doyle explain that to you."

Blondie placed a hand on the bars in front of her. There was no lock, but when the man touched the bars, she heard a click and the door swung open.

She didn't move. She didn't like the vibe blondie gave her. In fact, it took everything she had not to take a step back. The guy oozed disdain from his haughty look down to his immaculate suit. Lys didn't know who he was, why she was sitting in a jail cell or what they were going to do with her. She changed her mind and took the step back.

"Come on," the other man said, gesturing for Kamau to come out into the hall. "You too," he said when he saw Lys backing away.

Kamau followed the instructions. Lys hesitated. Really? Who were these guys? She caught Kamau's eye, and he jerked his head back, signaling for her to join him.

Being with Kamau would be better than ending up alone with the man standing outside her cell. Mustering her courage, Lys squeezed past the man, who didn't even bother to try to get out of her way, and went to stand next to Kamau. Lys didn't notice how bad she was trembling until she bumped up against Kamau's steady arm.

"Let's go," the man with the dark hair said, leading the way back toward the door at the end of the hallway.

Lys didn't want to move. Her heart pounded in her chest, and something inside of her told her that these guys were more likely to hurt her than help her. She didn't know why she felt that way, and that scared her more than anything.

She almost jumped off the floor when Kamau's fingers brushed her wrist. He gently wrapped his hand around hers and gave it a reassuring squeeze.

"We should stay together," Kamau said in a whisper.

Lys nodded and allowed him to tug her forward. They followed the dark haired man down the hall, with blondie bringing up the rear.

"May I ask where we are?" Kamau asked as they went through the door.

"Mr. Doyle will explain," the man in front said, biting off the last word. Silence descended and she glanced around the hallway.

This part of the building, or whatever they were in, looked more normal than the rooms they had just come from. The walls were still white, but they made a square instead of a tube. Framed paintings hung at regular intervals. Brass sconces threw patches of light onto the plain, white ceiling.

They went down the hall and turned left at a "T" intersection, past a few closed, wood doors. At the second one on the right, the man stopped and knocked.

Lys couldn't help her trembling. It felt like she might shake apart from the inside. Who or what was behind the door? Not Mr. Mason. Or aliens—she hoped. The police? Some government official? But why?

She didn't have to wait long to find out. The door swung inward, and when the man with the dark hair moved out of the way, Lys saw a large, wood desk with a man sitting behind it.

69

"Please, come in," the man said in an Irish accent. He gestured for them to enter as the dark haired man stepped aside. Kamau led Lys inside, still holding onto her hand.

The man stood, spreading his arms out. Two chairs stood before them. "Sit down."

Lys didn't move. As a physical specimen he didn't compare to the other two, but he had a hard look around his eyes that told Lys that he shouldn't be trifled with. His clear, blue eyes studied her for a moment. Lys held his gaze, and got the sudden urge to comb his curly, red hair.

"You can stand if you like, but with what you've been through, you should probably sit." He smiled, still looking at Lys.

Lys glanced at Kamau out of the side of her eye. He shrugged and they both moved to sit down. When he let go of her hand, Lys felt as if she'd just lost her life line. However, she rallied, and sat smoothly onto the chair, keeping her eye on the man across from her.

He nodded and sat. "My name is Rolan Doyle. You've met my associates, Erik and Jed." He waved the other two men out.

Kamau spoke. "My name is Kamau Matola. May I ask why we have been brought here?"

Mr. Doyle leaned forward, placing his arms on the desk. "I will tell you, after your friend introduces herself."

Lys swallowed. "My name is Lysandra Blake." She continued to look into his eyes. "Who are you?"

"I am here to help you."

Those were almost the same words Mr. Mason had said to her in the psych ward.

"Help us with what?" Kamau asked.

Mr. Doyle hesitated before he didn't answer Kamau's question. "What did Mr. Mason tell you?"

"How do you know Mr. Mason?" Lys asked.

He raised his eyebrows. "Jeremiah Mason and I have known

one another for a long time."

"What is your association with Mr. Mason?" Kamau asked, pressing the matter.

"I clean up Mr. Mason's messes. Try to salvage the lives he destroys."

For a moment Lys wondered if Mr. Doyle and Mr. Mason were rivals. Both trying to run treatment facilities?

"Messes?" Lys asked, the words slipping out. "What are you talking about?"

"Well," Mr. Doyle sat back in his chair and crossed his legs. "Which story did he feed you?" He looked at Kamau. "That you were suffering from a rare condition brought on by radiation from electronics use?" His attention turned toward Lys. "Or did he tell you that you were addicted to a drug that you've never heard of? Both are fatal, according to Mr. Mason."

"What do you mean?" Kamau asked.

"Which story did he give you?" Mr. Doyle asked again.

Kamau stared hard at the man across the desk. "Drugs."

Mr. Doyle nodded and looked at Lys. "And you?"

Her heart dropped into her stomach. "Drugs."

"I thought so."

Silence descended. Lys spoke. "I'm sorry, but I don't understand."

"Our good friend, Mr. Mason as you call him, is a sham." Mr. Doyle sat forward again. "He poisons people, and then swoops in to save them before their mysterious condition can turn fatal."

Poison? What in the world—Lys didn't know what to think. She didn't even know what to ask.

"It's ingenious, really," Mr. Doyle said. "He causes the symptoms, waits until he sees you are in the advance stages of the poison, and then comes to the rescue." He turned his attention. "Where are you from, Kamau?"

"I am from Mozambique."

"Interesting." Mr. Doyle nodded. "It's rare that Mason goes so far for people. He must have seen something special in you." He turned to Lys again. "What did he see in you?"

Lys didn't feel like this conversation was going anywhere constructive. "I'm sorry," she said again, "but who are you and why are we here? So far all you've done is sling accusations at someone who isn't here to defend themselves. Accusations, I might add, that we can't verify because we're being held prisoner."

There went her internal censor again. She'd only meant to spill about half of that.

"Oh, you're not prisoners." Doyle laughed.

Kamau frowned. "The cells that we just came from suggest differently."

"You're right about the cells; they don't seem very friendly, do they?" Doyle waggled a finger at Kamau. "But that's for your own protection. Mr. Mason gave you some tonic, if I'm right, and that stuff can really mess you up for a while. The cells are to keep you safe—a clean room environment that suppresses the effects of Mr. Mason's poison."

Lys was tired of this man telling her things that Mr. Mason supposedly did. "You haven't answered my question. Who are you? Not your name," she said quickly, "but what you do and who you work for." She was now channeling her inner attorney. Her dad would be proud.

Doyle nodded. "Fair questions. I've already told you that my name is Roland Doyle. We work for an independent branch of law enforcement. It is our job to track down people who deal in these..." He seemed to choose his next words carefully. "These crimes against youth who don't have any idea what they're getting themselves in to."

Lys took a breath to ask another question, and Mr. Doyle held up a hand. "Mr. Mason is a criminal. As far as we can tell, he searches out teenagers that have a mental or physical ability that he is interested in. He then poisons them, as I told you before, and swoops in at the last minute with the only available cure."

Whoever this guy was, he knew Mr. Mason. He'd just told Lys' story. Minus the poisoning in the first place part.

"What kind of abilities?" Kamau asked.

Doyle shrugged. "It depends on what experiment he is working on."

"What sort of experiments?" Lys asked.

"Well," Mr. Doyle said, "the 'hospital' that you were in had a laboratory in the basement. We think Mason was trying to gather select DNA in order to clone a perfect human being."

A perfect human being? Lys repressed an eye roll. Secret experiments? This wasn't a movie. Besides, she'd been in that basement. Dust practically encased the place; it obviously hadn't been used in ages.

"I know it sounds insane," Mr. Doyle conceded, "but he's been doing it for a few years. Our team has been on his trail, and yesterday was the first time we've ever caught up with him." A look of regret imposed itself on his face. "Unfortunately it was just an experiment site. We were hoping to find his main facility." He glanced back and forth between Lys and Kamau. "The two of you don't happen to know where that is, do you?"

Lys shook her head. Her thoughts flew in ten different directions, none of them good. She tried to line up Mr. Doyle's story with what had happened to her, with what Mr. Mason had said to her and then with what she'd experienced since all of this had started. It just wouldn't fall into place.

"Too bad," he said with a sigh. "I guess we'll just have to keep looking. It's lucky for you that we found you in time."

"In time for what?" Lys asked, sitting forward. "What did you save us from?"

Doyle looked into Lys' eye. He held her gaze for a moment. Lys felt the Need stir, wiggling under the blankets.

"A fate worse than death," he said.

Chapter 8

"A fate worse than death?" Kamau asked, raising his eyebrows. "Please explain."

Mr. Doyle nodded. "Yes, I know it sounds impossible. Mr. Mason has been performing experiments on people for years. Are you familiar with the mass suicides in Vermont about six months ago?"

Lys nodded. She remembered. Almost fifty teenagers had barricaded themselves into an old mansion for a month. They'd made some demands—Lys didn't recall exactly what—and had somehow got on the wrong side of the law. When the police or FBI or whoever took care of this stuff charged the mansion, all of the people inside had killed themselves.

"His people initiated that whole affair." Mr. Doyle pulled open a drawer and retrieved a picture. Lys immediately recognized a younger Mr. Mason. He and five other men stood in front of a wooden sign that said "Mending." The man on Mr. Mason's right was the leader of the people in Vermont. Lys had seen his picture a dozen times over the course of the standoff. Her social studies teacher tried very hard to keep her students up to date with the latest news.

"You recognize him?"

Lys nodded. Kamau shook his head. "I am sorry; I am not familiar with the event."

Mr. Doyle cleared his throat. "This man here was attempting a mind control experiment in Vermont." He pointed at the photo. "He and his people were harmless at first, but more and more innocent kids got sucked into the cult—for lack of a better term— and their parents grew concerned. When a handful of parents tried to come and retrieve their children, they found that their kids had been completely brainwashed. Not one of them would leave.

When law enforcement got involved, the man in this photo convinced everyone in his little cult to kill themselves."

Lys watched Kamau's reaction. His frowned deepened.

"How does this relate to Mr. Mason?"

Mr. Doyle turned the photo so he could look at it. "Mason was still in contact with this man up until just a few days before the whole thing blew up. We've been unable to find out what their communication consisted of, but we can only presume that Mason had a hand in suggesting that these people destroy any incriminating evidence against him."

That seemed pretty extreme to Lys. First off, the people in Vermont had made it very clear that the decision to end their lives was a completely individual choice. They left letters to their families, if Lys recalled correctly, that stated as much. Something about not being able to live in a world where being different made them outcasts. At the time Lys figured they were all mentally unstable, and had been led down the wrong path by someone who just wanted to either make money or revel in fame.

Thinking about the whole thing from a different angle, she had no way to tell what those people had been through or what their reasoning had been.

Kamau's voice interrupted her thoughts. "Forgive me if I seem doubtful, but this is all very strange."

"I realize it sounds insane," Mr. Doyle said with one of his now familiar smiles. "I'm just glad that we got the two of you out before anything permanent went wrong."

"What about Brady?" Lys asked.

"You mean the other boy that was with you outside the hospital?"

"Yes."

Mr. Doyle's smile faded. "I'm afraid he's in bad shape. Until he wakes up we won't be able to assess how much damage Mason's drugs did to him."

Drugs. Lys couldn't wrap her head around all of this. Mr. Mason said she was addicted to a rare drug. This man, this Mr. Doyle, someone she'd never seen before in her life, claimed that Mr. Mason had poisoned her so he could get her to his facility and then either use her for her DNA or brainwash her. This made less sense than Mr. Mason's original explanation. Thoughts of her first visit with Mr. Mason brought her memories back to her parents.

"Can I call my parents?" she asked. "They were planning to visit the hospital a few days after I got there."

"We have contacted your parents." Mr. Doyle looked back and forth between them. "They are aware that you are safe. Unfortunately we cannot let you speak to them, or release you, until this matter has been officially investigated."

"Release us? I just want to call my parents."

"I spoke to them myself," Mr. Doyle said. "They know you're safe."

A beep came from Mr. Doyle's watch, and he glanced down at his wrist. "Looks like I've got a meeting in just a few minutes. Why don't you let some of my people get you some food? I'm sorry to say that you'll have to stay in the cells for at least another day. The residual effects of the poison can be fairly nasty, if you know what I mean, and it's safer for everyone if you're locked up."

Wait, what? This guy was going to give them a snack and return them to their cells?

Mr. Doyle stood as Jed and Erik came back into the room. "Get these two back downstairs and bring them some food."

He looked at Lys and Kamau. "If you know anything about where Mr. Mason's facility might be, please tell me. We've been tracking this bloke for a long time, and it would put a lot of people at ease to know that he's been captured and put behind bars."

* * *

77

The short walk back to their cells felt like a thousand miles. Lys' mind was weighed down more than her limbs could ever be, and she didn't know which would give out first.

Had Mr. Mason lied to her? She had felt so sure about going with him. He promised to help her, and as far as she knew he'd kept that promise. Until this Mr. Doyle and his agency had kidnapped her.

Kamau's arm bumped hers, but the contact held no comfort. The world as she knew it a month ago lay in pieces. For a time she thought Mr. Mason could put it back together for her. Could he? Could anyone?

And Brady. Was he really too far gone? What did Mr. Doyle mean by all of that? The more that Lys thought about the basement at the hospital, the more she knew she had no idea what really happened.

If she believed her own version of the events she had seen a vision of Brady. Not a dream, not a memory, but a clear vision of either what was happening to him right then, or what happened a few minutes later. She'd seen it through his eyes. The only proof she had was the memory of going down into that basement and finding him in the room with the mirror.

That's when things started to get jumbled. She saw a light like he did, but when Lys saw it through her own eyes it looked different than when she'd seen it through Brady's eyes. So that didn't match up. Not completely, anyway. And Kamau had seen something totally different.

The issue of the door bothered her the most. Lys clearly remembered Brady crumpling the door like a piece of paper. With his bare hands. Kamau claimed he only saw the door open. Why would a barred, emergency exit that probably hadn't been used in years be open? Brady hadn't had a key. Kamau hadn't been close enough to be able to use a key. Had he?

She felt Kamau's hand brush her back as he led her through the door into the hall outside their cells.

"Are you alright?" he asked in a voice so quiet that Lys barely made out the words.

Not knowing what else to do, she shrugged. No, she wasn't alright! Was he?

Lys didn't even bother to speak as the two men put her back in her cell. They'd asked her what kind of sandwich she wanted just after they'd left Mr. Doyle's office. Another man arrived, handing them their lunches and leaving.

Turning to watch the men go, Lys stood at the barred door of her cell and wondered who to believe. She took a bite of her sandwich.

"You seem troubled."

Lys looked across the hall to where Kamau stood behind bars. "Aren't you?" she asked. "None of that seemed strange to you?"

To her surprise, Kamau smiled. "All of it seemed strange to me."

"Do you think he's lying to us?"

"Everyone lies," Kamau said. "Even people who think they are telling the truth, or doing things for the right reason."

Everyone lies? Lys wondered again if Mr. Mason had been lying. If Mr. Doyle had just lied to her. If Kamau really came from Africa. She supposed that she lied. Not a lot. Her parents had instilled a regime of truth throughout her childhood. Even when she did something stupid, if she told them the truth about it they would usually be reasonable. The few times Lys had tried to get away with a big lie, they'd caught her and she'd been punished.

"What do you think?" Kamau asked.

A harsh laugh escaped before Lys could stop it. "I think that anyone who leaves us in a dungeon, however bright and shiny it might be, isn't telling the whole truth."

"I agree," Kamau said. "He is hiding something."

79

Lys glanced around. The bars under her hands were cold metal covered in white paint. She couldn't reach anything else from where she stood; not even Kamau's hand if she'd wanted to. Turning, she studied her cell: sink, toilet, a pillow and a bed with sheets and a blanket. The sheets were fastened to the mattress, which was bolted into the frame which was encased in a steel box. Nothing there.

"What are you thinking?" Kamau asked.

"Just trying to figure out how to get out of here," she said. "If he would let me talk to my parents I might be inclined to stay, but he won't."

"You have a plan?"

She shook her head. "No. And we probably shouldn't be talking about it." She couldn't see any video cameras, but a place like this—a dungeon for some "independent branch of law enforcement"—had to have a camera somewhere. Maybe microphones too.

Kamau nodded. She hoped he understood. He'd seen movies, right? Didn't he say he'd been going to university before Mr. Mason had found him? It seemed strange to think that the boy standing right across the hall from her, someone she'd talked to and even been through danger with, lived half way around the world. Their differences should be more apparent than the color of their skin. But they weren't. They were both in the same boat. Did that make them friends? Or more?

Lys sat on the floor by the door and they both ate their lunch in silence—Lys not even tasting the food as she chewed.

"What does your father do?" Kamau asked.

"Uh," Lys said, "He's a lawyer."

"How long will it take him to realize that you are not where he thought you were?"

"I'm not sure," Lys said. "It depends on when they were planning to come and visit the hospital. It could be today or tomorrow or even the next day. They were supposed to call Mr. Mason and set up a couple of appointments."

That brought Lys back around to Mr. Mason. He had been very secretive about where he would be taking her. Her parents received some information from him, but Lys hadn't been privy to it. Not about the location of the facility anyway.

"I think that perhaps we should ..." Kamau started. Then stopped.

A low rumble filled the air, and the ground beneath Lys' feet began to shake.

"What is it?" Kamau asked, looking around.

"Earthquake." She shrugged. "Not a very big one."

"How do you know?"

"I live on the west coast. This happens all the time." Although when the shaking didn't subside after a few seconds she looked around.

When the wall on the other side of her bed blew open, she was so surprised that she didn't bother to duck. Rubble few at her, but most of it went to her left.

"Are you sure this is the right way?" a weak, but familiar, voice asked through the settling dust.

"I'm sure," Brady replied. "I can feel them through here."

"Brady?" Lys asked, coughing as a storm of particles enveloped her, rolling out through the ruined wall like fog.

"Hah!" Brady said triumphantly. "I told you we were going the right way."

Chapter 9

As the dust settled, Lys saw Brady holding up the slumping figure of Mark. They both wore the same plain, white outfits that she did, although someone had wrapped Brady's cut arm.

"What are you doing?" Lys asked, stepping forward to help Mark get through the opening. It was a hole at least four feet around.

"Busting you guys out of here," Brady said, supporting Mark from the other side. "Kamau is here, isn't he?"

"I'm here," Kamau said.

"Good, just let me get these doors open and we'll be on our way," Brady said.

Brady left Mark with Lys. As he stepped away, Lys noticed that Mark could barely stand. He leaned heavily on her, and Lys tried not to stumble. Fresh bruises adorned Mark's face and arms. Lys' eyes traveled down to his hands, which were encased in what looked like bright yellow hair gel. Solid hair gel.

"What is that?" she asked.

"Don't touch it, mate" Mark said, slurring the words together.

"Come on," Brady said, pulling the bars of her door apart like Superman would. "I'll grab Kamau and we'll get out of here." He looked back toward her with a grin.

"How did you do that?" she asked, shaking her head. Brady winked at her.

Lys stopped, noticing his eyes. They were the black, oily clouds again, just like when they got out of the basement of the hospital. But now the swirling vortex only filled in where the color of his iris should be.

The Need poked a hand out from under the pile of blankets.

Lys pulled her eye away from Brady's. He didn't seem to know (or care) that his eyes looked like pools of oil.

"Where are we going to go?" Kamau asked as Brady stepped through Lys' door and pulled the bars on Kamau's cell apart.

"Out," Brady said. "I heard some of the guards saying that only a few people are on duty tonight. A company party or something."

"And you think we can get past them?" Lys asked. She sent Kamau a grateful smile when he came over and pulled Mark's other arm over his shoulders.

"Brady can get us out," Mark said. "We have to go now."

"Why?" Lys asked as they started to follow Brady to the far door. "Who are these guys?"

"They're bad guys," Mark said. His head lolled around as if it might fall off any second. "They kill users."

Kill? Lys looked over at Kamau, who frowned down at Mark.

"Kill us?" Kamau asked, voicing the question before Lys could. "Why?"

"Because we can kill them. Don't worry, Brady will get us out," Mark said. "Just follow him."

The words garbled together. Mark's shirt came up as Kamau readjusted his hold. A dark, ugly, purple bruise, bigger than Lys' hand, covered his stomach.

Before she could ask what happened, Brady pulled the door at the end of the hall off its hinges and set it gently back on the floor.

"See," he said, looking back at Mark. "I told you I could be gentle."

"Good job," Mark muttered. "Now get us out of here."

Brady grinned. He seemed to be enjoying this a little too much.

They followed the younger boy out of the dungeon and into the more normal hall. The dim lights bathed the corridor in twilight. Brady waved them to follow as he crept along, keeping one hand on the wall at all times.

"How did he do that?" Lys asked, eying the door as they came through. Had Mr. Mason given him super powers?

"He's a chaos user. He can get through the field," Mark said. He jerked in their arms, and Lys almost lost her grip.

She exchanged a worried glance with Kamau. He shook his head—he didn't understand Mark's words either.

Brady waited for them at the next intersection. "There are a couple of people pretty close. I'm assuming that's the way out?" He directed his question to Mark.

"Dunno. I was out when they brought me in."

"I was awake," Kamau said. "The entrance they brought us through is that way." He pointed to the left.

Brady reached down and touched the floor with the palm of his hand. "There are a few people that way too, but they're much softer."

"That is the way out," Kamau said.

"Then we'll go that way," Brady said with a grin as he stood. "Follow me, and stay close."

Lys always imagined soldiers or action heroes saying things like that. The words seemed cheesy coming from a fourteen year old kid from Great Britain.

The implications of their flight started to sink in as Lys and Kamau dragged Mark through the hallway. They might escape, but where would they find themselves? And what would they do once they got out? Not that she wanted to stop and have a discussion about these things—she kept on Brady's heels as much as she could—but the questions kept surfacing.

Questions like, how could Brady suddenly bend metal bars like Superman? Or rip doors off their hinges? Put holes as big as her through walls? And what did Mark say? Chaos user? Field? What in the world was going on? The super power theory was starting to sound sane.

And this couldn't be a hallucination. No way. Lys had

dreamed some horrible things at the hospital when she'd taken the tonic, but this was different. More real, more sensory. Part of her wanted this to be a bad dream, but the realistic part of her knew better.

Each time they came to an intersection, Brady would squat down and touch the floor with his hand. After a moment he would stand and lead them the direction Kamau indicated. Lys lost track after two turns. She spent most of her energy trying to keep Mark upright.

The next time Brady stopped, Kamau spoke. "The entrance we came through is at the end of this next hall." He pointed. "But it opened up into a garage. I bet we can get out right here, if you wanted to avoid the guards."

Mark raised his head and he and Brady seemed to have a silent conversation. Brady nodded and looked back at Kamau. "Sure, I can get us through. No problem. You might want to move for a second."

Lys pulled Mark back as Brady stepped up to the wall. He closed his eyes and placed his palms on the concrete. He started to move his hands around like a mime, touching the surface in different spots.

"There we go," he muttered. Lys watched in amazement as Brady brought his hands back a few inches, and shoved them into the wall.

Shards of concrete shot out from around Brady's hands. Craters appeared beneath his touch. He curled his fingers under, and they sunk into the wall like it was made of sand.

Brady took a small step back. He pulled. As soon as the wall started to moan Brady shoved forward, pushing a section ten feet long away from him.

Bricks broke apart, and metal screamed. A chunk of the wall, at least six feet wide, shot forward, still in Brady's hands. Shards of rebar stuck out of the edges, and bits of brick cascaded to the floor.

Mark, who had raised his head to watch, said, "Not bad."

"I know, right?" Brady laughed, shoving his hands apart, ripping the chunk in two and tossing the pieces away.

"Stop right there!" a voice said from the end of the hall.

Lys turned her head to see two men in black coming toward them. Only these guys weren't in black suits, they were in black body armor. Just like the guys she remembered seeing outside the hospital.

Chapter 10

"Go!" Brady said, pointing at the hole. "I'll hold them."

"Hold them?" Lys asked.

"Trust me," Brady gave her another grin. "I've got this."

Mark shook his head. "Don't be stupid. You remember what I told you about the suits."

"Just so we can get away!" Brady said, bouncing on the balls of his feet like a boxer warming up. "Now get going."

Kamau started pulling Mark over to and through the giant hole in the wall. Lys had no choice but to follow. Well, she could have let Mark fall flat on his face—there was always a choice—but she didn't think that would be very nice. Or smart. So she kept going, trying to get them moving as fast as she could.

"Who are these guys again?" she asked no one in particular. She didn't expect and answer; she just wanted someone to validate the situation for her. The black body armor looked like something right out of the movies. It creaked like leather, but her fuzzy memory told her that they could take a beating. Their helmets resembled black bug heads with large, glossy eyes and pointed noses.

"The New," Mark said. "And they don't like us very much."

The dust settled and Lys saw that Kamau had been right. A small parking garage lay before them. Four cars and two vans occupied six of about twenty stalls.

"Where do we go?" Mark asked.

A blast sounded from behind, and Lys turned to look. More dust rolled at them, and she could hear Brady laughing hysterically.

"I told you to stay back!" his enthusiastic voice said. "I tried to warn you."

Two more figures ran toward them from the opposite

direction Brady had gone. "Brady!" Lys cried. "Watch out."

An alarm started to squawk, and strobe lights began to flash. The two figures ran at the hole. Brady arrived in the same instant they did. Both parties stumbled to a stop. Through the strobing lights, Lys could see that the two figures weren't men in black. They were kids.

Well, not little kids, although one of them wasn't even as big as Brady, but teenagers like her.

The taller figure grabbed the little one and got in front of him.

"Whoa," Brady said, holding up his hands.

"Who are you?" a girl's voice, accented in Spanish, demanded.

"I, uh ..." Brady stumbled over the words. Between strobe light assaults, Lys finally got a good look at them.

The shorter figure, a boy probably only twelve or thirteen, studied Brady through long, scraggly blond hair. The other figure, a taller girl with skin the color of caramel and dark hair that hung in loose curls down to the middle of her back, glared.

"Inez, look at him," the younger boy said, working his way out from behind her to get a better view of Brady. "Check out his eyes." He pointed.

"Who are you?" This time Mark spoke. He managed to use an imposing voice, and both figures turned to see who had addressed them. The girl grabbed the younger boy by the collar and shoved him behind her again.

"Cut it out!" he complained.

"Who are you?" Inez asked, glaring at them through the dust. She kept her eyes moving back and forth between Brady and Mark. "Are you with them?" She jerked her head back down the hall toward the last place Lys had seen the guys in black. Now the hall stood completely blocked by rubble.

"No," Mark said. He tried to stand up, but it didn't really work. "We're not with them."

Inez continued to glare. Her angry, haunted eyes seemed out

88

of place on her beautiful face.

Lys felt the Need kick a foot loose and looked away. Why had it felt so repressed before, and why was it coming out now?

"That one is using," the kid said, pointing at Brady.

"Shut up, Peter," Inez said. Although she did glance over at Brady, looking at his face for a moment.

"We need to get out of here," Mark said. "Before they bring reinforcements.

Inez glanced at Lys, Kamau and then back at Mark. When her eyes came to his hands they widened, and she muttered something in Spanish. Lys had no idea what she said.

"Inez," Peter said, tugging on her arm. "They're coming."

"I can get you out of here," Brady said, finally regaining the use of his tongue. "We were just leaving." He shot Inez a crooked grin, Lys thought he was going for charming.

Inez gave him a hard glare. "We don't need your help."

"We're all going to get caught if we don't move," Peter said. Lys noticed that he kept breathing deeply and looking back down the hall.

"You're on your own," Inez said to Brady, grabbing Peter by the arm.

"Wait!" he protested, pulling free. "We can't leave them here." He pointed at Brady, who stepped through the hole toward Lys. "He's using. You're always saying that we'd help anyone who—"

"Forget what I said," Inez said through gritted teeth. "We have to get what we came for and go."

"We can't go back," Peter said. "They're coming from there."

"We have to go," Mark said. "Now."

The tone of his words left no room for argument. He started to stumble away, pulling Lys and Kamau with him.

"You can't get out that way," Peter said.

"Maybe you can't." Brady looked back at them. "But I can." He shrugged. "You can follow us if you need to."

Kamau, who had been silent during the exchange, whispered, "There should be a door leading to the lobby in that corner. If I'm not turned around, there are a number of buildings right next to this one. We should be able to take cover."

Brady nodded, moving past them and into the lead.

"But Inez," Peter protested, "they're both using, and check out that guy's hands. Isn't that the stuff that you said we should--"

Inez shushed him. Lys glanced back just in time to see Inez dragging Peter down the hall.

"Do you think they'll be alright?" she asked no one in particular.

"We don't even know who they are," Kamau said. "Just as long as they don't draw attention to us."

Brady led them across the small parking garage. They wove through the vehicles, and no other people appeared. She could hear shouting, but she couldn't tell how close they were. The sound echoed between the walls, bouncing back and forth like a racquet ball.

"There," Kamau said as they came around a large van. "The door is behind that wall."

"How did you know that?" Brady asked.

"Someone came in the door when we pulled in."

"If you were awake, why didn't you try to escape?" Brady asked.

"Escape is difficult when your hands and feet are cuffed."

Brady shrugged. "Sure, I guess."

The door grew ever closer, but before they got there, a pair of armored men charged through.

"Don't move!" one of the men yelled, pointing a large gun at them.

Lys didn't know much about guns, but the barrels on these were huge. The bullets that came out of them must be the size of oranges. Lys did *not* want to find out what it would do to a person.

She didn't move.

"Yeah, right," Brady said, reaching out for the car next to him.

One of the men aimed his gun at Brady and pulled the trigger. Lys couldn't help it, she screamed.

A flash caused Lys to flinch, and then something the size of two baseballs stuck together came flying out of the end of the gun. It quickly spread out, revealing itself as a net. Before it could reach Brady, he grabbed the bumper and pulled part of it away from the car with a shrill screech of metal. He threw it and caught the net before it hit him.

The metal and the net flew back and hit the man in the armor, causing him to go sprawling on the ground. His helmet clattered off revealing Jed. He glared at them.

The other man fired his gun before Brady could do anything about it. Kamau pulled Lys aside just in time to avoid being buried in the net. The edge of it scraped her arm, and she cried out. A cold chill, not unlike when Brady had touched her in the woods, started up her arm and toward her shoulder.

"Are you hurt?" he asked.

"I don't think so," she said, her words slurring like Mark's.

"Can you move?" Mark asked.

Lys tried. She could move everything, but her right arm responded slowly.

"Missed again," Brady said, laughing at the two men with guns. He kept tossing bits of concrete, car parts and whatever else he could get his hands on in their direction. How *was* he doing that?

"Come on," Kamau said, "if we can get out that door then we can get to the street."

Lys nodded, and started to move.

"Hold it!" a voice said, sounding metallic coming through the helmet.

"You hold it," Brady said.

Lys didn't look back. She heard more grinding metal and a loud thump. Brady laughed again just as Kamau got them through the ruined door.

The short hall beyond led to a small lobby. Lys didn't much care about the furnishings, her focus landed on the wall of windows and the door that led outside.

"Out," Kamau ordered.

Lys did her best to keep up, heaving Mark along beside her and hoping that Brady would come after them.

The lobby sat void of people. Beyond the windows night had settled. Maybe they would actually get away.

She kept thinking back to the woods behind the hospital. These had to be the same guys. So why did Mr. Doyle try to convince her that he just wanted to help? The more people who came at them, the less Lys believed anything Mr. Doyle said. Who attacked kids with net guns? For that matter, who ran around in black combat armor, or whatever that stuff was?

"Brady!" Kamau yelled over his shoulder as they reached the front door. "Come on."

"Coming," Brady said, skipping through the door and into the entryway. His eyes still swirled black.

Just as they reached the exit, a net flew from the opposite end of the lobby. Brady didn't see it, and in mid skip it hit him, flinging him to the floor.

"Don't move!" a metallic voice said.

Lys looked into the lobby and saw Peter and Inez sprinting down the hall, heading straight for them. Another two figures in black chased the duo. Lys caught a glance of someone coming in from the garage. They were in trouble.

Kamau looked around, taking in their surroundings. "Cover your ears."

"Why?" she asked as she covered one of her ears and one of Mark's.

Kamau closed his eyes and opened his mouth.

A rumbling seemed to come from Kamau. It started in the air and then moved into the ground. The floor beneath Lys' feet began to buckle and shake. The air itself started to hum, vibrating her brain through her uncovered ear. She stumbled and almost went down. The windows of the lobby spider webbed, and Lys had to turn her face as the glass shattered. A wave of tile rose behind Inez and swept toward her pursuers. Peter looked back, but she grabbed him and they kept running.

The wave, now a foot tall, hit the figures in black and they scattered.

Peter and Inez ran through the broken window. She kept going, but Peter paused, looking at Kamau in awe. Kamau shut his mouth and the rumbling stopped.

"Dude, that was awesome!"

"Peter!" Inez said, coming back and grabbing him by the arm.

He slithered out of the hold and went over to Brady. "We can't leave them here!" He gave her a puppy dog look. "They saved us."

"They screwed us," Inez muttered under her breath. However, she ran to where Peter knelt next to Brady. She took a black, wicked looking knife out of her boot. Before Lys could object— why did she feel like the other girl might plunge the knife into Brady's heart?—Inez cut the net. It sizzled and flared, like a light bulb, and then went out, going from hard cords to slack. She then reached out and pulled it off Brady.

"Come on," she grumbled, tugging him to his feet.

Brady looked groggy, but he smiled when he saw who had a hold of his arm. "Hey," he said, nodding. "I told you we could get you out."

"Stupid." Inez said. She turned her fierce gaze on Lys and Mark. "Listen, you follow us and keep up. If you fall behind, we leave you."

Chapter 11

Before Lys could ask Inez any questions, Inez moved through the broken windows and out onto the street.

Kamau glanced at Lys. "I suppose we should follow her."

Lys didn't answer. Kamau's brown eyes were now silver and white, like clouds in the sky. The Need twitched again.

"Come with us," Peter said, leading a shaky Brady by the wrist. "We'll take care of you."

Kamau turned away to follow. Lys shook her head, not so certain that Inez would help. Inez didn't seem to want to have anything to do with them. She would probably ditch them the second she got the chance.

"Don't worry about her," Peter said, waving his free hand. "She's a softie."

Lys highly doubted that, but she followed anyway. Glass crunched beneath her slippered feet as she moved through the empty window panes and onto a small street. Low warehouses surrounded them, and the night sky blazed with light. Lys wondered where they could be. She wondered about a lot of things.

These kids seemed to know more than she did. Peter recognized Brady's eyes and hadn't freaked out. Did that mean Brady would be okay? Mark seemed a little concerned, but nothing like Lys would be if her eyes suddenly turned oily black. Inez and Peter knew something, and since Lys knew nothing, it seemed prudent to follow them.

Mark's head lolled back and forth, and he muttered something.

"What?" Lys asked as they made their way across the street and darted down the alley way between buildings.

"Where are we going?" he said, this time more clearly and

right at Inez.

"Away," Inez said, looking over her shoulder. "We should put some distance between them and us. There are plenty more guys where those came from."

Inez led them across the street and between the two nearest buildings. Broken crates, rampant clutter and garbage bins provided obstacles for them to dodge. Lys made them out easily, but everyone else seemed to be having difficulty. Kamau almost ran straight in to a pile of broken boards.

"Watch out!" Lys said, pulling Mark back so Kamau would stop.

"What?" he asked, turning his still silver eyes toward Lys.

The Need shook its head like a groggy dog. This was not good. Lys quickly looked back at the ground.

"There are some boards there," she said, turning them so they would go around.

Kamau reset his path and they set off again.

Inez, it seemed, may not leave them behind. Lys saw her exit the alley, but a moment later she returned and whispered something to Peter.

"Okay," he said, nodding. "You stay with Inez," he told Brady. "I'll be right back."

Brady nodded. The smile on his lips faded, and the color drained from his face. He lowered his head, shoulders slumping.

"Hey," Inez said, smacking him hard on the shoulder.

Brady slowly lifted his head. He never quite got it all the way up.

"Stay with us here," she ordered. "Do not shut down."

Odd words, but Lys didn't have time to ponder them, because she and Kamau got to the end of the alley, and Mark collapsed between them.

He'd been able to get his feet under him for a while, but the way he slumped to the ground made Lys wonder if he could get up again.

"What did they do to him?" Inez asked, squatting down as Kamau pulled Mark into a sitting position, shoving him against a nearby wall.

Lys took a moment to study their new ally. Tall and slender, Inez had just the right proportions and the long, glossy hair to match. If they went to the same school, Lys knew she and her friends would lament about how much they hated Inez for looking so perfect. Torn jeans and a baby doll t-shirt, which should look casual, only added to her appeal. However, the crease between her eyebrows deepened as she looked at Mark. She must make that face a lot, Lys thought, because the scowl lines never went away.

"I do not know," Kamau said.

"He's got bruises everywhere," Lys said, remembering what she'd seen before.

"Yeah, they do that," Inez said, her face showing a look of pity for a moment.

"Do what?" Lys asked.

Inez shook her head. "Nothing good."

Why would no one answer her questions? Inez went to get up, and Lys reached out to touch her arm. Just before she got there, Inez's hand grabbed her wrist, twisting it sharply.

Lys gasped, but managed not to cry out. Pain shot up her arm, and she moved to keep the pressure from breaking her wrist.

"Don't touch me," Inez said in a hard voice, her face a mask of disdain.

Lys returned the glare. For once the Need did her a favor; it gave her the guts to not back down. "Who are these guys?" she asked. "They kidnapped us; I want to know who they are."

Inez continued to stare for a moment before tossing Lys' wrist away like a used paper towel. "I don't have time right now to explain it." She cast a quick glance at Mark, who was watching them. "He probably knows more than I do anyway."

Mark shrugged, his pale face making him look like a ghost. "Can't explain now," he muttered. "Do you have a healer?" he asked Inez.

She frowned. "A what?"

"A healer," Mark said again, his voice cracking as he coughed. "I know you know what I'm talking about."

Inez shook her head. Peter ran back around the corner.

"Where are they?" she asked.

He pointed. "Most of them went the other way, but there are five headed right toward us."

"We have to move," Inez said, glancing down at Mark.

"I can lead them away from here," Kamau said.

"What?" Lys said.

"How?" Inez asked.

"He's in a tribe, he can probably see in the dark," Brady said with a tired grin.

Well, Lys mused, if he could see in the dark why did he almost crash into a pile of boards?

"I have some skill as a tracker," Kamau said. "And I have a few extra surprises up my sleeve."

"Can you follow us once we're gone?" Inez asked.

"Yes."

The two of them locked gazes, and Lys caught Kamau's silver eyes out of her peripheral vision.

"Do it," Inez said.

"Wait!" Lys said, turning to Kamau. "Don't go off by yourself! Those guys might catch you."

"Do not worry, I am an excellent tracker. I will find you."

"Come on," Inez said. She stepped over to Mark and pulled him to his feet with surprising strength. However, Mark stumbled, and even when Lys went to assist her, he almost fell back to the ground.

"I can get him," Brady said in an empty voice. He moved forward with purpose, gently pushing Lys aside and taking Mark under the arm. Lys stepped away, and Brady took all of Mark's weight. He grinned as Inez gave him a reluctant shrug of thanks.

"Where to?" he asked, a little of his bravado returning.

"Follow Peter."

Lys turned to look at Kamau and found only empty air.

"Where did he go?"

Inez shook her head. "He's good."

Lys continued to glance around, trying to figure out where Kamau could have disappeared to so quickly.

"Come on, princess," Inez said. "We can't stay here."

Lys could see the outlines of three figures coming at them from across the street. She followed Inez out of the alley and around the corner.

The sky to her left still pulsed with light. Not fire—she'd be able to smell it—so it must be a city. But which one?

As they ran across another street, heading for a wall of concrete, Lys realized that they could be anywhere in the country. Maybe even the world, although this place didn't smell foreign. She'd been to Mexico and England with her parents, and it was an entirely different experience. Everything looked, smelled and tasted different. Even the air. They passed a street sign and Lys saw that she could read the words. Well, at least they were in the United States. Probably.

Everyone else kept their eyes forward, but she couldn't help herself; she kept looking over her shoulder for either Kamau or the guys in black.

"Don't worry, princess," Inez said in a mocking tone, after she'd caught Lys looking back. "Your boyfriend will be fine."

Lys turned her eyes forward. "He's not my boyfriend," she muttered, not even wanting to go there right now.

Inez laughed.

"And don't call me princess," Lys said.

A huge mound loomed in front of them. Lys recognized it as the freeway. It must be the middle of the night, because hardly any vehicles drove on the road above them.

Brady stopped. He tilted his head to the side. "They're coming."

Lys glanced around. It took her a moment, but then she saw them. Two figures headed their way. "There," she whispered, pointing.

"Peter," Inez said, "you said you could find it."

"I can!" he said, turning a slow circle. "Just give me a minute."

"We don't have a minute."

"They're still coming," Lys said. "Can we at least get out of the open?"

Inez looked around. "Into the ditch," she said, pointing at the sandy area at the bottom of the freeway. They didn't have a lot of options; Lys followed the others, dropping to her knees, hiding behind the edge of the ditch.

"Not that it will help," Inez said. "They can see in the dark in those helmets."

"Do you have a flashlight?" Lys asked. She'd seen someone in a movie blind a guy who wore night vision goggles with a road flare. Then again, maybe the flashlight wouldn't be enough.

Inez didn't bother to answer. Maybe she'd come to the same conclusion.

"I can get rid of them," Brady said. He'd set Mark on the ground and crawled over to Lys and Inez.

"Not a good idea," Inez said.

The two figures got closer, coming down the road, moving their heads back and forth, searching.

Lys' breathing became ragged. Her hands began to shake—the world started to go gray.

Her vision fuzzed out for a moment, just like in the basement of the hospital.

Blinking, she shook her head. After a second the gray haze melted away, and her vision returned. Only what she saw didn't match what she knew she should be looking at.

Instead of seeing the two men coming down the road from the front, now she had a prime view of their backs. The perspective made Lys wonder if she was dreaming again—flying. The two men walked below her, not at eye level. The view swiveled from the backs of the men to the road beyond. Lys recognized the hill behind her, and when she noticed a shadow within a shadow she almost cried out. She could see herself crouched down in the ditch by the side of the road.

Closing her eye, she wondered if this would ever stop.

After a few seconds she opened her eye and found Inez watching her intently.

"What?" Lys asked, trying to sound nonchalant. Inside she breathed a sigh of relief.

"Oh I don't know. Just wondering if you're going to join us."

Lys glanced back at the two figures. They were gone.

"Where did they go?"

"Away." Inez jerked her head. "Peter found us our way under."

Lys followed Inez's gaze and saw Peter crouched on the ground, looking at something.

"Come on!" Peter waved them over.

Inez stayed bent over as she ran the fifteen or so feet to where the others waited. Lys followed, trying to spot either the men or Kamau, but couldn't see anyone.

"Are you sure this is it?" Inez asked.

"I'm sure." Peter folded his arms across his chest and looked at Lys. "I hope you guys don't mind the smell."

Chapter 12

Lys stopped and stepped back. "The sewer?"

"Storm drain." Peter corrected her. "It's different."

"I highly doubt that," Lys said, eying the grate. The two foot square lattice of metal lay nestled in the ground, the rusted bars held down with an old padlock. Up here Lys could see pretty well, but beyond the grate she only saw darkness. The kind of dark that liked to swallow people whole and never let them leave—like her dreams. She shivered.

"You're not afraid of the dark, are you?" Peter asked with concern in his voice.

"Uh, no," Lys said quickly. "Not really." She hated the dark.

"Well it's either the dark," Inez said, pointing down the drain. "Or those guys." She pointed back in the direction they had come.

"Where will we go?" Lys asked. She refused to crawl down there if this didn't lead to something helpful. Or at the very least, safe.

"Our place," Peter said before Inez could answer. He looked at Brady, who sat on the grass beside Mark and pulled on the grate. "Can you get it off?"

"Sure." Brady rose slowly to his feet, almost stumbling before he got up. Again it looked like he carried a heavy burden.

Brady came forward and pulled the old padlock apart with his thumb and forefinger. The u-shaped loop slipped out of the body with nothing more than a flick of his wrist.

"Wow," Peter said, eyes wide.

Inez grabbed the grate and pulled it up. "Come one, everyone in."

"But what about Kamau?" Lys asked. She would not leave him behind.

"He said he was a tracker, he'll find us," Inez said.

"I'm not leaving without him."

Inez raised her eyebrows. "You can do whatever you want, princess, but we're leaving. *He* can probably follow us. Can you?"

Lys hesitated. Could she? Duh, no. There was no way she could track them or follow them. What was it like down there? Dark? A maze? Creepy—yes. Terrifying—absolutely. She could imagine the thick water, the dripping walls, the corroded ceilings and the rats. There were always rats in the sewers. Storm drains. Whatever. It didn't matter. Nothing could stop the pang of fear that twisted her stomach up in a knot. She did not like the dark.

"He'll catch up," Brady said, rallying himself for a moment. "He's in a tribe."

Lys didn't like her options. She could stay and risk ending up alone, or she could go after Kamau herself, or she could go with them now, in the dark, and hope he found his way.

Inez didn't wait for Lys' answer. She jumped down, landing with a small splash.

"Peter," she said, her voice closer than Lys had imagined it would be, "you're next. Then lower that guy down and we'll catch him."

Peter looked at Lys. "Come with us." It was a plea, but didn't wait for an answer either. He jumped down after Inez.

Brady pulled Mark over to the hole. He blinked a few times before he spoke. "Kamau can find us again. Go with them now."

"But…"

"Just trust me."

Trust him? Lys didn't think she wanted to hear that again. Ever. The dark hole gaped before her, ready to welcome her to her doom. She took a breath, hoping it might help. It didn't. The warm, stale air caught in her throat and she had to stifle a coughing fit.

Brady helped Mark to the hole. She forced herself to walk over and grab one of Mark's arms. They lowered Mark down until

Inez said to let him go.

"You next," Lys said, waving a hand at the hole.

"You are coming, right?" Brady asked.

"I don't trust them to catch me," she said.

Brady smiled. "Right." He stepped into the hole, also landing with a splash.

"Come on down," he said.

Lys steeled herself. Every instinct she had screamed at her to run the other way. Dark hole, enclosed space and getting lost—she did *not* want to go down. Her shaking hands could attest to that. However, the image of the men in the black body armor came to her mind and Lys knew that she didn't want to stay either. So she sat on the dry grass and dangled her legs into the opening. A splash of light fell through the hole, and she could see the faint outlines of the people below.

"Just jump," Brady said. "I'll make sure you don't fall."

One deep breath didn't steady her shaking hands, so she took another with the same result. She could do this. Nothing bad lived in the dark. Really. Hopefully.

The soft footfall sounded on the grass nearby. Lys' eye, which she'd closed at some point, shot open.

"Come on!" Brady whispered.

She scrambled to her feet. Maybe she could stall them while the others got away. A shadowy figure stood about ten feet away.

"Who are you?" she asked, hoping to distract them.

"Lys?" Kamau's voice asked. "Is that you?"

The tension in her clenched hands bled free, and she almost giggled. Almost, but she managed to hold it in.

"Yes," she said, able to see him clearly now that his silvery eyes were toward her.

"What are you doing?" he asked in a whisper.

"We're, uh, escaping." Lys stepped back, and pointed at the ground.

Peter's head popped up out of the grate. "What's going—" He stopped when he spotted Kamau. "Oh, hey. Come on down."

Kamau looked at Lys. Lys shrugged. "Brady and Mark are already down there. They say this is the way to their place."

"It's one way to our place," Peter said.

"They will circle back to this area in just a few minutes," Kamau said. "Let's go." He held out his hands. Lys took them as he lowered her into the hole.

"Let go, I've got her," Brady said.

It took every ounce of Lys' courage to release her vise grip. She fell for a split second, then hands grabbed her around the waist and gently lowered her to the ground.

Not ground. Water covered, mossy, slippery concrete. What she wouldn't give for her hiking shoes about now.

Brady pushed her over to where Mark was sitting on a ledge. He seemed more alert.

"Are you alright?" he asked.

"*You're* asking me if *I'm* okay?" Lys laughed. This time the shrill giggle did come out, but she bit it off before hysteria could kick in. To distract herself, she looked around and found that she could see more than she had anticipated. This was both good and bad. The square-ish tunnel they stood in had stone ledges on each side. A rusted ladder hung down from the grate, and looked as if one step on it might break it in half. Ankle deep water ran down the middle of the channel. Cool air brushed her face, a relief from the parching breeze above. Lys didn't see any lurking rats. However, spiders were in rich supply.

If she could see the spiders then it wasn't too dark, right? She returned her attention back to Mark as Kamau lowered himself down the hole.

"What's happening?" Lys asked. "What's up with Brady? And those guys? And Kamau's eyes?"

Mark shook his head. "It's a really long story."

"No time for stories," Inez said, passing them. "We have to get moving."

Brady came to get Mark. Peter followed them.

Lys really wanted some answers, but it didn't seem like anyone else was interested in a Q & A session.

"Come on," Kamau said, moving up behind her. He placed a hand on her back and gently pushed her forward.

"Sure," Lys muttered. Why not follow these people down into the sewers so they could get away from the other people who were chasing them? Great idea. Wonderful day. What's for dessert?

Kamau looked like he wanted to talk, but Lys didn't feel like voicing any of her thoughts. So she turned and followed Peter's retreating form.

The dim light faded the farther they got from the grate. Lys felt her anxiety level rising, but she could still see. The others held their hands out in front of them, like mummies, groping in the dark.

"Peter," Inez whispered. "Get up here and lead us."

Lys watched as Peter walked forward, straight toward a random pipe that hung from the ceiling. Everyone else had passed on the right side of the channel. Peter was on the left.

"Whoa," she said, surging forward and snatching his collar. "You're going to run right into that."

"Right into what?" Peter asked, still searching with his arms.

"That," Lys said, taking his hand and resting it on the pipe.

"How did you know that was there?"

"I can see it."

Brady laughed. "You can see down here?"

"Yeah, it's not that dark," Lys said.

"It's pitch black!" Brady said, holding his hand in front of his face. "I can't even see my fingers."

Inez tilted her head. "You can see down here?"

"Yes." Hadn't she just said that?

"Get in front. Bring Peter, he can tell you which way to go if you tell him what you see."

"Uh, sure." She hoped her wavering voice didn't give her fear away. Why could she see when no one else could? She just hoped she wasn't hallucinating. This trip could get very interesting if she was seeing things that weren't there. Or not seeing things that were.

Lys grabbed Peter's hand as she went by and tugged him forward. They passed everyone else. "There's a tunnel that goes off to the left up ahead."

"Take us to it. I can tell you if it's the right way to go."

Lys led them slowly down the tunnel, warning everyone about stray pipes, cracks in the floor or anything in their way. They made good progress and got to the tunnel quickly.

"Here it is," Lys said.

Peter stopped, turned toward the opening and took a deep breath. He exhaled, and then took another lungful of air. Then he snorted.

"Nope. Keep going."

So they did. The cool air helped clear Lys' head. A thousand smells surrounded them, none as bad as she had imagined. Lys' feet were soggy, the slippers she'd woken up in just wet rags clinging to her toes and ankles. They finally found the rats. She stifled a shriek when the first one scuttled along the ledge and into a hole half its size.

"What is it?" Inez demanded.

Lys put her free hand on her chest, willing her pounding heart to slow. Fight or flight had kicked in. Maybe it had never left. "Sorry, just a rat."

"Afraid of the dark *and* rats?" Inez asked.

Lys muttered, "Who's up here leading?"

"I think she likes you," Peter whispered.

"Yeah, right." Lys didn't much care if the other girl liked her. Not right now, in this dark tunnel, being chased by some crazy guys in black body armor and trying not to think about her shattered life. Or what could be lurking around the next corner.

"We're almost to the strip," Peter said, taking another deep breath.

"The what?" Lys asked.

"You'll see."

She led them on. After what felt like thirty minutes, she began to see lights ahead.

"There's another tunnel leading off to the right," she reported.

"I bet that's ours. I can almost see it," Peter said.

Lys could see everything getting brighter. They came around a bend, and found light shining down into the tunnel from a grate above, creating a crisscross pattern. A soggy slide of pamphlets cascaded down along the wall and filled the channel in front of them with what looked like a mound of old newspapers."Where are we?" she asked.

"Vegas," Peter said, grinning and putting his hands above his head.

Lys looked at a flier that had managed to make it away from the others. Sure enough, an ad for a fun filled night with the lady of your choice. This was Las Vegas alright. Her mother had tried so hard not to let her see the pamphlets the last time they had come.

Thinking about her mother caused an ache in her chest, and Lys pushed her thoughts back into the present.

"We're in Las Vegas?" Brady asked. The excitement in his voice was almost back to its usual level. "Can we go up and see?"

"No," Inez said.

"Please," Brady begged.

"No."

"You're so mean."

107

"She is," Peter agreed. "Don't worry; I'll take you around later."

That's when it hit Lys. Peter's plan not only included taking them to his (or their) home, but he had it in his mind that Kamau, Brady, Mark and her would stay with them. Who took in perfect strangers? Especially the kind who exhibited signs of either genetic tampering or super powers? Lys wanted to look for the cameras. When was the show host going to jump out and say, "Gotcha!"

"Is this our tunnel?" Inez asked, squinting past the light.

"Should be, I'll see," Peter said, letting go of Lys' hand. He bounded forward, over the pile of pamphlets with a watery squelch.

"That's pretty sick," Brady said, moving to the nearest grate and looking up. Lys wasn't sure which form of "sick" he was referring to. "You guys have a secret lair under Las Vegas?"

Inez shook her head.

Mark spoke, his voice weak again. "Where are you taking us?" His eyes met Inez's, and she actually answered him.

"To where we live. We'll be able to get that stuff off your hands."

"Who do you." He hesitated. "Work for?"

Inez snorted and shook her head. "No one. We don't work for anyone."

Peter interrupted. "This is the right way, come on; we'll be there in just a few minutes."

Lys waded toward the pile of pamphlets and started over. With her feet already being encased in soggy slippers, Lys wasn't surprised when her foot slipped, but she hadn't planned to go flying backward. Her balance failed, her arms pin wheeled around, and her whole body started to fall. Lys braced for impact, but a pair of strong hands caught her by the waist and lowered her back to the bottom of the tunnel.

"Be careful," Kamau said, keeping his hands around her until Lys' feet stopped slipping.

"Thanks," she said, trying to smile and avoid his eyes at the same time. The Need tossed off another blanket, and Lys suddenly missed the dark where no one could tell where her eye was pointed.

"Here," Brady said from the other side, thrusting out a hand.

Kamau took one hand, and they helped her over the slippery pile. Much to her annoyance, Kamau came over after her without a single problem. He kept a hold of her hand after that. If the Need would stay down, Lys might have spent a moment thinking about that.

"Any day now would be nice," Inez said, her arms folded across her stomach.

Brady grabbed Mark and they set off down the new tunnel. More fliers swam on top of the almost knee-deep water. The angle of the floor sloped downward, and Lys felt herself grabbing onto Kamau's hand for stability. Part of her hated depending on him— she still didn't know why he had been in the basement of the hospital—but the other part smiled.

"How far down are we going?" Brady asked. The light gradually diminished, and soon even Lys had a hard time seeing much.

Peter didn't answer right way, but Lys saw him stop. "We're here."

A moment later a bright light filled the tunnel, causing Lys to flinch back, blinking her eye.

"Hey," Brady protested. "Easy with that thing."

The beam came from a flashlight mounted to the stone wall with rusty wire. It hit Brady right in the face.

"Sorry," Peter said, turning the light away.

A metal ladder, bolted to the wall, stood next to the flashlight. Rust covered its rungs, and Lys could see an empty hole where one of the bolts should be. Above that, in the ceiling, lay another grate.

"Move," Inez said, pushing past Kamau and Lys.

"Wait!" Brady said, leaving Mark to stand on his own. "It doesn't look safe. Maybe you should let me go first." He smiled at Inez. "You know, in case someone has infiltrated your secret hideout."

Inez turned an icy stare on him.

"I'm pretty handy in a fight," he insisted.

Inez stepped up on the ledge and put her hand on a rung. "I think I'll be okay." She started climbing the ladder. The ladder rose seven or eight rungs—the grate sat about ten feet above them. Inez reached the top and fiddled with a lock Lys hadn't noticed. After a few seconds Lys heard a click and the grate swung up with a tiny squeak.

The realization that Inez and Peter lived in a "secret lair" underneath Las Vegas hit Lys hard, and she wondered how long they'd been there. Did either of them have any family? Friends? Anyplace they could go? In all of this, Lys always kept in her mind that her parents would help her. What if she didn't even have that? What would she do?

Inez turned back, probably to say something, but she never got there. Instead her foot slipped and a rung of the ladder broke off.

The people that said near death experiences play out in slow motion were right. Lys watched as Inez slipped, then fell. Somehow she managed to keep one foot on a rung and it got caught. Her head started down for the ledge, and Lys flinched.

Everyone took a step forward, but Brady was faster. He got there before Lys had even fully realized that Inez might crack her head open against the stones. Like snatching a piece of fluff, he plucked Inez out of the air. She ended up parallel with the ground, one foot still stuck, cradled in Brady's arms.

"Easy, watch your step," he said, grinning.

For once Inez didn't have a scowl on her face. She stared at Brady for a moment before he wiggled her foot free. Holding her like a child, he turned and gently set her down on the ledge.

"Told you I was a handy guy to have around."

"That was awesome!" Peter cried, jumping up and down. "I've never seen anyone move that fast!"

Inez continued to stare at Brady, whose grin only got broader.

"Thanks," she muttered, tucking a stray lock of dark hair behind her ear.

"Anytime," Brady said. "Happy to oblige."

Maybe Lys should explain to Brady that people in Las Vegas didn't talk like old western movies. Then again, who was she to ruin the moment?

Peter tried to move past Inez, but she snatched him by the collar. "Oh no you don't." A moment later she climbed up the ladder and out the grate.

The warm pressure of Kamau's hand in hers got tighter.

"I wonder where we are going," he said in a quiet voice.

Lys nodded. She wondered the same—along with about a million other things.

"Come on," Inez said, her silhouette coming back into view.

Peter and Lys went first, leaving Kamau and Brady to help Mark.

"You're gonna love this!" Peter said, excitement oozing from his voice. He climbed the ladder and disappeared. Lys followed, gingerly avoiding the top two rungs and pulling herself through the square hole.

Chapter 13

Lys had expected a short, squatty room covered in moss with the sound of dripping water coming from one corner. Wrong on all counts. Just as she got her shoulders through, a light came on. She squinted for a moment, allowing her eye to adjust. When she could see again, Lys looked around.

The crumbling remains of a once grand ballroom lay before her. Lys stopped with both elbows through the hole, her mouth hanging open.

"Awesome, isn't it?" Peter asked, grinning. He offered Lys his hand, and she took it, getting up to her feet.

Twenty feet above her a chandelier the size of her bed hung, all brass and crystal, an echo of something she'd expect to see in a European palace. On the end of each arm the stub of a candle rested, the wax dripping down. The ceiling—what was left of it—had an intricate pattern of flowers and leafs carved into dark wood. The far quarter of the room lay in ruins, much like a Lego house would if you ripped part of it off. Dirt, bricks and stones cascaded into the ballroom, and it seemed to Lys that the place might be under excavation.

"Wow," she said finally.

Inez moved away from one set of electric construction lights to another. Her boots clicked on the stone floor, and Lys noticed that most of the dirt and dust had been cleared away.

"Lys?" Brady's voice came from back down the hole.

"Oh, sorry," she said, turning. Mark's head appeared and she held out her hand. He managed to get his arm up and Lys pulled.

"Maybe we should have planned this better," Brady said, grunting from under Mark.

"We've got him," Peter said. He grabbed the man's other arm and hauled him up. Between the two of them, Mark soon sat on the stone floor, panting.

Brady crawled through the hole, and the moment his eyes took in the room a wide grin split his face. "You live here? What is this place?"

"It's the ballroom of an old hotel," Peter said, grinning still. "The rest of the building is mostly gone, but this part and a couple of other rooms are okay."

"Nice secret lair," Brady said appreciatively.

"Thanks."

Kamau finally came up. His face betrayed nothing, but Lys thought she saw just a hint of wonder in his eyes. The Need jerked awake, and Lys took a step back.

"Are you two all alone?" Mark asked, looking around.

"Yeah, just Inez and me," Peter said.

Lys swiveled her eye to watch Inez turn on the other set of lights, beating back most of the shadows. Right behind Inez an arched doorway led away from the ballroom. Another smaller hallway sat beyond that. All of the other exits were either boarded up or sealed with cinderblocks.

"So what do you know about Brady's eyes?" Mark asked Peter as Inez approached.

"I, uh…" Peter glanced at Inez.

"We don't know much about it," Inez said. She stopped a few feet from the rest of them, folding her arms across her stomach. "What do *you* know?"

Lys kept her eye down, but the Need continued to insist that she pay attention to it. A gnawing started in her mind, and her fingers began to twitch.

"Do you even know what his eyes mean?" Mark asked.

Inez regarded him for a moment before she looked away. "Not really."

"It means we're special!" Peter said. "It's like super powers. Isn't that how Brady can do so many cool things?"

113

Super powers. Lys tried to think. Brady could do amazing things—all of them seemingly feats of strength. Could Peter do that? If so, why hadn't he? And what about Inez. A little voice in her head asked Lys, "What about me?" but she didn't get a chance to think about it.

A wave of dizziness hit Lys and she reached out to steady herself.

Brady's hand caught hers. "Easy," he said, "I am pretty amazing, you don't have to get all weird about it."

Lys couldn't help herself. Every sane bit of her screamed to keep her gaze down, but right now the sane bits were overrun by the Need. It forced her to look, demanded that she let it free from its prison. She tried to resist, but the strong arm of the Need slowly lifted her chin until she met Brady's eyes.

"Everything okay?" Brady asked, his smile fading.

Lys shook her head and backed away. "Fine," she managed to say. "I just…I just need to use the bathroom."

Those eyes! Brady's irises still swirled like black oil. Lys knew they were special. She needed them.

"Lys?" Kamau asked. He stepped toward her.

Her attention turned, and she saw Kamau's eyes still the color of wispy clouds. Without giving them a conscious order, Lys' backpedaling feet stopped, and she began to move forward, fingers reaching up for the first eyes she could get her hands on.

"Lys!" Mark yelled.

The word, or perhaps the tone, caused her to falter. Just as soon as she felt control return to her limbs, Lys stumbled to get away from temptation. She fell, landing hard on her butt. She crawled like a crab, and kept going.

"What's wrong?" Brady asked, concern in his voice.

Lys' shoulder bumped into the nearest wall, and she began clawing at the old wood. She had to get away from the Need.

Kamau took a step toward her.

"No!" she yelled. "Please, just leave me alone." The Need raged, furious with her weakness. She curled into a ball, trying to implode on herself. Maybe she would disappear.

Head to her knees, Lys squeezed her eye shut. She didn't want to hurt anyone. "Please, please, please." she begged, digging her fingernails into her legs.

Someone approached her and knelt on the ground. "Lys?" Kamau asked. He reached out and touched her arm.

She flinched back, pushing herself along the wall in an effort to put some space between her and Kamau. "Please, go away. I don't want to hurt you."

"Why would you hurt me?" Kamau asked.

Lys didn't get the chance to answer. Her eyes were burning. Not just the injured one, but both of them. It felt like she had smoldering coals in her eye sockets. Lys screamed—the same scream that Brady had emitted in the woods. She bit it back, trying to stop herself from going wherever she was about to go.

"She will lose control." Kamau's voice sounded like it was fifty feet away and underwater.

"No, talk to her, you can keep her from losing it. Use your power," Mark insisted.

"Listen to me," Kamau said. "Think about something nice. Someone you love. Maybe your parents."

Lys shook her head. "No." The image of her mother's bandaged face haunted Lys. She'd tried to take her mother's eye! What gave her the right to be alive?

"Let me die," she whispered. She started to shake.

"No one is going to die," Kamau insisted. "Listen to my voice. Breathe."

Lys tried. She curled up into a tighter ball, but she felt Kamau grasp her hand.

"Can you understand me?"

Lys nodded, but yanked her hand away, desperate to keep

from attacking him.

"She's going to lose it!" Inez said. "Knock her out. It's the only thing you can do. Or kill her."

Lys was good with that.

"Just listen to the sound of my voice. We can get you through this." He paused, and Lys felt his arms wrap around her. His breath tickled her ear as he spoke. "Do not let it wash over you. You are a rock, let it go around you. Rise above it. Look down on it. Do not let it touch you."

Lys took a breath. Her heart stopped its attempt to wrench itself from her chest, and her eyes cooled from a smoldering coal to a sunburn. The shaking continued—Lys felt as if she was breaking the worst fever of her life.

"Here," she heard Mark say. "Put a tiny bit of this on both of her eyes."

"But…" Kamau said.

"Trust me, it'll help her control it. Just don't put any near your mouth or ears. Then you'll be in trouble."

"Hold on," Kamau said to Lys.

She felt him turn. Even behind her shut eyelid, she saw the world go fuzzy gray. A moment later images of everything around her began flashing through her head: looking at herself from Kamau's eyes, seeing the room from the ceiling, running down the hall and going through a small space in the panel of a door, Mark glancing back and forth between Lys and Inez, who did indeed look like she would kill Lys. More hallucinations? Or something else?

Kamau was back. "Lys," he said, "I'm going to put some of this on your eyes. It will help, but it might hurt."

Lys nodded. It was all she could do.

A cold, clammy substance, something like hair gel, touched her eyelid. Lys drew back.

"It's alright," Kamau told her. "It won't damage you."

Lys didn't care much about damage; the Need roared inside of her.

Kamau lifted up her eye patch and applied the gel to the other eyelid. For a moment nothing happened, and then Lys felt something break inside of her.

The scream came again, and this time she was helpless to contain it. Visions, like those she had at the hospital, flooded her awareness. Other images crowded her mind. These filled her head like the wall of TVs at a department store. Each from a different person, each one overlapping the next. Like a thousand home movies playing all at once. Although how she knew that, was beyond her. Lys only knew that it hurt.

Hurt worse than anything else so far. Not so much physical pain as it was mental anguish. She was overwhelmed—overloaded. Like your first hour at Disney Land on a crowded day. There was too much to process, too much to see.

However, she wanted to see it all. Every little bit of it. A part of Lys ate it up. A small taste didn't satisfy her. No, she wanted—needed—more. Images flew through her mind, and Lys dove into them.

She saw people at a party having a costume contest for Halloween. She saw the shattered windows of the building they'd just run from. A horrible accident on the freeway had traffic backed up for miles. She watched a lovers' quarrel, she saw a baby born. Lys was engulfed. She swam in the visions, ingesting everything.

People laughed, people cried. More babies were born, and people died. Some quietly, others brutally murdered. Lys saw it from every angle, and her mind devoured it and longed for more. The Need gorged itself, and finally it waned, perhaps satisfied at last. With the gnawing hunger inside of her gone, the visions started to thin.

Lys rose, swimming back from the depths of the ocean into

shallow water. The images slowed, and she began to recognize people and places. After the inside hall of her high school disappeared, her own face resolved in three different perspectives. She looked horrible—bad hair, soggy scrubs and a grimace of terror on her face. The green color of her skin made her look sickly, as did her sunken cheeks. Was she dead? The more she thought about it, Lys decided she didn't want to die.

"Is she going to be okay?"

One perspective turned to look at Mark's face.

"She'll be okay," Mark said. "Lys!"

Lys felt her shoulder being shaken.

"Let me try," Kamau said. "Lys? Can you hear me?"

Lys could. Kamau's voice cut through the remaining overlapping images in her head.

"If you can hear me, follow my voice. Come back to us."

She did so; latching her consciousness onto Kamau's voice and following it back to the world.

Her eyes fluttered open. The scenes that filled her head left when her gaze fell upon Kamau and Mark, both looking worried. Lys was laying on a couch, her head in Kamau's lap.

"There she is!" Brady said brightly, his face coming into view.

"You okay?" Mark asked. "Any killing urges?"

Lys shook her head. That act alone sent her world spinning. The little man with the big hammer was back. "No," she said in a haggard voice. She thought she might vomit. "What happened?"

Mark took a breath. "You just broke."

"Broke what?" Brady asked.

"A barrier," Mark replied.

"Is this something to do with the drug?" Lys asked.

"Oh, it's not the drug," Mark shook his head. "There is no drug."

Mr. Doyle's words came back to her. Had Mr. Mason really

lied about all of this?

"No drug?" Lys asked.

"You're a science experiment!" Peter said, pointing at himself. "Just like me and Inez. That's what we think it is."

Mark furrowed his brow. "Science experiment?"

"Yeah." Peter pointed at Brady. "He has to be a mutant too. You saw what he did!"

"Mutant?" Brady looked at his hands. He nodded. "That would make sense."

Mark shook his head. "You're not mutants."

"But we're not drugged either?" Lys said. She struggled to sit up. Kamau helped her, keeping a hand on her shoulder.

"No, no drugs."

Lys looked around. She noticed that old, mismatched furniture filled the small room. Inez scowled at her while Brady looked at his hands, Peter glanced back and forth between people, and when Lys got to Kamau she found him watching Mark with interest.

Mark frowned at Inez. "You think you're science experiments?"

She shrugged and rolled her eyes. "How else do you get special powers?" She put the last two words in air quotes. "I don't go much in for the mutant theory." She waved a hand at Peter.

"You're not mutants," Mark said.

"So we're not freaks?" Peter asked, his eyes wide.

Brady laughed. "You're a freak, kid."

"So are you!" he shot back.

"No, you're not freaks," Mark said.

Still groggy, Lys watched and listened, trying to make sense of the conversation. It felt like she was missing a vital bit of information.

"So if it's not drugs," Brady said, "and we're not mutants, what is it?"

119

"You probably won't believe me even if I tell you," Mark said, shaking his head.

"After what we just went through? I'd believe it if you told me we were aliens," Brady said.

"No, you're not aliens, and you're not mutants." Mark grinned.

"Then what is it?" Brady wailed.

"It's magic."

Chapter 14

"What?" Lys said.

"Magic? I knew it!" Brady cried, pumping a fist in the air.

"Magic?" Lys wanted clarification.

"Magic," Mark nodded.

Lys noticed that his hands were clean—freed from the yellow goo. "What happened to that stuff on your hands?"

Mark held his arms out, wiggling his fingers. "We managed to scrape it off while you were out. Potent stuff."

"Is that so you wouldn't touch anything?" Brady asked.

"Yup." Mark shrugged. "The New know I'm a touch user."

"The New?" Brady asked, putting air quotes around the word new. "That's a really lame name."

"They're not concerned about being cool," Mark said. "They kill magic users. And that would be us."

"Kill?" Lys asked, still not convinced about the whole magic thing. "Why would they want to kill, uh, magic users?"

"They didn't seem particularly interested in killing us while we were there," Kamau said.

"They wanted information," Mark said.

"They'll kill you," Inez said in a hard voice "They've tried to kill us a few times."

Peter nodded gravely.

"Why?" Lys asked. Inez only glared at her, so she turned her attention to Mark. "Why would anyone want to kill someone who could supposedly use magic? We're just kids."

"Not all magic users are kids. They were after Mason at the hospital." Mark turned to meet her eye, and Lys flinched.

Before, with Mr. Doyle, Lys could still feel the Need, even if she couldn't get to it. Now it sat docile, waiting. But for what?

"And trust me, they'll come after us again," Mark said.

"Why are you suddenly so alert?" Inez asked Mark, eying him suspiciously. "Thirty minutes ago you were practically drooling."

Lys thought Mark might be angry—Inez's words were far from kind—but he laughed. "The effects of the New's dampening finally wore off. They've got technology that can repress magic. I'm sure their facility is packed with it." He jerked his head toward Lys. "Why do you think she broke so fast once we got away?"

"What do you mean, broke?" Lys asked. "I don't really feel any different."

"You might not feel any different now, but don't be surprised when your magic starts to manifest itself."

Brady turned to face Kamau. "Magic! Can you believe it? You should check out your eyes! Dude, I told you it would be awesome."

Kamau turned his attention Mark. "I think you owe us an explanation."

"Yes," Lys said. Maybe they would finally get some answers.

Mark opened his mouth to speak, then closed it again. He turned to Inez and Peter. "You don't know anything about magic?"

They both shook their heads.

"How have you survived?"

Lys didn't like the sound of that.

"We make do," Inez said, fixing Mark with an icy stare.

"Well you're still alive," Mark said. He looked them over. "That's something anyway."

"Come on!" Brady interrupted. "You're going to tell us about the magic."

"Fine, fine." Mark held up a hand. "Okay, this sounds a little crazy, but let me get through it." He took a deep breath. "It's is an old story—it goes back so far that no one even remembers the beginning."

Brady rolled his eyes. "What, like a long time ago in a galaxy far, far away?"

Mark smiled. "Not exactly. A long time ago the world was a different place. Before technology the world was filled with wonders most people can't comprehend."

"Technology?" Brady demanded. "Are you some sort of anti-technology freak?"

Mark shook his head. "No. Before technology people saw, heard, felt, tasted and smelled things on a different level than they do now." He paused. "I don't mean technology as in cars, the printing press and computers. I mean technology in the very rudimentary sense; simple machines and helpful tools started it all."

No one spoke; they were all listening intently. "Before technology, there was magic. Magic is divided into five categories. The categories are linked to our senses: touch, sight, sound, smell and taste."

"Mine has to be touch!" Brady said proudly.

"Just let me tell the story." Mark held up a hand. "Back then everyone had some form of magic. Everyone was particularly attuned to one of their senses over the others, giving them abilities beyond the norm."

"What kind of abilities?" Lys asked. What kinds of things did Mark claim this magic could do?

Mark shrugged. "Most of the accounts are gone—lost to society and progress—but the little we have uncovered is amazing. For instance, we have one journal that tells of a man who could punch holes through boulders. Another touch user could put his hand on the ground and feel what was going on around him through the vibrations."

"Wicked." Brady grinned.

"At one time magic was the most powerful force on the planet. There is evidence that the societies of the world lived in peace and harmony for thousands of years."

Peace for a thousand years? Lys couldn't even imagine a world without strife and war.

"Until someone got greedy?" Brady again.

"Along those lines." Mark said. "People who didn't have great abilities with their magic were jealous of those who did. A few of them banded together and started to make technology. Things that would help everyone be the same, so there were no advantages."

"Sounds like dystopia to me," Brady threw in. Lys was beginning to wonder what Brady did with his free time.

"Well it didn't go over very well. We don't have many particulars, but before too long there were two factions—one for technology and one against.

"Technology is powerful. You've all used tools: cell phones, computers or even a car. We can do so much more than the generation before us just because of the technology we have.

"Magic is powerful as well, but it works in a completely different way. Magic is personal. No two people wield magic in the same fashion. Every cell phone or pencil works the same no matter who is using it. Magic is different. The man who was so powerful in the sense of touch could do amazing things, but he could not heal. Others with their sense of touch could heal any wound."

"Wow," Lys breathed. If this magic thing was real, all she'd seen of it was destruction. All she'd felt from it was horror, terror and violence. Could there be a good side to it?

"Wow is right. " Mark looked back at her, meeting her eye.

Lys looked away.

"So people back then had super powers? Like the X-Men?" Brady blurted out.

Lys blinked. Seriously, what did Brady read and watch?

"Kind of," Mark answered.

"So what happened?" Brady asked, leaning forward.

"The people with the technology won," Mark said, shrugging. "They built tools and machines and discovered medicine. Soon no one had to wait for a healer to arrive to mend a wound nor did they have to wait for a powerful touch user to move large objects or build great structures."

Inez leaned forward. "What does this have to do with us, and where has this magic been? Why doesn't anyone know about it?" She watched Mark intently, but with a frown on her face.

"You," Mark said, glancing around, "are all magic users."

Silence followed the announcement.

Lys cleared her throat. "Uh, is that why Brady can crumple metal doors like newspaper?"

Mark nodded. "He already guessed his sense."

He flexed his fingers as he looked at his palms. "It's gotta be touch, but you said touch could heal people. Can I do that?"

"Not everyone," Mark grinned. "I couldn't heal a paper cut, but I can push things with my feet as well as my hands. Everyone is different."

Lys tried to process this. Magic? Really? The logical side of her brain didn't want to entertain the idea. However, she'd seen Brady destroy doors and cars, and she'd seen Kamau send a wave of tile floor at the guys in black. The whole world as she knew it was changing faster than she could keep track.

Kamau, who had thus far been silent, spoke. "What is the origin of the magic?"

"Good question," Mark said, pointing his finger. "Magic comes from the world—mostly from living things. Kind of like the Force, but on a very specific level."

"So we're Jedi?" Brady asked, bouncing in his seat.

"No."

"Where has this magic been?" Inez asked again. "Why do we suddenly have it?" Her tone still betrayed her disbelief. Lys was right there with her.

"Technology has," Mark hesitated, "disrupted the magic of our world. The ability to use magic sits dormant in blood lines for a long time. It's likely that one or more of your ancestors was a powerful user."

"User?" Lys asked. Peter had said Brady was using. "You make it sound like drugs."

"Not drugs." Mark shook his head. "But some of the effects are the same. It's different for everyone."

"Speaking of different," Brady started. He was staring into Inez's eyes. "Why are everyone's eyes a different color? I like the red better."

Lys risked a look. Yes, Inez's eyes were indeed swirling red, just like Peter's. Why hadn't they been doing that the whole time?

Inez smacked him on the shoulder. "Stop staring."

Brady's face lit up like he'd just got a new video game.

Mark went on. "Besides being divided into the five senses, magic is also divided into five levels. The levels range from complete chaos to neutral to anchored."

"More lame names," Brady said.

Mark ignored him. "Some call the levels infancy, adolescence, adulthood, middle-age and ancient. Either way works."

"What do they mean?" Inez asked, her swirling red eyes regarding Mark with renewed interest.

"They coincide with a person's raw power versus their control capabilities. Black eyes are an indicator of chaos. More power than most, but also a lack of precision that can be dangerous. Red, like Inez, means adolescence or chaos neutral. Not quite as much power, but more control. Gold, like Lys, means she is adult or neutral."

"My eyes are gold?" Lys asked. Her hand flew to her bad eye. The fingers appeared in her vision. The eye patch she'd been wearing was still pushed up on her head, right where Kamau had left it.

"Check it out, they look cool!" Brady said, pointing to the wall behind her.

"They?" Lys asked. "But my eye...the doctors said I would never see out of it again."

No one spoke. Lys steeled herself and turned, gazing at her reflection in the cracked, oval mirror on the wall. Lys could still see the scarred gouges around her right eye. Most of them had faded, but the two deep ones probably wouldn't ever disappear. Nervously, Lys turned her attention to her eyes. Her normally blue irises were swirling gold, like a paintbrush moving through a vat of sparkling, golden paint.

"Wow." They were beautiful. Both of them. "But how?" She looked at Mark.

He shrugged. "I have no idea. A good question for Mason maybe."

"So what does gold mean again?" Brady asked.

"Users with gold eyes have the best balance of control and power." Mark waved a hand. "Light blue is middle aged or neutral stable—they lean more to the control side with less power. And finally, those with silver eyes are ancient or stable—master of control, but not much power."

"So what I'm hearing is that I'm a baby touch user?" Brady asked, wrinkling his nose.

"That's right," Mark said, laughing.

"Why would you want to be ancient?" Brady asked.

"Think of it like the martial arts. There are those who can hit or kick so hard they can hurt anyone, but it takes a lot of energy and it's not very precise. A master who can hit someone in exactly the right spot doesn't need as much power to get the same effect. Both ends of the spectrum have their pros and their cons."

"Can you change your, level?" Lys asked.

"No. At least not that anyone has ever heard of. Your level is born inside of you. There is some leeway in learning more control

127

or more power, but it doesn't go far. You get what you get and you learn to work with it."

"Which level are you?" Kamau inquired.

"Chaos, like Brady."

Lys remembered Kamau's eyes in the tunnel. "You're anchored," she said.

"I guess so." Kamau shrugged. "Brady said my eyes were silver."

"So," Brady propped his chin in his hand, looking at Inez. "I can see that you're eyes are red, but what is your sense?"

Inez's eyebrows knit together. "I don't know."

Mark asked, "What happens to people when you use on them?"

Before Inez could answer Brady put his head in his hands. "Oh man, not again," he said, moaning.

"What is it?" Lys asked.

"He used too much," Peter said, shaking his head.

"I didn't use anything," Brady said in a flat voice. His hands started to shake, and Lys saw him curl in on himself. "I just feel so bad."

Inez, who sat next to him, stood. "He's going to lose it."

"He's not going to lose it," Mark said.

"That's what you said about her." Inez jabbed a finger in Lys' direction.

"She's fine. Breaking is rough." Mark turned his attention to Brady. "What's wrong?"

For a moment Brady didn't answer, and when he did, the despair in his voice broke Lys' heart.

"I just can't stop myself," he said, gripping his hair in his fingers and pulling. "I'll hurt someone."

Those words—the tone of his voice; they all combined together in Lys' mind, and she knew exactly how he felt. This must be his own Need. After seeing what he did to inanimate objects, Lys had no desire to find out what happened if he lost control.

"Can't you help him?" she asked Mark.

"He needs to learn to control it."

"Control what?"

"The magic," Mark said. "If you can't control the magic, it controls you."

Chapter 15

"You can control it?" Inez asked, shooting Mark a questioning look.

"Sure," Mark said. His eyes stayed on Brady, who started to rock back and forth. "Can you handle it?" Mark asked.

Brady shook his head. "I don't think so."

"Try," Mark said.

"How?" Brady whimpered.

"Channel the energy to where you can deal with it," Mark said, leaning forward. Lys noticed one hand poised, ready to touch Brady.

"There's so much, and it wants me to…" Brady trailed off. He didn't have to say it. Lys knew what he was talking about. Maybe they all did.

Well, everyone except for Kamau. Lys stole a glance at him and found no recognition or understanding emanating from his eyes. Instead he looked curious, like Brady was an exhibit at the zoo.

"I can't," Brady said, his voice almost a sob. One of his hands jerked down to the chair, and his fingers closed over the arm rest. The cloth and wood splintered and caved under his touch, the arm breaking off with a crunch. His head came up and his other hand jerked forward, reaching out for Peter. Peter jumped up and into the chair, out of reach. Mark's hand shot in and a flash of blue appeared as he touched Brady's arm.

Brady froze. His fingers twitched, then his reaching arm went limp, falling to his lap.

"Better?" Mark asked, hardly a trace of concern in his voice.

Brady didn't say anything, but Peter pointed and said, "What did you do?"

Mark shrugged. "It's a shock of static electricity. One of my specialties."

"And it stops you from using your powers?" Peter asked.

"Only for a little while. Usually long enough for someone to get back in control."

Inez frowned. "If you just used your magic, what happens to you?"

"Same thing that happens to anyone else. I'm sure the two of you have experienced the side effects of using." Mark looked at Inez and then Peter.

"Yeah, you could say that," Inez said.

"How do you cope?" Mark asked as he turned his attention back to Brady, who had his head in his hands again.

"Depends," Inez said, glancing away. "It just depends on what we have to work with."

Mark nodded.

Lys listened to them. She looked at Brady, then over at Kamau who still seemed more interested than concerned. "What just happened?"

Everyone turned to look at her. Maybe the words came out harsher than she intended, but it didn't matter.

"Well?" she asked. "Sorry, but I don't get it." She turned to Kamau first, but he just shook his head.

Next she set her sights on Mark. "What's going on?"

Mark sat back, sighing. "Using magic isn't free."

"Okay," Lys said, "so what does it cost?" The comment was supposed to be flippant, but Mark studied her for a moment before answering.

"Good way to put it." He paused. They all waited. "Using magic is better than anything you've done before. It enhances your senses in ways you can't even imagine. But..." he trailed off, narrowing his eyes. "But it takes a toll. It leaves you wanting more, and the more usually involves something, unsavory."

Lys knew immediately that he had to be talking about the

Need. "Using magic feels good?" she asked, trying to understand.

"It sure does," Peter said. "Really good."

Nothing about the Need felt good, except when she hurt people. "Wait, whatever I just went through didn't feel good."

Mark shook his head. "No, breaking isn't fun. When you learn to channel, that's when it gets better."

"Better?" Lys didn't like the turn this conversation just took. "What do you mean?" The image of her living the rest of her life battling between the Need and magic (if that's even what was going on) left her shaking her head. No, Mr. Mason promised to help her. He promised to cure her.

"Better," Mark agreed. "It still takes work, but I haven't met anyone yet who can't learn control."

"Learn control?" Inez asked. She shot icy daggers at Mark. "We've been searching for a cure."

"A cure?" Mark cocked his head to the side. "You don't need a cure, just some training."

"There's no cure?" Lys asked. An invisible hand reached out and socked Lys in the stomach. She hadn't realized just how much hope lay in that little word. Cure. Hope. An end to all of this. The slippery footing her mind had been perched on fell away, and with it the possibility of ever being normal again.

"No," Mark said. "Mr. Mason thought you were a magic user, and when he knew for sure he came for you. He trains magic users—helps them through breaking and then teaches them how to use properly."

Lys didn't hear anything after the no. No cure. Her heart fell through her body and landed at her feet with a resounding thud. No hope. The last string that lead back to normality had just been cut, and as the end fluttered around her mind, she broke again. Only this time there wasn't any magic involved. This time she felt her sanity give way.

"I have to use the bathroom," Lys said as she shot to her feet.

"Where is it?" She could hear the crazy in her voice, but didn't care. She had to get out of there.

"Down the hall, to the left," Inez said, pointing.

Someone said her name, but Lys ignored them. She walked briskly from the room. Passing the bathroom, Lys dredged up a vision she'd seen when she broke. Another way out of this place lay at the end of this hall. A bolted door greeted her trembling hands, but Lys didn't bother with the handle. Instead she knelt down and pushed on the bottom panel of the door. It gave way, and she wriggled through.

Fear and anger pulsed in her veins. Her mind rushed ahead, thinking about what she would do as soon as she got to a phone. First she'd call her parents. Her dad knew plenty of people in Las Vegas. Someone would come to pick her up. Or at least take her to the hospital where she could be properly chained down.

The rough surface of the Velcro straps still chafed Lys' wrists in her dreams. She unconsciously rubbed one of them as her feet tried to catch up with her mind. The dark hallway ended abruptly, but another door stood in front of her. This time she tried the handle. It turned.

Without a thought as to who or what might be on the other side—frankly a police officer would be welcome right now—Lys pushed the door open and went through.

This time she found herself in a storage room full of costumes and boxes. Racks of dresses, feathered boas, sexy shoes and skimpy undergarments crowded most of the space. Another door, on the far wall stood open. Lys looked back and found that the door she had come through didn't have a handle on this side. In fact, as she let it swing closed, it almost entirely disappeared, blending into the wall and leaving only a small seam.

In another time and place she would have been thrilled to find a secret door into the basement of a Vegas night club, or theater, but now she didn't care. All she wanted to do was get out of here.

If Mr. Mason couldn't cure her, then maybe someone else could.

Lys walked through the storage room, her shoulders brushing the gaudy costumes, and her eyes glued to the far door. If she got lucky, one of the performers would be down here and they would let her use their cell phone to call her parents.

A haze settled over Lys as she moved. The hallway outside stood empty, and Lys walked down it, looking for someone to help her. Or at least a way out. However, her brain seemed to be disconnected from her actions, and she had a hard time making decisions about which way to go. The lights were on, but no one was home.

The basement soon became a frustrating maze for Lys. The haze morphed into gray which turned into different perspectives, and Lys shook her head. She stumbled through the hallways, trying to figure out which view from her eyes was her own. Panic threatened to bring her to her knees, but Lys fought it.

Finally, after forever, Lys saw a green and white sign that said "EXIT." She stumbled toward it, tears streaming down her face. Stairs led up and Lys couldn't climb them, so she crawled, her hands groping for the handle. Freedom and escape from the madness her life had become lay just beyond that door. If she could get there, she could get help.

Her hands brushed the bar, and Lys pushed. Her fingers slipped off and she almost face planted into the door. A snarl of frustration escaped and Lys threw herself at the bar, pushing with everything she had. The surface gave way, and she fell, hands crashing onto a cement landing.

Light touched the night sky, but only from one direction. Stale, desert air blew through her hair, filling her nostrils with the stench of body odor, alcohol and tobacco. Lys got to her feet, still holding on to the door, and caressed the concrete wall of the building. For a moment Lys forgot the horror of her life and reveled in the normality that lay before her. Then a car went by the alley, tires screeching, and snapped her out of it.

Lys let go of the door, hoping that allowing it to shut behind her would rid her of the world of magic and men in armor. She could deal with the Need, just as long as it was the only thing she had to deal with.

Crazed euphoria filled Lys, and she felt her lips curl up into a manic grin. She lurched down the three, concrete stairs and kept going for the end of the alley. Vegas never slept. Someone had to be around.

She heard humming and didn't realize the sound came from her until she got close to the end of the buildings. The random tune came from her lips unbidden, and she laughed at herself.

The scrape of feet on asphalt behind her brought her up short.

"Hey, what we got here?"

Dread washed the euphoria away, and Lys suddenly felt more grounded than she had in days.

"She's a looker," a guy's voice said from behind her.

"And she looks lost."

Lys closed her eyes. Crap.

"Hey little lady," the first voice said in a heavy, southern accent. "You need some help?"

Right, like they were going to help her. Lys didn't stop walking, but she did turn so she could see her "helpers."

Four big guys occupied the alley behind her. All of them walked with an over confidence that only came with getting exactly what you wanted, and all of them leered at her with the hungry eyes of animals in heat.

"Oh, I'm good," Lys said, trying to sound nonchalant. Her heart started making its way up into her throat. Thirty feet to the road.

"What are you doing out here all alone, darlin'?" the guy with the southern accent asked, stepping after her.

"Just meeting a friend." Lys shrugged. "For coffee." Twenty

feet to the road.

"Where at?" another of the guys asked.

"Starbucks." There had to be a dozen Starbucks in Las Vegas, right?

The end of the alley lay about fifteen feet away, but now the guys were closing fast.

"Forget your friend, darlin'. You come get some coffee with us."

"Uh, no thanks." She managed a forced smile, glancing over her shoulder. "He gets kind of jealous if he sees me with other guys." Ten feet to go. She wasn't' going to make it.

The southern guy raised his eyebrows. "Well then, we'll just have to avoid the Starbucks for a while."

They all closed at once, lunging forward, hands outstretched for her. Lys cried out, turning—hoping she could make it to the end of the alley before they got her. However, she didn't encounter open air. Instead her face crashed into another guy's chest.

Chapter 16

Lys tried to push away from him, but he wrapped his arms around her. Before she could begin struggling in earnest he spoke.

"There you are, baby. You're late."

The words seemed so absurd that Lys' eyes flew up to the face of the voice's owner. To her complete surprise, Kamau stood above her.

"I've been waiting." He smiled, but it spoke of disapproval, as did the possessive tone in his voice.

Lys couldn't talk. Her mouth opened, hinging up and down, but no words came out.

"Really, baby," he said in a low voice. "You hanging out with these guys?" He shot a withering look at the four figures in the alley.

Finally she got a word out. "No."

Kamau continued to glare at them. "I didn't think so."

The tone in his voice caused the four guys to step back. Kamau's presence towered above them, even though he had to be a few inches shorter than the tallest of them. Lys found herself clinging to him, and hating herself for it—hadn't she just vowed to leave his world behind? Her hands wouldn't stop trembling, and her heart pounded so hard against her ribs that she was sure Kamau could feel it.

"Why don't you guys go find someone else to help?" Kamau said.

The words lashed out like a whip, and the four guys jerked, shaking their heads. One of them started to stutter something, but another grabbed his arm and they backed away. Kamau continued to stare at them until they turned and ran.

A breath she didn't realize she'd been holding escaped from Lys' lips in a stuttering exhale. She inhaled, gulping in the much needed air.

"Are you alright?" Kamau asked, pushing her away, hands on her shoulders.

Lys swallowed. She had to be strong. She leveled her eyes at his chest before she spoke. "Thanks for helping me, but I'm not going back."

Kamau digested this. "What are you going to do?"

"I'm going to call my parents and…" And what? Go back to where she started? Right now it seemed like the only option. "I'm going to call my parents," she said again. Tears threatened to begin cascading down her cheeks,.

"How?" Kamau asked.

The question struck Lys as funny, and she let a short laugh escape. "With a phone."

"You don't have any money."

Lys had an answer for that one. "I'll call collect. I just need a pay phone." Or someone's cell phone.

"Why?"

Lys shook her head. He wouldn't understand.

"Lys," he said, leaning down to try to look into her eyes. "Why do you want to leave?"

The Need didn't rear its ugly head, but Lys only looked at his eyes for a moment. "Because I don't want this." Now a tear did come. "Mr. Mason said he could cure me. He lied." The last two words were packed with all of the betrayal and loss that Lys carried in her. She lowered her head and began to sob. "I just want to go home."

Kamau wrapped his arms around her and drew her to his chest. At first she couldn't respond. All she could do was cry.

"Shhh." Kamau said, stroking her hair. "It's okay."

She didn't believe him, but the words gave her the strength to cling to him. The tears and the sobs continued—an unstoppable wave of emotion that tried to wash away the hurt she'd been carrying around with her.

The flood engulfed her. Lys had no idea how long they stood there, in the dawning morning, this boy she barely knew trying to comfort her when true comfort was impossible. She tried to let the pain wash away, but not all of it would go. Part of her knew that this would never be over. Part of her knew that the magic existed, and that it lay inside of her like a disease.

Kamau didn't say anything more. He just held her, resting his chin on the top of her head. When the sobs died down, and Lys ran out of tears, Kamau stroked her hair again. "Do you want to go home?"

Lys looked up at him and nodded.

"I will help you."

"You will?" Lys expected that he would try to talk her out of it.

"Yes." He stepped back, releasing Lys.

For a moment she felt naked and alone—the barrier against this new world gone. But then she remembered that she'd made this decision. She wanted to go. She did.

Kamau glanced behind him at the road. "I believe I saw a gas station just around the corner. Would they have a pay phone?"

"Yes," Lys said. A gas station. Good.

"Come on," he said.

Gratitude for his understanding filled Lys, but when he took her hand a different emotion came into play.

No, she thought to herself. This is not the time. But that thought didn't stop her from intertwining her fingers with his before they walked to the end of the alley and onto the street.

Vibrant pink filled the eastern sky, silhouetting the hotels. A cool breeze blew past them as they emerged, and Lys felt her spirits lift a little. She saw the gas station immediately, and true to his word, Kamau led her toward it.

"What did Mr. Mason tell you when he found you?" he asked

as they walked past the entrance to a seedy-looking club.

Lys sniffed. "He came to the hospital and told me that he could help me."

"Help you with what?"

She shot a look at Kamau. Was it possible that he didn't feel the Need? Mark said everyone exhibited different symptoms. "Help me stop wanting to hurt people." She didn't want to discuss it. Apparently Kamau caught the hint.

"And he said he could help you?"

Lys nodded. "He's the only person who didn't think I was crazy."

"Were you using your magic?"

"I don't think so." Lys hoped that the urge to rip people's eyes out did not constitute using magic. "It's something else."

"Did he say he could cure you?" Kamau asked as they walked across the small parking lot that surrounded the gas station.

"I asked him if he could help me, and he said he could. I asked if he could cure me and he…" Lys thought about it. Did he ever actually say that he could cure her? "He didn't say he couldn't." She finished.

Kamau said nothing as he opened the door and held it for Lys.

Inside the gas station, a skinny man sat behind a counter in front of a display of cigarettes. He didn't bother to look up from texting on his phone as they entered. The news played on a flat screen TV in one corner, but the sound was drowned out by the loud rap music that came from a radio next to the clerk.

"Do you have a pay phone?" Lys asked. She'd checked outside and saw nothing.

"It's in the back." He pointed toward the restroom signs, still not looking up.

"Thanks," she said automatically.

Kamau followed her through the little store and to the doorway in the far corner. The pay phone sat huddled in a nook, right around the corner from the fountain drinks. Patches of the white paint on the walls and ceiling peeled back, revealing a dull, gray color underneath. Cracks riddled the linoleum and Lys could smell the toilets from the end of the hall.

Suddenly Lys realized that she hadn't used a toilet in ages. The thought of going into the bathroom here made her cringe, but this need couldn't wait much longer. She looked over at Kamau and saw him eying the men's door with suspicion.

The phone lay just a few feet away, but Lys decided that she'd rather talk to her parents without having to cut it short or do the "I have to go" dance.

"I think I'm going to—" Lys jerked her head toward the women sign.

"Good idea," Kamau said. He released her hand and Lys quickly strode into the bathroom, before she could think too much about Kamau, magic, her parents or Mr. Mason.

The solitude rattled her resolve. The smell kept the trip short. As she washed her hands, Lys noticed her eyes. They still swirled gold—beautiful really. She stared at herself in the mirror, wondering absently why she never felt the need to go after her own eyes. But that's not what she wanted to dwell on. She had to get out of here and find someone who could really help her.

But could anyone do that? If she was a magic user, what would happen to her? Did anyone besides Mr. Mason and the guys trying to kill them know about magic? Surely someone had to. A secret society maybe, or ancient guardians? Brady probably had a few ideas.

The gold in her irises mesmerized her for a moment before she shook her head and grabbed a paper towel. Too much thinking.

Out in the hall Lys found herself alone. Her stomach constricted at the thought that Kamau left her, but she took a deep breath and decided it didn't matter. She'd be leaving him in a little while. Why prolong the agony?

She walked back toward the phone and found Kamau browsing the shelves. He gave her a smile when he saw her. Unable to stop them, her lips curled into a grin as well. Heartened, she turned and picked up the phone. With the age of the cell phone Lys could honestly say she'd only used a pay phone one other time in her life, and that had been on a dare. However, she did remember that to get an operator all you had to do was dial 0. She pressed the button and waited.

Silence filled the receiver, and Lys wondered if she'd done it wrong. Her hand hovered over the flap to hang up, but just before she pressed it a woman's voice came on the line.

"Hello, may I help you?"

"Yes," Lys said, and she could hear the excitement in her own voice. "I'd like to make a collect call please."

"What is the number you are trying to reach?"

Lys recited the number and waited. As she did so, her thoughts turned to magic. Could it be true? And if so, why would people be trying to kill her?

A hand landed on her shoulder.

She spun around, heart racing, hoping the guys from the alley didn't follow her.

Kamau stood, watching the television in the corner. Following his gaze, Lys felt her jaw fall open.

She couldn't hear the commentator over the hum of the coolers and the music from the radio, but she could clearly see Mark's face on the screen.

"What?" Lys asked.

Kamau held up a hand. He seemed to be listening. "They say he is a dangerous criminal. He is reportedly armed and suspected to be involved in a kidnapping," Kamau whispered.

The picture on the screen changed from Mark's face, to Lys' face. She groaned. Was it her year book picture? No, they'd used one that had been taken when she went to Sea World. She was soaked—they'd been sitting in the splash zone.

"Oh no!" Lys whispered, the implications cutting through her mortification. "What are they saying?"

Kamau kept watching. "That you disappeared from a private camp. Mark is supposed to be a counselor, and they are saying he forced you to go with him." Kamau looked down at her, an amused smile on his lips. "What were you doing in that picture?"

"Don't ask," she grumbled. She heard the phone start to ring in her ear. Her parents would take the call, and then she could explain.

After two rings a familiar voice answered. "FBI, can I ask who is calling?" Lys' blood ran cold.

The operator started off on the collect call spiel. Lys slammed the phone down into the cradle and stepped back like it might bite her.

"Was that Doyle?" Kamau asked.

Lys nodded. "He must be at my parent's house."

Kamau's still silvery eyes swiveled back to the television. Then he glanced at the clerk, who was now watching them intently.

"He's looking right at us," Lys said through clenched teeth, shifting to the side so Kamau's body hid her. "We have to get out of here. If Doyle's at my parent's house, and I'm on the news, the police will be looking for us. I wonder if they know Doyle just wants to kill me." And what was he doing at her parent's house? Posing as FBI?

Kamau put a hand on her shoulder. "Look, I think I can get us out of here, but I'll need to get close to the clerk, and I'll need his undivided attention."

"What do you mean?"

"I can use my magic on him," Kamau said, glancing over her head at the clerk. "But we'll need to hurry, and we need to be convincing."

"But…"

"What do you like to eat?"

"What are you talking about?"

Kamau glanced back at the clerk. "If we buy something we'll seem more normal. I can work better with that."

"We don't have any money!"

A twenty dollar bill appeared in Kamau's hand. "I picked it up in the alley. Now grab something to eat. Then you're going to have to play along."

Lys let Kamau guide her to the nearest shelf where she grabbed a bag of pretzels. Kamau took two candy bars and a box of gummy worms.

"What do you mean play along?" Lys asked. She caught the clerk watching them again. He still held his phone in his hand.

"I have an idea that might work."

"What?" Lys asked.

"We will pretend to be, uh, together. If he believes we are a couple traveling through town I can get him to forget about his interest in you."

"Forget?" Lys asked.

Kamau studied her face. "I know you do not believe wholly in magic, but I do. It exists. Can you trust me?"

"Sure," Lys said, not quite understanding if she meant it.

Kamau wrapped his arm around her, twisting her to face him and pulled her very close. He handed her the candy. "Help me dump this stuff on the counter, but stay facing me. Pretend we're together."

"What?" Lys hissed. Her face was buried in his shoulder, the rest of her pressed right up against him.

"You're going to have to act a little more interested than that," Kamau whispered in her ear.

Oh, he meant *that* together.

Before she could react, Kamau had them moving. Lys tried to

keep her feet in synch with his, mirroring his steps so they wouldn't tread on one another. Just before they got to the counter, Kamau leaned down and kissed her ear. "Giggle," he whispered.

Well that wasn't hard. The brush of his lips on her ears tickled. Not to mention the fluttery feeling blossoming in her stomach.

"Dump the stuff," Kamau said softly.

A small squeak escaped as Lys felt her back side collide with the counter. Without turning, Lys shoved the candy and pretzels at the clerk. Kamau's now free hand went around her shoulders. Trying to look convincing, Lys returned the favor, her hand having to stretch to get around his neck. She never realized just how tall he was.

"How you guys doing?" The clerk asked, curiosity in his voice. Lys heard the beeping sound as he scanned their items.

"Good," Kamau said as he stroked Lys' hair. Lys could practically hear the sneer in his voice. Like he knew he was about to get lucky. For a moment Lys thought about pushing him away. What kind of girl did he think she was! But then she remembered they had a plan, and that Kamau could somehow influence people. She berated herself for not asking him what his supposed sense was. Touch, like Brady, or sight like her? If she could use magic, she'd bet she used sight.

"Where you guys from?" the clerk asked.

"San Francisco," Kamau said. "Road trip." As if that explained everything.

"You traveling alone?"

"Yeah, just the two of us," Kamau said. "All alone. On a road trip."

"Where are you headed?"

Lys heard the clerk ask the question, but Kamau's hand slid up her back. To both her horror and her delight, Kamau's face came toward hers. She met his eyes. They were so dark, so intense, and so locked on her that Lys was helpless to resist the kiss that he gently planted on her lips.

Electricity exploded within her. Everything else in the world melted away, leaving her here, alone with him. Lys felt her lips respond. She slid her hand up into his hair, grabbing hold, afraid he would pull away. His lips parted, she allowed hers to do the same. One breath of his scent and Lys' mind whirled. Her stomach turned into butterflies. This was better than satisfying the Need. She could feel like this forever and be happy about it.

Their lips separated for a moment, coming up for air. Ready to go in again, Lys dug her fingernails into Kamau's neck—she felt him pull her closer, if that was possible. Their lips met again, and Lys felt herself melting into Kamau. The world could end now, she was happy.

"That'll be $8.73," the clerk said in a bored voice. "You want a bag for this stuff?"

The spell broke. Kamau drew back. Lys tried to hold him close, but he pulled free.

Lys reluctantly withdrew her hands. Kamau took a tiny step back—Lys felt like they were parted by the Grand Canyon. The spike of bliss suddenly fell away, leaving Lys feeling rejected and unfulfilled. She reminded herself that this was only an act. They were trying to get out and back to the others. It meant nothing.

Kamau handed the money to the cashier over Lys' shoulder.

"Sorry," Kamau said to the man, "what were you saying?"

The question must have been rhetorical. To Lys' relief (and satisfaction) Kamau stepped in close again, but not quite as close as before. His fingers traced a path down both sides of her face. When his hands reached her shoulders, he leaned down and kissed her neck. His lips lingered—she could feel his breath in her hair. Lys melted. None of the boys she'd gone out with before had made her feel like this.

"Oh, nothing," the clerk said, handing Kamau the change.

"Wait, I asked you where you were headed."

"Denver," Kamau said. "We are going to Denver. Just a young couple in love."

The cashier snorted. "Yeah, whatever."

Lys listened in amazement. Even she could feel the pull of Kamau's voice. She almost believed that they were going to Denver.

Kamau kissed her one more time before slowly pulling away.

"Thanks, man," Kamau said in a casual tone. He retrieved the bag. "Come on, baby, let's go."

Kamau turned, catching Lys with an arm and leading her away from the counter. The radio went off behind them, and the news announcer's voice filled the station.

"If you have any information regarding this man, or if you have seen this girl, please call the number below on your screen."

"Oh no," Lys whispered. She tried to walk faster.

"Don't draw his attention," Kamau said, holding her back. "Just walk."

The news announcer went on. "Police are looking for help from everyone. They ask you be alert to strangers in the area."

Ten more steps to the door. Lys found herself counting down. Seven, five, three...

"Hey, guys," the clerk said.

They stopped three steps from freedom.

Chapter 17

Kamau handed the bag to Lys. "Yeah?" he asked, turning his head back around.

"Do you want your receipt?"

Lys' heart pounded against her ribs.

"Oh," Kamau disentangled himself from Lys and walked back to the counter. "Thanks."

Lys didn't move. She didn't even dare breathe. She heard Kamau's footsteps coming toward her. When he arrived, he put his arm around her shoulders. They took one step forward.

The news announcer was still going. "The girl's name is Lysandra Blake. She's just sixteen years old from California."

"Oh, and guys," the clerk said.

Kamau squeezed her shoulder.

"Next time, wear shoes," the clerk said.

Lys glanced up at the doorway—now just an arm's length away. Sure enough, a sign that said "Shoes Required" hung next to the door.

"Sorry, man," Kamau said. Lys almost jumped out of skin when Kamau's hand wandered to her rear and gave it a squeeze. "You know how it is."

"Sure." He did *not* sound convinced. "Hey, can your girl please turn around for me?"

"You trying to hit on my girl?" Kamau demanded. Suddenly he seemed like a force to be reckoned with.

"No, man, we've just got this Amber Alert, and I'm a concerned citizen, okay?"

"A concerned citizen?" Kamau asked. "Okay, that's very good of you. I'm grateful for your vigilance. You saw the girl when she came in. She's nobody."

Nobody! Lys was still trying to figure out if she should be mad about the butt squeeze. Now she was nobody?

"Well I didn't get a good look—"

Kamau actually interrupted the guy. "Sure you did. Just as she walked in. She looks a little like the girl on TV, but this isn't her. Not quite."

"I don't know." the clerk said, his voice hesitant.

Lys stood stone still. She only took a breath because she felt herself getting dizzy. Would this guy fall for it?

Kamau went on. "And next time we'll be sure to read the signs more carefully before we come in." He paused. "Thank you for the receipt."

"Sure, whatever," the guy said. Maybe back to texting on his phone. "Just remember next time. Socks don't count."

The news announcer's voice disappeared, replaced by a sports caster. "It's been a wild day today for college football."

"Let's go!" Lys whispered the moment they cleared the doors.

"Just keep walking." Kamau's hand moved up to her back. He kept a firm hold around her as they moved through the gas pumps. It had to be the longest, slowest walk of Lys' life. She expected the cashier to run out after them. Or he could be calling the police.

"We need to get out of here," she said, twisting out of his arm when they finally reached the sidewalk.

"I apologize," he said, releasing her and taking a step away. "I hope I did not offend you."

"Uh," Lys had more hormones rushing through her than she knew what to do with. "No, no offense." A tiny part of her wanted to smack him for squeezing her butt—the other part of her wanted to go back to kissing right away. What did she want? Lys didn't know. She didn't look at him.

"I did offend you."

"No!" Lys said. She changed the subject. "What are we going to do?" She wasn't sure which she should worry about more, her

149

face on the news or Doyle answering her parent's phone. "We should get back to the others," Kamau said, steering Lys along the sidewalk to put some distance between them and the gas station.

Lys stopped. "But I'm not going back."

Kamau stopped as well, looking down at her. "Lys, if Doyle is with your parents then you can't go home."

"I could just go to the police." As soon as she said it she knew the idea wouldn't work. So she tried another approach. "Or I can call the FBI and ask them…" She shook her head. The words "I want to go home" echoed through her mind, but Lys knew that it wasn't possible.

"Come back with me," Kamau said. "Mark can help us get to Mason, and if he said he could help you, maybe he can."

The smooth sound of his voice, coupled with his hands on her shoulders and the concerned look in his eyes stopped her panic.

Wait, the sound of his voice? "You're a sound user," she said.

"I didn't think you really believed in the magic," Kamau said.

She didn't let him dissuade her. "You just used magic on that guy!" She pointed her finger back the way they had come.

"Yes," he said.

"Did you just try to use your magic on me?" For some reason this infuriated her. Had she been manipulated from the moment she first met Mr. Mason?

"No." Kamau shook his head. "I did not."

"Have you ever used your magic on me?"

Kamau nodded. "Only when you broke. I tried to help you."

"Help me?" Lys stuttered.

"Yes."

At that moment, when their eyes met, and the butterflies in her stomach overpowered everything else, Lys knew she was in trouble. After running from a ghost (or whatever that had been in the basement of the hospital) and then escaping from prison together she found it hard not to at least like the guy. But he always took time to make sure she was okay. His smile turned his otherwise polite face into something she could get used to looking at every day. And he was brave. She'd always been a fan of the knight in shining armor. She couldn't deny the desire to let him hold her forever.

Forever? Or just because the last few days had proven to be the most terrifying of her life? The sound of Doyle's voice on the phone echoed in her ears. She couldn't go to her parents for help.

She pulled her eyes away from Kamau's. "I guess we should get back to the others."

"You'll come?" he asked. "I won't force you."

Lys laughed a bitter laugh. "As you so aptly pointed out, I don't have anywhere else to go at the moment."

"I did not mean to make you—" Kamau started.

Lys interrupted, holding up a hand. "Don't worry, I don't feel coerced." She smiled, lowered her hand and reached for his.

Kamau's lips stretched into a broad grin as their fingers intertwined. "Good."

* * *

They walked back toward the alley, but Kamau turned into a small security entrance for the building. He led her through a hallway to a supply closet and then through a crawl space where his wide shoulders touched both sides. When they emerged, Lys found herself down the other hall leading from the old ballroom.

"Did they tell you how to get out?" Lys asked.

"Peter did," Kamau said. "After they found you missing. How did you get out?" He dusted off the knees of his scrubs as he stood.

Lys pointed. "There's a loose panel."

Before she could show him, Brady's voice filled the hallway. "You're back!" he said, bounding toward them. "We were starting to get worried. Mark was ready to send out a rescue party."

He stopped short when he saw the serious looks on their faces.

"What's wrong?" he asked. "You two have a lovers' quarrel?"

Lys shook her head. "Where's Mark? We've got problems."

Brady led them back into the main ballroom where Mark and Peter sat in a set of old chairs, playing a card game on a rickety, wood table. Mark looked up as they entered.

"Found her?" Mark asked.

"We have news," Kamau said.

"Bad news," Lys added

Mark put his cards down. "What?"

They all walked to the table, and Kamau told Mark what they'd seen and what had happened. He left out the part about the guys in the alley. And the kissing. When he finished, Mark's lips were turned down in a frown, his eyebrows knit together in a scowl.

"On the news?" Mark asked.

"An Amber Alert," Lys said. "Which means it's going all over the country." She paused. "And how is Doyle at my house? Is he FBI?"

"I doubt it. He's probably got connections in all of those agencies, but I don't think he's employed by any of them." Mark shook his head. "Doyle is working pretty hard for this one. I wonder what he thinks he'll find."

"He wants to find her." Inez's voice filled the large room with disdain. She walked across the floor, came to the table, folded her arms across her chest and glared at Lys. "Why don't we give her to him?"

"Inez!" Peter and Brady protested together.

Peter persisted. "Why would you say that? You know what those guys do to people!"

Inez nodded. "Yeah, I know what they do." Her eyes swiveled

to Peter. "And I know that they don't ever stop looking."

The younger boy shrunk back a little, but didn't lower his eyes. "But they can help us." Peter's head jerked at Mark.

"Right," Inez said, her gaze darting at Mark before once again settling on Lys. "Like she helped us?"

Lys, still riding the emotional roller coaster of almost being attacked by a gang of thugs, to being rescued, to seeing her face on the news, to the warm feeling of Kamau's lips on hers, Lys' filter didn't engage before she spoke. "Me? What did I do?"

"You just leave?" Inez said, pointing back down the hall. "Without explanation and without telling anyone?"

"I didn't know you cared." Lys said. Her mind wailed at her to stop talking, but her emotions kept her mouth moving.

"I don't. Not about you." Inez took a step toward Lys. "Apparently the only thing you care about is yourself. Spoiled little rich girl." Inez practically spat the last words out, throwing them to the floor like the proverbial gauntlet.

"What?" Lys asked, taking a step of her own.

Inez glared. "If anyone else's picture had come up on that screen, would you have come back?"

"Would you have even told anyone about it if you knew?" Lys demanded. Anger filled her, and Lys saw only one outlet for the moment. "No, I doubt it. You probably would have turned me in for a ten dollar reward so you could get your next fix of whatever it is you do." The harsh words felt foreign coming from her lips. They also felt good.

"Well at least I work for what I get."

"You'd probably sell him out if it gave you what you wanted." Lys pointed at Peter.

Inez reeled back as if she'd been physically assaulted. "You bitch!" she shrieked. Lunging forward, Inez reached for Lys, but in a flash Peter, Mark, Brady and Kamau all stood between them. Kamau planted right in front of Lys, his hands on her shoulders so she couldn't move. It took Lys a second to realize that her fingernails were gouging into her palms. Her throat felt dryer than the desert.

Inez yelled at Peter and Brady to move.

Lys shook her head. "What's wrong with me?" she whispered, feeling the anger drain away. Why did she want to annoy Inez? Sure, she didn't much like the other girl, but Inez and Peter had helped them—were still helping them—and she'd just purposely provoked Inez.

"Get her out of here!" Inez bellowed. "Get that little bitch out of our home."

"Inez!" Peter said, trying to overcome her volume. "Calm down. You know what it's like."

"I don't care what it's like!"

"Inez." This time Brady spoke. "Give her a break. She just found out that those New guys are at her parent's house. That means her whole family is in danger."

"She's put us all in danger," Inez said through gritted teeth.

"How many times have I put us in danger?" Peter asked. Lys thought he sounded a lot more mature than his eleven or twelve years.

Inez said nothing, and a tangible wall of anger floated between members of the group.

Mark broke the silence. "I think that maybe I should try to show you guys a control technique for magic."

* * *

The announcement brought everyone's eyes to Mark, who stood in the middle of the two groups, watching the exchange of verbal gunfire.

"A control technique?" Brady asked.

Kamau stepped out of Lys' way. Inez glared at her.

Mark nodded. "Yeah, it's the only one I know that works for every sense."

"You're going to teach us to use our magic?" Peter asked, stepping forward.

"No." Mark shook his head. "I'm going to teach you all to channel your magic in the right direction. Once you can do that, it's easier to actually use your magic." He stopped and looked from Inez to Lys and then back again. "Plus, it minimizes the effects of using."

"I haven't been using," Inez said.

Mark didn't answer, he just stared her down until she lowered her eyes. Then he slowly looked around the room at them all. When his gaze met Lys' (which she kept to a fraction of a blink) she saw that he looked tired. Tired, sick and injured.

"Are you mates willing to listen to me before someone really freaks out?"

Lys nodded. Everyone nodded, although Inez did so reluctantly.

"Great, have a seat."

Brady went to sit on a chair, but Mark waved a hand at him. "On the floor everyone. Make a big circle over here. Give yourself plenty of space."

Kamau and Lys went to the far side of the space Mark indicated. They left enough space between them that their fingers couldn't touch if they both stretched out their arms. Inez ended up right across from Lys. The other girl continued to glare, and for once Lys didn't lower her gaze. She felt the Need growl, and much to her shame she almost urged the monster on.

Mark stepped between them, breaking the moment. "First off, let me make sure I know what I'm dealing with." He looked at Brady. "Chaos, touch." Brady grinned. Mark moved on to Kamau. "Ancient, what?"

"Sound," Kamau said.

"Sound." Mark nodded and turned to Lys. "Neutral, what?"

"Uh." Lys didn't want to say it. Saying it made it real. However, hiding from it wouldn't make it any less real. "Sight," she said. "I think."

"Okay," Mark said, looking at her as if he were sizing her up for the first time.

"Peter," Mark said, pointing at the younger boy.

"Well, my eyes go red."

"So Adolescence." Mark nodded.

"And it has to be smell."

"Smell?" Brady blurted out. "What good is that?"

Peter scowled. "I can track any person within a hundred miles. And I got us through the tunnels didn't I?"

Brady held up his hands. "Sorry, all this hocus pocus stuff is new to me. I didn't know." He turned to Mark. "Can't we rename the levels? Something cool, like maybe the planets?" His eyes lit up. "You know, Mars for the red eyes, Venus for the silver eyes and maybe Saturn for Lys' gold eyes. Although I'd like Saturn for chaos because I like the rings."

"Really?" Inez asked, throwing a hand up into the air.

"Yeah," Brady said. "It would be like your horoscope. Mars, uh…" He trailed off. "What's your sense?"

Mark turned to her. "I've been wondering that myself."

Inez didn't meet anyone's eyes. Instead she glanced at Mark's feet. "I'm not really sure."

Mark nodded. "That's okay," he said kindly. "What happens to people when you use your magic on someone?"

"I, uh." She cleared her throat. "People usually do things that they wouldn't normally do."

"Like what?" Mark prompted.

"Like falling all over themselves to help me when I want them to," Inez said.

Brady snorted. "Pretty sure you don't need your magic for

that."

Inez shot him an annoyed look.

He held up his hands. "I'm just sayin'."

"She makes me think of food all the time," Peter said.

Mark nodded. "Ah, so you're a taste user."

"Taste?" Inez asked, her eyebrows knitting together again.

Brady made a face. "Is that any better than smell?"

"Shut up!" Peter said. Brady laughed.

Mark held up a hand. "It's different. Taste doesn't just deal with food, but with people's appetites." He turned his attention back to Inez. "So things like greed, lust and anger are probably pretty easy for you to bring out in people."

Inez nodded.

"Okay," Mark said, "So no one here is the same sense as anyone else but Brady and I. That will make things more difficult, but we'll give it a try."

He sat down at the head of the circle. Lys noticed that he moved slowly, and she remembered the bruises on his stomach. How badly had the New injured him?

"Everyone close your eyes." Mark waited a few moments before speaking again. "Take a deep breath."

Lys did so, and she could hear the others doing the same.

"Make sure to breathe from your stomach and not just your chest. Fill your lungs to capacity, hold it for three seconds and then let it out—slow, like air coming out of a balloon through a pin hole. Keep going."

From her stomach? Lys took another breath and found that only her chest moved when she breathed. She let the air out and tried again. Starting from her navel, Lys slowly drew air into her lungs, amazed as the bottom of her lungs filled before the air topped off in her chest. Three seconds of holding the air in made her mind scream in protest. Then she slowly let it out, imagining it as a thin wire of air coming from her nostrils, hitting her legs and curling back up around her like smoke. She'd taken a self-defense class for a while, and she'd never quite got the hang of meditation.

"Use your mouth to breathe out if it helps," Mark said after a few seconds. She tried it and found that although it was louder, it seemed easier to control coming from her mouth.

In her mind, Lys started to count the number of breaths she took. When she reached twenty-three Mark spoke again.

"Good. Now keep breathing. As you exhale, try to rid yourself of excess thoughts and worries."

Lys tried not to shake her head. Excess thoughts and worries? That's all she had!

"Keep breathing," Mark said. "If you can't empty your mind, imagine a blackboard. Toss everything you've got at it. Take a look at each item—problems, worries, distractions, everything—and erase them one by one as you exhale. If it won't go on the first try, do it again. Keep it up until there is nothing left but a blank board in front of you."

"Do we use an eraser, or what?" Brady asked.

"It's your subconscious," Mark said. "Do whatever comes to your mind. If the blackboard analogy doesn't work for you, think of something else. Some people use sitting on the bottom of a pool as their meditation platform."

Lys tried to come up with her blackboard, but got caught up in what it should look like. Did it have to be black, or could it be a white board? Could she use different colored markers to write with? And was it okay that she wanted to wipe the items off with her hands and then clean her hands on a pair of old jeans that she loved?

"Try not to get too caught up in the details," Mark said. "Just let your subconscious take you where it wants to go."

How did he know? Was he listening to her thoughts?

Finally Lys had her board; about a million problems covered it, leaving hardly any of the white showing. With an internal sigh,

Lys started to wipe them off, letting them go. Sometimes it worked, other times it just made her think of three more things she needed up there, and any space she'd cleared filled with new concerns.

"Does everyone have a clear mind yet?" Mark asked.

Lys didn't say no out loud. She'd just gotten to Kamau's name, and a whole new world of issues popped up. However, she kept listening to Mark.

"Now open up a hole in the middle of your board. Let it represent magic. It's not an outside problem, it's something that comes from inside of you, therefore, you can control it."

After a moment of satisfaction when she allowed herself to think of Kamau's strong hand around hers, she exhaled and blew all of the remaining words off the board. It stood white and clean, ready for use.

Imagining the center of the surface, Lys placed a hole the size of a pin. Golden light surged from it, reminding Lys of the end of a firecracker as it lifted into the air.

"Is there energy coming out of the hole?" Mark asked.

Lys nodded. Did everyone else?

"Good." Mark seemed pleased. "Now, put your hand on the board, and move in front of the energy."

Lys' ethereal body placed both hands on the board before she moved her face in front of the beam of energy. It tossed her hair back and tickled her cheeks. She took a breath before scooting over until one of her eyes looked directly into the beam.

A surge of pleasure filled her. The golden energy connected with her eye and Lys felt the Need cringe back. The beam was light and the Need was dark. They couldn't be in the same place at the same time.

"Everyone there?" Mark asked. Lys didn't hear anyone answer—she nodded again.

"Good, now let the energy go through you. It's very important that you don't let it fill you, because if that happens you'll have to break all over again." Mark paused only for a second. "Find it an outlet. Use the end of your finger or your eyes or your hair or whatever."

Once Mark warned her not to let the energy fill her, Lys noticed that this is exactly what it was trying to do. She looked down and saw her hands first. She imagined them filling with the energy, and as she did so they started to glow. Turning them to the sides, Lys shot the energy away from her, just like she saw super heroes do in the movies.

Lys stood there, eyes taking in the beam of energy and channeling it out through her hands, for what felt like an hour. However, with each passing second Lys found a better balance than she'd had before. The energy began to leave a song in her head—a buzzing of unfamiliar but not discomforting tunes that she almost recognized.

"Once you think you've got that," Mark said, "try to use your magic."

Chapter 18

Use her magic? How exactly did he expect her to do that?

At first nothing came to her, but then she remembered what happened when she broke, and all those times she thought she'd been hallucinating. Seeing through other people's eyes.

She didn't want to end up seeing through a million eyes at once again, so Lys concentrated on one person. And since the only person in the room that might have their eyes open was Mark, she tried to find him.

At first nothing happened. The light continued to go through her, and Lys did her best not to panic. She told herself to concentrate—focus.

Once again she tried to find Mark. The magic curled around her, vulturing, looking for a path. She thought about Mark's dark eyes and the magic shot to her right. Lys let her mind follow it, and a moment later a gray haze—like back at the hospital—surrounded her. It lifted almost as fast as it came, leaving Lys with a clear view of the ballroom with Inez and Peter sitting on the floor. Lys grinned.

Peter sat taking deep breaths and Inez's scowl had almost disappeared. Almost. Her perspective turned, following Mark's gaze, and moved past Kamau until it settled on her. She laughed when she saw her own, smiling face.

"What's funny?" Mark asked.

"I can see myself." Okay, seeing herself talk but not looking in a mirror had to rank up with the strangest things she'd ever done.

"You can?" Mark looked around.

"Well, not when you move your head."

"What do you mean?" Mark turned his attention back to Lys.

"I can see through your eyes."

Mark blinked. "Through my eyes?"

161

"Yeah." Lys suddenly felt like she'd done something wrong, and tried to pull out. Nothing happened. She saw her own face go from laughing to scared.

"What's wrong?" Mark asked.

"How do I get out of it?" She felt her breath catch as she tried to push herself away from the energy coming from the hole. "I can't get out of it!"

"Don't panic," Mark said, standing and taking a few steps toward her. "If you can't get yourself out, I can do it. But first, try this. Let more out than you're taking in."

More of the energy? Lys tried to concentrate on the beam, but couldn't with Mark looking down at her grimace.

"Close your eyes," she said.

Mark did, and she was able to once again focus on the hole. With all of her might, she pushed the magic out of her. Unfortunately it felt like trying to shove a watermelon through a smoking pipe. Nothing happened, so she pushed harder, using every ounce of willpower she could find. Still nothing.

"It's not working," she said, panic rising in her voice.

"Keep trying."

Lys pushed, she pulled, she fought—all to no avail. The balance she had so carefully constructed began to break down, and the energy filled her.

"It's really not working," she said, this time through gritted teeth. The view through Mark's eyes opened again, as did about fifty others. Most showed only black or shadows, but plenty of others filled her mind. Lys saw herself flinch back.

"Okay," Mark said. "This might not be comfortable."

A jolt of white hot electricity seared through Lys. It raced to the hole in her board and struck, leaving the board a smoking, charred mess. Lys felt herself yanked from her meditation and thrown back into the real world.

Gasping for breath, she doubled over, squeezing her eyes shut in an attempt to get rid of the fading images that crowded her mind.

"You okay?" Mark asked, squatting down in front of her. His hand lay on her bare forearm.

Lys slowly opened her eyes, her vision returning to normal. "Yeah, I think so." She looked up at Mark. "That's scary."

Mark smiled. "Sure is, mate." He stood and looked around. Lys followed his gaze and found both Peter and Kamau watching her. Inez and Brady still sat with their eyes closed.

"Not bad for your first time," he said.

Lys felt like a fish out of water. "That's magic?"

"Yes, it is."

"How do you feel?" Kamau asked.

Lys thought about it before she answered. "Good, actually." And she did. The remaining buzz of the magic echoed around in her head. The Need lurked in the shadows, unable to come out. Both resided inside of her?

She opened her mouth to ask Kamau how he felt, but Inez's eyes shot open, and she gasped, looking around frantically.

"What is it?" Mark asked, moving to her.

Inez took in her surroundings, and as soon as her eyes settled on Peter she calmed down. "Nothing," she said to Mark after a breath or two. "I just had a hard time getting out of it."

Mark nodded, then turned his attention to Brady. "Hey, Brady, come up for some air."

Lys noticed that Brady's eyes moved back and forth behind his eyelids. He didn't say anything.

"Hey, mate," Mark said, striding across the circle. "Get out of it."

Brady moaned. "Can't," he said softly.

"Try," Mark ordered.

"Don't want to."

A scowl moved over Mark's face. "Now."

This time Brady's eyebrows knit together, and his face screwed up in concentration. Sweat broke out on his forehead. "But I can feel everything."

"You can feel everything later," Mark said. "Right now I need you back here."

Brady nodded. His shoulders shook like he had the chills, and a moment later he opened his eyes. Lys noticed that his oily eyes swirled the fastest of anyone, and his hands shook like an old man's.

"You okay?" Mark asked.

He nodded. "I think so." A small grin broke out on his face. "That's pretty damn cool."

"Isn't it?" Mark said with a knowing smile.

Kamau frowned. "Why is it hard for some people to come out of the magic?"

Mark looked at him for a moment before answering. "Magic is different for everyone. Some people can access it easily but have a hard time getting out. For others it's the opposite. Did you have difficulty breaking away?"

"No," Kamau said, shaking his head. "Not at all."

"Ancients have more control in general," Mark said before looking around. "Why don't we break for lunch. Inez, we need to get a hold of Mason. Do you have a cell phone?"

"I can steal one."

"That works. I need to tell him where we are and find out when someone can come pick us up."

Inez didn't look particularly happy with the idea of calling Mr. Mason, but for once she didn't argue. Instead she just stood and pointed down the hall. "There's some food in the first room. Help yourselves. I'll go get a phone." Her eyes briefly flickered to Lys as if to say "Don't even think about following me."

Right, like Lys would put herself in a position where she'd be alone with Inez.

164

Lunch went quickly. Lys inhaled some chips and a small sandwich, hardly listening to Brady throw out ideas for renaming the power levels, and barely noticing Kamau's leg pressed up against hers. She wanted another go at her magic. Sure, it terrified her, but on the other hand for a few minutes she'd actually felt like she was in control of her own destiny. Maybe she could go on. Maybe her life wasn't over after all.

Before they'd finished, Inez returned with a cell phone and a bag full of fruit.

"Here," she said, dumping it on the table. "The phones usually get reported stolen within a few hours, so you should use it now." Without another word, Inez snatched up an apple and left the room, gracing Lys with yet another withering gaze.

"Don't worry, she'll calm down soon," Peter said, following Lys' eyes.

Lys shrugged. She didn't care much about what Inez thought or did. At least that's what she kept telling herself.

Mark took the phone and left the room, dialing as he went. His voice faded after the word, "Hello, Jeremiah?"

Lys stood and made her way back to the ballroom. For some reason she felt better about dabbling with magic there. Inez sat on the floor in a far corner, her eyes closed. Going back to her previous spot, Lys settled down and tried again.

This time it was easier to clear her mind, but getting to the magic took a while. She heard the others shuffle back in, but no one said anything.

When she finally got the hole in her board, and the magic began to fill her, Lys had to have Mark get her out because she couldn't open an outlet. Magic poured into her body like water filling a glass, and when it got to her waist hysteria kicked in. That happened twice before she got it right.

As soon as she found a balance, she opened her sight and

searched for someone's eyes to look through. She didn't want to use Mark again, so she looked farther away. It took a few minutes, but she finally found a person. Although she had no idea how she did it—the whole thing felt like a video game that she never read the directions for.

The view from the person's eyes came into focus, and Lys recognized that they were in the supply room. There might be a lot of bad costumes in Vegas, but how many could claim the purple and white bodice on a dress made of feathers and slabs of tire. Right, no one.

She found her perspective moving toward the wall where the door lay hidden. She expected them to hang up an outfit and leave, but instead they walked to the wall and put a hand on it. A glove appeared. A black glove.

Lys hissed in a breath. Lots of costumes had gloves—must be someone from the show. However, when the perspective swiveled to the left, Lys caught sight of two policemen, one talking into his radio and another drawing his gun.

Maybe the club got busted. Lys wished she believed that.

Pulling out of someone's sight seemed easier than getting out of her magic. It felt like squeezing part of her mind through a funnel. Lys retreated from the policemen and searched for another set of eyes to look through. It didn't take long, and as the now familiar gray haze cleared, Lys found herself in a hallway, standing at the back of a line of four other policemen. She wished she could hear what they were saying, but Mark had told her that being a sight user meant she probably would never hear anything when she did this.

"Get me out." The words blurted from her mouth as she recognized where this set of policemen were standing.

Mark started to say something about her doing it on her own.

"Now!" she said, raising her voice.

The shock hit her and Lys flew back into her own eyes, the

scene around her shredding into ribbons. She blinked and shook her head, trying to clear the remnants of the magic from her sight.

"What is it?" Mark asked, arms crossed over his chest.

Lys gulped. "The police. They're right outside the doors."

The words no sooner left Lys' lips than a crash came from the end of the hall. Everyone sprung to their feet.

Lys watched in horror as a police officer ran into the ballroom. The gun in his hand followed his gaze, traveling from her to the others and settling on Mark.

"Freeze!" the officer said as another man burst from the hall.

Lys saw everyone put their hands up

"I think we found what we're looking for," the second officer said.

"Call it in." The first officer returned his gaze to Lys. "You alright there?"

Lys nodded. "Yes, sir."

This guy thought she'd been kidnapped. By Mark. That explained the guns.

"I'm fine. I think there's been a misunderstanding." Lys said.

"These guys aren't all police officers," Peter said in a hushed whisper. He inhaled deeply. "The New."

To Lys' surprise, Kamau stepped forward, speaking before either man got to their radios.

"Officers, I'm so glad you found us. We've been lost down here for hours, and couldn't find our way out." He smiled brightly.

The first officer looked around at the construction lights. "Lost?"

"Yes," Kamau said, "and you found us. We're grateful."

The others shot sidelong glances at Kamau, and Lys returned a reassuring smile and gave her head a little shake.

"You are?"

Kamau nodded. "Absolutely." He took a step forward. Neither police officer twitched. They both had their eyes glued to

167

Kamau, and they listened to his voice intently. "We're glad that your superiors sent you after a group of lost tourists."

"Lost tourists?" Inez muttered.

The first officer's attention turned toward Inez, and the look of serenity on his face screwed back up into a glare.

"Yes, officer," Kamau said, glancing at Inez out of the corner of his eye. "We were on a tour, and the guide brought us into this room. He told us a ghost story and then disappeared."

"A ghost tour?" the second officer asked.

"Yes." Lys noticed Kamau flick a finger at Brady. He nodded and shifted his weight. "It was horrible. The girls were scared, but now you found us."

Both police officers nodded in unison with Kamau. Their eyes sort of glazed over and they swayed back and forth.

"You should put your guns away. You're heroes."

The second officer lowered his gun, then they both put their guns away, grinning madly.

"My goodness, what is that on the floor?" Kamau asked.

As both officers looked down, Brady's hands shot into his pockets. He pulled out two pieces of broken tile and threw them at the police officers. Each one struck its mark in the head, and both men slumped to the floor.

Inez swore.

"Nice," Mark said.

"Dude!" Brady said, turning toward Kamau. "You totally just used a Jedi mind trick on those guys! I had no idea you could do that."

"Jedi mind trick?" Inez asked.

Brady turned to her. "Yeah, you know, like Luke Skywalker in *Star Wars*?"

Inez blinked.

"Oh come on," Brady said. "You know, the force, *Star Wars*, Princess Leia...These aren't the kids you're looking for." He waved his hand in front of Inez's eyes.

"I know what a Jedi is," Inez said, swatting his hand away.

Brady turned to Mark. "We could use Jedi names for the magic! Padwan, Jedi Knight, Jedi Master—stuff like that!"

Mark shook his head.

"There are more coming," Kamau said, interrupting Brady before he could really get going.

Mark turned to Inez. "Are there any other ways out?"

"Just back through the storm drains."

"Then that's the way we go." He pointed at the far corner. "Now."

Lys jogged behind Brady, who led the way. Inez and Peter brought up the rear. The room began to tilt back and forth, and Lys almost lost her footing.

The magical buzz from a few moments earlier swung the other way—filling Lys with the gut-wrenching need to sit down and cry.

"I told you they'd bring us trouble," Inez muttered to Peter as she strode toward the grate in the floor.

Peter shrugged. "We'll be okay."

"We'll all be okay if we can get to the rendezvous point and meet whoever Mason sends to get us," Mark said.

"Get over here," Inez said. "I'm going to cut the power."

Everyone hurried to comply, and just as the pounding on the doors down the hall began, the room went pitch black. Lys felt Kamau step closer. The sound of the grate being lifted squeaked in the silence, and Lys cringed.

"They're coming through the second doors," Kamau whispered.

"I'll go first. The rest of you follow," Inez said. Lys heard her jeans rubbing against the side of the grate, then the click as her boots hit the concrete below.

"I can't see a thing," Brady complained. "Where's the hole?"

Lys looked around. She couldn't see anything either. Wait. She'd been able to see in the tunnels before. It must have been magic. Taking a breath, Lys closed her eyes and willed the board into existence again. It jumped to life, clear and clean—ready for use. Lys opened a tiny hole and moved in front of it. Instead of concentrating on other people's eyes, she tried to imagine what it would be like to see in the dark. When she opened her eyes, the pitch black room sat bathed in a dull gray. She could see. Not only that, the desire to cry was crowded out by a happy buzz.

"Right there," she told Brady, taking his arm and steering him forward.

Lys didn't need Kamau to tell them that one set of policemen had broken through the door. She heard the pounding right before the splintering of wood. "Go!" she whispered, putting Brady's hand on the edge of the hole.

Brady didn't even hesitate. He jumped down, landing right next to Inez.

"Have everyone jump, I'll catch them," he said.

"You can't see," Lys pointed out.

"Don't need to see, now I can feel you guys moving around up there."

Brady looked up and Lys could clearly see his swirling eyes. She glanced at Kamau and found his bright, silvery eyes focused on the hallway across the room.

"Mark," Lys said, moving him forward. "Go."

She didn't bother to watch him drop. Footsteps sounded from down the hall, feet crunching on dirt and rocks from the cave in.

"Go," Lys said, pushing Kamau forward.

Indistinct words came from the hall, following the flashlight.

"They're looking for us," he said.

"Just go!" Lys said, wondering if the gas station clerk had turned them in. Maybe Kamau's little trick didn't work as well as he thought.

"You should go first," Kamau said.

Okay, Lys had to admit that the knight in shining armor routine made her weak in the knees, but now was not the time for chivalry.

"I can see, you can't. Go." She maneuvered him over to the hole, placing his toes on the edge.

He looked at her. Lys knew he couldn't see her face, but his eyes bore right through hers. *Could* he see? She reached out to squeeze his hand, but before she got there another flashlight joined the first, and from the way the beam spread across the floor, Lys could tell the policemen were getting close. So instead, he got a nudge. He only hesitated for a heartbeat before he jumped.

Lys and Peter dove to the floor, narrowly avoiding the flashlight beam. A fresh set of officers hit the end of the hall—a different hall than the first set. And with them came a pair of men in black body armor. Lys felt Peter squirm beside her.

"What happened?" one of the officers asked.

"Quiet," one of the men in armor said.

Betting against those helmets not being able to see in the dark would be a bad idea. She gently pushed Peter toward the hole. He started to army crawl his way backward.

Maybe she could distract them while Peter and the others got away. Lys steeled herself and prepared to jump up.

Peter beat her too it. Springing to his feet, he bounced away from Lys.

"Hey, who are you guys?" he yelled, waving his arms.

All eyes turned toward Peter. The police officers trained their flashlight beams on him, and his sprinting form moved in and out of the light as he ran.

"Freeze!" a police officer said, gun following Peter.

"That's one of them," a synthesized voice said from under a helmet.

The other figure in armor raised a weapon. It looked like a crossbow from the future. The figure pointed it right at Peter and pulled the trigger.

Lys found herself on her feet as the weapon fired, launching a large c-shaped projectile at Peter.

She tried to move, but something had a hold of her ankle. She tried to break free, but the scene around her seemed to slow. She saw Peter running, arms still waving. The projectile followed him. When it hit him, it clamped around Peter's middle like a crazed Pac-Man, locking shut with a click.

* * *

White light burst from Peter, blinding Lys. A scream full of pain rang out. The ballroom filled with anguish as Lys cried out as well.

"No!"

But her cry got cut short. Someone grabbed her from behind, putting a hand over her mouth, and lifted her off her feet. Before she could begin to struggle in earnest, her captor jumped and they both went down the hole.

"They got Peter!" Brady whispered as they landed. He set Lys down.

"Go get him!" Inez said, panic in her voice.

"It's the New," Lys said. "They got him with some kind of weapon. It clamped around his stomach and then there was a bright light." She could hear the hysteria in her own voice. Peter's scream echoed down the hole.

"That's a dog collar," Mark said. Everyone turned to look at him, even though they probably couldn't see him.

"Dog collars don't capture," Mark said. "They kill." The scream from above cut off.

Lys watched Inez's eyes go wide. She shook her head and

started to reach for the ladder.

Mark's hand shot out and grabbed her. "He's gone."

"I have to go get him," Inez said, trying to wrench her arm free.

The synthesized voice spoke. "He's done." A pause. "The rest of them can't be far."

Rage shot through Lys. They killed Peter? They really killed him? Then the realization hit—if she'd jumped up before him, she'd be dead.

It should have been her.

She turned to the ladder, ready to go up after Inez, but Brady grabbed her arm.

"We have to go," Mark whispered.

Inez struggled, and Lys could see the tears in her eyes.

"Come on, you've got to get us out of here," Brady said.

Footsteps approached from above. Brady shoved her to the front of the group. "Go!"

How could he be so callous?

"We'll all die if we don't move," Mark said, his eyes traveling back up the hole. Lys could see the beams of the flashlights getting brighter.

Offense, attacking, didn't suit Lys' style, but rage bubbled up from her gut, filling her with the desire to climb back up the ladder and face the men there. The fact that she'd never fought with anyone before in her life didn't matter. She'd find a way to hurt them. Or worse.

"Come on," Kamau said in a whisper. He reached out and took her hand. "You're the only one who can get us out of here."

Lys shook her head as tears gathered in the corners of her eyes. She glanced around at the others. Mark still had Inez by the arm, and Brady's face told Lys that he wanted to do the same thing she did.

But Mark said they'd killed Peter. It should have been her. She couldn't let anyone else get hurt.

"This way," she said, her voice barely audible. She stepped past Kamau. "Join hands, I'll get us out of here." The dark pressed down on her, and Lys felt a tug of emotional anguish coming from her heart. Instead of storm drain tunnels, Lys saw a burial chamber. Who would care if they died down here? Who would even know?

Kamau's hand gave hers a squeeze, and Lys shook her head. They were not going to die down here. Not if she had anything to say about it.

She opted to stay on the ledge instead of climbing down into the channel. Ankle deep water still ran through it, and she thought they'd make more noise in the water. Lucky for them, the ceiling gave everyone plenty of head room. Moving as quickly as she dared, Lys took them to the end of the short tunnel and got them around the corner before halting.

"Which way?" Lys asked. She heard whispering behind her, but Lys didn't listen. Instead she kept her head moving, making sure they were alone. If the New had found their way to the ballroom, then they might have someone down here. She'd never underestimate them again.

"Left," Inez said in a harsh voice.

Lys started to walk, stepping as quietly as she could. Behind her Kamau moved like a ghost, not making a sound. She could hear the others scraping their feet and shifting their weight.

Eventually they had to step down into the water. Lys felt her heart pounding, and her hand became clammy in Kamau's. Every scrape they made and every slosh of water caused Lys to jump.

Fear had become commonplace for her over the past few weeks, but this time she found that her body's reaction to fear started to interfere with the little control she had over her magic. She had to concentrate to keep the world gray instead of having it plunge back into the darkness. Half of her still wanted to go back and attack the New, while the other half of her wanted to let the magic wash over her like water at the beach.

They came to a four way intersection and Lys stopped.

"There are four tunnels here, which way?"

"We should get above ground soon," Mark said.

Lys opened her mouth to ask why, but Inez's voice interrupted her.

"Let me go!"

"Inez," Brady said, "he's gone. If you go back, you'll get killed too."

Lys turned to look at them. Brady had Inez's hand, but she was trying to wriggle free.

"What if I don't care?" Inez asked, glaring in Brady's general direction. Her eyes started to swirl red.

"We care," he said.

"I don't care if you care." She blinked, the red orbs disappearing for a moment. "Let me go."

The look on Brady's face changed, and Lys saw Brady's eyes go wide. "What are you doing?" he asked.

"Just let me go."

Mark let go of Kamau's hand and turned back toward Inez.

"Inez, stop it," he said.

Brady jerked back, throwing Inez's arm away from him. "Fine! Go do whatever you want."

Inez didn't say anything. She started sloshing away.

"Stop her," Mark said.

"Inez," Lys said, going after the other girl, who climbed up on the ledge. "Stop. Please." When Lys caught up she reached out and grabbed Inez by the arm.

Inez turned. "Don't touch me, princess."

"Come on," Lys started.

"Let me go!" Inez screamed, the words reverberating through the tunnel, shattering the quiet dripping of water.

"No." Lys didn't know where it came from, but she wasn't about to move for Inez. "And don't call me princess."

Inez laughed, a harsh sound that grated like rock on rock. "Why not, princess? That's what you are. A spoiled, rich girl. A princess in a castle with servants to do your every bidding."

"You don't even know me." Lys glared. She felt the Need stirring, fighting its way through the magic.

"And you don't know me." Inez said. "Now get out of my way." One hand came up and began to pry Lys' fingers off her arm.

"You can't go back there," Lys said. "You'll end up like Peter."

"Never mention his name," Inez said, growling. "You don't deserve to even speak his name."

Something warm and wet hit Lys right below the eye. She reached up a trembling hand, and the world stood still for a heartbeat.

Inez spit on her. Her. What had she ever done to deserve that? What had she ever done to deserve any of this? The precarious balance in her mind tilted dangerously to one side, and Lys felt the darkness and the Need barreling to the forefront of her conscious.

In an instant, faster than she thought she could move, she was reaching for Inez's face, clawing for flesh and hoping for blood.

Lys felt nothing but pure hate. The Need blossomed anew, bigger, meaner and more terrifying than ever before. Adrenaline fueled her actions, and she knew that she could kill Inez. She could take the other girl's eyes for her own and then kill her. The thought didn't bother her; it exhilarated her– drew her in, seduced her and caused her to act.

Inez screamed, but not in terror. In fury. She tried to grab Lys' hands, but Lys twisted away. Before she could reach Inez's eyes, Lys felt a kick to her thigh. Her leg exploded in pain, and then went numb, causing her to stumble.

Lys held on to Inez for support; the other girl keeping her upright. Inez finally got Lys' hands off her face, and she tried to hold Lys' wrists.

Being an only child, and a girl, Lys' dad made sure she could defend herself. She'd taken a year of self-defense classes, and while she wasn't proficient at anything, she did remember a few moves. Lys twisted her hands out of Inez's grasp, easily pulling free. Then she stepped back and kicked Inez as hard as she could in the stomach.

Inez stumbled backward, hitting the ledge and rolling off. She landed in the channel with a splash. Lys didn't give her a chance to recover. She sprung down after Inez, going for her eyes.

Voices yelled. Someone's hands tried pry the two girls apart. Lys ignored them. She would get to them in a minute—Inez was first. Everything and everyone else sat outside her rage, but they would get their turn.

Her fingers inched toward Inez's eyes. Her nails cut in the other girl's cheeks. Hands held her back, Lys could only move in slow motion. But it was enough. She moved steadily closer. The fear in Inez's eyes goaded Lys on. To have someone fear you was almost as intoxicating as satisfying the Need.

So close, just an inch more and she would have them—she licked her lips in anticipation…and then she was being flung up and away.

She hit the rock wall hard, cracking her head and seeing black spots. She slid down, landing unsteadily on her feet.

"Keep her back!" a voice yelled, breaking the spell.

Lys gasped, but couldn't breathe. However, she could see. She could see blood on her hands.

"Grab them!"

Lys convulsed. Spasms of pain and fear lanced through her limbs, causing her to go to her knees.

Kamau arrived, hands groping in the dark to brush her arms,

but he didn't have to hold her. She curled into a ball and started to sob as she continued to twitch. Lys couldn't live like this—didn't want to continue existing.

"Please," she sobbed as Kamau knelt down next to her. "Let me die."

"You're not going to die," Kamau said.

"I'm sorry," she said, "I couldn't stop myself."

"It's not you, just don't move," she heard him say.

All thought, all reason was gone. Her world shattered around her. Lys truly wanted to die.

And then it went away. Not just the relief of shedding tears, or the release of adrenaline, but the feeling evaporated. Her sobbing stopped, but the shaking didn't.

"That's better," Mark said. She felt another hand on her shoulder. "Come on, Lys, calm down."

Calm down? She'd just tried to kill someone! And she'd wanted to do it. She curled into a tighter ball—Lys tried to shut out the world.

"Don't do that," Mark said. "Kamau, talk to her. Give me a second."

What would Kamau think of her? Even in her own eyes Lys knew she was a monster.

"Shhh," Kamau said, rubbing her back. "You're okay."

Lys shook her head. First she got Peter killed, and now she'd attacked Inez. "Just leave me here."

"That's awfully dramatic," Kamau said.

"Please."

"No," Kamau said.

She heard Mark coming back. "Here," he said. A moment later Lys felt another jolt of electricity, and her mind cleared. She unclenched her arms from around her knees.

"Better?" he asked.

Lys opened her eyes and slowly raised her head. Kamau

tugged her into a sitting position. "How's your head?" he asked.

The throbbing there paled in comparison to the roller coaster her emotions were on.

She made the mistake of looking down at her hands. Blood covered her palms, and she could feel chunks of flesh under her nails.

Revulsion filled Lys and she tried to back away from her own hands, running into the wall. Her hands! She'd tried to kill someone.

"It's okay," Mark said, grabbing her wrists. "It's okay, everyone is fine."

"No," she whispered. "No, I..."

"It was Inez's magic. She lost control. It's not your fault."

Lys felt herself balanced on the edge of a knife. Part of her wanted to believe Mark's words, but the other part of her wanted to revel in her attempt to get Inez's eyes. Two sides of her fought for control, and she didn't know which one would win.

"We need to go," Brady said.

Lys looked over and saw Brady kneeling next to Inez, who had her face in her hands.

"Someone's coming," Brady said. "I can feel them."

"Come on," Mark said as he and Kamau pulled Lys to her feet. "I'd love to let you rest, but we have to go."

Before anyone could move, splashing came from two of the tunnels, and six members of the New appeared, running right at them.

Chapter 19

Mark turned first, blue light flaring from his hands.

"I wouldn't do that if I were you," one of the New said. "Electricity in water? Doesn't seem like a good idea."

Lights turned on from six points, and Lys blinked, trying to get her vision to adjust.

Brady stood, but one of the New had a gun leveled at Inez's head.

"No one move. Hands up and open. Don't make me collar you," the synthesized voice said.

Inez stiffened, and started to stand, but the man with the gun proved faster.

Lys screamed.

The gun didn't launch another collar. Instead a dart flew from it, burying itself into Inez's shoulder. She stopped mid-stride and spun around. Brady caught her twitching form before she hit the stone floor.

"No one else moves unless I tell them to," the figure in the lead said. "If you do exactly what I say, we won't have any more unfortunate accidents."

Lys glared at the man. She could feel his eyes on her through the helmet. She tried to redirect her magic from seeing in the dark to looking through people's eyes, but got nothing from him. Either magic didn't go through the helmets, or she'd reached her limit.

The other five members of the New spread out, each taking one of the magic users. The leader grabbed Lys roughly by the arm and dragged her into the middle of the channel. The others got the same treatment. As soon as the man touched her, Lys felt her connection to magic cut off.

"Now, we're all going to go up to the surface. I don't want any trouble." He emphasized this by shoving the barrel of his gun hard into the base of Lys' neck. "I'll just use this one to make sure the rest of you behave." He pushed her forward. "Move."

Every inch of Lys shook and trembled. She stepped forward and didn't know if she'd be able to shift her weight from one foot to the other. The ankle deep water threatened to sweep her away, and if not for the iron grip around her arm, Lys would have gone down.

The man who shot Inez shoved Brady away and hauled Inez to her feet. The other girl stumbled, shaking her head. Lys couldn't keep an eye on her, because her escort led her out first.

With the bobbing lights, they moved much faster. Lys trudged forward, the barrel of the gun still at the back of her neck. The process of thinking didn't exist—her brain felt disconnected, and she could barely manage putting one foot in front of the other. She tried to stop looking at her hands. Blood dried on her fingertips, and she could still feel chunks of Inez' skin beneath her nails. A shudder joined the shaking and she wondered what would happen if she threw up. Would they shoot her? Or let her drown in her own vomit and the four inches of water at her feet?

Light—real light—began to tease her eyes. After going around two more corners, Lys could see even without her magic. The man holding her arm led them to a ladder.

"You first," he said, releasing Lys.

Not knowing what else to do, Lys reached out a shaking hand and started to climb. It took her three tries to get her foot on the second rung, and when someone reached down and drew her out of the hole she almost didn't care that he wore black armor.

"Here she is," a voice said from under the helmet. "I knew they were down there. Where's our boy?"

Lys shrugged away from the man, getting her arms out of his grasp. She watched as the leader of the men climbed up the ladder. Without one of them touching her, she felt her magic stir.

It pulsed, bowing the barrier that held it back. But Lys didn't want the magic. Not this time.

With a thought she allowed the Need to resurface. It writhed, angry at having been denied Inez's eyes. Lys let it fill her as the others climbed out of the hole. Inez slumped to the ground, dazed. Just as Brady stood up, Lys willed the Need to take control. Red fury burned before her eyes, and Lys knew just where to direct it.

The leader from the tunnels, and the man who helped Lys out of the hole, stood conversing. One of them took his helmet off, revealing Jed underneath. Good enough.

She locked gazes with Brady, who must have been thinking along the same lines. He smiled as she turned.

Lys let out a scream and ran at the two men. The Need saw Jed's eyes and filled Lys with a desire she could not control. And instead of trying to hold back, she reveled in it.

The world slowed as she got closer. Jed turned in surprise while the leader brought his weapon up. Five steps away. Three. Two. The gun fired, and she screamed.

Only nothing hit her. Instead, something hit the gun and tossed it through the air.

She kept running. If they planned to kill her, she would give them an easy target. If not, they'd hesitate. Either way, they had to go through her to get to the others.

Jed seemed surprised when Lys kept coming, and even more unhinged when she started clawing for his eyes. His big hands couldn't contain her wiry arms. People started to yell around her, but Lys ignored them. She focused on Jed's clear, blue eyes and let the Need do its thing.

The sheer fact that Lys wanted what the Need did made things so much easier. She ground her teeth together as she kept trying to get around his arms to his face. Only a few inches remained. She had him!

Then the wind got knocked out of her. She felt a screaming pain in her ribs, and she flew backward, hitting the ground with a hard thud.

A rib cracked on impact. Lights danced before her eyes, and she couldn't move. Couldn't breathe.

Tears of pain streamed down her face. Screaming filled the air around her, and after a moment someone grabbed her hand.

"Lys?" Kamau's face came into view.

Lys opened her mouth to reply, but still couldn't breathe.

"Can you get up?" His words slurred together in her mind. She shook her head.

"We need to move," he said, grabbing her hand and tugging her up.

Lys cried out, the sudden change in position releasing her lungs. A ripping pain filled her right side, but she didn't have time to think about it. Kamau pulled her to her feet and started to lead her toward the others. She stumbled, trying to keep up.

Around her lay a dusty field covered by used cars. A black van sat with its doors open, one more member of the New inside.

Only a few feet separated them from the others when a loud pop sounded, and Lys saw a net fly out of the end of Jed's gun. Brady dodged behind a car so quickly that Lys could swear she didn't even see him move. A second pop followed, and Mark had to dive out of the way. The net grazed him, but he didn't get caught up in it. Still, he fell, hitting the ground hard, rolling away with a grimace of pain on his face.

The two armored men advanced.

Mark rose to his hands and knees. Brady tossed a piece of metal at their assailants. It bounced off harmlessly as one of the men turned on Brady.

"Move!" Kamau said, pushing everyone apart. They scattered, and the small harpoon-ish looking projectile that came from the gun rocketed through them, sticking in the ground a few yards

183

behind.

"What is that?" Lys asked, crouching behind a car with Kamau.

"I don't think we want to know," Kamau said.

Jed held up his hand and his two cohorts stopped.

"We're not here to hurt you," he said, the same look of disdain on his face as he'd had in Doyle's office. "If you come quietly, we promise that no harm will come to you."

"You're full if it, Jed," Mark said, stumbling to his feet.

Jed's eyes turned to Mark and a dark smile creases his lips. "It'll be a pleasure taking you in."

"Right, like that's going to happen." Mark shook his head. Lys could hear the bravado wavering as Mark took a step forward. "Why don't you and your boys back off and let us be on our way. We already took care of your little friends."

Jed snorted. "I don't think so." He glanced around. "You're outnumbered, and I'm pretty sure these kids don't have any idea what they're really dealing with."

"All they need to know is that you're trying to kill them."

"Would I do that?" Jed asked, placing a hand on his chest.

Lys watched the exchange. The two men looked like gunslingers from an old western movie, faced off with nothing in between them. Only Mark didn't have a gun. Still, Jed hesitated. Why?

A flicker of movement caught Lys' attention, and she saw the two armored men turn their guns on Mark.

"Yeah, mate, you would." Mark's hand came up just as Jed's gun did. Jed fired and Mark shot blue light from his palms, creating a visible shield in front of himself. The net hit the shield, spread out, twitched and fell to the ground.

The other two fired as well, but Mark threw himself backward, landing hard again.

Lys got to her hands and knees and crawled with Kamau to

where Inez waited behind a car. She didn't want to make herself a target, and she didn't have anything to offer a real fight. Her ribs protested, and she could feel herself getting light headed. She risked a look back.

Brady appeared, crouching in front of Mark, his hands kneading the dirt like dough. He grabbed the ground like a rug and raised his hands. The earth came up and Brady flicked it like a towel. A wave rolled toward Jed. He tried to get out of the way, but Lys watched as he rose to the top of the wave and then down the back side.

The two men in armor converged on Brady. He squat down, grabbed clods of dirt as big as his head and threw them across his body, each hitting a man in armor in the chest. They both flew back, landing thirty feet away on the ground.

"Brady!" Mark yelled. "That's enough!"

Lys turned her attention back to Brady. He knelt down, his hands still kneading the ground. Only now they were in elbow deep.

"It feels so good," Brady said. "This is awesome!"

"Hey!" Mark said, moving toward Brady. "Cut it off now. We need to go."

"Okay, okay," Brady said. He tried to pull his hands free, but wasn't able to.

"Uh," he tugged again with the same result. "I don't know what..." Brady lunged forward, like something had grabbed him from beneath the ground.

The dirt around Lys started to shake and jump. She got to her feet and stepped back. The ground gave way, sucking her down like a whirlpool. One leg went in to her upper thigh. She screamed.

Inez backed away.

Lys' other leg began to sink as well. Clawing at the dirt she tried to stop herself from being inhaled by the ground. Rocks scraped at her through the thin pants, and she felt a scream of pure terror rising from her lungs. The smell of the dark engulfed her, and Lys clawed faster, trying to stop from sinking. Her breath became shallow, and she felt the world closing in around her. Not the dark. Please, not again.

Just as her hips passed into the dirt a strong hand reached out and grabbed hers.

"Hold on," Kamau said. His other hand clung onto a car bumper.

Lys couldn't speak. She just kept struggling.

"Brady!" Mark bellowed. "Cut it off!"

"I can't," Brady said, fear rising in his voice. "It won't let me."

Mark growled and ran toward Brady. He started to sink, and was up to his knees before he leaned down and touched the ground around him. Brady's vortex hit a chunk of solid stone where Mark stood. The earth beneath Lys solidified, holding her fast.

Lys watched as a wave of earth came from under Brady's hands. It crackled and groaned as the ground pitched and rose, coming straight for them. Cars slid aside, metal hitting metal.

Lys couldn't move. Kamau struggled in vain to pull her out.

"Go!" Lys said, shoving Kamau away.

Before he could argue, Mark stepped in front of them. He thrust his hands into the oncoming wave, and it crashed against him, the middle of it falling. The edges kept going. One of them just missed Kamau and took out a line of cars. The other hit Inez straight on. She rolled to the top of it and got bucked off, flying through the air. She screamed.

"Inez!" Lys said. She looked at Brady. "Brady, you have to stop!" She glanced at Kamau. "Can you help him?"

"I got it," Mark said, literally pulling the ground up in front of another wave and stopping it. Mark ran to Brady and touched him on the side of the neck. Lys saw a familiar flash of light and Brady

186

collapsed.

"Are you hurt?" Kamau asked.

"I'm fine." Lys shook her head. "Where is Inez?" Kamau looked in the direction Inez had gone. "Go look for her!"

Kamau jumped to comply. Lys tried to wiggle free, but to no avail. She'd let her friends bury her under the sand at the beach a few times; it had taken her quite a while to get out of it. That paled in comparison to this.

"Inez is hurt!" Kamau said.

Mark swore. "Is anyone else hurt?"

"No, just stuck," Lys answered, her voice trembling. She heard Brady groan.

"What happened?" Brady asked.

"You lost control," Mark snapped. "I told you not to mess with it. Now stay there while I go check on Inez. Don't even think about using."

"Inez?" Brady's voice was small, desperate.

"You hurt her," Mark said. "Let me go take a look."

"But I…I didn't mean to." Brady stammered, stumbling to his feet.

Lys cranked her whole body around in order to see Inez. Her middle wailed in protest. Kamau and Mark knelt next to Inez. Brady fell to his hands and knees. Lys thought she could hear him crying.

"Is she okay?" Brady asked, pleading.

"She's breathing," Kamau said, "I don't see any blood, but I'd bet her arm is broken."

"Her arm?"

"Nothing we can do about that here," Mark shook his head. "I'm no healer."

"We need to splint it," Kamau advised.

Brady continued to babble; Lys couldn't make out his words.

A black van came around the far corner of the lot

"We have company," she yelled.

Everyone looked up. Mark swore again.

"Get her behind that trailer," Mark ordered Kamau and Brady. "Lys, what's wrong with you?"

"My legs are stuck," she said, trying again to pull herself free. And it felt like someone had punched her in the ribs.

"I can fix that." Mark ran over and placed a hand on each side of her leg. "Grab my shoulder and pull yourself out just as soon as the dirt is loose enough."

Lys felt the ground rumble and then loosen, but it didn't turn to sand like it had for Brady. Rocks and dirt funneled around her legs, scratching and biting. "Ouch," she said through clenched teeth.

"Sorry," Mark grunted. "My precision isn't great. It would be easier for me to make the whole field loose than just this bit."

"It's okay," she said. "Just get me out; the van will be here any second."

The ground became loose, but not fluid. Lys pulled on Mark's shoulder. She felt a deep gouge forming as she wiggled one leg free. Ignoring the pain (knowing they were about to be caught) Lys clawed her way forward, finally getting the other leg out. She rolled over on her back, gasping. Flinching as she breathed.

"Looks like the touch users aren't being very nice to you ladies," Mark said, glancing at her leg.

"Let's go," Lys said. She didn't even want to look. Lys could feel blood flowing freely from her leg to the ground. The warm, sticky fluid changed directions as Mark helped her to her feet.

"Come on," he said. "Let's get out of here.

The adrenaline pumping through her veins began to wane. She heard Inez stifle a scream and she heard Brady saying he was sorry over and over. Mark half carried her through the maze of tangled cars to the others. He still didn't seem very steady on his feet, and Lys tried to support her own weight as much as she could.

They weren't there yet when the dark van came around the nearest row of cars. It came straight for them.

"Oh great," Mark said. "Kamau!"

Lys tried to move faster. Kamau started back toward them.

"Better get out of the way," Mark said to Lys, gently pushing her to the side.

She didn't argue; especially when she glanced down and saw the deep cut that ran from the front of her ankle, up and around to the back of her knee. Lys didn't usually have a problem with blood, but that was deep, and she felt herself getting lightheaded.

Oh no, Lys thought, *I'm not passing out*. She grit her teeth and limped away from Mark.

Kamau ran to help her, and he reached her just as the van flipped around so the passenger door stopped right in front of Mark.

"More New?" Kamau asked.

"I don't know. But you'd better go help Mark. Use your Jedi mind tricks, or whatever."

Kamau hesitated.

"Just go," Lys said, pushing him away. She heard the click of a door opening. She tensed, looking back over her shoulder, ready to dodge a flying net or whatever else might be shot at her.

Chapter 20

Lys almost cried with relief as Ayden and a woman Lys didn't recognize appeared when the window rolled down.

"You guys need some help?"

"It's about time you got here," Mark said.

"What happened?" the woman asked, glaring at Mark. "What did you do?"

Mark looked like he wanted to say something smart, but he held up a hand. "We have to get out of here. There are three of the New over there, and Brady just lost it."

"Jump in," Ayden said.

"Wait!" the woman said, eying Lys. "Let me grab the first aid kit. She's going to bleed to death."

Those were not the words Lys wanted to hear.

"She's not going to bleed to death," Mark said,. Then he took a good look at Lys' leg. "But it probably wouldn't hurt to wrap it." He accepted the kit from the woman. "Let's go."

Kamau got Lys' arm around his shoulders and helped her limp to the van. They put her in the back seat with Inez and Brady.

"You know how to wrap that up?" Mark asked Brady.

Brady looked a little sick. "Uh…"

Inez, sweat pouring down her face, rolled her eyes. "Just do it," she said, looking at Lys' leg, actual concern in her eyes. Well, concern mixed with pain. The way she held her left arm Lys wondered how she wasn't screaming. "Who are these guys?"

Mark turned as they pulled out after Ayden. "A couple of Mason's people. Friends of mine," he added, seeing the dark look on Inez's face. "They're here to help."

"Sure they are," Inez muttered, closing her eyes.

"Hold on, try not to pass out," Mark said to Lys.

The words began to blur together as Brady pulled a long roll of gauze out of the first aid kit. He started at her ankle and wrapped up Lys' entire leg. The dizziness increased as she had to move her leg, and soon all she could see were little patches of reality through the black blotches that spotted her vision.

"Lys?" Mark said. "Do *not* close your eyes."

It didn't much matter if her eyes were closed. Black engulfed her. Sound continued to distort, and Lys soon slipped into oblivion.

It didn't take long for the magic to call to her. Lys could feel it trying to get through the barrier. It whispered softly, caressing her emotions and enticing her to use it. Just for a minute. It would feel so good.

Someone tried to talk to her, but Lys ignored them. Instead she pictured her board. The white surface appeared—bowing out like a giant ball rolled behind it. She wanted to put a hole as big as her head in the board. The magic would fill her. The brilliant light would sing to her.

The idea both seduced and repulsed her. Could she get back out of it if she allowed the magic to overflow? Would it block out the Need if she did? Which was more dangerous?

Darkness took her, and Lys let it. Her mind filled with overlaying images, and she watched as they played on a dark screen. They started slow, increasing in speed like a rock rolling down a hill. Lys tried to concentrate—the pure quantity overwhelmed her. She willed the magic through her in an attempt to balance it. The images slowed and dwindled until she saw only one—someone looking at her picture. Fingers stroked the frayed edge of the photo, and the perspective got blurry. The view went dark for a moment—blink. Lys understood. Someone was looking at her picture, and crying.

A knife cut through the scene and yanked Lys awake. She sat

up, dizzy and gasping for breath.

"There we go," Ayden said.

Lys blinked a few times in order to clear the picture of her from her vision. Faces formed around her, and finally Lys recognized Ayden sitting on wooden bench next to her. The woman from the van sat on the other side.

"Where are we?" Lys asked, glancing around and finding herself in a picnic area of some sort.

"Outside Vegas," Ayden said. "Jodi here is about to heal your leg. You should be awake for it."

Jodi smiled. "Healing broken bones in a moving vehicle isn't easy." She shot a worried look over at another picnic table where Lys could see Inez lying down and Mark sitting with his head in his arms. "So we stopped."

Lys felt disconnected, like she'd just taken an afternoon nap that she couldn't wake up from. Raising a hand, she could see her fingers shaking.

"Shock," Jodi said, her blue eyes swirling. Her short, blond hair lay plastered to her head with sweat. "Don't worry; I'll have you fixed up in a second." She smiled and then looked at Ayden. "You might want to hold her."

"Why?" Lys asked, her voice shaky.

"It doesn't really hurt," Jodi said. "But it's a little uncomfortable. It's always wise to keep you from thrashing around, especially since you've never been healed before."

"I'll hold her," Kamau said, stepping into view.

Ayden and Jodi exchanged a glance and Jodi shrugged. "Doesn't matter. She'll probably be fine."

"Can I watch?" Brady asked, walking over to the table.

Kamau replaced Ayden, sitting down next to Lys and taking her trembling hand. He smiled.

A small part of Lys finally grounded. She tried to return the smile, but didn't manage it.

Jodi had Lys put her foot up on the bench and pulled the gauze away from her leg. Lys couldn't help a gasp of pain. The big gash still oozed blood, and she could see dozens of other scrapes that didn't look like they were going to get better anytime soon. "Ooh, nasty. Did he do this?" Jodi asked, glancing at Mark.

Lys shrugged. "I was stuck. He got me out."

Jodi rolled her eyes. "Never trust a chaos user to do what someone more mature should take care of."

Lys didn't know what that meant. "What are you going to do?"

"Heal you," Jodi said, placing her finger at the top of the biggest gash.

A cool, clear feeling started in the cut, right where Jodi touched it. The blood in and around the wound got warm, uncomfortably so, until Jodi's finger moved on. Once her finger was gone, a cool sensation, not unlike peppermint gum, replaced it.

It didn't hurt, but it was uncomfortable, like having one side of you next to the fire while the other side stood in the snow. Lys could feel herself squeezing Kamau's hand hard, but she couldn't let go. As Jodi's finger moved the wound closed up, just like a zipper.

"Is that hard?" Lys asked through gritted teeth.

"Not really," Jodi said. "I'm a natural healer. It just takes some energy. Now hold still. Give it a minute to settle down," Jodi said, her finger still tracing the gash.

Amazement kept Lys' eyes riveted to Jodi's finger and the clean, pink skin that it left behind. Kamau leaned forward so he could get a better look.

"Amazing," he said. "We couldn't see it when she healed Inez or Mark."

"Inez?" Lys' thoughts were drawn away for a moment: bloody hands, the fight after the sewers, Peter. "Is she okay?"

"She's okay," Brady said, his eyes not moving from Jodi's work.

"Hold still," Jodi warned. "Just a few more seconds."

"Sorry," Lys said, turning her eyes back to her leg.

"There you go," Jodi said a moment later. The hot-cold feeling traveled down the rest of the wound until there was nothing left of it. Not even a pucker of welted skin.

Lys noticed Jodi's hand shaking. "Are you okay?" Lys asked.

Jodi smiled. "Just a little tired. I haven't done this much healing at once in a long time."

"Thank you," Lys said.

"I told you," Mark said, "some of the touch users are very skilled at healing. I'm just not one of them."

Lys glanced over to see Mark propped up on one elbow. Inez too.

"I told you to rest," Jodi said, frowning at Mark.

"Sorry, I just wanted to watch." Mark's innocent face didn't seem like it was doing much for Jodi. He still looked bad, but the color had returned to his cheeks.

"Do you want me to do the rest?" Jodi asked, glancing at Ayden.

"Do the other big ones, if you're up to it."

Lys held up her hand. "It's okay, I'm fine. You're tired, and the rest aren't that bad." She was grateful, but Ayden's mention of "if you're up to it" made Lys wonder what price this woman paid for using her magic. Lys didn't want to be the reason for anyone losing it. Mark told them he could control the consequences, but Lys wasn't sure.

"It's not a problem," Jodi said, reaching her hand to start again. "I already did your bruised ribs, let me finish."

"No!" Lys said, jerking away. Jodi's eyebrows knit together, and Lys said, "It's okay, really. I've had worse." Not entirely a lie.

Jodi and Ayden exchanged a questioning glance. She didn't

194

care what they thought. "Okay." Jodi stood. "Whatever you want. You're going to need to wash the rest out and wrap it up again though."

Lys nodded. "Yeah, I'll do that. Thank you." She smiled. "Sorry, it's been a long day."

"I bet."

Ayden looked at Mark. "We should get out of here."

Mark nodded. "Sure, I'm ready. Lys needs to clean up."

Lys' leg still oozed blood, and her thin pants hung in shreds. She glanced around and spotted the rest stop building. "I'll go wash this off. Are there any more bandages?"

Kamau got up. "I'll get them."

Standing hurt, but Lys could do it. She put a little weight on her leg and found that it held without too much shaking.

"Do you want some help?" Jodi asked.

"Let me do it," Inez said.

Lys blinked. Inez's face still had scrapes from where Lys had tried to claw her eyes out, although it looked like some of the bigger ones were gone.

Go to the bathroom alone with Inez? Inez who spit on her? Inez who she tried to…this couldn't end well.

Inez climbed off the table and stood on shaking legs. "I have to pee anyway."

Jodi shrugged and Ayden nodded. Mark watched Inez as she walked toward Lys.

"Come on," Inez said to Lys when she didn't immediately follow. "We haven't got all night."

Fear didn't stop her, it was more like complete embarrassment. What did you say to someone after you'd tried to rip their eyes out? "Oh, hey, sorry about your face. My bad." Lys didn't know. However, she did want to clean up, and she didn't want to look like a baby in front of everyone, so she took the first aid kit from Kamau and limped off after Inez, hoping someone would have the sense to check the bathroom for her dead body if Inez exited alone.

The sun shone over the building, blinding Lys until she entered the shadows. Against her better judgment, she followed Inez inside.

To Lys' relief, Inez went straight into a stall. Lys set the first aid kit down on the semi-clean counter and turned the water on in the sink. She pulled five or six paper towels out from the dispenser, got them wet and started to wipe.

The smaller scrapes stung, but Lys knew that the big one Joni had healed would have required stitches. She ran her finger over the new skin; it didn't show any sign of abrasion.

The first aid kit held some antibacterial wipes, and Lys used them to finish cleaning her leg. Gritting her teeth together, Lys made sure to wash every bit of dirt out that she could see—she wondered what happened to the dirt inside the big wound that Jodi healed.

"You okay?" Inez asked.

Lys practically fell off the counter. She'd been so engrossed in cleaning and trying not to whimper that she hadn't even noticed Inez coming out of the stall.

"Uh," Lys said, wiping a strand of hair out of her face with the back of her hand. "Yeah, good." Yeah right. Blood still flowed down her leg, creating a puddle on the counter top, she wanted to cry, everything hurt, and she didn't know how to tell Inez she was sorry.

The two young women regarded one another. Lys could see pain in Inez's eyes—deep and wide, it spread from the corners of her eyes and onto her whole face, tightening the muscles of her jaw and pulling her lips into a thin line. The hate that Lys expected to see was absent.

"Here," Inez said, pulling a few more paper towels out. "Dry off. I'll help you bandage it."

Lys took the paper towels and pat her leg, trying to soak up as much blood as possible. "How's your arm?" she asked, still not knowing what to say.

"Hurts," Inez said, rummaging in the first aid kit. "But it works."

Silence descended as Inez found a roll of gauze and some tape. The last moments before Peter fell into that trap replayed through Lys' mind. She held the end of the gauze as Inez taped it down and started to wrap.

"I'm really sorry about Peter," Lys said in a whisper. This felt like sacred ground—she didn't know if she had the right to be there. But she had to say it, and she needed Inez to believe it.

Inez stopped wrapping. Her jaw muscles rippled before she took a breath. "I know, me too."

The raw acceptance that Inez displayed brought tears to Lys' eyes. She took a breath and tried to steady her voice. May as well get it all over with at once. "And I'm sorry about your face."

To her utter surprise, Inez looked up. A tiny grin tugged at one corner of her lips. "I didn't know that a spoiled little princess like you had that much fight in her."

Lys blinked. She had no comeback for that.

The other corner of Inez's lips twitched. "I'm sorry I blamed you." She paused, going back to wrapping. "And I'm sorry I went after you with my magic."

More silence as Lys held the gauze and Inez wrapped.

"What do you know about this Mason guy?" Inez asked after she ripped the gauze apart and taped the last bit.

"Not a lot," Lys said. She climbed down and turned to wipe the counter and wash her hands. "He came to me when I was in the hospital after I—" she still couldn't talk about it. "After I attacked someone like I did you. He said he could help me, that I was addicted to a deadly drug."

Inez washed her hands and they both pulled out more paper

towels. "So he lied to you."

"Yeah," Lys said, staring at her golden eyes in the mirror. "I guess he did."

"And you want to go back to him?"

Lys thought about it. "I want to know how he can help me. I can't live like this. I don't want to hurt anyone else." She turned and looked at Inez, only meeting her eyes for a second.

Inez opened her mouth to say something when a pounding came on the door. Bam, bam, bam!

"You ladies alright in there?" Brady asked. "We're getting worried."

Inez sighed and said, "Give us a minute!"

"Okay, just making sure, sheesh. Just trying to be a gentleman and all that."

Lys laughed.

"What are you laughing at?" Inez asked, some of her usual fire returning.

"Oh, I just think it's funny how much he likes you." The topic may not have been entirely appropriate, but Lys brought it up anyway. Mostly because she did think it was pretty cute.

"Likes me?" Inez asked.

"Yeah, he's got a mad crush on you."

"Mad crush?" Inez asked, sampling the words like a new flavor.

Lys shook her head. "He's been trying to get your attention since the first second he saw you. How could you not notice?"

"I've got bigger things to worry about," Inez grumbled.

Lys shrugged, conceding the point. "Come on, we should get back."

Inez didn't move. "Do you think Mason will do anything against the guys that got Peter?"

"I don't know, it sounds like he's tangled with them before." No other insights came to her mind. The pain returned to Inez's face. Maybe bugging her about Brady hadn't been the best thing to do. Inez didn't need anything else to worry about right now.

The answer seemed to satisfy Inez. She grabbed the first aid kit with her good arm and pushed out the door. Lys followed, limping slightly and wishing she could restart this whole day—week—all of it.

Kamau and Brady stood outside, not far away.

"Finally! We thought you might have crawled out the window and ran," Brady said, grinning.

"Tempting," Inez said.

Brady took the first aid kit from her. "You'd regret it."

Inez snorted.

Kamau walked next to Lys. "Are you alright?" he asked.

Lys wished he'd put his arm around her, even though it threw yet another spin on the direction her life was going.

"I'm okay," she said, walking forward. Her leg throbbed, so she went slow, not wanting to provoke it into bleeding everywhere.

Inez and Brady moved faster, leaving them with a little space and time alone. Sort of alone.

Lys swallowed, and found her throat dry as the desert around them. "Is there a drinking fountain around here?" Lys asked.

"On the other side of the building," Kamau said, jerking his head.

"I'm thirsty," Lys said. She changed direction. "Do you think we have time?"

Kamau looked back toward the van. "Mark and Ayden are having a fairly serious discussion. They won't notice."

"You can hear them from here?" Lys asked.

"Yes."

"Are you listening to everything they say?"

"Would it bother you if I was?" Kamau asked, looking down at her.

She caught herself staring into his dark eyes and pulled her gaze away. The Need had been silent since she attacked Jed, but she knew it wasn't gone. "I, I don't know. Maybe. Did you listen to me and Inez?"

Kamau managed to look a little ashamed. He put a hand on her arm. "Yes. I admit I was worried when she offered to go with you. So I thought I would, uh, just make sure everything was okay."

Lys felt her good knee go weak. Seriously, this guy was unbelievable. And all in a good way. "I admit that I was worried too. Thanks." She smiled.

They'd reached the drinking fountain. It took everything she had to turn away from Kamau and lean down to get a drink. Her mouth had gone even drier than before, and after several good gulps of water she didn't feel satisfied. As she stood back up the world tilted and she staggered.

Kamau reached out to steady her.

"Easy," Kamau said, keeping her upright and moving in front of her. "I thought you said you were okay." He had a hand on each of her shoulders.

Lys rubbed her face with a hand. "I was. Am." She closed her eyes. "Just dizzy."

"Do you need to sit down?"

The world continued to spin, and she reached out to put a hand on Kamau's chest. She didn't mean to, but he was the only steady thing around. "Maybe. Maybe we should get back to the van."

"Okay." Kamau sounded worried. He put his arm around her shoulders and she wrapped an arm around his waist. They walked slowly, and every step made the world tilt back and forth like a seesaw.

By the time they got to the van, Brady, Inez and Mark were sitting in the back. Ayden climbed into the driver's seat.

Jodi narrowed her eyes at Lys. "Are you okay?"

"Just dizzy," she said, glad that Kamau still had his arm around her.

"You lost a lot of blood," Jodi said. "You should probably get some sleep."

"I doubt that will be a problem," Lys said as Kamau helped her climb into the van. She took the spot right behind the driver.

Kamau sat at the other end of the bench. "You should put your leg up," he said, patting the seat between them.

At the moment she didn't care much about her leg being up— she'd rather be snuggled up with her head on Kamau's shoulder. But maybe he didn't feel the same way. Or maybe he didn't want to lead her on, or maybe he didn't want to show too much in front of the others. Lys shook her head and ordered herself to stop reading into it. She put her seat belt on and swung her legs up, propping her back against the wall and the window.

Her legs were just long enough that by stretching them out her feet would be on Kamau. Even after sort of washing them off in the bathroom Lys didn't want her feet on anyone. She kept her legs bent so she wouldn't bug him.

The van started backing out. Kamau reached over and gently lifted her feet, setting them on his leg. His warm hands rested on her ankles and his fingers squeezed. "Get some sleep."

Chapter 21

Lys dozed. Her head lolled against the seat as her mind wandered through nightmares. Peter disappeared again and again. Her parents started coming into her dreams as members of the New, with guns, trying to kill her. Darkness kept swarming her, and the Need battled with a desire to use magic that she couldn't control. She let the magic out, and it consumed her. Of course she could see through everyone's eyes, and the sheer volume of input scared her. Pleasure swept through her—exhilarating. Then came a sharp pain, and the magic cut off so fast it felt like she had been thrown off a cliff onto sharp rocks below.

She jerked awake, gasping for breath, her whole body screaming in agony. Bringing her legs to her chest, she curled up into a ball, buried her face in her knees. She tried not to cry.

Lys felt someone move next to her. Kamau's arm went around her shoulders.

"It's okay," he whispered in her ear as he rubbed her back.

Lys didn't believe him. Which meant at least he wasn't using magic on her. However, none of that helped the way she felt—like she'd just lost the whole world and all of her emotions had been replaced by a black void.

"She probably crashed," Ayden said.

A crash? Lys tried to use the problem to bring her mind back into focus. Kamau continued to rub her back, and she leaned in to him, needing to feel someone near her. He pulled her closer and held her tight.

"What do you mean by crash?" Kamau asked.

"How much did Mark tell you about the magic?"

Kamau's rumbling voice reverberated through Lys as she listened, her head still down and her eyes squeezed shut. "He told us about the power levels and the different senses. He explained a little bit about the New and then showed us a control technique."

"He didn't explain about the addiction?"

The word made Lys' head shoot up. Addiction?

Kamau shook his head. "He and the others said something about magic having a price, and about it feeling good to use it, but nothing specifically about addiction."

Lys glanced in the back seat and found everyone there asleep. Mark's head rested on a jacket wadded up against the window. Inez leaned against the other window while Brady's head lolled on her shoulder. The still lucid part of Lys smiled. Inez would be mad when she woke up—Brady would be in heaven.

"Magic does have a price," Ayden said. "For some people it's much worse than others."

"What do you mean?" Lys asked, finding her voice trembling almost as much as her insides.

"Have you used your magic enough to get how good it feels?" Ayden asked. He waited and Lys shrugged while Kamau shook his head. "Then maybe you haven't noticed, but the more you use, the more you'll want to use."

"Like drugs?" Lys asked.

This time Jodi spoke. She turned around. "For some people. Drugs are a good analogy. Only once you start, you can't stop using."

"What do you mean?" Lys asked.

This time Ayden took the question. "Once you break into your magic it becomes a part of you. The power will slowly fill you, and if you don't use it, letting some of it out, it will overwhelm you."

Lys thought about the exercise Mark had taught them. He said to keep a balance, letting as much in as you were letting out. Did the magic fill her even when she hadn't opened up to it?

"What will happen when the magic overwhelms you?" Kamau asked.

"At the very least you'll lose control with your magic, like Brady did back there" Jodi said. "At the most you'll go completely crazy and then lose control."

"How do you stop it?" Kamau asked.

Ayden shrugged. "Training."

"Mason's got a few tonics that help until someone can get themselves under control," Jodi said.

Lys listened, anger growing inside of her. The fact that a cure didn't exist made her grind her teeth together and wish to be obliterated from off the face of the earth. The Need wiggled.

"What did you mean by crash?" she asked.

"If we stick to the drug analogy then it's easier to understand," Ayden said. "Drugs make people high and when the substance wears off people crash. Magic is like that too. You use it and it feels good—stop using and you'll feel like the world just got yanked out from underneath you. More than a few people have committed suicide because of it."

Lys found Ayden looking in the rear view mirror at the three in the backseat. "I'm surprised that Inez and Peter lasted this long. They've probably been self-medicating with either drugs or alcohol."

"Or both," Jodi said.

The mention of Peter's name added a whole new dimension to her despair. She shuddered.

"Looks like you're crashing right now," Ayden said.

Lys shrugged. She didn't want to talk about it.

"Well, whatever you do, don't start using." Ayden shared a glance with Jodi. "Wait until we get to Mason. He's got a few things to help, and there are some people who can give you advice on crashes."

The nonchalant way they spoke about the whole situation made Lys wonder if either of them had ever crashed. It should make her feel better, knowing that they weren't all that concerned, but it didn't. Instead, as she caught the two of them sharing a worried glance, she wondered if she should be afraid.

"Do you have a lot of people who don't crash?" Kamau asked. He moved his hand to the back of Lys' neck and ran his fingers through her hair.

"Everyone crashes to some extent," Jodi said. She turned to look at Lys again. "Just ride it out. Think happy thoughts and stay away from your magic."

"Won't it fill me until I go crazy?" she asked, biting out the words. Hot anger was swelling within her, and it kept getting worse and worse.

"What if someone else uses their magic on you?" Kamau asked, reaching out to take Lys' hand with his free one. She let him intertwine his fingers with hers, and then hung on for dear life. Her emotions continued to plunge into anger and darkness, and she wanted nothing more than to scream.

"What do you mean?" Ayden asked.

Kamau shrugged. "Well, Mark used his magic on Lys and Brady when they could not get out of it. Does someone else using magic on you help at all?"

Ayden shook his head. "Not that I know about. Mark's little talent is good for disrupting the flow of magic through a person. It works the best on breakers."

"I wonder if it goes through those suits," Jodi asked, changing the subject.

"Good question, we'll have to try it out when we get back."

"Try what out?" Kamau asked.

Jodi smiled. "We caught a couple of the New in their suits at the hospital. We've got them at the cabin. Mark would be a good test for those suits. We're trying to figure out how much magic they can take."

Lys had tried to get through the helmets, but with no luck. How could the New be so powerful? It didn't seem fair that they could do or go wherever they wanted.

Lys' mind raged, and her emotions barreled down into a dark abyss. She spoke only so she could think about something besides wanting to let the Need loose and hurting everyone around her. "Where are we going?" she asked.

"Mason's got a couple of retreats. We're headed for one of them." Ayden glanced down at the clock on the dashboard. "Should be there in about an hour."

An hour? Lys didn't think she could wait that long.

Ayden and Jodi started talking about the black armor suit again, and Lys reburied her face in her knees.

"Have you tried meditation?" Kamau asked, his lips so close to her ear that she felt his breath move her hair, tickling her neck.

Lys shook her head.

"It might help."

His voice alone helped, but he could be using magic on her. Part of her didn't care.

"Take a deep breath," Kamau said, rubbing her back.

Lys tried, but being curled into a ball didn't make it easy.

"Again," he said when she exhaled. "Close your eyes and let your emotions drain away, just like Mark said."

That wasn't going to happen, not with Peter's smiling face looking at her and the memory of her attacking Inez so fresh. Did happiness still exist?

"Come on," Kamau said, "you have to relax."

Lys snorted. "Sure, right."

"Try." The word bore through her, knocking away a few layers of darkness.

She nodded, taking another breath. A small layer of tension eroded.

"Good," Kamau said. "Keep going."

Lys did. She exhaled and tried to let go of everything. Faces of people she cared for swam before her, and the darkness kept blotting them out. She grabbed the light and pressed it forward, crowding the black back into a corner of her mind. Each breath helped, and Lys clung to the light and the feel of Kamau's hand in hers.

Kamau continued to whisper encouragement in her ear, and Lys followed the words back into the real world. After what felt like an hour, Lys opened her eyes and raised her head—the anger now confined to a small corner of her mind. The Need occupied another corner.

"Better?" Kamau asked.

Lys nodded. She felt even more tired now than she had since this whole thing had started. Exhaustion made her eyelids droop, and her legs were so heavy that they slid off the seat and onto the floor.

"Come on," Kamau said, "you look spent. Try to get some sleep."

She didn't resist as he gathered her in his arms, resting her head against his chest. The thump-thump of his heart filled her ears, and Lys closed her eyes, drifting off into oblivion. The sensation of Kamau kissing her lightly on the top of the head might have been her imagination, but she hoped not.

* * *

The rocking of a bump pulled Lys from sleep. She closed her eyes again, not ready to face reality, but another jolt jerked her awake. For a moment she couldn't figure out where all of her appendages were, then she remembered Kamau and found one of her hands in his and the other wrapped around his waist. His cheek pressed lightly on the top of her head, and she could tell by the depth of his breathing that even after the bumps he was still sound asleep.

The van bounced and Lys barely managed to keep her head

from colliding with Kamau's chin. She extracted herself and put Kamau's head on her shoulder, hoping she wouldn't wake him.

Everyone in the back seat still slept, although now Inez's head rested on top of Brady's, which lay on her shoulder. She'd love to see the look on Inez's face when she woke up.

Ayden's eyes regarded her in the rear view mirror. "Feeling better?" he asked.

"A little," Lys said.

Ayden had pulled the van off the main road, and they were winding up a steep mountain trail. Now might not be a good time to mention that she got car sick. Lys leaned over and could see the edge of the road mere inches from the tires. Below her, the hill fell away like a steep ski slope full of rocks.

"We're almost there; it's just around this next bend."

The "next bend" turned out to be a slight understatement. The road continued to wind in and out of trees, just avoiding the edge of the drop off. Ayden took the van around a sharp curve, and Lys' view of the road ahead disappeared for a few seconds.

When it came back into view she gasped.

Two figures stood in the middle of the dirt road. They were both dressed in black body armor, and they were both pointing guns at the van.

Chapter 22

Ayden slammed on the brakes, the van fish-tailing as it crunched to a stop.

"Mark!" he bellowed, waking the other man from his nap.

"What the?" Mark said, blinking. He glanced out the front windshield and swore. "Where did they come from?" He looked one hundred percent better, like he'd just spent the last three days loafing around doing nothing. He sat up and reached for the door handle.

"I don't know," Ayden said, undoing his seat belt.

Bellows of disturbed dirt whipped around the front of the van. The cloud rolled over the two figures.

The side door to the van opened, and Mark jumped out. Lys could see his hands crackling with electricity. "Get up, Brady," Mark yelled over his shoulder.

The two figures in black followed Mark with their guns.

Mark wound up like a baseball pitcher.

Lys didn't even get the chance to choose her reaction. Fear triggered rage, which opened up a path that led from deep inside of her. Magic exploded outward, and she could see not only each and every leaf on the trees around them, but she could see the van from two different angles and then everything inside the van from five different perspectives. She couldn't tell how many of the New there were, because she didn't know how many people's eyes she was looking through.

Ayden was half way out of the door when Jodi yelled, "Wait!"

Jodi rolled down her window. "Guys, what are you doing?" She addressed this to the two figures in black.

"Probably trying to kill us," Brady said, following Mark.

Jodi shook her head. "Not worth it Mark."

Lys frowned. These were the bad guys. If she'd had any

offensive weapons in her magical arsenal she'd have pulled them out in a second.

"Mates, you're rotten." Mark said, shaking his head and allowing his hand to fall to his side.

"It's about time you got here," one of the figures in black took their helmet off, revealing Genni, the councilor from the hospital. "We need to figure out how much these things can handle."

Ayden scowled. "We've got injuries in here! Why don't you go play off the road?" He did not sound happy.

"Oh relax," Genni said, smiling. Lys wondered if that smile meant more than just hello—it sure looked like it. *Especially from Ayden's point of view.* "We saw you coming up the road and we wanted to make sure everything was okay."

Ayden didn't reply.

She ignored his lack of vocalization, and waved her arm in front of the black suit she wore. "Can we keep Mark? We really want to test these things."

"Sure," Ayden shrugged. He put the van back in gear. "Keep him. If he's up for it. Just get out of the road."

"Thanks!" She grinned. Ayden gave a half wave.

Inez groaned from the back seat.

"Sorry about that," Ayden said, moving the van forward once again. "Some of us are a little more rambunctious than others."

Jodi turned around. "Inez, how is your arm feeling?"

"Ugh," Inez said, rubbing her face with her hand. "My arm feels fine, but I think I might throw up."

"Oh no," Brady said. "No cookie tossing in here."

Lys tried desperately to get out of her magic. The fact that she hadn't opened it in the first place, at least not consciously, made it harder to visualize a way to shut it off. As she searched she noticed what Ayden had been talking about. He and the others were right—using magic felt good. She'd felt it a little before, but now the golden energy thrummed through her veins, pulsing and filling her with a sensation she'd never known. She couldn't even compare it to satisfying the Need, because it was different. Different as in kissing a boy she kind of liked versus the memory of Kamau's lips brushing hers. To put it simply, this feeling was better. Better in every way imaginable.

And that made it difficult to want to break out of it. Mark said that as long as the magic didn't back up that she'd be fine, right?

But despite her efforts to release the magic, Lys could feel the overload coming. Like too many sweets at Christmas, Lys knew that she couldn't keep this up for long without suffering the consequences. Whatever they might be.

So she closed her eyes and tried to picture the board. Too much magic, she couldn't make it work. Instead she focused the energy into a stream. When she had it all going in the same direction, she slammed a dam down in front of it.

Her body screamed for her to let it go, while her mind reveled in how good using felt. However, just as she slammed the dam down, she had one last vision.

The perspective looked up, and settled on Doyle's face. His eyes shot daggers and his jaw jut forward—teeth clamped shut. The view swiveled and Lys caught the reflection of the person whose eyes she was looking through.

Peter.

That wrenched her out of the magic, vomiting her back into the van just as it rolled to a stop.

She gasped, feeling as if she'd been physically struck. Peter. He wasn't dead.

"Here we go," Ayden said. "Home sweet home."

Lys blinked, trying to clear her mind and vision.

"Come on," Ayden said, throwing the van into park. "We'll find you guys a place to stay."

Lys found herself leaning forward with her face in her hands. Once again her insides shook like she'd been out in the cold for too long.

"Are you okay?" Kamau asked.

"Yeah," she said, looking up. She opened her mouth to tell him about Peter, but Kamau's taunt, pale face stopped her.

The immediate thoughts of Peter fluttered away. "Are you okay?"

"I'm fine."

Brady and Inez climbed out of the back seat and exited the van.

"You sure?" Lys asked. She resisted the urge to put a hand on his cheek. "Are you crashing?"

Kamau shook his head. "I do not know."

"Come on," she said, grabbing his hand and leading him outside. "We'll ask Ayden what to do."

Kamau followed, and when the two of them steeped out of the van Brady met them with an eye roll.

"Why don't the two of you just get the snogging over with?"

"What?" Lys asked, confused.

Brady glanced over at Inez. "They're killing me."

Inez nodded. "Yeah, I can see it."

Lys blinked. Had Inez just been nice to Brady? She tried to get Inez's attention, to tell her about Peter, but the other girl looked at Ayden, who gestured them forward.

She'd been expecting a compound of some sort, judging by the amount of people Ayden said would be there. Reality turned out to be a huge cabin and a separate three car garage with a loft over it. Lys caught a glimpse of a handful of tents out behind the cabin.

"Come on," she said, gently tugging Kamau forward. His unsteadiness unnerved her, but it also made her feel better—more normal. If normal could be applied to any part of this situation.

Inside the cabin made Lys feel claustrophobic. The large entry hall led into a gigantic great room. Sleeping bags covered half of

212

the floor while all of the plush furniture had been pushed onto the other side. Eight or ten people lounged in the furniture, talking, and three of the sleeping bags were occupied. Although, with all of the noise, Lys didn't know how anyone could sleep.

"Did you bring Mark back with you?" a woman—one of four on the couch—asked.

"He's out playing," Ayden said. "Genni and a couple of others are out there trying to figure out those black suits."

The entire couch of women seemed very disappointed by Mark's absence. Lys wondered if he knew he had a fan club.

"Oh, hey," Ayden said, holding out a hand as a man with dark hair and caramel skin walked through the room. "Daya, this is Inez. She just arrived."

The exotic looking man turned to smile at Inez. "Taste user?"

Inez nodded. "That's what they say."

Ayden pointed between them. "Inez, this is Daya. He's our most experienced taste user. When you've had a chance to settle in you'll need to find him. He can help you sort through how to use your magic."

Lys wondered how much of Inez's story Ayden knew. Had they talked when she passed out the first time?

Daya nodded. "I can see that you're an adolescent, your eyes are still quite red."

Inez nodded again, not saying anything.

"There are a few of us here. Once you get settled in just ask anyone where I am. We have a lot to talk about." Daya continued to smile as he held out his hand.

"Thanks," Inez mumbled, taking his hand and shaking it.

"Whew," Brady said, putting his arm around Inez. "It's been a long day; I bet you want to sit down."

Lys had to stifle a laugh at the look of surprise on Inez's face.

"I'll let you get to it then." Daya nodded and moved past them.

213

Ayden led them through the great room and to the left. "The kitchen is that way," he said, pointing behind them. "And most of the girl's bedrooms are this way and upstairs."

"Where are the boys'?" Brady asked.

"Outside in the tents or over the garage."

"Tents?" Brady asked.

Ayden shrugged. "Mason's old-fashioned. He believes that the ladies need to be comfortable."

Jodi, who stood just behind Lys, laughed. "He's pretty smart, you know?"

"I guess," Ayden grumbled. "Did you say that you had a couple of spots in with you and Genni?"

"Yeah, we've got a set of bunk beds that no one is using yet. Come on," Jodi said, moving down a short hall that branched off the main one. "We've got some clothes in the closet that will probably fit you. You can shower and change. I'll check on Inez's arm again and finish with your leg."

Kamau still looked shaky. Lys gave his hand a squeeze. "Ask Ayden about it."

He nodded and tried to release her hand. Lys held on and looked into his eyes. "Promise me you will ask him about it."

"I will," he said in a tired voice.

Lys gave him her best mothering look as he slipped his hand out of her grasp and walked away.

Lys watched him go before she and Inez followed Jodi to their room. "Take either of those. That's Genni's bed." She pointed

Lys made a note of which bunks were hers and Inez's. Maybe Jodi would leave them alone for a minute so Lys could tell Inez about Peter.

"Why don't you both sit down?" She looked at Lys' leg. Blood seeped from the gauze in a few places. "On second thought, why don't you go shower first. Grab some clothes, get cleaned up and come back here."

"Sure," Lys said, trying to catch Inez's eye, but the other girl was looking out the window So Lys grabbed from the closet a pair of loose sweats and a t-shirt that should fit.

"Towels are in the closet next to the bathroom. Help yourself. Wrap your leg up in one after you're finished." Jodi pointed down the hall.

"Okay," Lys said. She lingered in the doorway for a second, but Inez still didn't look at her. Lys left, wondering when she would get a chance to tell Inez that Peter was alive.

* * *

Lys felt one hundred percent better after a shower. Allowing the water to cascade from the top of her head, over her entire body and washing away through the drain left her feeling clean. Clean from running, almost dying, wading through storm drains, using magic, attacking Inez, losing Peter—everything washed away.

The magic called to her. It came from the tiniest corner of her mind and whispered for her to open up to it. Lys refused. She didn't want to go anywhere near the magic again. Before, she hadn't noticed either the high or the low, but that last time had been bad. Really bad. What Mark said about using magic feeling better than anything else was right. What Jodi said about the crash was right too. Why did this happen? What was magic, anyway?

As she toweled off, trying not to get blood on the floor, Lys thought back to the first conversation they'd had about magic. It came from the world around them? Like the Force? Why would something natural be addictive? Would the world make magic addictive? If so, should humans even be using it?

A knock came at the door, interrupting Lys' thoughts.

"You in there?" Inez asked.

"Yeah, I'm almost finished." Lys pulled the sweats on, keeping a towel wrapped around her leg. "Don't leave, I need to talk to you."

"Sure, whatever."

Lys smiled. Inez sounded interested. Strange how things worked out sometimes.

After pulling the shirt over her head, Lys ran her fingers through her hair and opened the door. Inez stood outside, a pile of clothes in one hand and a towel in the other.

"How's your arm?" Lys asked.

"That's what you wanted to talk to me about?"

"No." Lys took a breath and looked up and down the hall.

"What is it?" Inez asked, shaking her head.

She blurted it out. "Peter's alive."

Inez started at her, eyes hard and jaw set.

"I saw him," Lys said. "I used my magic accidentally and saw him."

"Where?" A tremor of hope filled Inez's voice.

She hesitated. "He's with Doyle and the New."

Inez swallowed that.

"Maybe Mr. Mason will send someone to get him out," Lys said. She'd thought about this in the shower. Surely Mr. Mason would want to help Peter—get him away from the New. Peter could use magic, and didn't Mr. Mason try to save magic users?

"Do you believe that?" Inez asked.

"It never hurts to ask."

Their eyes met, and Lys saw the slightest hint of a tear. "I wanted you to know."

Inez blinked, a tear disappeared and her normal, haughty expression returned. "Go see Jodi; she's dying to fix your leg."

"Right," Lys said, moving so Inez could get into the bathroom. As she walked away, Inez's voice came down the hall.

"And Lys."

"Yeah?" She didn't turn.

"Thanks."

When Lys got to the room she found Jodi waiting.

"Sit down," she ordered. It didn't sound like she would be taking no for an answer this time.

Lys sat, peeling the towel away from her leg. Her heart began to race as Jodi studied the wounds.

"Not too bad," Jodi said. "This should only take a few minutes."

Lys watched in fascination as Jodi's fingers trailed up and down her leg, transforming the wounds to smooth, pink skin. When she finished, Lys didn't even have any pain. Only the strange, peppermint sensation lingered.

"Anything else?" Jodi asked.

Lys studied Jodi, waiting to see sweat break out on her forehead or her hands clench together as she either crashed or was assaulted by her own Need, but nothing happened. Jodi just kept smiling. Lys pulled together her courage and asked, "Don't you crash?" The words tumbled out.

Before Jodi could answer, the sound of footsteps came down the hall. Lys expected to see Inez come through the doorway. Instead Mr. Mason appeared. A smile spread across his face when he saw Lys.

"I'm so glad to see that you made it. We were all worried."

Lys' heart sank into her stomach. Mr. Mason. She hadn't figured out what she wanted to say to him. So she said, "Thanks to Mark, we're fine."

"I hear that Mark wasn't the only one who helped get you here."

"Uh, no, I guess not." Lys shifted on the bed. Could she trust him? As if in answer, a trickle of water came from her hair, flowing all the way down her back, causing her to shiver.

"I was hoping I could speak with you," Mr. Mason said.

Chapter 23

Lys' blood went cold, and she willed Inez to shower faster. "Yeah, but we should probably wait until Inez gets back. She wants to meet you."

"I'd like to meet her, but I only have a few minutes." He sighed. "I think I owe you an explanation."

Oh sure, *now* someone offered to explain—now that she was full of conflicting information and half-formed opinions. Lys wondered if she should try to get out of the conversation, but then her brain kicked in. She shouldn't pass up the opportunity to get some facts out of him.

"I spoke with your parents this morning," Mr. Mason said.

That caused her throat to constrict, and she searched his blue eyes for truth behind the statement. "You did?"

He nodded. "Why don't we go to my study?"

The possibility of talking to her parents overrode her trepidation, "Okay." Lys turned to Jodi. "Will you please tell Inez where I went?"

"Sure, but I'm betting that the other taste users will be in here before you get back. Everyone loves the new kids."

Good thing Inez could take care of herself. Lys smiled. "Thanks."

Mr. Mason led her back through the now quiet great room, and up the stairs next to the front entrance. They went past two rooms, both filled with more sleeping bags and back packs, before Mr. Mason stopped in front of a larger set of doors. They looked heavy—carved wood and ornate, brass knobs. Lys felt like the doors didn't belong here in the mountains, but that they should be guarding the library of an old estate house.

"This is my study. We'll have some privacy up here." Mr. Mason removed a key from his pocket and inserted it into the knob. He opened the door and gestured her inside. "As you can see, the rest of this place is pretty crowded."

Lys swallowed. Stepping inside the study felt like a Herculean effort. Questions weighed her down like chains, and she had to concentrate on moving her feet. Were the Fates tugging her back, trying to keep her from entering?

"Let me flip the lights on," Mr. Mason said.

Light filled the room, and Lys stifled a gasp. Before her lay a beautiful library. Intricately carved shelves covered two walls of the small room. Tattered spines lined the rows with titles in languages that Lys couldn't read. A table stood under the curtained window, laden down with stacks of tomes. The smell of old paper and glued bindings filled Lys' nostrils, bringing a thousand memories of sitting in the library down the street from her house to her mind. She could practically hear the crackle of turning pages.

"Wow," she said.

Mr. Mason chuckled. "A modest collection."

She glanced over at him and raised her eyebrows.

"I've got quite a few more at another location."

"What are they?" Lys asked.

"Books regarding the magic of our world," Mr. Mason said. He gestured Lys to a couch that sat facing a low, square table.

"Books about magic?" Lys asked, slowly going toward the couch. Her eyes darted back and forth, trying to find a single title she could read.

"Well," Mr. Mason followed her. "The largest that I know about anyway."

"But how?" Lys stopped herself. "These are *all* about magic?"

Mr. Mason shook his head. "No." He indicated that she should sit. "Only a few are *all* about magic, others mention magic." When she finally sat down he followed suit, settling at the opposite end of the couch. "Considering when we started we knew very little, any bit of information was important."

Lys allowed him to meet her gaze before turning away. He sighed. "I apologize for what happened. I usually like to explain the magic myself."

He was apologizing for not telling her about the magic? What about the attack? Her being kidnapped? The New? Her parents? There were so many other things she wanted to discuss. Right now magic sat at the bottom of the list.

"You said you talked to my parents." Lys wanted to know about this first. The thought of having them worried out of their minds about her was unforgivable.

"Yes," Mr. Mason looked as if he'd been expecting a different question. "I spoke with your father yesterday, after Ayden picked you up."

"But Doyle is at my house!" she said.

Mr. Mason held up a hand. "He's not at your house. Ayden told me what happened. Doyle got onto the phone lines and rerouted any call that he thought might lead you to him."

"How did he do that?"

"The New rely heavily on technology. I have no doubt that this was an easy task for his people."

Lys digested that. "You talked to my dad? What did you tell him? Can I call him?"

Mr. Mason shook his head. "We're too far up here in the mountains to get a clear signal. We're sitting as far away from technology as we can, for obvious reasons." She opened her mouth to retort, but Mr. Mason held up his hand again. "I spoke with him and told him that you were fine. He was relieved. He told me to tell you that he loved your guts."

Lys closed her mouth. That was an inside joke between her and her dad. Her mom knew about it too, but no one else would. Mr. Mason had talked to her parents. That was a relief. She turned her worries in a different direction. "How did my face get on the news?"

"I'm afraid that was the New. As soon as you all escaped they sent the word out to the local police."

Well, that made sense. "Who are those guys?"

Mr. Mason sat back. "What did Mark tell you?"

Lys related the conversation they'd had with Mark. "All he told us was that the people who used technology won, and that they were the New. He didn't explain much more."

"Then he only told you half of the story which, considering the circumstances was probably wise."

So there *was* more to the story. Lys met Mr. Mason's eyes, wanting to see the truth there. "What's the other half of the story?"

"We don't have a lot of details," Mr. Mason started. "Most of the information from the time of magic is gone—lost to history and those that wanted the rest of the world to forget about magic. However, we have learned a few things.

"When the New made their play, a small group of those who wielded powerful magic fought back. They almost beat the New, but in the end they lost, and the New hunted them down and killed most of them."

"But not all of them?"

Mr. Mason shook his head. "A handful survived, but they were forced into hiding."

"What about the rest of the magic users?" she asked. "Mark said that everyone in the world used magic in one way or another, even if it was just a tiny amount."

"After the Old—those that opposed the New—were defeated, most people hid their magic abilities. It didn't take long for magic to fade away almost completely."

"The Old?" Lys asked. Brady was going to choke on that name.

"We don't really have a word that matches the translation, so we just coined them the Old."

"So if people stop using magic, it fades away?" Lys didn't understand. Her thoughts turned to her earlier musings. "And why is the magic so dangerous now? If everyone wielded it at one time, why is it so, horrible?"

"Good questions." Mr. Mason stood and walked over to a shelf on the far wall. He pulled a book as long as Lys' arm out from between two others with the hiss of leather on leather. He brought the volume with him and placed it gently on the table before he sat down.

Cracks spider-webbed the green, faded leather of the cover. Cream colored frays could be seen through the worn edges of the spine, and the binding looked as if it may not survive many more openings. A single yellow scrap of paper dangled from the bottom of the pages. Mr. Mason placed his finger on the yellow marker and swung the book open. Lys heard the leather creak and the pages crackle. A musty smell filled her nostrils.

"The New disrupted the flow of magic in our world," Mr. Mason said.

"Flow of magic?" Lys asked, distracted by the beautiful artwork on the pages before her. Lys had no idea how detailed the old book would be. Flowing calligraphy and intricate drawings of flowers, trees and ivy covered the two pages before her. She leaned closer. None of the words were English, but she could decipher the pictures.

A map of the world took up most of the left page. At least, it looked like their world. The basic shapes were similar enough to make the connection.

Black, red, gold, blue and silver lines crisscrossed the map.

"This is the most informative book I have found on how the magic of our world works," Mr. Mason said. "I believe this represents the flow of magic as it was in ancient times."

Lys followed the lines with her eyes. Different symbols

accompanied any place the lines crossed: a hand, a nose, an eye, an ear or what must be a tongue. However, on five of the crossings, where more than two gold lines intersected, a gold star appeared.

Scrawled notes surrounded the map, some of them in the margins of the book and obviously added long after the original text—Lys couldn't read any of them.

Her eyes turned to the next page. More indecipherable text covered the top portion, but a set of five drawings occupied the bottom half of the page. One looked like that big rock in the middle of Australia. Another was clearly a volcano topped by snow. The third was a cave and the fourth looked like a lake full of giant, gray rocks. The last one resembled a tripod made of huge, red slabs of stone. Each picture had a star next to it.

"Do these match up?" she asked, pointing at the stars on both pages.

"I believe they do."

Lys' eyes wandered back to the map. "This one is close." A star sat in North America, a short distance below the Great Salt Lake, although the lake appeared much larger than it did today.

"It is." Mr. Mason smiled.

"What does it mean? What are these places? Are they places of magic? Do the colors of the lines have to do with power?"

"I don't know about the lines, although I have to assume that they correlate with the power levels of magic, as you said." He sat back, pointing at the right hand page. "As for these places, I believe those are the outlets of magic into this world."

"Outlets?" Lys asked.

Mr. Mason traced one of the gold lines with his finger. "There are very few places where more than two lines cross. The stars mark where at least three gold lines cross one another. From there, the flow branches out to the rest of the planet."

Lys followed a few of the lines with her eyes. "So the stars indicate outlets?" She still didn't understand that part.

"Outlets for magic," Mr. Mason reminded her.

"If there are outlets for magic, why don't people know about them?"

"Because," Mr. Mason said, sighing, "the New plugged them."

Lys took a moment to think about that. "They plugged the outlets? How?"

He shook his head. "We have no idea. I doubt those of the New today know how it was done."

"You know them? I mean, the New?"

"They have hunted me since I was young. There are a few I know personally, but not many." He shifted in his seat. "We have tried to reconcile our differences, but each time we try, tragedy follows."

"So why did they plug the magic?" Lys asked.

"To keep magic users from defeating them. The Old fought for a long time, even when their numbers dwindled down to almost nothing, but in the end only five of them remained."

"Five?"

"Five users, each a different sense—all neutrals."

Lys was a neutral user. "What's so special about being neutral? Mark said that each power level had its advantages but that one wasn't better than another."

Mr. Mason nodded. "Mark is correct." He leaned forward and turned the book over a few pages. A single illustration filled the right side.

Five people—two women and three men—stood in a circle around a glowing depression in the ground with a tree carved into it. They were dressed in flowing robes, and Lys could clearly see the golden eyes of the three facing her.

The people had their hands raised above them, and on their arms they wore leather wrist guards. The guards bore the same symbols from the map: hand, nose, ear, eye and tongue. Lys leaned closer.

The drawing twitched. Strings of gold tugged at the lines, and for a moment the drawing scattered into a million bits of color, all pushed out to the edge of the page. Then, as if resetting itself, the lines came together to form a new picture. This one swept across the page, showing the inside of an enormous cave, filled with people, all of them fighting.

Lys couldn't tear her eyes away as the little figures fought and died in front of her, like a rough sketch of a computer generated battle from a blockbuster movie. The perspective slowly zoomed in to reveal four people standing around a fifth, who lay on the ground in a pool of inky blood. A man with the symbol of a finger on his wrist stepped forward and touched the injured figure. The red ink drew back into the body, and the injured woman got to her feet. The five of them moved to surround the depression in the ground and raised their hands.

Mr. Mason's voice yanked Lys back into the present. "This tells us that the picture shows five magic users, all neutrals as you can see, regulating the amount of magic that comes into the world." He gestured toward the text on the opposite page.

Lys blinked, and the figures froze—just as she had first seen them. She tried to process Mr. Mason's words. "Regulating the amount of magic? But why?"

"I'm no scholar, but what we have been able to translate tells us that the outlets of magic to our world had to be…maintained. Not constantly, but this book speaks of a group of neutrals that traveled to these spots and used their power level to keep the magic from getting out of balance."

"But why?" Lys asked again, giving the book one last hard look. "If magic was part of this world, why would it need to be balanced?"

"Fire is part of our world, so is rain, wind, earthquakes and a thousand other things that can throw the balance of an ecosystem off. Given time, the environment will right itself. According to the texts we have found, magic often spiked through one outlet, temporarily leaving the others with less power. The magic would eventually re-balance itself, but the magic users of this world discovered a way to keep it from spiking in the first place. Preventative medicine, so to speak."

"Why are you telling me all of this?" Lys asked, shaking her head. This happened a long time ago. If the outlets were plugged, why did any of this matter?

Mr. Mason sat back again, giving Lys an appraising look. "The Old are gone. All killed except for me, and I wasn't even one of their official numbers, which is why I'm still alive. The New kill anyone who exhibits signs of magic use."

"Why?" Lys asked. "Why do they care? Why do they have to kill people?" She didn't want to believe that the New killed anyone. If they were really killers, she would be dead. And they hadn't actually killed Peter.

"The magic in our world is now unstable. It leaks out around the plugs the New put in the outlets, but there is no balance to it. They don't want magic users to find that balance. With it, magic would flow as it did before."

"It would?"

Mr. Mason pointed at the drawing in the book. "With five neutral users, each a different sense, I believe we can undo what the New have done. We can bring magic back into our world."

"B-but," Lys stammered. "Magic, back into our world?"

"It belongs here," Mr. Mason insisted. His eyes glimmered with excitement. "Our world itself is out of balance without it. Consider global warming, ozone layer problems and pollution."

Now he was beginning to sound like those crazy environmentalists that Lys saw on the news.

"Most of these things would be eliminated if magic were to return."

"But what about breaking?" Lys asked. "And the high and the

crash?"

"Those would be gone too. I realize that your newfound powers might be overwhelming and that you have just inherited a great deal of responsibility." He smiled. "But most kids dream about this—about being special."

Lys didn't answer. He was right.

Mr. Mason leaned toward her. "You are the only neutral sight user that we've found. Our goal is to bring magic back into this world so that people won't have to go through what you did. If we can free the outlets of magic, no one will go through breaking. The magic will once again be balanced. As it should be."

Lys swallowed hard, her mind going a thousand miles an hour. "When the men from the New were interrogating me, they told me a few things that I didn't understand."

"Did they?" Mr. Mason raised his eyebrows.

"They told me that you were involved with that mass suicide in Vermont a few months ago. Is that true?"

Mr. Mason sighed and sat back. "Unfortunately, that is partially true."

How could it be partially true?

"The man who started that cult was, at one time, a guest at my facility." He waved a hand. "It's been years, the man was one of the first people I helped. Most users who come through camp stick around, but he didn't. He went back out into the world to try and live a normal life."

A normal life? Lys didn't even know what that meant anymore. Her life was gone, replaced by something so different that Lys couldn't even compare the two. How did anyone think that they could live a "normal" life after finding out they could use magic? After they found out they were *addicted* to magic?

Mr. Mason's eyes seemed to be seeing things from his past. Regret registered on his face. "I didn't know what was going on—we don't have much access to technology up at camp—until I saw

227

it on the news. By the time I got there, everyone in that mansion, including my friend, were dead."

"They were all magic users?" Lys asked.

He nodded. "My friend was trying to do the same thing I was—helping those whose magic abilities manifested. Unfortunately he never did learn that you can't fully control anyone through magic. At least not with taste. He lost hold on his people and they started to break. Violently." He paused. "One by one, they went insane, and in the end my friend's own unstable mental state meant ruin for them all. What they did not do themselves, the New took care of." He bowed his head, "Lys, I can't keep seeing these things happen. I've waited a long time for this. Some of the people here have devoted their lives to it."

Lys studied him for a moment. "And now you need my help?"

"Yes," he nodded.

"Well," Lys took a breath, feeling the thud of a bowling ball hitting the bottom of her stomach. "I'm sorry, but I'm not sure I can help you."

Chapter 24

Mr. Mason frowned. "Can I ask why not?"

Everything she'd been through up to this point rushed through her head. The Need, the magic, the crash, the pain, the suffering, her loosing Peter. "I'm not very good at this magic thing."

"Control is often difficult at first."

She looked at his eyes. The Need stirred. She could feel the magic stirring too—a desire to let it flood her tickled the back of her mind. "I just don't want to hurt anyone else."

"What do you mean?" Mr. Mason asked. "It was my understanding that the injuries were not your fault."

She shook her head. "No, they weren't, but it's my fault that Peter got caught."

"Caught?"

Oops. "Yeah."

"Mark said Peter got hit with a collar."

Lys swallowed. "Well, that's what we thought, but then I saw him."

"Saw him through your magic?" Mr. Mason asked. "Mark told me that you can see through other people's eyes."

Lys nodded.

"And he's alive?"

She nodded again. Her thoughts turned to Inez, and the anguish that filled the other girl's eyes every time someone mentioned Peter's name. "Doyle has him."

Mr. Mason sat back on the couch, steepling his fingers. "If they haven't killed him, that must mean they want him for something. Do you have any idea what that might be?"

Lys shook her head. She decided to go out on a limb. "Can we help him?"

He shot her a sidelong glance. "We're not exactly equipped to take on the New. Not right now." He sat forward. "But if we could get more power we'd have no problem getting him back."

The whole set up was so juvenile that Lys almost rolled her eyes. Seriously? If she agreed to try this magical unplugging thing he'd agree to go help Peter?

"Lys," he said, shaking his head. "It is not my goal to keep magic users in the dark, or to make them forget about their powers—that they're special. It is my goal to bring magic back into our world." He gestured to the book that lay open on the table. "Our world needs magic to survive."

She swallowed, thinking. Did she want to help him? He said that people wouldn't go through what she went through if the magic of the world was balanced. But would the world know what to do with magic?

"I don't mean to shock our world," he went on, as if reading her thoughts. "But to gradually bring magic back into society. It might take years, generations even, but I believe it's the right thing to do."

He did believe it. Lys could see it in his eyes and hear it in his voice.

What if he was wrong?

What if he was right?

"Are you willing to trust me?" He sat forward. "Give us a week. Work with some of our users to see if you feel more comfortable with your magic, and then the decision is entirely up to you."

Lys thought about Peter and Inez. What had they gone through? Breaking without having anyone else around to help them or explain to them what was going on? They made it through, but Lys wouldn't have. Not even close.

She searched Mr. Mason's face, looking for deceit or malice. Her eyes found a man concerned about people and the world as a whole.

The doubts Mr. Doyle had planted still inhabited her mind, but Mr. Mason had explained. And hadn't the New proven that they were the bad guys? Hunting them, throwing them in prison, trying to use force to bring them back and taking Peter? They killed magic users. How many innocent people—people who didn't understand what they were going through—had they murdered?

Her mother's face swam in her mind, as did her aunt's. Had Aunt Della been addicted to magic? Is that why she could never break free of it? If doctors knew about magic then they might have been able to help.

Slowly, deliberately, Lys nodded. She looked at Mr. Mason. "I'll think about it."

"Good," he said, lips pulling back into a thin smile, although she saw disappointment in his expression. "I'll make sure you get introduced to our other sight users. They'll be able to help you through the first few weeks of using."

A knock came at the door. Mr. Mason didn't look surprised.

"Come in," he said.

The heavy door swung open, and Ayden stuck his head inside. "You ready?" Ayden asked. He frowned when he saw Lys. "Sorry, I didn't know you had anyone in here."

"We're finished," Mr. Mason said, standing. Lys followed suit. "Please think about it. I'll be around whenever you want to talk."

Lys knew a dismissal when she heard one. She moved across the room and slipped through the door while Ayden held it open.

Something didn't feel right. Too many stories—possible lies— swam in her head, and nothing added up. Lys couldn't make the puzzle pieces fit together. Her mind reeled, and she needed someone to talk to.

She ran down the stairs and to her room, hoping to find Inez there. When she found it empty she grabbed a pair of boots and headed back out the front door. Stepping outside felt like emerging from a dark tunnel. The sun hung just above the trees, and a dozen or more people milled around. Some were using magic—Lys could see the touch users tossing a tire in the air—while others sat in small groups talking. She didn't recognize anyone.

Lys sat down on the front porch and laced her boots tight, tying a double knot bow. A few people stole glances her way, and a set of girls not much older than herself said hello as they went into the cabin, but most people were engaged in something more interesting than ogling the new girl. Good, Lys thought, the less attention the better. What would these people think of her if they knew she might not help them? They were just people; most of them kids. Who was she to refuse to help them make their dream come true? Mr. Mason's dream.

She stood and walked down the wooden stairs. At the bottom she turned and followed a path to the back of the cabin. When she cleared the corner Lys caught sight of the small tent city pitched within the trees. At least a dozen tents, in varying colors and sizes stood scattered around a large fire pit. Lys walked straight toward the nearest group of people that she saw.

Six or seven older teenagers stood chatting. She caught the eye of one of the boys as she approached. He stopped talking to his friends and looked up.

"Hey," he said.

"Hey," Lys said, trying to seem shy.

"You just came in, didn't you?" one of the girls asked.

"Yeah." Lys nodded. She went on before anyone else could speak. "I was wondering if you knew where they put the two boys that came in with us. I've got a message for one of them."

"Sure," the boy continued to smile. "They put them in the green tent over there, but I think the touch user is already gone off to play."

Lys laughed. "Sounds like him. What about Kamau?"

"The guy from Africa?"

Lys nodded.

"I haven't seen him come out yet."

One of the girls in the circle shook her head. "He came out a few minutes ago and went that way." She pointed. "I think all of the other sound users are up the hill right now. He is a sound user, isn't he?"

"He is," Lys nodded again.

"What kind of user are you?" the boy asked.

Lys tried not to hesitate. "Sight."

"Oh, awesome!" The girl smiled. "I am too. With you, we now have two girls that are sight users."

"Oh, great," Lys tried to make it sound sincere. "Cool." Before the conversation could go any further Lys walked away, waving. "Thanks. I'll see you guys around."

Her feet felt heavy again. All of these kids used magic? None of them looked like they were suffering any adverse effects from it. They all seemed happy, and excited. Did they all know about Mr. Mason's plan? Is that where their hope came from? Lys felt her own heart sink—they would all hate her if she didn't try.

The trail the girl had indicated rose steadily through the trees. Lys found herself short of breath as she climbed. It must be the altitude, she thought to herself, or the fifteen pound hiking boots.

She didn't meet anyone on the path, although she could hear things moving around her. The thought of wild animals made her cautious, but with this much human activity, she doubted if any animal would be willing to get close.

The trees here were pine—tall and slim with bare trunks for a dozen feet up. A canopy of boughs and branches spread over her head, spotting the trail with moving light as a breeze lifted the limbs.

Lys finally found Kamau standing with a group of five other

people. They all turned as she entered the clearing.

"Sorry," she wheezed, forcing a smile. "I'm probably kind of loud."

"Lys," Kamau said, stepping toward her. "What are you doing here?"

She almost whispered that they needed to talk, but if these were the other sound users, then it would be useless to try to be soft enough that they wouldn't hear.

Before she had to answer, a tall woman clapped her hands. "Take a break everyone, but be back here in fifteen minutes."

Lys gave her a grateful smile. Kamau said a few words to his group before he came to meet her. Most of the others filed by, nodding or saying hello. A lump formed in her throat as she watched them pass. They would all hate her when they found out that she wouldn't help them.

Kamau walked toward her, smiling, but the expression faded when he saw her face.

"Can we talk?" she asked, looking around.

"That might be problematic," he said.

"Yeah, I kind of figured." She sighed. "It's important."

Kamau took her hand and tugged her further up the hill. "Why don't we go this way? We might have more privacy."

Oh great, Lys thought. If the other sound users just heard that, they would for sure think that she and Kamau were going to make out.

Lys followed Kamau up the hill for a few minutes, grateful for his hand in hers, but also afraid of what she wanted to ask him. To their left, the setting sun lit the horizon with beautiful orange and red hues. When they could no longer see anyone behind them, Kamau stopped.

"What is it?" He placed his hands on her shoulders. "You look upset."

Lys drunk in his dark eyes. "Does any of this scare you?"

234

"What do you mean?"

"I don't know." Lys waved a hand. "This! Being addicted to magic. People trying to kill us. Having all this power…" She trailed off as her emotions shot straight into her throat. Swallowing didn't help. A tear gathered in the corner of her eye, pooling until it overflowed down her cheek. Kamau placed a hand on the side of her head, smearing the tear with his thumb.

"I didn't realize that you could be afraid," he said, stepping closer.

Lys laughed, but only a pinched squeak came out. "Whatever."

"Really," he said. "The girl that dragged me around in the basement of what she thought was a haunted building to find a boy she hardly knew but thought might be in trouble? That's not exactly cowardly behavior."

More tears streamed down her cheeks, but Lys smiled at the words. "Brady was in trouble."

"And what about the girl that was ready to take on a handful of thugs in an alley in Vegas?"

Lys shook her head. "You saved me from that one."

"You were doing just fine," he said, putting his other hand around her back.

Butterflies started in her stomach. Lys looked into his eyes and found peace there. She lifted her face as Kamau lowered his lips to hers. That same feeling of electricity ran through her as their lips brushed. He took his time, kissing her once, twice and then pulling away. They held each other's gaze for a moment. Lys thought that in his eyes she could see the wisdom of ages. He leaned down and kissed her on the neck, slowly making his way up to her ear.

Is this what love felt like? Real love? Or was this just primal attraction? Kamau stopped, looking down at her again. Lys wrapped her arms around his neck, pulling him closer. She rose upon her tip toes, and this time she kissed him.

All of the books and movies that described the world standing still when two people kissed were right. Lys had scoffed at them, even after having kissed a few boys, but now she knew better. For those few seconds, only Kamau mattered to her. She hoped she was the only thing that mattered to him. They were, in that moment, a perfect match. It felt like they had forever. They could be the only two people in the world.

She had to come up for air, and they studied one another.

"What did you want to talk to me about?" he asked softly, hands stroking her neck.

Right now Lys didn't care what she'd come to talk to him about. "Just something Mr. Mason asked me." She snuggled into him, wrapping both arms around his waist.

"What did he ask you?"

"He asked me to help him. It's hard to explain." She paused, rearranging her thoughts. "I asked him about the people in Vermont."

"And what did he say?"

"He said that he knew the guy who initiated it, and that he tried to stop them, but got there too late. And he said that the New do kill magic users."

Kamau pushed her away so he could look into her eyes. "Do you believe him? Do you trust him?"

"I don't know," Lys said.

Kamau nodded. "What did he ask you to help him with?"

She took a deep breath. "He asked me to help him unplug the magic so it can return balance to the world."

"What does that mean?" Kamau asked.

"He had a book that showed the flow of magic in our world. There are five places where a bunch of the gold lines crossed, and he said that the New plugged the magic that came from the outlets."

"I don't understand. What did he tell you exactly?"

Lys gathered her thoughts. She told Kamau as much as she could about the book and the explanation.

"He needs neutral users?" Kamau asked.

"That's what he said." Lys went on. "He asked for my help, and I asked him if we could go after Peter. But then he said we needed more power to beat the New."

"Peter?" Kamau asked, his fingers tightening on her arms.

Lys nodded. "I saw him. I mean I saw through his eyes. Doyle has him." She started stumbling over the words. "Right before we pulled up to the cabin. I saw him."

"Does Inez know?" Kamau asked before she could ramble anymore.

"Yes."

"We need to go find her," Kamau said, grabbing Lys' hand and starting back down the hill.

"Why?" Lys asked.

"Because," Kamau said, "she'll go after him."

Chapter 25

Lys hadn't thought about that.

"When did you see him?" Kamau asked.

"Right as we pulled up here," Lys said.

"Be very quiet," Kamau said, pulling them to a stop.

Lys watched Kamau close his eyes. His chest rose and fell to his deep breathing, and after ten or fifteen seconds, he turned his head to the right. Another few seconds went by before he opened his eyes.

"This way." Kamau tugged Lys behind him as he set off down a faint trail. The sunset glowed brightly above them as they made their way through the trees. "Brady's with her," he said after a few dozen steps.

"Can you hear them?" Lys asked.

He nodded. "We need to hurry."

They started to jog. Kamau's feet flew over the trial, never touching a branch, a leaf or a twig. He didn't make a sound. Lys, on the other hand, made enough noise for the both of them. She tried to follow his lead, but couldn't keep up and be stealthy.

The path turned down the slope, and Kamau slid to a stop. Lys grabbed a tree branch to keep from crashing into him.

Before them lay a small, cement building surrounded by a barbed wire fence. The structure couldn't be more than ten feet square, and the clearing around it reached only a few feet beyond that. A chunk of the fence had been torn away, leaving a gaping hole. The barbed wire hung down, waiting for someone to step into its lair.

An angry voice came from the building. "Where is he?"

Kamau let go of Lys. "Stay here," he said just before he went through the hole.

Yeah, right. Lys followed, taking care not to get her clothes caught and also eying the forest for anyone who might be around.

"I said, where is he?" Inez's unmistakable tone filled her voice with menace.

Kamau ran around the front of the building.

"You'd better tell her what she wants to know," Brady said.

Lys found a barred window and looked inside.

Inez was in the middle of the small room. Brady stood on the creaking cot, holding a man about three feet off the floor. The man's hands clawed at the iron grip Brady had on his throat.

Kamau stepped inside. "He probably can't talk with you cutting off his air supply."

Inez spun around, rage on her face. When she saw Kamau her expression softened a small degree. "What do you want?"

"Lys told me she saw Peter. We came to find you." He shot Lys a look through the window. She grinned.

As she walked around the side of the little building, she almost tripped over someone lying in the dirt.

"What the?" she said.

"Don't worry," Brady said from inside, "he's only knocked out. I think"

Lys moved to the door and stepped in. "What did you do?"

Brady shrugged, tossing the man on the floor and climbing down. "Inez hit him."

The man got up and tried to hit Brady, but Brady swatted the blow away. He grabbed the leg of the metal cot, ripped it off and twisted it around the man's chest and arms. The cot fell, now a tripod. "Nice try, buddy."

The man grunted.

"Who is this?" Lys asked.

"He's one of them," Inez said, pacing around the room like a caged tiger. "He knows where they'd be keeping Peter."

"I don't know what you're talking about," the man said.

"Don't lie!" Inez screamed the words, lunging forward and

grabbing the man by the hair. She yanked his head back and forced him to his knees. The next words came out in a dangerous whisper. "You can tell me where you keep the prisoners."

"We don't take prisoners."

"Funny thing, that." Brady said, imposing himself between the man and Inez. "They took us prisoner, and we're here to tell the tale."

Lys glanced at Inez and saw that her eyes swirled red. Inez shoved Brady aside, and the man began to tremble.

"Why don't you tell me where they'd take a prisoner." She leaned down, her face only inches from the man's. "You'll be much more comfortable if you do."

Lys wondered what Inez could do with her magic when she was really trying. Sweat beaded on the man's brow, and the trembling cranked up a notch to the shakes.

"I told you, I don't know." His voice cracked.

"Think hard," Inez said, yanking the man's hair back again.

Tears formed in the man's eyes. "I'm not sure. It could be anywhere. We've got lots of places out west."

"We were in Las Vegas."

The man shook his head. "They can't hold users there for long. He's probably been transported to Denver. Or maybe Phoenix."

"Which one?" Inez asked in a low voice.

A sob escaped, and the man shook his head. "I don't know."

Inez turned to Lys. Their eyes met, and Lys once again saw the consuming pain that simmered behind the swirling red.

"Can you try to find Peter again?" Inez asked.

Lys wanted to refuse. To tell Inez that Mr. Mason would help them, but Inez's haunted eyes cut through Lys like icy water.

"Yeah."

"Are you sure?" Kamau asked.

Lys nodded. "I'll try."

She took a deep breath and cleared her mind. The golden energy battered against the flimsy barrier surrounding it. The small hole Lys opened barely held against the onslaught of magic trying to break free.

Following what Mark taught her, Lys channeled the magic and forced it through her consciousness. To her surprise, it didn't take more than a few seconds to find a precarious balance. Close enough. Lys turned her thoughts to Peter. Images from all around her sprung up, and she grit her teeth together as she filtered them out. She kept Peter's face in her mind, and after a few more seconds the magic found him. Or so she hoped.

She'd been expecting to see him lying in a white cell, like the one she'd been kept in, but instead Lys saw the sunset. The same sunset that lit up the sky outside the building.

Okay, Lys reasoned, the sunset would be everywhere in the west. Luck made her play and Lys' perspective moved, catching a glimpse of Peter's reflection in a window. She'd found him!

He swiveled his head again and Lys saw the inside of a vehicle. Two figures in black body armor sat in the back with Peter.

Lys wanted to recoil, but then reminded herself that the men in black could not see her.

The now familiar buzz began to fill Lys' mind, and she started to feel like she was flying through the air.

"Do you see him?" Inez asked.

"Yeah," Lys said, trying to ignore the buzz in her head. "He's in a van with a couple of guys from the New."

"Where?"

Lys shook her head. "I can't tell. They're driving."

Inez started in on the prisoner again, but Lys didn't listen. More images crept into her peripheral, magical vision, and suddenly she could see Mr. Mason's cabin. She tried to focus, knowing that she was probably seeing through some of the users there.

Before she got out of all of them, one perspective turned from looking at the cabin to looking at three figures in black body armor.

"Oh no," she said aloud.

"What is it?" she heard Kamau ask.

Lys didn't answer. Letting more magic through the hole, Lys opened her awareness and found dozens of perspectives, all of them looking at figures in black armor. Some from above and some from below. Some made her wonder if she was seeing through the eyes of insects—the black figures towered over them.

"They're here," Lys said. Her heart began to race, and she tried to shove her way out of the magic.

"Who?" Brady asked.

Lys frantically threw a plug at the hole. The magic poured out, forcing the plug away. She saw herself shake her head and grit her teeth. This time she put everything she could get into it, and the magic abruptly cut off. She slumped forward, stumbling.

"The New," she said, reaching her hand out for Kamau's steady arm. "They're outside, and they're everywhere."

Chapter 26

"Now?" Kamau asked.

"Right now," Lys nodded.

Kamau cursed under his breath. "Not now."

"We have to warn the others!" she said. "Will the sound users hear them?"

"I'm not sure," Kamau said. "Probably. Where did you see them?"

"Everywhere," Lys said, looking out through the door—half expecting to see a gun pointed at her face. "Can you talk to the other sound users? Tell them the New are here!"

"Do they have Peter with them?" Inez demanded.

Lys shook her head. "I'm not sure, maybe."

Inez took a step toward the door, but Kamau grabbed her. "Your best shot at finding him is to stick with Mason."

Inez shook off his hold. "Why? You don't trust him."

Kamau shrugged. "Maybe not, but his people can stand against the New. We can't. Not by ourselves."

"I'll go alone," Inez said, lunging for the door again.

"Yeah, right," Brady said, on her heels.

The sound of running footsteps from outside cut the conversation short. Lys, who stood closest to the door, caught a glimpse of Mark and Genni running through the trees.

"What's going on?" Mark asked, skidding to a stop just outside the door. His eyes rested on the unconscious man.

"The New are here," Lys said. "I just saw them, they're everywhere."

"What?" Mark asked.

Genni frowned. "Are you sure you didn't see me?" She still wore the black body armor.

"No," Lys shook her head. "Not you. Lots of them."

"What did you see?" Mark asked.

"Dozens of them, coming from every direction."

Mark swore. "How did they find us?"

"They have Peter," Inez added. "Lys saw that too."

"We'd better get back." Mark glanced at the member of the New on the floor. "He's not going anywhere. Come on."

They all exited the building and took about seven steps before the world exploded around them. Lights flashed and a blaring sound worse than a fire engine trapped in a gym filled the air. Kamau went down to his knees, covering his ears.

"What was that?" Lys yelled, not sure how loud her voice was.

"It disrupts the sound users. They're cutting off our communication. Or trying anyway. It'll wear off in a few minutes," Mark said.

In the twilight, Lys saw a handful of figures in black armor coming through the trees about a hundred yards away.

Lys pointed. "There!"

"Great," Mark said. "We have to get back to the cabin. Kamau, can you move?"

Kamau looked up, leaving his hands on his ears, and nodded.

"Good. Run."

Lys ran, shoving Kamau in front of her. They followed Mark, who took them on a faint path that wound between the trees. Around them, the sunset started to fade into twilight. They ran down the hill, getting closer to the cabin.

How had the New found them so fast? Why didn't the New just leave them alone? The ancient war with the Old—is that what kept them coming? Or was it something else?

Bright flashes of the tents started strobing through the trees, and they met a group of users coming up the hill.

"Get behind the line!" a man with red, swirling eyes shouted. He waved to Brady. "Why don't you join us."

A net flew over Lys' head, entrapping a boy who went down

in a heap. Everyone ducked as three more went by.

Fear jolted the Need and her magic. She tried to keep them both back, but the barrier in front of her magic bowed. The Need snarled. Lys decided that she'd rather have the magic than the Need, so she let it out. A thin stream, pouring straight into her mind. She made a split screen so she could see out of her own eyes.

"They're not killing today?" someone asked.

"Apparently not," Mark answered. He gestured for Lys, Kamau and Inez to join a group of users who were running for the tents. "Follow them, they'll take you out of here."

Lys knew Mark would want to stay and fight. She glanced around and saw movement through the trees. The twilight from above, and the shadows from below made it difficult, but not impossible, for Lys to spot the New as they approached.

"There!" she said. "There's one right there."

Brady was ready. He had a rock in his hand, and following Lys' finger, he threw it, striking the figure in the body armor.

"How can you see that?" someone asked.

"She can see in the dark!" Brady said proudly.

"Darlin'," the man with the red eyes said, waving her over. "Why don't you stay here right behind me and tell us where they're coming from."

"Cody," Mark said.

"It's okay, I can do it," Lys said, wanting to do something.

"Mason is going to have a fit," Mark said.

"Behind you!" Lys pointed as she spotted more intruders. "Two of them."

Mark didn't have time to argue. He crouched down and spun in a circle, like a discus thrower in the Olympics. However, Mark didn't throw a stone, he spewed rocks and dirt that came right up off the ground, driving the two figures in black back.

"Keep your eyes moving, darlin'!" Cody said in his southern

drawl. "Kind of hard to see out here for the rest of us."

Lys took up position between Cody and Brady. "There are three up in those trees and two more almost to the tents over there."

Cody grinned. "Go flush them out, boys!" He looked like he was having the time of his life. He had a belt full of marbles and one in each hand. Lys didn't have to ask him what they were for after he threw a barrage of them toward the three figures in black up the hill. They exited his hands so fast that Lys couldn't actually see them until they hit a target.

"Nets!" she yelled, pulling Cody and Brady down. The breeze from the cables ruffled Lys' hair.

"Nice!" Brady said, grinning almost as big as Cody.

"What about the other side?" Lys asked, looking over her shoulder. "There are three going toward the tents!"

"Got it," Mark said. "Come on Brady, I think we can use your towel trick on these guys."

"Yes!" Brady said with a fist pump. "And can we call them the BG's? You know, for bad guys? Just until I think of something better."

Brady's words faded as she watched them go. All around her dirt flew in chunks. Nets whizzed through the air. So far there had been no gun fire. Well, except for Cody. He was like a gun by himself.

"I wonder what the rest of them can do," Kamau asked, looking at Cody and the others in the line.

Lys jumped; she hadn't realized he had stayed.

He smiled. "One of the sound users is coordinating everyone. I can hear her now, so she asked me to stay with Cody."

Where did Inez go? Lys glanced back, but couldn't see the other girl.

Cody nodded. "Good. Tell me whatever they tell you to." He tossed another volley of marbles into a black figure that Lys pointed to. He frowned. "They're usually more brutal."

Lys shook her head. Was he complaining?

"More nets!" Lys shouted as soon as she saw another volley coming their way. She glanced over at the boy the first net had caught. Someone had dragged him behind the line. His still body made Lys wonder if the New had decided to kill today after all. Four others lay under nets as well.

"They cut off magic use, and if you mess with it, sometimes they hurt the person inside," Cody explained, following her gaze. "Don't worry, someone will get him out of it eventually. For now he's safe."

Inez had a knife that could cut through those nets. Lys focused her magic, searching for the other girl.

A wave of images assaulted her, and it took her a second to sort them out. Most resembled the chaos that surrounded her, and before she found Inez something caught her attention. "Uh, Cody," she said, trying to make out what she was seeing. "They've got something really big up the hill."

"How big?" Cody asked, sending a round of marbles at a set of black clad figures that got too close. The black armor must be tougher than it looked, because they kept getting back up, even after being hit by Cody.

"Kind of looks like a surf board," Lys said, trying to get into the vision of those around her so she could see Cody and herself.

Cody swore. "Sound guy, tell the others that they're going to pulse us." He didn't wait for a response.

"Get ready to jump people!" he shouted. Cody placed a hand on Lys' shoulder. "Darlin', just as soon as they lift that thing up, tell me. When it starts to come down, yell 'now' just as loud as you can."

"What is it?" Lys asked

For the first time, Cody looked concerned.

"Nothin' good," he said.

A crackling sound behind her caused Lys to turn. A wave of earth rose, headed straight at the New near the tents. Lys saw Brady and Mark, shaking patches of ground like you'd shake out a towel.

"Pay attention people!" Cody said, squeezing her shoulder. "Those two can take care of themselves. Don't worry, they've got our backs. Just tell me when that thing comes down."

Lys concentrated. Four figures in black surrounded the surf board sized object. When they lifted it into the air Lys said, "It's up."

"Get ready!" Cody said. "Relay that to the others," he told Kamau.

Projectiles continued to fly around her. Another net caught a victim—this one a girl who couldn't be any older than Lys. She went down with a scream, but it sounded more like anger than anguish. A blue flash lit up the twilight behind her, and Lys saw Mark through another perspective. All of this came through other people's eyes, and Lys knew she was about to hit the overload point.

So she shut down everything but the images of the object and her own view. She watched intently, but still had a hard time discerning when the gray cylinder began to fall. The instant she could tell Lys yelled, "Now!"

Lys loved roller coasters. She loved being thrown around every which way, and she rarely got sick on them. The sensation of leaving her stomach fifty feet behind her made her scream in delight.

This, however, made her scream in terror. One second she stood on the ground, watching the cylinder fall, and the next she had been yanked off her feet. Not just off her feet, but off the ground and up past the trees—completely ruining her concentration. Like a claw from one of those toy vending machines in the mall had reached down and plucked her into the air, at the speed of light. Not only did it feel like her stomach was still on the ground, it felt like her soul had been ripped from her body, leaving the flesh and blood behind.

Only the screaming proved that she still had both lungs and vocal cords.

Cody didn't just have her by the waist, but he held two others by the arms. She saw half a dozen more clusters of people jumping into the air, and she wondered if Kamau was still on the ground or if someone had a hold of him.

"Go get em, boys!" Cody yelled as they reached the apex of the jump. He literally launched the two people he held in his other arm out over the trees. Lys could see a cluster of the New along with their gray cylinder—Cody's guys were headed straight for it.

Lys tried to watch, but she started to fall, and the tree tops got in her way. Wait, they were falling! She took a breath so she could scream again, but before she had to, Cody landed on the ground with no more than a light thump.

"Good job," he said with a grin.

Screams filled the air. Not yelling, like before, but screams of pain and terror.

"What's going on?" Lys asked, flinching at the noise.

"Some of the other groups didn't get out of the way in time," Kamau said as a woman set him back on the ground. Lys noticed that his dark skin was a shade or two lighter than it had been a moment before.

"Pulse is a nasty business," Cody said. "It messes with our magic. Makes it feel like your head is going to explode if you don't get out of the way."

"Did we…did we get out of the way?" Lys asked, her hands shaking a little. Too many feelings ran through her and she couldn't tell magic from pure fear.

"Sure did, thanks to you."

Kamau held up a hand. "They say to fall back to the outside

of the cabin. Mr. Mason's orders."

"Okay," Cody ducked as a clod of dirt the size of his head buzzed by. "You two follow those two." He indicated a pair of touch users who were whipping projectiles out of the air with tree branches. "We'll be right behind you."

Lys felt Kamau grab her hand.

"Fall back!" Cody yelled. "Left side first."

Kamau led Lys toward the left side of the line. She barely kept her feet under her as they ran, following the two touch users as they made a break for the tents.

"We're clear," Kamau said.

"Of what?" Lys asked.

Kamau didn't get a chance to answer. A wave of heat hit Lys in the back, pushing her forward and causing her to fall to her hands and knees. A ringing filled her ears as smoke and heat engulfed her. Lys shook her head in an attempt to stop the world from spinning.

Lys blinked, trying to clear her vision. She coughed and inhaled smoke. Behind them a wall of fire raged. Dirt, burning branches and rocks fell all around them.

"We need to move!" Kamau shouted, pulling on her hand.

Lys barely heard him. She looked back to where Cody had been standing only moments before. Flames engulfed the entire line of touch users. Were they gone? Really gone?

"Lys!" Kamau shouted again. "We need to move."

She allowed herself to be hauled to her feet. Smoke and screaming filled the air. One of the screams she recognized.

"NO!" Brady's voice cut through her shock. "Mark!"

Lys followed the sound of Brady's voice with her eyes. On the other side of the tents she could make out Brady's slight form, crouching on the ground next to someone else.

"This way," Lys said.

"But," Kamau said.

"Brady's over here!" Lys snapped. "We have to help him."
They were not going to leave him.

Kamau didn't argue, but she had to drag him behind her. They ran through the remains of burning tents to where Brady knelt next to Mark.

"You need to get out of here," Mark said, his voice haggard.

Lys skidded to a stop and knelt on the ground next to Brady.

"What happened?" she asked.

"I got hit," Mark said through gritted teeth. "You need to get out of here. Brady, get Lys out of here."

"I'm not leaving you!" Brady protested, placing a hand on Mark's chest.

Lys's eyes traveled to Mark's leg. The bone in his thigh stuck out of a gaping wound. Blood poured from it, creating a dark pool on the ground.

"Mark!" a new voice yelled.

Lys turned to see Ayden running toward them. His eyes were swirling gold, like a cat.

"What happened?" he asked. Then he noticed Lys. "You need to get back to the cabin right now! Brady, Kamau, take her—" He stopped, looking down at Brady. A dark glow had begun under Brady's hands.

"What are you doing?" He asked. Brady didn't respond.

"Hey," Ayden said, pushing Lys to the side. "I said what are you doing?"

Kamau grabbed Ayden's shoulder. "Wait."

Brady moved one hand to Mark's injured leg. He took a deep breath and closed his eyes. The dark glow increased before Brady said, "I can fix him."

Chapter 27

"What do you mean you can fix him?" Ayden asked, his golden eyes traveling to Mark's wound.

"Someone come get ready to pull on his leg," Brady said softly, sweat beading on his brow. No one moved. "Now!"

The urgency in his tone provoked a response. Lys backed away as Ayden and Kamau knelt on the ground. Kamau went to Mark's shoulders and Ayden went to his leg.

"Set it. Do it fast." Brady said in almost a whisper.

Kamau clamped down on Mark's shoulders and upper body while Ayden took his leg. "One, two…"

Lys turned away. The crunch made her flinch, but Mark's scream brought tears to her eyes. Pain lanced through the air, and Lys buried her face in her hands.

"Hold him! Just a little longer," Brady said.

Mark groaned. Lys raised her head. The exposed bone had been replaced by a wound as big as her hand. Blood continued to pour out, but almost as she realized this, Lys watched as it first slowed and then stopped.

"How?" she said, stepping closer.

They all watched in fascination as the wound sealed up. Just like what Jodi did to Lys' leg, only on a much larger scale. An angry, red welt replaced the wound. Another crunch, this one softer, sounded as the bones meshed back together—or so Lys imagined. Mark's eyes fluttered open as Brady removed his hands.

Mark seemed confused. "What in the?" He looked down at his leg and then back up to Brady.

"You healed him," Lys said, amazed.

Brady nodded. He sat back, swaying. "I could feel it. I could feel everything. And when I pulled him over here, I knew I could fix it."

"Fix it?" Ayden demanded.

Brady nodded again. "But it's not healed. At least, not all the way."

"I've never heard of a chaos touch user being able to heal," Mark said, his voice strained.

"Can you heal?" Lys asked.

"No." Mark shook his head. "Like I said before, not even a paper cut."

Ayden looked hard at Brady. "How did you know you could heal him?"

Brady's pale face regarded the man. "I just knew I could. The bone is back together, but I don't know how good I did on the rest of it."

Lys flinched as a burning ember flew past her cheek, searing her flesh, reminding her that they were standing in the middle of a war zone.

"We need to get to the cabin," Ayden said. He studied Brady with a guarded expression.

"We can carry him," Brady insisted. He stumbled to his feet and took one of Mark's arms.

"Why don't you let us take him," Ayden said, indicating to himself and Kamau. "You make sure Lys gets to the cabin in one piece. We'll be right behind you."

Brady didn't look like he was going to be much help. He limped over to her as the other two lifted a groaning Mark to his feet.

"Come on," she said, putting her shoulder under one of Brady's arms. He didn't resist as she started off toward the cabin.

All around them people ran. Some fought back, but most were headed in the same direction as Lys. Small explosions filled the air with debris while the loud siren sounded again. Lys flinched, but the sound wasn't as powerful as before—Kamau didn't go to the ground.

She wound them through what remained of the tents and back toward the front door of the cabin, almost retracing her steps from earlier. Probably less than thirty minutes earlier, Lys thought to herself. How quickly things changed.

"Over here!" Inez's voice cut through the noise.

"Hey!" Brady put on his winning smile. "What's up?" He stumbled, only staying upright because of Lys.

Inez jerked her thumb over her shoulder. "They've got some people working on an escape route down at the garage. Mr. Mason said he wanted us there as soon as we found *you*." The last word was addressed to Lys.

Lys swallowed. "Me?"

"You two best buds now?" Inez asked as she took Brady's other arm.

"I thought you were leaving," Lys shot back.

Inez shrugged. "I need to live through the next hour if I want to see Peter again."

A group of people ran past them, back toward the hill where Cody and his line had been. She hoped they were healers.

"Go to the garage!" Ayden said from behind them.

"We're going," Inez said. "What was that thing?"

"Someone called it a pulse. It disrupts magic, or so he said," Lys said.

"You didn't get hit by it?" Inez asked, wiping her face with a hand. She looked pale.

"Uh, not exactly," Lys said. "Did you?"

"A little, but some of the sound users blocked most of it."

They were almost to the end of the cabin. The ground rumbled beneath their feet. Lys hoped it was magic, and not the New. Inez in the lead, they rounded the corner. Lys expected to find more fighting. Instead, a handful of the New had fifteen or twenty magic users surrounded.

The magic users were on their knees—a few lay unmoving on

the ground. Lys tried to pull Inez back, but one of the New heard them and turned around.

"There he is. We were worried that you'd been caught in the crossfire," a metallic voice said through the helmet.

Without visible eyes, Lys couldn't tell who the member of the New was talking to. Not her, surely.

"Where is Mason?" the voice demanded.

"Like we'd tell you that," Brady said with disdain.

"I wasn't talking to you," the man said. "Net them."

Everyone scattered. Brady surged forward, trying to tackle the man in the black armor. Inez dove one way and Lys went the other, hitting the ground with a grunt and rolling to avoid the net she could hear coming through the air. She didn't roll far enough.

The net landed on her torso and upper legs. It pinned one arm, leaving the other free. She tried to crawl forward, but found that she couldn't move anything under the net. Rolling over didn't work either. Her free hand grabbed a hold of the edge of the net to try to push it away. A wave of dark energy engulfed her. She couldn't see.

Lys let go of the net and balled her fists together. Not the dark. She shook her head.

Blinking, Lys found that she *could* see, but not in the dark and not from other people's eyes, like someone flipped the switch off her magic.

"Don't struggle," Kamau's voice said. "It'll only make it worse."

Lys nodded. She lay face down with Kamau behind her. Without her magic she could only make out the boots of someone lying near her, maybe Mark. The flickering light from the fires didn't penetrate this far around the cabin.

"Is this the one?" a metallic voice asked.

"Yes," Kamau said.

"Good. Leave her until we get these others taken care of.

She's not going anywhere."

"Kamau, what's going on?" Lys craned her neck as far as she could. Did they mean her?

"Oh don't worry," the metallic voice said as a dark figure crouched down near her head. "Kamau made us promise to take good care of you."

"What?" Lys demanded. Her stomach constricted into a knot.

"He's working for us." He shook his head. "I told you not to trust Mr. Mason."

"Doyle?" Lys asked. "What are you talking about? Why are you doing this?"

"We wanted to know Mason's plan, and Kamau wants his sister back. Since we knew that Mason hoped you were something special, we sent Kamau in to keep an eye on you."

To keep an eye on her? Lys turned her head, trying to find Kamau. She couldn't see him. They sent him in to keep an eye on her? To discover Mr. Mason's plan?

Images of the past few days flew through her mind. Kamau had always been right there, ready to help. All concerned eyes and soft touch—he'd been keeping an eye on her? But, he kissed her.

Had everything between them been a lie?

Anger flared through her, and she began to struggle, determined to get out of the net.

"Don't bother," Doyle said. "You're not going anywhere." Before he could go on, an invisible hand threw Doyle back. He hit the log wall of the cabin with a thud.

"Get Ayden! Burn that net off Lys!" Mr. Mason's voice shouted.

Lys heard footsteps stomping around her.

"Don't move," someone said, "at all."

Lys held her breath. She felt pressure from the net, closing in on her—constricting. For a second she thought it might cut through her as it got tighter and tighter, but suddenly the pressure disappeared. Cold enveloped Lys and she began to shiver.

"Up," the voice ordered.

Lys got to her hands and knees. Shards of ice, leftovers of the net, fell to the ground with a tinkle. A pair of hands helped her to her feet.

"Get her to the garage," Mr. Mason ordered. "I'll be in the van."

Darkness still surrounded her. For having not been able to see in the dark for her whole life, Lys was surprised at how much she missed it. She couldn't even clearly see her rescuer.

"What's going on?" she asked weakly.

"Mr. Mason is getting us out of here."

"What about everyone else?"

"They'll be behind us." A pause. "Close your eyes for a second."

Lys did so, and even through her eyelids she saw the flash of light that must have lit the entire mountain up. She hoped it blinded the New in their technology helmets.

"Okay, this way, we're almost there," her helper urged, dragging her forward.

Lys glanced back the way they had come. Someone started a fire close by, and she could see at least ten people trapped under nets, including Inez and Mark. Almost everyone else in the clearing was on the ground or just getting to their feet.

She pulled her arm free and turned back. She would not leave Brady and the others.

"What are you doing?" her helper demanded.

Lys ignored her, taking a few steps toward Mark.

A dark shape came out of nowhere and blocked her path. Lys stopped in her tracks. Even without her magic she could see Kamau's broad shoulders.

"Lys," he started, reaching for her.

Tears sprung to her eyes as she backed up. "You used me."

257

Used her to get to Mason, to get his plan.

Kamau shook his head. "Lys, you have to listen to me. Mason has my sister."

Lys could hear the worry in his voice, but now she knew the concern had never been for her. Kamau was a cold, calculating predator, and she had been his prey. The feel of his lips on hers, of his arms around her started an ache inside that blossomed into fury.

"Leave me alone!" she shouted, slapping his hands away. "You lied to me!" She hardly recognized her own voice. "None if it meant anything!" Her hands shook, but this time hate flowed through her. The meaning and truth of her own words sunk in, and Lys knew that he had used her. All of the attention, sticking close to her all of the time and pretending to care about her; it was all part of a plan to betray her—to betray Mr. Mason and his ambition to save magic users.

"Lys," he said, grabbing her wrist.

She jerked her hand, and when it didn't come free, she stepped forward and stomped on his foot as hard as she could.

Kamau let go. Someone grabbed him from behind.

Her escort pulled her away. "Come on!"

She allowed herself to be dragged down the road to a waiting van.

Her escort shoved her through the door and into the nearest seat. "Ayden is right behind us," she reported.

"Good," Mr. Mason said from the driver's seat. "Are the others prepared to help us get out?"

"They're ready."

Lys watched as her escort, whose name she didn't even know, helped Ayden into the van and shut the door, staying outside.

The van had three benches in the back. With her and Ayden, most of the seats were taken. Ayden took the passenger side. The woman sitting next to Lys smiled, but it felt empty. Everything felt empty. Lys felt empty—betrayed and alone. She wanted to cry. But it didn't seem like she had time for it.

Mr. Mason put the van into drive. "Hold on everyone."

Chapter 28

"You'd better put your seat belt on," the woman next to Lys said.

Lys' fingers fumbled with the pieces, trying to connect the metal end into the receiver. If she hadn't preformed the action thousands of times she never would have been able to do it.

Four magic users jogged in front of the van. Lys thought they would all be touch users, but when the low hum began she changed her mind. She recognized that hum—Kamau had made the same noise in Las Vegas. Were all the people in front of them sound users?

Underneath the van, directly in front of the sound users, the earth lay still. However, a wave of trembling, jumping earth fanned out to the sides. Cracks formed around them, but never in the road. Lys heard a crackling sound and saw the side window across from her break, spider-webbing.

One of the figures waved as they scattered, and Mr. Mason stomped on the gas. The van jumped forward like those roller coasters that shot you from the platform. There must be a touch user or two behind them.

The small, winding, dirt road that they'd driven in on lay before them. Lys glanced out the back windows of the van and saw several members of the New running after them. She shifted her gaze out the front windshield. The dirt road ran straight for maybe twenty yards before making a turn so tight that if they tried it they would surely fly right off the mountain side. Could touch users fly?

Special effects had nothing on what she saw next. In front of them, just before the wheels rolled over it, the headlights illuminated a new road—dirt and gravel solidified into smooth rock before her eyes.

Mr. Mason didn't take the corner. Instead, he drove forward, the road forming in front of him. The nose of the van angled forward, and they started down the mountain side.

The lap belt held Lys hanging with her back at least six inches away from the seat. Her feet and hands dangled free as the belt dug into her stomach.

In front of them, the road continued to form. The curious side of Lys wanted to know what was happening behind them, but she couldn't look back. The van began to drift to the left, and the road went with it, keeping them from tumbling down the hill.

A loud thump hit the back of the van, pushing the front wheels off the formed road. The hood of the van dropped down, the axle hitting the rock with a squeal. A huge crater caved in the roof, forcing people to duck. Lys stifled a scream.

"Hold on," someone said.

Sure, Lys thought, I'll do that.

The van literally flew off the end of the road, scraping the entire undercarriage as it did so. Another loud thump sounded from the back. A barrage of voices filled the air.

"Hook us!"

"Get them off there!"

"Keep the door open!"

"Do it now!"

Those were the last words Lys heard, and at that particular moment she decided that sitting near the front sucked. The bottom of the cliff grew steadily closer. They continued to fly away from the mountain side. The world slowed to a crawl, and Lys could see the ground coming, getting brighter in the headlights. Her heartbeat thump-thumped in her ears, the tang of mountain air and old leather seats filled her nostrils. The voices behind her started to sound like the teacher in *Charlie Brown* cartoons.

The van stopped.

If she thought the seat belt had hurt before, now it was an ax, chopping her at the waist, attempting to sever her in half. This time she couldn't scream, as a matter of fact she couldn't breathe at all. Time sped up again, and Lys struggled to inhale. People around her were hollering, but the blood pounding in her ears overpowered them. Darkness began to gather at the edges of her vision. The pressure on her abdomen did not ease. Lys couldn't breathe. She clawed at the seat belt, trying to give herself some room. It was too tight, her fingers couldn't get in there. They stopped working. Her vision fuzzed, went gray and then started to tunnel.

Someone cut her loose. She fell forward, face planting into the back of the driver's seat.

"Get out!" A voice said as someone pushed her out the door. The ground lay fifteen feet below, and Lys wondered how bad it would hurt to hit, but a woman caught her and set her gently on her feet.

The roar in her ears abated, but now she could hear another roar. A helicopter hovered overhead.

"Bring it down!" Mr. Mason ordered.

Lys looked up. The van dangled headlights first, ten feet off the ground. An overhang of rock held the back of the van.

Above that a helicopter hovered, with members of the New hanging out each side. Nets flew at magic users, but a blast of wind buffeted them away. The helicopter bucked, and the pilot had to back off.

"Why don't you come over here? In a second there will be a lot of falling debris," Ayden said, taking her by the elbow.

Ayden wasn't kidding. She watched in fascination as a couple of magic users started tossing giant chunks of the ground at the helicopter. A sound user climbed on top of the van and sang a note that vibrated everything down to her teeth. Within seconds the helicopter fell to pieces around them.

A figure in black crashed into the cliff side, rolling down like a barrel.

Lys looked away. Bile rose from her stomach. People were dead. That guy would not be getting up and walking it off. Cody, along with who knows how many other magic users—all dead. The New killed people; Mr. Mason killed people. Lys didn't know how she should feel about any of it.

Kamau's face swam before her eyes, and Lys grit her teeth together. He betrayed her! He betrayed them. If not for him, no one would have died today. If not for him, the New would never have found them.

A poking memory reminded Lys that if not for Kamau she might be dead or crazy already, but she thrust it out. He used her to get Mr. Mason's plan. That thought brought enough anger to snap her out of it.

"Our ride will be here in two minutes," someone reported.

"Is everyone okay?"

Then a voice Lys recognized. "Did we lose any neutrals?" Mr. Mason.

"No, we're all here." Ayden put a hand on Lys' shoulder. "You still with us?"

Lys nodded. She didn't trust herself to speak. She still couldn't breathe very well—it felt like she had a five gallon water cooler sitting on her chest. She wanted to sit down, but Ayden kept her upright.

"Anything broken?" Ayden asked.

Lys considered this. Her hands responded when she moved them, so did her legs and arms. The muscles in her neck throbbed, but nothing felt broken. She shook her head.

"Good." Ayden glanced up at the van. "We should probably move."

Behind her, Lys could hear crackling and the groaning of metal. She managed to turn her head—not a pleasant experience she decided at once—so she could see what Ayden was looking at.

The van dangled above them, windows smashed and wheels mostly gone.

"Come on," Ayden said, taking her by the elbow. "It's not going anywhere." He paused. "Probably."

Lys followed. She flinched as she tried to take a deep breath. The people from the van, including Mr. Mason, were all looking back up the hill.

"Are they coming after us?" Lys asked.

A few of the people laughed. Genni, who Lys had not noticed before, shook her head. "Not for a while."

Out of the corner of her eye, Lys saw lights. She turned her head and spotted a vehicle coming toward them.

"Uh," she said.

"Not to worry, that's our ride," Mr. Mason said.

Lys decided she must be in shock. Everything felt surreal, like she was watching a home movie. Her body must be really beaten up, but Lys didn't mind. She felt...good.

Wait. Lys narrowed her eyes and tried to think. What senses were there? Touch—she'd seen what that could do. Sight; she hadn't been able to influence people's emotions. Kamau did with sound, so it could be that. But what had Mark said? Taste dealt more with physical appetites and smell dealt with the emotional? She glanced at Ayden—a smell user.

The group gathered loosely. One girl stood apart from everyone. She was young, not very tall and extremely slender. Lys couldn't see her face because she had a hijab wrapped around her head and pulled down to cover everything but her eyes. The girl never looked at anyone else. She kept away from the group, gazing back up the hill.

Gravel crunched as two off-roading SUVs pulled up. The drivers unrolled their windows and greeted Mr. Mason. Lys didn't bother to listen, lost in her own thoughts.

Kamau. His face, his smile, his hands, his lips…could it all be a lie? Did he use her? Was he really working for the New? She'd seen the evidence with her own eyes. Heard it as they were talking. All for his sister? Did Mr. Mason have his sister? Did the New? Was she already dead?

Lys felt tears forming in her eyes. She brushed them away; no time for crying now. She followed the smaller girl's gaze back up the hill. What happened to the others? Did Mr. Mason get them out?

"Come on," Ayden said, squeezing her shoulder. "We'll go in this one."

"But what about everyone else?" she asked in a small voice.

"Don't worry, they'll be okay."

Lys allowed Ayden to steer her to the second vehicle. A short man crawled in the very back while Lys, Ayden and Genni took the middle seat.

They would be okay? Lys thought with one last glance up the hill. No, Lys didn't think so. And as the SUV started to move, the cliff side grew farther and farther away, and so did the chances of Lys ever seeing her friends again.

"How do you think they found us?" the driver asked. Lys could see his square jaw and his golden eyes in the rear-view mirror. Deep lines etched his cheeks, making him the oldest person Lys had seen with Mr. Mason.

"They must have followed someone," the passenger said—a woman with long red hair and blue eyes.

"Inside job," the guy from the back said.

Lys' heart dropped into her stomach. Kamau—she couldn't deny it.

"You saw?" Ayden asked, watching her.

Lys nodded.

"Saw what?" Genni asked.

"Kamau," Lys said. "He's with the New."

"Who?" the driver asked.

"One of the kids that came in with Lys. They were with Mark at the hospital when the New caught them," Ayden said.

The New *had* caught them. Could the whole thing have been a set up? Mark told them that the New usually killed magic users. Even he had been baffled that they were all still alive at the New's headquarters. Did Kamau have something to do with that? Did he have everything to do with it?

"He was with you the whole time?" Genni asked.

"The whole time," Lys said numbly. How could Kamau be a traitor? He'd helped them get away from the New. He'd saved her life. He'd kissed her. Was it all a lie? The question would not stop plaguing her, and even though she thought she knew the answers, Lys didn't want to believe it

"You think he led them to us?" Genni asked.

Ayden shrugged. "Probably. I mean, everyone else had been there for days. This group comes in and a few hours later we're on the run again? Too convenient."

Genni nodded. She leaned around Ayden to speak directly to Lys. "Did he say anything to make you think that he was with them?"

"No," Lys shook her head. Kamau had said plenty of things, but nothing to indicate that he supported the New.

"You guys were all together right before the New attacked. What were you talking about?" Genni asked. She said the words kindly—it didn't quite feel like an interrogation.

"I, uh…" she trailed off. Did everyone here know about Mr. Mason's plan? He hadn't indicated that she should go telling everyone about it.

"Did you tell him what you and Mason talked about?" Genni asked.

Lys nodded.

"Lys is a neutral. Mason asked her for help with the outlets,"

Ayden said to the others.

So they did know.

Ayden looked hard at her. "Did you tell Kamau about that?"

She wanted to lie. No one would ever be able to prove otherwise, but she didn't think that would be right.

She nodded. "I told Kamau about it." Her purpose had been for him to him help make sense of it all. She wanted him to tell her that it was okay that she didn't want to use her magic anymore. All she wanted was a friend—someone to talk to. "I told him everything Mr. Mason told me." She looked up at Ayden. "I'm so sorry. I didn't know."

He waved a hand. "They've suspected what we're up to for months. It won't come as a big surprise."

"But now they know for sure," Genni pointed out.

"That's probably why we're headed for Utah."

"What's in Utah?" the woman in the passenger seat asked.

"The nearest outlet. Did you see it on the map?" Ayden asked Lys.

"We're going there?" Lys asked.

"That's the direction we're headed. Mr. Mason's orders. From what I understand, we've got a time limit," the driver said.

Ayden pulled his hand up and pushed the light button on his watch. "What's today?" he asked himself, bobbing his head up and down. "Yeah, if Mr. Mason wants to hit this window, we'll have to do it by tomorrow night."

"That's a tight schedule," Genni said. "We don't even have supplies, and it's a long hike."

"I'm sure Mason's got that taken care of," Ayden said, lowering his arm. Lys noticed Genni's hand reach out to take his before their arms disappeared between them.

Lys' thoughts were immediately taken back to Kamau. He must have led the New to the hospital in the first place. And when he didn't know much Kamau probably told them that Mr. Mason wanted Lys, but he didn't know why. That had to be the only reason they got away from the New. Sure, Brady, Mark and Kamau had been amazing, but seriously, the six of them against a dozen or more people in black body armor? Why hadn't she seen it earlier?

Another part of her mind still protested. Kamau had been so kind to her. She liked him, and she thought he liked her. Why else would he do all those things? To find his sister? He would surely do almost anything to get her back. Did that make him bad?

Kamau *had* done horrible things to try to get his sister back. People were dead—he'd led them to Mr. Mason, and people like Cody were gone, forever. How many more people would die if they couldn't beat the New?

"Have you ever fought the New before?" Lys asked.

Ayden shrugged. "Sure, but it's been a while. They've never found us before. The only other time I fought the New was when we jumped them."

"I've taken them on a few times," the driver said.

"Neil has been around for a while," Genni said with a smile.

"Age before beauty," he said with dignity.

Lys cleared her throat. "Uh, have you ever beat them?"

"The New don't go down easy," the man from the back said. "We've won some battles, but never the war."

"Do they really kill magic users?" Lys asked. "I mean, if they find them?"

Ayden nodded gravely. "They do."

The tone of his words indicated to Lys that she'd hit a nerve.

"Would they have killed me?"

Ayden regarded her. "Your parents let Mason take you from the hospital just in time. Doyle arrived the next morning. The week before, Mason missed a girl in Oregon by mere hours. The New made it look like a drug overdose."

Lys swallowed, suddenly not feeling well. "What will they do

268

to the others?" Brady's easy grin filled her mind, along with the way he looked at Inez—like she was the most beautiful creature he had ever seen. She wondered if Mark's leg would be okay.

Kamau's dark eyes tried to invade her thoughts, but Lys refused to let them. He'd thrown himself in with people who would kill her if they caught her. She didn't understand exactly why he did it, but Kamau was on the other side. The wrong side.

Even the questions that Mr. Doyle had asked her made sense. Had he been trying to turn her so she would rat out Mr. Mason. Sow discord to make it possible for them to get Mr. Mason's plan from her. And she'd given it to them without even knowing! Because of her, the plan got handed to the New on a silver platter. How many more people would die because of the New, because of her?

The SUV finally found a paved road, and the driver hit the gas, accelerating fast. She could practically smell the burning rubber from the tires.

"How can we beat them?" she asked.

Chapter 29

Neil, the driver, snorted. "Only one way."

"More magic," the man in the back said.

"More magic?" Lys asked

Ayden spoke. "Mason is convinced that if the magic portals are unplugged magic users would be more powerful. And not only that, but there would be more of us."

"Would everyone know about magic?" Lys asked. She'd never considered the possibility that her parents would know about her magic, and that the neighbor down the street could be a taste user or a guy at school could be a sound user. Would the government have to make special laws against magic? Would they use touch users for war? Lys had just seen how effective they could be.

"So you're a neutral sight user?" Genni asked.

"Yes," Lys said, nodding.

"You're the first one we've ever found," the man in the back said.

"So Mr. Mason told me," Lys said, her mouth going dry.

"How's that for timing?" Genni said with a smile.

"Yeah," Lys managed. Great timing. And she might ruin the whole thing because she feared magic almost as much as she feared the Need.

Lys glanced over and caught Genni giving Ayden a smile. Love glittered in her eyes. Ayden grinned back. Lys tried not to think about Kamau, but she couldn't help it. She still felt the warmth of his arms around her, and she could smell the slightly wild scent that always accompanied him. What would he do in her place? Would he sacrifice everything to help these people? To help her?

For that matter, what would Brady do? Lys almost laughed out loud. Duh, he'd be the first to volunteer for the job. Brady wanted to save the world, this would be right up his alley. Her thoughts turned to Inez. What about Inez? The other girl didn't trust anyone, and considering even the little bit Lys knew about Inez, she didn't blame her. Would Inez help Mr. Mason save other magic users? For Peter? Even if she might lose herself in the process?

Kamau fought for his sister. What would Lys fight for?

The question derailed her train of thought. Fight? Her? Lys wasn't a warrior. After seeing the battle with the New, Lys never wanted to be a warrior. Did that make her a coward? What if the only thing she could ever contribute was helping Mr. Mason release the magic? How would she feel knowing that she didn't take the chance when she had it? How many more magic users would die because of her selfishness?

Was it selfish to cherish your sanity? Did it make her a bad person to want to keep from despair so deep and so dark that it scared her to even think about it? Did it make her crazy to want to be with Kamau even though he brought the New down on them?

"Lys?" Ayden asked.

Lys sniffed. A tear slid down one cheek. When did she start crying?

"Are you okay?"

"Yeah," she nodded, wiping the tear away. Just a few days before Lys had been tied down to a bed, unable to wipe her tears from her cheeks. Her life had turned upside down since then. Friends at school were just faces and names. Lys missed them, but she honestly hadn't thought about them much since arriving at Mr. Mason's hospital. There hadn't been time.

Her parents were another matter. She thought about them constantly. How was her dad? He had a big trial for work the week after she left—had he won? Did her mom's second eye surgery go well? Would she be able to see again?

The memory of Jodi healing her leg surfaced. The icy-hot

sensation that Lys felt as Jodi moved her hand up the wound would never fully fade. It didn't hurt—hadn't pained her at all actually—and she would always be grateful.

What if someone could heal her mother's eye? Suddenly the possibilities of what magic could bring into the world burst through the mental clouds of confusion and pain. Could touch users heal cancer? What about sound users? Could they vibrate tumors apart? Or soothe people who were trying to jump off buildings? Taste users, could they help soldiers be brave? Would the world even need psychologists if smell users could help them access their memories and deal with them? And what about sight users? Lys could see in the dark. What could others do?

She knew so little about magic, but a thousand wonderful possibilities filled her mind. So much good could be done with magic. Her mother could be whole again.

"You sure?" Ayden asked, still looking at her.

Lys sniffed. "I'm okay, just shock I guess." Tears came from both eyes—two eyes, not one anymore. Magic hurt her, but magic also helped her. Other people's magic had done more than help her, it had saved her.

What if she could help people?

She'd never been terribly outgoing. Not like her dad. Of course he was a lawyer, he loved to talk and he liked people. But mostly he loved to help others. He always told her that the reason he'd become a lawyer was so that he could help people with problems that they couldn't solve themselves. And to make sure that the little guys didn't get trounced by the big guys. His words, not hers.

Little guys and big guys. Lys didn't know if either party here was big, but it was pretty obvious that the New were out to get magic users. And she didn't feel good about that.

One of the most important lessons Lys had ever learned from her dad was to listen to her gut. When she was little he'd fill his stomach with air and stick it out so he looked like a pregnant woman. Then he'd wander around the house, looking for some trinket Lys had hid for him. Later she realized her mom probably gave the hiding place away, but her dad always put on a big show about following his instincts.

And when he felt strongly about a case, he could get lost in it for months at a time. She remembered one year when he'd missed her art show for school along with her first, and only, dance recital. But Lys didn't remember feeling upset, because she knew that if her dad put that much time into anything, that it must be important. He taught her sacrifice.

It had always been a powerful lesson to Lys. Now she faced her own hard decision. Her sacrifice.

Lys closed her eyes and tried to listen to her gut. What would accepting the responsibility to help Mr. Mason do to her? It would hurt her, she couldn't deny that. But would it be worth it? Was it worth it to help everyone else? Not to mention saving innocent magic users, people who wouldn't understand their situation until far too late?

She glanced over at Ayden and then around at everyone else in the vehicle. Would she do it for them, for Brady and Inez and Kamau? The image of her mother's smiling face came to her mind again. Would she do it for the people she loved? To keep help them and keep them safe?

Yes.

She didn't have to ask herself again. She would do it. Not for Mr. Mason, but for everyone else it would affect.

Chapter 30

"I thought deserts were made of sand," Genni said.

Ayden, who hiked right in front of Genni turned around and laughed. "Not all deserts are the Sahara."

Lys followed Genni, but she hardly noticed the people in front of her. Instead Lys took in the scenery, and wished she had a camera.

"Have you ever seen anything like this?" the man behind her—originally from Italy—asked no one in particular.

"It is beautiful," Genni said. "And I'm not complaining about the lack of sand."

In the distance, huge monoliths towered, making Lys feel like a tiny bug in tall grass. No two spires looked the same—some had bulbous tops, but most thinned as they rose. Rings of red, orange and white stone piled on top of one another. The map called this place the Needles, and Lys could see why. They were stalagmites without a cave, rock teeth growing from the center of the earth. From farther away, the towers looked like the back of a giant porcupine with its needles sticking out everywhere. As they'd driven closer, some resembled decaying castles or fortresses, while others looked like deformed sticks with marshmallows melted on top.

Their path wound in and out of a maze of canyons and up and along the tops of a set of plateaus.

"Here's your sand," Ayden said as they started to descend.

Lys turned her attention from the towering rocks back to the trail. The people in front disappeared through a gap between the steadily narrowing cliff walls. She could see them as their heads bobbed away, like they were going down a staircase.

Ayden passed through the gap. Genni and Lys followed. They descended and found themselves on the gravelly floor of a canyon. Before they had been hiking on hard, unyielding rock, and the change to the shifting, chunky dry river bottom was jarring. The few trees she saw—stunted things, more bushes than trees—grew right out from between the rocks. She had no idea how they survived or where they sucked their water from. Still, they were there, looking as if they would be sticking around for a long, long time.

Even in the late fall, the temperature had Lys sweating. Not scalding, and certainly not humid, just a dry heat that pulled the water right out of her. She wouldn't be surprised if she heard the sucking sound as the skin on her hands cracked.

"Let's stop for a break," Mr. Mason said. He hiked at the front of the line, leading them all to a place called Druid Arch.

Lys stopped in the shade of the canyon wall and took a pull from her canteen. Thank goodness for Mr. Mason's hidden supplies. Sometime the night before, they had pulled off in a little town that Lys didn't even catch the name of. Mr. Mason took them into the middle of nowhere, where a friend of his had an entire barn full of food, water, clothes, sleeping bags and other survival gear. Lys wondered if Mr. Mason believed society would collapse.

While they had been loading supplies from the barn, Mr. Mason had come to talk to Lys. She told him she would help before he got a word out. He'd tried to hide his elation, but the giddy look in his eyes gave him away.

Less than an hour later, they'd been back on the road, driving fast for the Utah border. Lys hadn't bothered to try to stay awake. She'd slept until a sliver of light from the rising sun crested the horizon. By that time they were close. The view of the red rocks that made up this part of Utah kept her occupied while they made their way into Canyonlands and to the trailhead where they started hiking from.

"How you holding up?" Ayden asked.

"I'm good." Lys looked around. "I just wish I had a camera."

"No kidding," Genni said, standing close to Ayden. Lys noticed that they didn't touch when Mr. Mason was around. She wondered why.

The small girl with the hijab on hiked right behind Mr. Mason. She didn't speak to him or anyone else. Lys had tried to go over and talk to her, but Ayden had warned her against it, telling her that he'd never heard her speak to anyone, although she seemed to understand Mr. Mason's orders. Lys still hadn't seen more of the girl's face than her dark, brown eyes.

The girl wasn't the only one not from America. They had one man from Italy and one woman from somewhere near Russia that Lys couldn't pronounce. Neil, the SUV driver, said he lived in Norway before Mr. Mason found him, and it turned out that Genni grew up in Canada. Two other people didn't speak English very well, but everyone understood. There were ten of them in all, counting Lys. She'd tried to casually ascertain what kind of magic they all used, but no one had mentioned it, and she didn't want to be too obvious that she basically knew nothing about what they were here to do.

They started again, and Lys fell in line behind Genni. If Lys didn't know better, she would think they'd landed on a different planet. The rock formations reminded Lys of a futuristic world. All they needed were shiny exteriors and little cars flying around them.

In California the trees thrived. She'd been to the Redwood forest, and that made her feel small. This place made her feel alien. The only hints of humanity were the few wooden signs that labeled the trails and carrions—little pyramidal rock piles that kept you going in the right direction when the trail wasn't evident. A space ship could land in front of her, and Lys wouldn't be surprised.

"It feels like we're the only people on the planet," Genni said, as if reading Lys' thoughts.

Lys nodded, glad that someone else felt like an intruder as well.

"I can feel the magic getting stronger as we get closer," Genni said. "Can you?"

Lys shrugged.

"I feel it," the man behind her said in his Italian accent. "Pulsing, practically beneath our feet."

"It almost feels like this place is alive," Genni continued.

"I don't feel it at all," someone else said.

Conversation erupted around her as everyone tried to express how the magic felt to them. Genni, who knew French, dropped back to try to translate for someone. Left with Ayden, Lys moved closer to him.

"How come some people can feel the magic and some can't?" she asked.

Ayden thought about it. "I'm not sure. Magic is such a personal thing."

"Can you feel it?"

"Oh I can feel it. I'm surprised you can't see it."

"See it?"

"Well, I'm a smell user, and I can smell that this place is different. It's on the wind and in the rocks and even in the water sitting in those pools down there." He studied her for a moment. "You don't see anything?"

"I haven't tried." She gave him a weak shake of her head.

"Oh, right. You didn't get much of a chance to practice, did you?" He shrugged. "Probably a good idea, but be ready. I have a feeling you'll need it before long."

Ayden stopped as Mr. Mason approached.

"We're almost there," Mr. Mason said. "I wanted to warn Lys."

"About what?"

"I sent a small group out ahead of us yesterday. Ayden told me that Kamau is aware of our plans. It is likely that our people have neutralized the New that were sent here to protect the outlet." Lys had no doubt what the word "neutralized" meant.

"Okay," she said.

"I didn't want it to come as a surprise." Mr. Mason raised his voice. "We're almost there people. Hopefully we won't run into any problems, but just in case, I want our neutral users in the middle of our formation, surrounded by those of you who are here for protection."

He turned to Lys. "Stay with Ayden."

Lys watched Mr. Mason walk away. As he did so two other people came over to stand by them—the man from Italy and Neil. Mr. Mason walked to where the small girl stood alone. He leaned down and whispered something in her ear. The girl nodded and slowly came to join Lys and the others. Two more came over as well. That made seven.

So these were the other neutrals. "I thought we only needed five," Lys said.

"We've got two taste users and two touch users," Ayden explained quietly as they started to walk.

Mr. Mason kept them going at a fast pace. A few people looked completely worn out—stumbling down the canyon floor, just barely keeping up. All the walking she and her friends had done through the summer had paid off after all. The air here felt thin, like skim milk compared to whole milk, and Lys felt herself breathing hard, but she could keep up.

When the arch first came into view, she thought it had fallen. The drawing from the book showed the arch resembling a tripod, but when Lys saw it from the side it looked flat. Well, thick as a house, but still flat.

The trail wound around until Lys could kind of see the arch from the front. It looked like the rocks from Stonehenge in

England, only rougher, less finished. The arch resembled an "M", with one leg squished, thinning the space between two legs into a ribbon. There was nothing delicate about Druid Arch. It rose hundreds of feet into the air, looking as if its plateau pinnacle could hold up the sky. The stones, only slightly worn away by gritty sand carried on the wind, stood solid and imposing. Nothing less than a bomb could force this mighty monolith to fall.

"I've never seen anything like it," Lys heard a woman say behind her.

Lys nodded, still following the line of people in front of her. They had to slow when Mr. Mason took them off the path and up a narrow crevasse in the opposite side of the canyon.

"Aren't we going the wrong way?" someone asked.

Mr. Mason shook his head. "The only way to access the magic portal is from here. We'll need our sight user for that. Come on."

She swallowed. He needed her? It took a moment for Lys to get her feet to move. Only reflex kept her going forward.

The group followed Mr. Mason up through a spot where the canyon walls met and made a "V". They clamored up the steep, rocky path and over a landslide of huge boulders before a gap two feet wide greeted them. Lys let Ayden help her across and she followed the others to the far side of the jutting plateau.

"Over here, please," Mr. Mason said, waving the neutrals closer to him. Lys followed the others, wondering what was coming next.

"Lys, I think we're going to need you to find our path," he said.

Her heart skipped a beat. Find the path? She slowly inched forward, passing through the group. No one spoke, everyone watched her.

When Lys made it to the end of the rock, she stopped. Looking out over the gap, Lys saw nothing but air and a quick fall to her death.

Chapter 31

"Anything?" Mr. Mason asked.

Lys didn't answer. She tried not to notice how far below her the bottom of the canyon sat. Stacks of orange, red and white rocks lay below the precipice where she stood. She closed her eyes. The magic stirred. Her board appeared and she poked a hole in it. Golden energy shot into her mind, and Lys opened her eyes.

The layers of rock below twisted. An invisible paintbrush took the colors and pulled them across the landscape between where Lys stood and the arch. To her amazement, a path appeared—the end of it just a few feet below the edge of the cliff.

"I see it," she said.

"Good girl," Mr. Mason said, patting her on the shoulder.

"I don't see anything," someone complained.

Lys looked around. "Can anyone else see it?"

Everyone shook their heads.

"Can you step onto it?" Mr. Mason asked.

"Sure." Lys swallowed hard. "It's a few feet down." She sidled closer to the edge

"Here." Ayden offered her a hand.

Lys grabbed Ayden's hand and hoped he would forgive her for crushing his fingers. She tried to ignore the empty air below the path as she stepped to the edge and lowered one leg off. Toes grasping, Lys reached out, and the moment she touched the stone a buzz of magic filled her mind.

Someone behind them gasped. "Wow."

"Extraordinary," Mr. Mason whispered. "The path spreads from wherever you touch it."

Lys sat on the cliff edge and put her other foot down. Ayden kept a hold of her hand as she shifted all of her weight on the new path.

"You okay?" Ayden asked.

She nodded. "Can you see it now?"

"I can see it," Ayden said. "It's growing, moving to the arch."

"I can see the whole thing." Lys let go of Ayden's hand and took a tentative step forward. The winding, rock path was just wide enough for two people to walk next to each other on. She leaned over the side, trying to see if it connected to the ground. As far as she could tell, it floated above the canyon floor, supported in only a few places by thin rock pillars that hadn't been there a moment before.

"Can everyone see that?" Mr. Mason asked.

"How is it there?" someone asked. "Is it an illusion?"

"No," Mr. Mason said. "It resides in the magical realm of this world. Physically it may not exist in ours."

Lys turned back and saw everyone looking at Mr. Mason with raised eyebrows or thoughtful scowls.

"Magical realm?" Genni voiced the question.

Mr. Mason nodded, studying the path below Lys' feet. "The two are together in the same place, but they do not use the same space."

"How can that be?" someone asked.

Mr. Mason shook his head. "I'm not sure. There are gates through which we can enter. Magic users of old would say they slipped into the magical realm. There are only a few places where it still exists so substantially. The outlets are some of them. More gates will return after we free the magic."

"Is it dangerous?" a man asked.

"No," Mr. Mason said. "As magic wielders, it should feel familiar to you."

"Can *we* walk on it?" Ayden asked, squinting down at the path.

Mr. Mason smiled at him. "Why don't you find out?"

* * *

281

Ayden took a deep breath and sat down on the edge of the cliff. Groping with his foot, he didn't let the air out of his lungs until his toe scraped the path. After a moment, he gingerly lowered the other foot and put all his weight on his legs. A smile spread across his face as he let go of the cliff wall.

"Feels solid."

"Good," Mr. Mason said, pointing at the group. "You two go first, put Lys right behind you."

Two men climbed down, one of them shaking a little. Lys and Ayden held on to them as they passed. The longer she stood on the path the more giddy the thin ribbon of magic that she had let out made her feel. She wanted to shut it off, but if the path disappeared for her, would anyone be able to see it? The last thing she wanted was to have everyone fall to their deaths because of her.

Lys felt someone take her hand from behind. Heights didn't really bother her, but she decided that she didn't mind the contact, even if the illusion that it would help her stay on the path was a lie. She reached out and took the trembling man's hand in front of her. He immediately clung on.

They moved slowly. Lys risked a glance back and found that the young girl with the hijab was walking right behind her. The rest of their party trailed along like a snake, winding on top of the rock ribbon. Druid Arch got steadily closer, even though the path took an indirect course.

Below the rock pillars rose, creating spikes that waited for someone to fall on them. Lys shook her head, trying to clear the image from her mind. No one would fall. They would all make it to the arch in one piece. Never mind the fissures—glowing gold—that spread across the path just ahead.

She started to warn everyone, but a cracking noise erupted in front of them. Before she knew it, the first man in the line

282

disappeared in a shower of rock chips. A huge chunk of the path followed.

"No!" Lys cried. Faster than she could follow, the man in front of her let go of her hand and lunged forward, catching his friend by the wrist. With super human strength he flung the other man over the gap, where he landed twenty feet away on his hands and feet, like a spider.

The rock kept crumbling, the edge coming toward Lys. The man in front of her backed up, herding Lys with his arms. "Move!" he yelled.

Lys bumped into the girl behind her. She felt the line jam up as they moved back.

"Toss them!" the man on the far side yelled.

Golden cracks appeared under Lys' feet, causing the stone to chip.

"It's still coming!" she said.

Before she could protest, the man had her by the waist. Lys left the ground and she flew through the air.

The moment Lys' feet lost contact with the path, it began to get fuzzy. Lys screamed, hurtling toward the touch user who was on the other side. He jumped, and the path became translucent. Lys expected a messy collision, but the man caught her gently.

Without a path they were all going to fall.

The man maneuvered Lys so her feet came down first, and the path solidified beneath Lys' feet. The man crashed down beside her, and they both went sprawling.

Lys rolled. Her legs dangled out over the air—she scrambled, trying to get a hand hold on something, anything. As fingers brushed the opposite edge of the path, Lys grabbed hold, lying with the top half of her body on the path and the other half in the air.

The man who saved her skidded to a stop—one hand holding firmly to the edge.

"Stay there," the man said to Lys.

More cracks appeared around Lys. The layered rock under her stomach crumbling.

"I don't think that's a good idea."

A terrified scream cut through the air. Lys' attention was drawn to the other half of the group. They'd backed up into a crowd, two people dangling off the edge and another being pulled up by Genni.

"Keep Lys on the path!" Mr. Mason bellowed. "Don't let her lose contact with it!"

That could be a problem, she decided. Each edge she touched started to give way under the pressure of her grip or her weight. She scrambled up until she had her knees on the narrow path. The touch user still dangled by one hand.

"Get behind me!" he said. "This section is going to collapse."

"But," Lys said, crawling toward him.

"I can get up, just get on the other side of me," he insisted. "Keep touching it."

Shaking so hard her head hurt, she went past the man. When she reached a spot where the path met a needle, she stopped and turned around.

The others had climbed up. The man with her now knelt on the stone, slowly backing toward her.

"Be ready to help people when they get here," he said.

"They're going to toss them?" Lys asked.

The question answered itself as Lys saw Ayden flying across the gap. Terror twisted his face, and his lips parted in a silent scream. The touch user stood and caught Ayden's arms and twirled him around like a little kid, setting him right in front of Lys.

Ayden teetered. Lys reached out and grabbed him, pulling him back. The next person sailed at them.

"How will the last person get across?" Lys asked, helping

284

Ayden steady Neil as he landed.

"Some of the touch users can jump pretty far." Ayden said noncommittally.

Lys watched in fascination as Genni—it took her a minute to figure out that the slight woman was the one tossing people—got everyone across. Lys kept stepping back, making room for people to land.

When everyone was across, Lys glanced over her shoulder. They didn't have far to go.

"We should get moving," Mr. Mason said.

"What about Genni?" Lys asked.

He shook his head. "She can't make that jump."

"We're just going to leave her?"

Mr. Mason frowned. "You have to enter the path through the gate. Once she leaves it, she won't be able to get back."

Genni stepped off the path and fell. Lys cried out, but Genni landed on the ground below with a gentle thud. She waved and yelled, "Good luck!"

Ayden waved back. Lys noticed that he looked worried.

"Come on," Mr. Mason said. "We need to get to that arch."

The remaining section of the path stayed stable. Lys and the others moved quickly toward Druid Arch. When they got within a hundred feet, Lys noticed the had arch changed. Before it looked two dimensional, practically flat. Now Lys thought it may have been an optical illusion, because the arch was no longer a squashed "M". It now resembled a tripod, with three legs that all came together at a blunt point, five hundred feet above them.

"The arch, it's changed," she said to Ayden.

He glanced up. "It doesn't look different to me. But you're the sight user."

Lys saw movement. From the shadows between the tripod legs four figures emerged. "There are people in there!"

"I see them," Ayden said, frowning.

The touch users in front of Lys tensed, and she saw one of them pull a small club out of their jacket.

"Hold on," one of the neutrals said. "They're with us. I can hear them." He added in explanation.

The figures waved. Ayden and a few others waved back.

"How did they get up here?" Lys asked.

"Mason sent a sight user with them," Ayden explained. "He wasn't sure what they were going to run into."

When Lys and the others reached the base of the arch, the four magic users helped them off the path and onto the roughly hewn rock stairs that led the rest of the way. Ayden exchanged a few words with one of the men about the collapsed path, but Lys didn't bother to listen. The towering stones had her full attention.

Standing at the base of the arch Lys felt like a familiar tug, like she'd spent time here as a kid, but she couldn't remember the details. The rocks shot into the sky—impressive in their own right. Dark streaks stained them, as if the stone itself wept. The smooth ground beneath the arch sloped gently down to a lower center point. Lys looked up and could see a small hole situated at the pinnacle. Well, it looked small from here, but the hole itself could be as wide as she was tall.

Gold tendrils of magic reached down from the hole, wrapped through the stone and continued to the ground. Once they reached the bowl, the vine-like magic followed the circumference of the depression, spiraling downward into the center.

She looked around in wonder. The magic ebbed through the stone, lapping at her feet like the ocean brushing a sandy beach. She could see every crack in the rocks and every ray of sunshine that penetrated the arch. The light seemed to linger in the arch, giving the entire scene an unearthly glow. The place felt alien, but it also felt like home.

"Alright everyone," Mr. Mason said. "Those I sent ahead only found four of the New here—good thing we learned a little bit about their suits. We know that there are plenty more on the way. The rest of you, keep your eyes open and keep the neutrals safe. Neutrals, drop your packs and get a drink. It's time."

Chapter 32

Lys didn't have much in her pack. She shrugged it off, hardly noticing the lightening of her load. The other neutrals did the same, setting their bags around the edge of the huge arch leg. Lys took another drink before placing the canteen on the ground. What happened next?

"I think you'll find your places around the bowl." Mr. Mason pointed.

Lys and Ayden stepped forward, toward the center of the depression. Being a sight user, Lys understood how she could see the magic embedded in this place, but she wondered what the others could see. Or if they felt the magic in their own sense, like Ayden talked about earlier.

"What are we looking for?" Ayden asked, addressing his question to Mr. Mason.

"You'll know it when you find it." Mr. Mason stood on the far side of the bowl, smiling at them.

"That means he doesn't know," Ayden muttered to Lys under his breath.

"Can you see the magic here?" she asked.

Ayden shook his head as they slowly walked around the bowl. "No, I can't see it, I can smell it."

"What does it smell like?" Lys made a face. For some reason she couldn't imagine that the raw energy she could see smelled very good.

Ayden stopped. He closed his eyes and inhaled. "It smells like power."

"It feels alive," the touch user said. He knelt down and stroked the stone with his hand. "Alive and excited."

"What does it look like?" Ayden asked.

Lys let the scene ingrain itself into her memory. "It's

beautiful," she said. "The magic is like vines made of light, wrapping around and going through the stones." She pointed. "I think it starts in the bowl and goes up through to the top."

The magic pulsed and Lys saw what they were looking for. "Right there," she pointed. "Ayden, I can see the symbol of an eye, just like in the book." Lys walked over and stood on the eye. The magic surged beneath her, tickling the souls of her feet.

Ayden moved to the spot on Lys' right and stopped. "Oh yeah, I can sense that now."

The young girl moved on the other side of Lys. She stood silently, waiting. Lys could see the symbol of an ear right in front of her feet.

They gathered close to the center of the bowl. Close enough to reach out and touch fingers. The other two found their places. They waited.

Mr. Mason moved in, circling them.

"Join hands," he said. "Be prepared to keep tight control on your magic. It will use you as a channel."

Lys felt a lump form in her throat. Could she keep control over her magic? The tiny stream seemed manageable, sort-of, but if they needed more she didn't know what would happen. She took a breath and reminded herself that she wanted this. This would help a lot of people, including her and her mother and any other innocent magic users that the New would hunt and kill.

Slowly, the five around the circle joined hands. As soon as the last two hands touched, Lys felt a surge of power—like the revving of a big engine in a truck—go through her body. Her mind tingled and she blinked as her sight went first fuzzy and then brighter than the sun reflecting off the ocean. The light from the bottom of the bowl increased in intensity. Lys could just make out an intricate symbol that resembled a tree carved into the rock.

"Don't break the circle." Mr. Mason ordered. "Can everyone sense the symbol in the middle?" They nodded. "Good, now try to reach out with your magic. Focus on the symbol."

Lys had to close her eyes. The light made it impossible for her to concentrate. Even behind her eyelids, Lys could see the flickering magic. She took a deep breath and doubled the size of the hole in her board. More wanted to come, pressing against the barrier.

"Neil, Lys, we're not balanced, I need more from you," Mr. Mason said.

Nothing got done if you never tried anything, right? Lys took another breath and doubled the size of the hole again.

Images exploded in her mind. The brightest came from the people watching her. Different perspectives overlapped, and Lys could see herself from almost every angle. For the first time she, felt like she could handle it. It could be because of their scant numbers. Maybe she could do this.

A crack appeared in her board. It started at the hole and ripped through the void, releasing a river of magic that Lys was helpless to contain. Thousands more images filled her mind, some of them so alien that she wanted to scream. This time she knew she was seeing through the eyes of animals, bugs, birds or whatever was close. Colors she'd never seen came with some of the perspectives, along with images she couldn't understand at all. Some showed her only darkness.

"That's better," Mr. Mason said.

She had to stay like this? Lys didn't believe she could. The magic roared in her ears and burned her closed eyes. Her mind wouldn't be able to keep up for long—this would drive her insane.

"When you get in balance, concentrate on that symbol."

Balance? There was no balance here! Lys wanted to tell him, but her lips wouldn't respond.

"Redirect it," Ayden said.

Lys pressed her lips together and concentrated on the magic beneath her. She thought back to Mark's lesson and tried to redirect her magic through those vines and into the symbol in the stone. She opened her eyes. The light around her flashed as her magic bent—the tendrils flaring as they inherited more power. The stone pulsed, matching Lys' beating heart.

"Good," Mr. Mason said after a moment. "Now concentrate on that symbol, and pull."

The words didn't make sense, but Lys knew what to do. She reached out through the streams of magic and sunk into the symbol, like sticking her hand into a bowl of cookie dough and squeezing. The plug shuddered as the others did the same. They pulled, tearing the stone apart and flinging the pieces aside.

Lys expected the plug to be gone. The only symbol she'd seen in the book was the tree. But beneath that lay the scrawl of runes and the representation of a tongue.

Neil, the taste user furrowed his brow and closed his eyes. The vines of energy beneath him started to get brighter, and a moment later a halo of golden energy surrounded him.

"Do it," Mr. Mason said.

Neil nodded but didn't open his eyes. His skin started to glow and his hair stirred, as if a breeze had wandered through the arch. Lys tore her eyes away and glanced down at the runes. Tiny cracks appeared, expanding as if the stone itself were drying out and crumbling to dust. The breeze picked up, turning into a gale force wind. The remnants of the plug got caught up and carried away like leafs in the fall. Neil sagged, and if not for the others holding onto him he may have gone to the ground. Sweat beaded his brow, and his swirling, golden eyes looked hollow—almost dead.

Below the taste runes lay the symbol of an ear. Sound. Lys shifted her feet and glanced around. Did they each get a layer? What was she supposed to do when her turn came?

Mr. Mason walked around the circle and stopped behind the young girl. "You can do this."

She nodded, and Lys felt the girl's grip tighten.

Lys watched in fascination as the vines between the girl and the plug pulsed with the thrum of magic. Like blood through veins, the power diverted to the girl, and like the man before her, she started to glow. The effect was beautiful, but as Lys' fingers got crushed beneath the girls grip, she was sure that whatever was happening to the girl was not pleasant.

"A little more," Mr. Mason said.

The girl started to tremble. Lys could feel raw power building beside her, and had to force herself to stay in her spot. The song from the magic called to her, and Lys wasn't sure she could resist.

We shouldn't do this, a voice said in Lys' head.

Mr. Mason stepped closer to the girl, his lips just inches from her ear. For moment he said nothing, just stood there. The girl shook her head once before she stiffened. Then opened her eyes and nodded.

"Do it," Mr. Mason said.

A sonic boom—at least that's the only way Lys could describe it—emanated from the outlet. It rocked the very air around them, and the plug shattered into a million pieces, too small to see anymore.

The glow around the girl faded, and she stumbled.

"Keep her up," Mr. Mason said to the others.

Lys hardly heard him. Instead she stood staring down at the plug. Despite the water she'd just drunk, Lys' mouth went dry, and her heart missed a beat or two.

An eye. The symbol of an eye surrounded by more runes sat carved in the stone at her feet.

What was she supposed to do?

"Lys," Mr. Mason said, now behind her. "You need to take all the magic from the plug into yourself, then release it. That will break the seal."

Take it in? Release it? Lys shook her head. This didn't sound like a good idea.

Without warning, the power started toward her. The magic streams shifted, and the ones coming in her direction got brighter. She watched without breathing as the first wave reached out for her feet.

Lys already felt like a water bottle with a hole in the bottom. The magic she'd been channeling poured through her, and she didn't think she could handle much more.

"Do not release it," Mr. Mason said in her ear. "Let it build up inside of you."

Lys' throat closed, and she swallowed hard as she looked around. Everyone but the girl beside her was watching her, waiting. The young girl had her head down, and Lys thought she might be crying.

The magic forced her to act before she wanted to. It blasted through her body like a bullet. Out of reflex she shut down the outlet she'd been holding open. Golden power started to fill her from the souls of her feet, up to her knees and then her hips. It felt a thousand times stronger than a roaring sugar high. Lys couldn't stop shaking, and part of her didn't want to. It felt so good!

There weren't words or thoughts to describe it. Satisfying the need—the frog's eyes—paled in comparison, like the light and warmth of a match versus the blazing sun beating down on you in the desert. Every bit of her body tingled in pleasure and joy. Kamau's kiss couldn't ignite one nerve ending like this did. She was on fire, but the burning caused pure ecstasy.

"Keep taking it in," Mr. Mason's voice said from about a hundred miles away.

Lys didn't much care what he said, all she cared about was how she felt. How much power she had! She closed her eyes and reveled in it flowing through her veins alongside her blood, as if it should have been there all along. Mark had said that magic was part of her, and now she believed him.

Up through her chest, then down her arms and to her fingertips, the magic filled her to capacity. Lys felt her skin start to tighten up, like a balloon right before it burst from too much pressure.

"A little more," Mr. Mason said.

Lys would take all that the magic would give her. Her scalp tingled as the last unoccupied space filled with magic. The world around her sang.

"Now, release it," Mr. Mason said.

Release it? Lys shook her head.

"Release it before it consumes you," Mr. Mason said.

Lys didn't care if the magic consumed her. That sounded like a great idea.

"Do it now," he said.

The smell of her house filled her nostrils. It got past the song and poked a part of her brain that still cared about something besides magic. Memories of her parents, her friends and growing up flashed through her mind.

"If you want to see them again, you need to release it."

Dark thoughts of her parents being hurt or her friends dying—nightmares she'd had as a kid—flew at her, and Lys mentally shook herself, putting some distance between her and the magic.

She could still see through the others' eyes, and Lys found herself glowing twice as bright as either the taste user or the young girl. More images of fear kept her lucid, and Lys looked for a place to punch a hole in herself.

At first she couldn't find a spot—her skin providing a barrier stronger than rock or steel. Panic started to set in as her heart throbbed in her chest. Her chest. Lys concentrated on her belly button and wormed her way through until she found a thin spot. With all of her mental might, she threw herself at the weaken bit. The first attempt failed, and she bounced back.

The magic continued to fill her, and Lys could feel her body and spirit becoming overloaded. She tried again, ramming the spot as hard as she could. It cracked, but did not break.

She conjured up a wicked looking knife. It dropped into her hand, she took a proverbial breath and stabbed the spot, ripping through it like a pirate did with a sail. The knife penetrated the wall, and Lys pulled it down, releasing all of the magic she could, straight out her belly button.

The plug burst apart, the remnants rising up and through the top of the arch.

The rune disappeared, as did all sense of sanity.

Lys no longer only saw through the eyes of those close to her; now she could see everything. She didn't know how, but she knew that's what it was. The world lay around her, above her, below her and inside of her. She saw families having picnics at the park, soldiers fighting in the jungle, people working in cities and farmers tilling their fields.

Magic, the light from the portal, overwhelmed the world. She saw it come from all directions, touching everyone, leaving nothing unaffected in its wake. Lys tried to cry out, to warn them, but she had no voice. Only her eyes. She was forced to watch.

A man in Tokyo fell to his knees, screaming and writhing. The eyes Lys saw through ran toward him. The man looked up, his face contorted in anguish. His eyes swirled black. Lys' perspective changed. She now watched a little boy running toward his father, who held out his arms to keep the boy away. Magic flamed from his hands, cutting everything they were pointed at in two, including the little boy.

The scene changed. A man with a camera in a helicopter watched as a woman ran up the side of a volcano. Every step she took left behind puddles of molten lava. When she looked up at the camera, Lys saw that her eyes were churning, burning red. The woman tore her gaze from the helicopter and threw herself into the volcano. Before they could get out of the way, a geyser of lava as big as a sky scraper engulfed the helicopter and everyone on board.

Another place. Lys recognized it as the smoldering ruins of Los Angeles. Below her sat a little girl, all alone in the middle of the street. She knew this dream. Only now she understood. This wasn't a dream. It was real. The little girl looked up, revealing her oily, black eyes.

Touch users. So many broke at once that the world broke too, leaving nothing but pain and terror behind. Military and governments no longer had power. Now the touch users had control. They fought one another. Some of them tried to help others, but most just wanted more power, more magic. They used until they killed their perceived enemies, then they died. One man was everywhere, his sapphire blue eyes swirling. His influence was that of a god, and he used it to send the world into further chaos. She saw his face and screamed.

The sound jerked Lys back into her own awareness.

"Keep the circle closed," Mr. Mason's voice said. "Ayden, this one is yours."

Lys didn't want to open her eyes, afraid that she would find the world destroyed.

"Is she going to be okay?" Ayden asked.

"She's fine," Mr. Mason said. "We need to finish this."

Finish it? Lys forced her eyes open and found herself on her knees, still holding onto Ayden's and the young girl's hands. It took a moment for the wall of perspectives to resolve into a half dozen or so. Lys was still at the arch. They hadn't finished the ritual.

They could stop it. They could stop the future that she'd just witnessed.

"Don't," she said, the words coming out as a raspy whisper. She looked up at Ayden. "Please, don't do this."

A golden glow already surrounded Ayden, but he looked down at her. "What?"

Tears poured from her eyes. "If we finish this, it will destroy the world."

Ayden narrowed his eyes. Lys could see the elation there from the magic, but somehow he had more control than she did. "What do you mean?" he asked.

Mr. Mason stepped over Lys and Ayden's arms, going inside the circle. "She's crashing," he said. "We have to finish this now." He moved between Ayden and the plug. "Do it, now."

Rage cut through her fog. "I know what I saw." She clenched her teeth together. "If we do this, the world ends."

"The world will not end." Mr. Mason's eyes went from their brilliant blue to a swirling pool of sapphires. "You will all finish this, now."

Those eyes! She'd seen those eyes in her vision. Mr. Mason was the man controlling the world.

"It's you." Lys said, leaning back. "You're the one who—"

"Finish it," Mr. Mason interrupted. The words obliterated Lys' conviction.

When Lys heard Kamau influence the gas station clerk with his voice, Kamau had been smooth and evocative. Leading, guiding and suggesting rather than forcing. Lys never considered the possibility that he could impose his will on anyone. Maybe he couldn't do it with sound.

Apparently Mr. Mason could. Obligation overran Lys' emotions. More memories of her family and friends surfaced— smells from her house, school and growing up coming through her nose—but so did the irrational fear that they would all die. She didn't want to do this, but her emotions had control, and Mason must have control of them, because Lys couldn't find the courage

297

or energy to resist.

Beside her, Ayden stiffened. He nodded, and Lys felt the power in him gathering. Mr. Mason put a hand on each of Ayden's shoulders. The power spiked, light spilled out of Ayden's mouth, but instead of going to the plug and the runes—which cracked but did not break—most of it went into Mr. Mason.

Lys didn't know what the others could sense, but with sight magic Lys could see the golden power fill Mason. Only he didn't let it go. Instead, once the transfer was complete, he stumbled back, now glowing like Ayden had been.

The hold Mason had on her mind stuttered, and Lys used every bit of will power she had left to wrench her hand free of Ayden's.

The young girl next to her jerked her hand out of Lys'. As she did so, her hijab fell away, revealing who could only be Kamau's sister underneath. Mason had had her all along.

Ayden fell to his knees, watching Mr. Mason. "What have you done?" Ayden asked, fear in his eyes. "We're supposed to be freeing the magic."

Mr. Mason laughed. "That's right, son. Soon I will have more magic than anyone else has ever had."

Lys looked between the two men. Son?

More perspectives blossomed in her head, revealing the black-clad figures of the New, a moment before they attacked.

Chapter 33

A dozen of the New along with Mark, Inez, Brady, Peter, Kamau and a handful of other magic users appeared. Lys could see everything at once. The New, in their black body armor, trying to net the magic users. Mark appeared behind the touch user in the circle. Blue light flashed, and the man fell to the ground. Brady faced off with two of Mason's users. He started throwing rocks that Peter gave him. Lys could see Inez's magic—red and jagged—leaving her hands as she pointed at other users. Two of them went immediately to their knees. The others got caught by Brady's rocks right before he flung them off the cliff using his towel trick. Kamau ran to his sister as Ayden reached out to his father, who now stood in the middle of the cracked runes, bathing in the power.

Faster than Lys could make out, one of the touch users snatched Mason from the bowl and spirited him away.

"Where is he going?" one of the New asked Lys.

"The path," she said, pointing.

Six users joined Mason. Lys could just make them out through the blinding light coming from the outlet. Mason and the others ran toward the entrance to the path. They were going to get away.

Five members of the New, along with Brady, Peter and Inez advanced on them. Mason's sound user opened his mouth, and two of the touch users held their hands out in front of them. A wave of pain hit Lys like a truck, causing her to double over.

Mason. The man from the end of the world. They couldn't let him get away.

She scrambled to her hands and knees. To her horror, she saw Mason being tossed into the air like a rag doll. He arched far along the path only to be caught by a touch user. A moment later they were all gone. Several of the magic users, and four of the New, went after them.

Chaos erupted around Lys. The people with the New yelled back and forth, trying to figure out if they could re-plug the outlet. Kamau held his crying sister in his arms. Inez and Peter tried to help a struggling Brady to his feet, but the magic, which had started to latch onto people like clinging rose vines, had him so entwined that he could hardly move. Lys tried to stand but couldn't. So instead she scooted along the ground until she reached Ayden. He hadn't moved since Mason had been swept away.

"Ayden?" she asked. He sat staring after the retreating form of his father. "Ayden, we have to plug this back up."

He slowly shook his head. "We don't have the right people." He turned to look at her. "And even if we did, I'm not sure we could do it. Can you do that again?" Pain filled his swirling, golden eyes.

Lys turned to the seal. "We have to try."

"I can't even move," Ayden said.

"That magic is going crazy," she said. Bits of stone kept breaking off and rising to the top of the arch in the fountain of power.

The crash hit her without warning. She gasped, and the magic pulled her down, hitting the ground with a hollow thump. The abyss within her opened up, dark and inviting. It whispered for her to become one with it. The world was going to end anyway, she didn't want to be around for that.

Fear dissipated, only to be replaced by defeat. What could she do to help? She only wanted one thing—to be erased from the universe. Maybe if she had never existed she would be able to stop feeling pain and loss. The darkness began to intertwine with the magic. Part of her burned from heat and the other from cold. Her mouth went dry, and she could taste death. At some point she must have closed her eyes, because black engulfed her. Not even overlapping images or the sight of a destroyed world came into her mind. The darkness called to her, enticed her and promised that it would be more kind than the world she would leave behind. She believed it.

"*Lysandra.*"

The voice came from the darkness. No, it came through the darkness.

"*Lysandra, don't leave us.*"

She didn't recognize the voice; it belonged to a young woman.

But I want to go, Lys said in her mind. I just want to rest.

"*We need you,*" the voice insisted. "*Kamau needs you.*"

Kamau? The name hardly meant anything to her. Nothing did.

"*I think he likes you,*" the voice said. "*He'll be sad if you leave us.*"

Likes me? Lys tried to concentrate, no easy task with the darkness blocking out the light. Kamau. A pair of dark eyes appeared, then a smile. She could see him, but he betrayed her.

"Lys," a deeper voice prompted. "Stay with us."

The sound brought her back. It cut through the dark like lightning, leaving Lys an escape route. She mentally propelled herself toward the opening, reaching for what lay beyond.

Gasping, Lys opened her eyes. She lay on the hard stone, her head in Kamau's lap with his sister holding her hand. Cold still filled her, and Lys started to shake.

I told you we could get her back. The words came from Kamau's sister, only Lys heard them in her mind.

Kamau smiled in relief. "Are you alright?"

Lys sat up, shaking and dizzy. The magic in the rocks beneath her began again to twine up her arms and legs. Before it grabbed her, Lys rose shakily to her feet. The runes, were they gone?

Please don't let them be gone, Lys thought.

"Lys!" Kamau said, following her. "What are you doing?"

She didn't answer. She lurched over to the plug, and stopped. More than half of the rune pattern had been blown away. The magic leaked out through the missing chunks.

"Lys," Kamau said again, coming up next to her. "We need to get out of here." His hand brushed her arm. She wanted to bury her face in his shoulder, but instead she turned away. She couldn't think about him—about them—now. Her eyes found his sister. Maybe she would understand.

"We can't leave it like this," Lys said. "It will destroy everything."

The girl nodded.

"We don't have the right people to stop it," Kamau argued. "And the New can't do it." He waved a hand, and Lys saw that the New had retreated, back beyond the arch.

"Kamau," Lys looked into his eyes. She didn't know what she felt for him, or which side he worked for, but he was a decent person, and surely he didn't want to world destroyed. "We have to try." A tear trickled down her cheek. "Everyone will die if we don't. I saw the future. If this thing blows all of the touch users in the world will break at once."

Kamau frowned down at her.

She's right. Kamau's sister's voice came in her mind again.

"But we don't have a taste or a touch user," this was Ayden, who walked over to them.

"I'm a touch user." They all turned to see Peter and Inez dragging Brady toward them. The magic had Brady encased like a second layer of clothes. "And Inez here is a taste user."

"But you're not neutrals," Ayden insisted.

Brady shrugged. "We could try, or we could leave." He looked at Lys. "But if what she just said is true, if she saw the future, and all of the touch users break at once, leaving is pointless."

"You really saw the future?" Inez asked.

Lys nodded.

"Will you help us?" Brady asked Inez. He held her hand.

Inez looked first at the leaking magic—Lys wondered if Inez

could even see it—and then at Brady. "Why?"

"Why?" Brady raised his eyebrows. "Because even though this world can be terrible, that doesn't mean it should end. Not like this."

Inez gazed at him for a moment before her eyes turned to Peter. A tiny smile tugged at the corner of her mouth; then she looked over at Lys. "You're going to try?"

Lys nodded. "Yes."

"And you?" She directed this question to Ayden. "Why would you help us? Aren't you still with your daddy?"

Ayden shook his head. "It wasn't supposed to happen like this," he said softly. "My brother was a smell user, just like Mason and I. When he broke—he was just seven years old—he never came out of it." He stopped, taking a deep breath. "We had to kill him. No one else was supposed to have to go through it like that. That's why we...at least that's why I thought we were doing all of this." He glanced around at each of them. "I guess I was wrong."

Mark appeared in the circle. "Why don't you let me do it?" he asked, looking at Brady.

In her mind's eye, Lys could see the book from Mason's library. The five magic users. The fighting. The one that was saved.

"Brady has to do it," Lys said. Everyone looked at her. "Because we need a healer."

"A healer?" Mark asked. "How do you know?" His gaze bore into Lys.

"I saw it," she said, "in Mason's book. In the scene I saw the touch user heal one of the others."

Ayden and Mark exchanged an eyebrow-raised glance.

"You didn't see it?" Lys asked, a lump rising in her throat.

Brady bent down and placed his fingertips on the pulsing stone. He closed his eyes. "I can feel it," he said. His eyebrows furrowed together. "I can feel the cracks like Mark's leg." Eyes opening, Brady looked at Lys. "I think I can fix it."

A burst of magic forced them all to flinch away. Lys saw another chunk of the runes disappear.

"If we're going to try, we need to do it now," she said. "The plug is almost gone."

"I will do it," Kamau said, looking at his sister. She shook her head. Neither spoke, but after a moment Kamau nodded. "Please, be careful."

The girl stepped forward and took Lys' hand. She held out her other hand for Inez. Inez accepted and Brady gave her a quick peck on the cheek. Lys saw the other girl smile. Why was it that in the midst of saving the world that she would be so happy for those two? Lys felt Kamau's fingers squeeze her shoulder as she took Ayden's hand.

Mark and Peter stepped back, and the moment the others got into position and linked, Lys felt an even more overwhelming force assault her than before. The magic felt more demanding this time. Like the Need and the frog—a primal instinct, and something she wasn't sure she could control.

Inez gasped and Brady stood stunned for a few seconds.

"Try to balance the magic," Lys said.

"Balance?" Inez asked, her voice strained. "You want me to balance this?"

Whereas before the magic had been beautiful, now it was flaring and pulsing. The vine-like tendrils jerked back and forth, writhing like snakes. Even the golden light changed, turning more brown.

Ayden spoke. "Brady has a lot of extra power. Try to dial it back a bit kid, and the rest of us will have to let it loose."

Let it loose?

You can control it. The words came in Lys' mind—Kamau's sister again.

Lys wondered how the girl spoke directly into her thoughts,

but didn't ask. She didn't believe the words anyway. She couldn't resist the pull. If she had to go in again, Lys knew she wouldn't come back out. She wished she could tell her parents she loved them one last time.

Before she could change her mind, Lys obliterated the wall holding her magic back. Power rushed through her body like a song. Every nerve ending tingled, and her senses exploded. She felt like she was glowing brighter than the sun.

"This first one is mine," Ayden said. His voice came as a surprise. Lys had almost forgotten their purpose.

Lys watched Ayden's face as magic that had been shot through the top of the arch got pulled back and into him. The glow returned, now angry brown instead of golden. Ayden's features contorted in pain and anguish. His hand clamped down around Lys', and sweat trickled down from his hair.

"What did they look like?" he asked in a raspy voice. "The runes," he said, looking at Lys.

Lys found that she could recall the symbols with exactly clarity. She fixed them in her mind and did her best to infuse them into the stream of magic. It must have worked, because he closed his eyes and shot the magic from his body back into the plug.

In an almost reversal of what had happened a few minutes before, the chunks of stone dropped from the magical fountain, back onto the plug. The stones glowed red hot for a moment, looking like cooling lava, before the runes resealed, and the symbol of a nose settled in place.

Ayden went to his knees, but his hands did not let go.

"You're next," he said, looking up at Lys.

In her whole life, she never imagined that she would be called upon to bear a burden such as this. She remembered all to clearly the way the magic made her feel as she pulled the plug, and Lys was certain that she would not be able to go through it again. Not and be sane afterward.

As she closed her eyes, she silently said goodbye to her life, her family and all that she held dear. The magic would consume her, leaving nothing behind but want and need. But if the rest of the world could go on, she would do it.

Lys called the magic back to her. The flow from the arch slowed, and as she continued to pull, it reversed directions. Power started to fill her, and it took only a few seconds before she once again felt like a balloon about to pop.

The thought of letting it go hurt more than Kamau's betrayal had. Her stomach wrenched inside of her body, and tears poured down her cheeks.

"Do it," Ayden said.

Lys let the power linger for a split second, before she shoved it back at the plug, putting the image of what the symbols looked like with the magic.

A stream of magic shot from her and hit the plug like a fist against a board. The runes reappeared, as did the stone, and a moment later, her part was done.

As soon as the last of the power left her, Lys knew why people killed themselves. Not one scrap of happiness, light or hope remained in her.

"Just let me die," she said in a whisper as she too went to her knees.

"Sound is next," Ayden said, his voice hollow. Lys wondered how he could keep going if he felt anything like she did.

"I am ready," Kamau's sister said.

Lys knelt on the ground. Her head weighed a ton, and her eyeballs would barely swivel to look at Kamau's sister's feet.

"You have to hold on," Kamau's voice said in Lys' ear. "You must help them finish."

Lys didn't even have the energy to shake her head, or tell him to leave her alone. He didn't understand. How could he? He'd never really been affected by the crashes.

"Lys," Ayden said. "The runes."

Allowing her hundred pound eyelids to close, Lys pulled up the mental picture of the sound symbols and infused them into the magic that burst from Kamau's sister toward the bowl.

It must have worked, because Ayden said, "Inez, you're up. Can you feel the taste magic?"

Inez muttered under her breath.

"Draw it back to you."

Lys opened her eyes and forced her head up so she could look across at Inez. The other girl stood wide-eyed with her lips pressed together. Jagged, dark magic rained down on her from above, almost like lightning strikes.

"How much of this do I have to take in?" Inez asked, gasping for breath.

"Until there's no more," Ayden said.

Inez shook her head, but gritted her teeth. More magic came back to her, and she started to glow red.

"Lys," Ayden said.

Lys didn't care if they won. She didn't care about anything but being filled with magic again.

"Be strong," Kamau said in her ear. "You have to finish this."

Irritation caused her to shoot the symbols into the magic for Inez. How dare Kamau betray her, come back and think that he could use his magic on her. Not only that, she could feel his body heat, as if he stood within inches of her.

"Leave me alone," she managed to say.

He didn't get a chance to retort. The magic surged beneath their feet, shocking Lys back toward normalcy. Before her, the plug bowed up, like someone was pushing on it from under the ground.

The surge cleared Lys' head enough so she could think. She remembered the scene she saw from the book. "Everyone hold their part."

"Not sure how long that will last," Inez said.

Lys looked over at Brady. "You have to use touch to seal it," she said. "Can you do it?"

He nodded, his long, pale face already covered in sweat. Lys recalled how hard it had been for him to control his magic before this. She bit her lip as he closed his eyes.

The ground rumbled, and Lys saw rivers of magic being pulled back through the arch and into Brady. She felt her own magic spark back to life, and the oppressive emptiness retreated a step. In her mind, images of everything around her filled the wall of television sets. Once again, some were her, others showed her the world as it was now, and yet others whispered of a new future, where no one blew up volcanoes.

"Hold the plugs." Brady said, his voice rich and deep, like he belonged with the ancient stones. "Just a few more seconds." He glowed like a spectral ghost. The light from the seal now looked like it resided inside of Brady. The magic swirled around him in oily, black clouds, attached to him with tendrils of golden light from the plug.

Lys pulled her attention from the images in her mind and turned it toward the sight plug. The energy beneath it tried to throw off the seal, but Lys held it firm, using pure willpower to keep it from breaking.

"That's it, almost there," Brady said.

One perspective from her mind drew her attention. Lys saw them all at the arch, just like they were now. But she saw herself from behind. She stood, yanking Kamau's sister up with her. Brady pulled away from the others. Inez yelled something. Brady shook his head, smiled and threw himself onto the plug.

Sounds from the here and now filled her ears.

"Brady? What are you doing?" Inez asked, the pitch of her voice rising.

"I can't stop. Not now. I need the magic. You know how it

feels."

Lys knew how it felt—the elation followed by the dark abyss. To have everything and then feel like you have nothing. It was too much.

"Please," Inez said through a sob. "Please. Try to stop."

"I can't. I want to keep it, and if I give it up, I'll always want it back. I told you I could fix it, I just didn't mention that I would die."

Lys' eyes shot open. She stood, pulling the young girl beside her to her feet. "No!" Lys shouted, realizing that she'd seen the future a moment before.

Brady yanked his hands free, his body still pulsing with power.

"What are you doing?" Inez asked, grabbing for his hand.

Brady shook his head and smiled. "I love you. Remember that."

Before anyone could move, Brady stepped into the hole.

Chapter 34

"No!" Inez screamed, reaching for Brady, but he was gone. For a moment nothing happened, then a force like the wind, only made of energy and magic, shot straight up from the outlet. It flowed through the hole at the apex of the arch, filling the sky, strangling the magic already there. The edges of the outlet began to crackle and spider web.

"Get back!" Ayden yelled to Inez.

Inez didn't move. She looked into the outlet, tears streaming down her face. "No," she said again.

The flow of magic slowed and the crawling vines dimmed. The light pulsed through the tendrils, but it began to wane. When the magic holding her to the ground ebbed, and Lys fell to her hands and knees.

"Brady," Inez cried, rushing forward. Ayden proved to be faster. He grabbed her, not allowing her near the plug.

Lys crawled. She had to see. The runes had filled in. The top layer reforming as the pieces gathered back to the plug. A great wind blew straight down from above, and Lys saw the magic returning. Golden trails in the sky retraced their path back to the arch. She watched as the magic squeezed through the gaps in the plug. As the top reformed, there were tiny spots that didn't seal.

The runes settled in place. The tree symbol reappeared in the bottom of the bowl. The magic stopped. Silence descended.

"Did he do it?" Kamau asked.

She turned to look at him, finding his sister at his side. "I don't know. I think so." She didn't know what the tiny cracks meant. Maybe nothing. Maybe everything.

Lys felt Kamau's fingers reach for hers, but she couldn't take his hand. She managed a weak smile.

Mark, who appeared beside Inez, wrapped her in a hug as she

sunk to her knees. "I'm so sorry," he whispered in a choked voice. Inez continued to cry. Eventually she grabbed Mark and clung to him. Peter crawled over, hugging Inez with tears streaming down his face.

Kamau's sister moved around Lys and took her other hand. A slight smile creased her exhausted face.

Lys had so many questions, but she didn't want to ask them. She didn't want to think about what just happened, nor did she want to think about what would happen later.

"Lys," Kamau said, "this is my younger sister, Damisi. She has some very unique abilities."

Didn't they all? Lys smiled down at the girl, but she had nothing of substance to say. "It's nice to meet you."

Damisi's voice came in her head again. *You and Kamau make a good couple.*

Lys didn't want to think about Kamau either, but she felt herself blush despite all she had been through in the last few days.

"Damisi." Kamau's voice was serious.

"Thank you for coming for me," she said to her brother, this time aloud.

"Mother was upset."

Lys sensed a story, but again, she didn't want to talk. An emptiness filled her—a black hole that sucked her will away. Magic, Brady, her vision of the future. All these things combined into a puzzle that Lys couldn't put together. The longing for magic lay inside of her, almost as powerful as her need, but right now exhaustion washed over her, allowing her to ignore it. The loss of Brady broke away the barriers around her heart. She could hear Inez still sobbing into Mark's shoulder, and Lys knew that Inez had to be suffering even more. She let go of Kamau's and Damisi's hands and stumbled over to Inez.

"I'm so sorry." Lys didn't have anything else to say. She reached up and stroked the other girls' hair.

"He's gone," Inez said, the words muffled by Mark's shoulder.

"He's gone." Lys repeated the words as her heart broke. Could she have stopped him?

It was too much. Lys felt herself fading. She lurched to the side, barely catching herself with her hands.

"Lys!" Kamau was there immediately.

"Sorry," she whispered. "I think I'm done."

Chapter 35

She woke to the soft murmur of voices. Cool, fresh air filled her nostrils. When Lys opened her eyes, darkness greeted her.

Darkness! Where was she? Panic forced her into a sitting position, her hand reaching out in front of her. To her relief, her fingers came into view, but they were blurred, and everything around her lurked behind a black curtain. What did the magic do to her?

Magic. Once a word symbolic of wonder: Princesses, castles, wizards, knights, unicorns, love...now Lys felt a heavy weight inside of her—the word magic a curse. She lay back down, pulling a sleeping bag up to her chin.

"Lys?" Inez's voice asked. She turned her head to find Inez lying across from her. "Are you okay?"

"Yeah." The image of Brady stepping into the hole caused a lump to form in Lys' throat—what could she say? "Where are we?" Inez would kill her if she knew Lys had known what Brady was going to do. She asked herself again if she could have stopped him.

"Some campsite in the desert." Inez sat up, pulling the sleeping bag tight around her.

"What about Mason?" Lys propped herself up on one elbow facing Inez.

"He got away, those guys from the New went after him."

Should she be rooting for the New? Did they still plan to kill her when they got the chance?

"I kind of hope they catch him," Inez said.

Lys nodded, her mind returning to the events at the arch. "I'm sorry I collapsed. Not much of a help." Lys looked away.

"Kamau brought you back."

Silence descended. The mention of Kamau turned Lys to

another subject she didn't wanted to think about. Kamau had betrayed her, betrayed them. But then he saved them. Lys didn't know if there were good guys and bad guys anymore.

That thought brought Lys to who really saved them. "I'm sorry about Brady," she said.

Inez nodded. "He did it to save us." Her voice cracked. "Why would he do something so stupid?"

"Because he's a hero. Because of the magic. Because he loved you."

"Don't say he did it just for me!" Inez said, quickly wiping a tear away.

Lys shrugged. "He cared about people. He did it because he loved you and wanted to save everyone." It was a good answer. A true answer, but not the only answer. The other part of the answer included magic and being able to live without all that power. Lys shook her head. "What time is it?"

"It has to be almost morning." Inez shifted in her sleeping bag.

"Did everything happen yesterday?" Lys hoped she hadn't missed several days.

"Yes."

Lys considered her magic. "Do you feel," Lys paused. "Empty?"

"Yeah."

The past week felt like it had been a year long. First Mason at the hospital, the recovery facility, the New. "You guys showed up with the New," Lys said. "What happened? Did they have Peter?"

Inez nodded. "They used Peter to track us. After they got you out of camp, Kamau explained things to, what's his name? The guy with the red hair?"

"Doyle?" Lys ventured.

"That's him. Kamau explained Mason's plan. He said you told him." Inez raised her eyebrows.

314

"I did tell him," Lys said. "Right after I talked to Mason. Right before we found you."

"Doyle told everyone Mason's plan. He explained that opening the outlets would cause an imbalance, or something. He asked for volunteers to go and stop Mason." She grinned for a second. "Naturally I said I would help."

"How did you convince Mark to come?"

"He decided to come on his own," Inez said. "Six or seven users came with us."

Lys tried to digest this. "But don't the New kill magic users?"

"They do." Inez shrugged. "But you know, the enemy of my enemy and all that. At least they didn't kill Peter."

"I'm glad he's okay." Lys smiled. She could feel Inez's pain and joy through her words.

"Me too."

A rustling from outside startled Lys. "You girls up? Why don't you come out and help us with breakfast? Everyone else is awake." Ayden's voice came through the tent, his usual joviality gone, replaced by a beaten down tone that made Lys sad.

Lys looked at Inez and they pulled themselves out of their sleeping bags. Their boots sat near the door, and Lys took her time lacing hers up. Inez sighed and Lys unzipped the door. Crisp, morning air greeted them, and after Inez helped her out of the tent they both stood with their arms wrapped around their stomachs, teeth chattering.

"Here." Ayden handed them each a hooded jacket. "These were in the van."

"Thanks." Lys took the jacket and pulled it on over her clothes.

"Kamau is working on a fire. Come help us cook."

She didn't really cook, but it might be good to have something to do. Something to keep her mind off of Brady, magic, and death.

A handful of people from the cabin stood a little way from the fire, talking to Mark in low voices. Kamau and his sister coaxed a blaze from the fire pit just as Lys and Inez walked over.

A dull gray hovered in the air, waiting for the sunrise to burn it away. They were still in the desert, surrounded by the Needles. Each step she took on the rocks sounded like a stampede. The silence made Lys believe that they could be the last people left in the world.

Kamau stood as they approached. He had a bucket in each hand. "We need some more water for breakfast." He met Lys' eyes. "Would you like to help me?"

Not the smoothest get away line in the world, but it would have to do. Lys took one of the buckets. "Sure."

They walked down a path lined with stones on each side. Kamau waited to speak until they were a good distance away.

"I'm sorry I didn't tell you," he said, glancing over.

"I'm sorry I stomped on your foot." Not the best way to begin, but at least she started.

"I deserved it."

"Yeah."

Their feet crunched on the path. Lys had a thousand questions, but she didn't trust her voice.

"You probably hate me."

"No!" Lys said, turning her head to meet his eyes. "I mean—" She looked away. "It would be easier if I could hate you."

They arrived at the water spigot and Kamau turned it on, watching as his bucket filled.

"My sister disappeared three months ago." His eyes continued to watch the water. "My parents asked me to find her."

Lys didn't have any siblings. She didn't even have many cousins, but she could feel the despair in his voice. Now that she'd lost Brady—a friend—Lys understood. "How did you find her?"

"It is a long story." He moved his bucket and held out his

hand for Lys'. She gave it to him, their fingers brushing.

Kamau went on, "At first I didn't find Mason, I found Doyle and the New."

"Did they try to kill you?" Lys asked, glancing around as if expecting the New to appear.

"They did," Kamau said, his mouth tugging into a small smile. "When they failed at that, and I convinced them that I wasn't with Mason, we struck a deal. They got me to Mason in exchange for me finding out what Mason's plan was."

"Which I handed over on a silver platter," Lys grumbled.

"Doyle knew that Mason wanted you specifically, so he told me to stick close to you."

"Which you did," Lys said, hitting him with a flat stare. It hurt more coming from his lips.

"I couldn't help myself," he said, holding her gaze.

Okay, Lys had to admit that was good. "And?"

"And I wanted to tell you a thousand times, but Mason had my sister. When you found me in the hospital basement, I was looking for her."

That, at least, finally made some sense.

"Until you and Brady came along, I didn't know what Mason expected of a magic user—the breaking. So I'd been stuck in my room for a few days."

"And the New? Did they follow you?"

Kamau's dark eyes went cold. "They weren't supposed to attack, but someone got antsy and nabbed us. In their hide out I told Doyle he had to let us go because I still didn't know anything."

"So they let us go?" Lys asked.

"No," Kamau shook his head. "Doyle wanted us around for another day so he could try to convince you to trust him and not Mason. Mark and Brady broke us out unexpectedly."

Water sloshed to the top of the bucket, and Lys watched it

slowly settle. Finally the pieces of the puzzle fell into place. The New followed Kamau from Vegas, maybe using Peter to help them. Having Mason so close turned out to be more tempting than they could handle, so they attacked in force. Hurting people. Trying to hurt her. And Brady.

Lys swallowed, blinking away a tear. She steered her thoughts in a different direction. "How is your sister?" Lys asked, picking up her bucket.

"She is well, and she is safe." Kamau's eyes searched hers. Lys wondered what he found there.

"I'm glad," she said, turning away.

"Wait," Kamau said, reaching out to put his hand on her arm. "I *am* sorry I didn't tell you."

Lys felt more tears coming. "I'm sorry too," she said, stepping away. He had used her, misled her—was everything a lie? She wanted to ask, but couldn't find the words, and part of her didn't want the wrong answer from him.

"How are you?" he asked.

Curse him, why did he always have to be so concerned? "How am I supposed to be?" she asked, her voice cracking. "Brady's gone, I'm addicted to magic, I've got a need to rip people's eyes from their sockets, the man who said he could cure me lied and then left, and you—" She swallowed. "You're gone too."

"I'm not gone," he said, stepping around in front of her.

Lys shook her head; she couldn't handle this right now. "You said it was all a lie."

He put a hand under her chin, tilting her eyes up to meet his. "I didn't say it was all a lie. I never lied about you, or the way I feel about you."

She wanted to believe him. Wanted it so bad that her body ached for it to be true. But she didn't want to let him in. Not again. Not now.

His eyes searched hers. "You're like no one I've ever met

318

before."

"What, you've never had to seduce a girl before?" The remark slipped out. She wanted him to feel as bad as she did.

Kamau smiled. "I'd have to say that you seduced me."

"What?" Lys asked, jerking her chin from his hand. "What are you talking about?"

"I guess I have a soft spot in my heart for girls who try to get me killed."

Lys looked away. "Yeah, well I don't have any place in my heart for guys who pretend to like me in order to use me."

Kamau reached out and brushed a tear from her cheek. "What about a guy who is sorry he used you, and now he can't stop thinking about you?"

More emotions. More tears. Lys blinked and stepped away. "I'll have to think about it." She turned, walking back down the trail. Kamau moved up beside her, and she didn't shift away when he walked so close that their arms bumped.

"G'day," Mark said when they approached.

Lys moved to the fire and set the bucket down next to a table made of rocks and a plank of wood.

"Let's eat," Mark said.

They cooked pancakes and hash browns on a griddle over the fire. Lys almost let the hash browns burn, but Damisi saved them. Peter took up a spot next to Inez—he smiled at Lys but didn't say anything. His eyes kept wandering to Damisi.

Lys tried not to think about how good it would feel if Kamau put his arm around her as they sat next to one another. A gap stood between them, something far worse than a physical obstacle. And Lys knew that she needed to make the next move.

She turned her attention to the far side of the circle and saw Mark wince as he sat down on the ground to eat.

"How is your leg?" Lys asked him, remembering that he'd been injured just a few days before.

"Sore, but good," he said. "Thanks to Brady." Mark didn't hesitate to mention Brady's name. Lys found that comforting.

The four users that Lys didn't know sat down as well. They served breakfast on tin plates and ate in silence until Ayden cleared his throat.

"I think we should all go through what's happened. We've got a lot to talk about."

"And you've got some explaining to do." One of the magic users said.

Ayden nodded. "Why don't we start with Lys? Will you tell us what Mason told you at the house?"

Lys did so, repeating again about the book, the magic being bottled, the outlets and Mason's plan to let the magic back into the world. "He didn't mention anything about destroying everything."

"What happened at the arch before we got there?" Kamau asked.

She told them, weariness tugging her emotions down to despair.

Damisi spoke for the first time. The girl looked even smaller with an over-sized hoodie on that went almost to her knees. Her slender figure belied her strength. "Will you tell us what you saw?" she asked Lys. "The future, I mean."

"It was terrible." Lys took a breath—everyone leaned forward, listening. "I was jumping around from person to person. I saw a man in Japan tear his little boy in half while he was breaking. I saw volcano's erupting because of touch users." Lys went on, repeating everything she could remember. "And at the end, I saw Mason. He was happy that the world was wrong." Lys glanced at Ayden. "I'm sorry."

Ayden shrugged. "I guess you all know by now that Mason is my father." He looked around. "It wasn't a big secret or anything, we just kept the relationship quiet. We both liked it better that way."

"Did you know what his plan was?" Kamau asked.

"I knew about the magic. He told a lot of people about that, but he needed me specifically because I'm a neutral smell user. He also told me about Lys when he found her. Almost everything at the hospital was aimed at forcing her to break so Mason could identify her power level."

"Did he know what would happen if we unstopped the magic?" Damisi asked, bringing them around to their original subject.

"I don't know. He hardly talked with me about it, and I never got to read his books. He kept them under lock and key. I don't even think he showed the one he showed to Lys to more than a dozen people."

"He showed me." Damisi said.

"Because he needed you. He's good at using people." Bitterness filled the words.

Ayden turned to look at Kamau. "You have some explaining to do as well. How did you get to the hospital?"

Kamau retold his story about meeting Doyle and their bargain.

"So you staged everything?" Mark asked.

"Yes," Kamau nodded. "I faked that my magic was emerging so Mason would come for me."

"You've been using your magic since you arrived at the hospital?" Mark asked.

Kamau shook his head. "No, I've been using magic, although that is not what we call it, since I was a child."

"How did you manage that?"

"There are legends in our tribe, legends about what you call sound users. My father is not a wielder, but my grandmother was. She passed her talents onto my sister and I, although Damisi is more powerful than I am." He smiled at her.

Lys' heart practically wrenched itself from her chest. The love

321

in his eyes convinced her that Kamau would do anything for his sister. Could he think of her the same way? He said he did. Could she believe him?

"Did you know about the other senses? Or the power levels?" Ayden asked.

Kamau shook his head. "We thought the different eye colors were due to gender or family relations, and we have no other senses mentioned in our heritage songs. Ancestors of my family have been wielders for more generations than anyone can remember."

Ayden exchanged a glance with Mark. "So magic in the world isn't quite as dead as my father thought."

Mark sniffed. "Do the New know about all that?"

"No." Kamau shook his head. "I convinced them that only Damisi and I knew about the magic."

"So, what do we do now?" Lys asked, glancing around the circle. "Do you think they'll come back for us?"

"The BG's?" Mark asked.

Lys smiled. "Yeah, them."

"The BG's?" Ayden asked, raising his eyebrows.

"Brady's name for them. Bad guys," Lys explained. "Do you think they'll stop hunting magic users?"

"They won't," Kamau said. Lys turned to look at him and found his eyes on her. "When I was with them I saw how much they hated magic users. They think of themselves as heroes— saving the world from the evil of magic. Even if Doyle has had a change of heart, which is doubtful, he is only one in a chain of people. People who hate magic users and will do anything to eradicate them from the earth."

Peter spoke for the first time. "Who will help the new users?" He glanced at Inez. "We did it together, but it wasn't fun. We almost died like twice a month."

"I don't have a good answer for that," Ayden said, sharing a

322

look with Mark. "But it's not my plan to abandon everyone."

"We can't leave the other users out there to go through this alone," Inez said.

Ayden raised an eyebrow. "Are you with us then?"

Inez sent him a scathing glare. "Brady just died to save us. What do you want me to do, go back to my life and forget anyone ever loved me enough to die for me?"

Ayden studied her for a moment. "No."

"I'm in," Peter said. "Brady was my friend too. And I'd like to help other kids."

Damisi's small, clear voice came from her lips. "Our tribe deals with the magic quite differently than Mr. Mason did." She glanced at Kamau. "Perhaps we can help figure out a way to control it."

"Yes, I've been thinking the same thing." Kamau looked around the circle. "Our wielders use their gifts on one another. A combination of that and some mental exercises keep the addictive side of magic at bay." He met Lys' eyes again. "I don't know if it will work for the other senses, but I'm sure we can provide some insight."

"Magic doesn't have to be addictive?" Ayden asked.

"The pull is always there," Kamau said, "but there are a number of ways to control it. I'd never had a problem until I came here, away from our tribe and their lands."

"You're really in a tribe?" Peter asked. A spark of enthusiasm shot from his eyes, and Lys smiled, feeling yet another round of tears. Brady had said the same thing.

"It's a secret tribe," Damisi said, wiggling her eyebrows.

Lys looked at Kamau. "A secret tribe?"

He shrugged. "Yes."

"Do you have to kill us now that you told us about it?" Peter asked, looking at Damisi.

"We'll see."

Lys caught the hint of a smile on Inez's face. Inez saw her looking and scowled. Her eyes went from Lys to Kamau and back again. Pain replaced the momentary amusement, and Inez lowered her gaze.

For a moment Lys didn't understand. Did Inez not trust Kamau? Was she angry that Kamau lived and Brady didn't? But as she watched Inez the true meaning hit her. Lys had another chance with Kamau. Inez would never see Brady again.

Lys slid her hand across the gap between her and Kamau. She slipped her hand on to his, hoping he really had feelings for her. His eyes fell on their hands, and he looked up. Lys managed a small smile, and she tried to fill it with hope. Turning his hand, Kamau opened his palm and intertwined his fingers with hers.

The others were talking about who to contact. Lys ignored them. She watched Kamau as he pulled the back of her hand to his lips and gently kissed it. A butterfly stirred in her stomach. She smiled—this time without hesitation.

"We should probably contact every user we know," Mark said. "See who's still loyal to Mason, and who would be willing to help us."

Ayden nodded and turned to look at each of them in turn. "None of you have to stick around."

"Where else would we go?" Lys asked. She glanced at Mark and Ayden and saw teachers, she looked at Inez and saw a friend, in Peter she saw a little brother; she didn't know what Kamau meant to her yet, but she didn't want to do this without him.

Magic. It had ripped her world right out from underneath her, replacing it with horrors and wonders she had never imagined. But Lys couldn't go back. Not now. Not after everything that had happened. She nodded at the others and her eyes fell on Kamau. She'd stick around.

A Note from Jo

If you enjoyed reading about Lys and the rest of the crew, and you want to stay in the loop about my latest releases, and updates stalk me on my website

joannschneider.com

One of the best parts of being an author is knowing that my story captured your imagination. If you have a minute, please leave a review on Amazon or Goodreads. A few lines about your overall reading experience would be appreciated.

Also By Jo Schneider:

New Sight Series:
New Sight
New Powers

New Sight Short Stories:
Persuasion
Potential

Jagged Scar Series:
Fractured Memories
Severed Ties
Shattered Dreams
Crippled Hope

Babes in Spyland

Acknowledgements

This poor book went through more revisions than a girl's hair before a first date with the hottest guy around. If not for a few key people, this novel would still be floating around on my computer, in the "I don't want to talk about it" folder.

First off, I must acknowledge PD, my mean editor. Without her, my characters would be contradicting themselves every three pages. So you should thank her as well. And trust me, I don't use the term "mean" lightly here.

There are a slew of writing buddies that deserve a shout-out, including: The Accidental Metaphores and the 3-Million Group. Jane and Taryn specifically smacked me around when I needed it.

Also, there are the dozen or so troopers who read revisions of New Sight three or four times. You know who you are, guys. Call me, I still owe most of you dinner.

My family may or may not have had something to do with me becoming a writer. I think they secretly want me to become rich off my writing job so I can support all of them in their old age. I'm down with that. Love you guys!

Also, a shout out to Alfred Stringer, who brought you and I the shiny new cover art for this book.

I suppose I should be grateful for my boring drive home from work, in which the idea for New Sight leapt down from the heavens and implanted itself in my brain. Still not sure if that's healthy, but there you go.

About the Author

Jo Schneider grew up in Utah and Colorado, and finds mountains helpful in telling which direction she is going. One of Jo's goals is to travel to all seven continents—five down and two to go.

Another goal was to become a Jedi Knight, but when that didn't work out, Jo started studying Shaolin Kempo. She now has a black belt, and she keeps going back for more. An intervention may be in order.

Being a geek at heart, Jo has always been drawn to science fiction and fantasy. She writes both and hopes to introduce readers to worlds that wow them and characters they can cheer for.

Jo lives in Salt Lake City, Utah with her adorkable husband, Jon, who is very useful for science and computer information as well as getting items off of top shelves.

Made in the USA
San Bernardino, CA
15 August 2018